THREE AND OUT
Murder in a San Antonio Psych Hospital

A Work of Fiction

By

John C. Payne

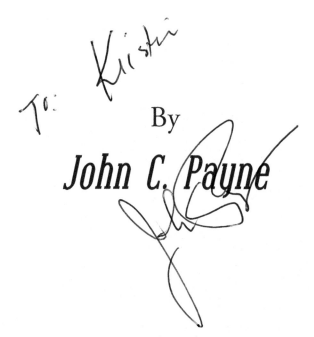

Other Books Written Under the Name of John C. Payne

The Three and Out Trilogy

*The Saga of a San Francisco
Apartment Manager
*The Chicago Terminus

The Stage Series

*Stage Three: Rod Richards Returns
*Stage Four
* Stage Five: The Reincarnation
*Stage Six: The Infidelity Murders
*Murder in A San Antonio Psych Hospital,
Revisited
AND
* In Defense of Patch Schubert (A Historical Romance)

NOTE: These books are available through
www.johncpayne.com OR Amazon.com

If you enjoy the books, I encourage you to post a comment about the novels on Amazon.com. Thank you.

THREE AND OUT
Murder in a San Antonio Psych Hospital

A Work of Fiction

By

John C. Payne

THREE AND OUT, Murder in a San Antonio Psych Hospital
Copyright © 2021 by John C. Payne

The book (ISBN 9781482525823) was reprinted September 15, 2011, and revised several times.

AUTHOR'S NOTE

THIS book is dedicated to the conscientious professionals who work with the mentally challenged individuals across America. Without the support of these "giving" persons, the less fortunate would have no one or nowhere else to turn to for their daily support. Most of them would plunge into hopeless despair.

There are numerous mental health clinics and hospitals in the United States. A large number are municipally-owned, tax-supported facilities. On the other end of the spectrum, there are private, for-profit mental health care clinics, and hospitals with multiple types of ownership.

Management of each facility varies based on their legal status. The tax-supported organizations are strongly influenced by the political process. The others must depend on innovative marketing, creative programming, and careful husbandry of financial resources.

The primary setting of this story focuses on an unusual hospital in an urban setting. The facility had been an old, two-story hotel near the famous San Antonio River Walk. It wasn't affiliated with any of the national hotel chains and became insolvent. A private, for-profit mental health hospital replaced the shuttered hotel. One unfortunate day a murdered patient was found in the hospital dayroom. Rod Richards is appointed the administrator in the midst of the intensive investigation by local and federal agencies. A number of the patients and several staff members are pegged as "persons of interest" by the law enforcement authorities. The case is ultimately solved and Rod Richards moves on.

This story is a complete work of fiction. Names, characters, places, and incidents are products of this writer's imagination. Any resemblance to any persons living or dead is purely coincidental. The hospital's name and location are also fictional.

PROLOGUE

SHE was lying nude in a fetal position underneath the ping pong table in the dayroom on the second floor of the hospital. A huge pair of scissors was embedded in the center of her chest. Her yellow, hospital-issued pajama bottoms were wrapped around her neck. A trail of blood began at the opened door and ended in a huge pool on the tiled floor beneath her shoulders. There were fingernail etchings carved out in the congealed blood. While difficult to interpret correctly, they seemed to depict a series of nine or ten numbers.

Did the assault happen in another location, maybe in one of the patient rooms next to the hospital dayroom? Was she dragged here by the assailant, or did she manage to crawl in here on her own? Did anybody witness the murder or even hear loud pleas for help?

She was discovered the following morning at approximately six-thirty by janitorial personnel making their rounds sweeping and mopping the floors on the second level. They exercised common sense not to walk near the crime scene and reported it immediately to their supervisor. He, in turn, called the police.

How could something like this take place in a mental health hospital? All patients are required to be closely monitored by staff personnel. Why was the life of this particular patient so violently snuffed out?

CHAPTER 1

ROD Richards was exhausted. Although his six-foot athletic frame and light-colored hair belied his true age of fifty, he was run down. His reputation to reach out for new challenges and the dynamics of change had caught up with him. It used to be fun and adventurous. No more.

Janice had been a willing accomplice in their hectic lifestyle till now. She'd not been feeling well since they decided to leave San Francisco. Janice didn't share her feelings with Rod because she knew he'd insist on staying in the city until their family doctor cleared her to travel. Both were anxious to relocate to San Antonio and join up with their son. Larry Richards and his family were waiting for their day of arrival.

Janice thought the reason for her lethargy was related to everything that had to be accomplished in preparation for the move. She could rationalize the bruising displayed on her arms and legs from bumps received packing and stacking heavy boxes. She didn't feel like eating because of the mountain of stress related to the relocation. Janice hid her pain and discomfort.

She tried to act positive and even humorous about the move as they began their long journey southeast. Larry told them they would be arriving in the middle of Fiesta San Antonio. He told them this historic event started in 1891 and is deemed a "party with a purpose." The eleven-day celebration began as a community function to recognize the heroes of the battles of both the Alamo and San Jacinto. Larry assured them that no other municipality in the country could generate citizen participation approximating this event.

"Rod, I feel as though we're going to a foreign country," Janice told him.

"Why so?" he asked with a quizzical look.

"Well, there are so many Mexicans living there. I heard they're still fighting that dang Battle of the Alamo! Larry said uniformed soldiers are still guarding the entranceway to the mission. Was he kidding?"

"*Buenos Dios*, Janice! No, those folks are American citizens with a Hispanic heritage. The battle fought on the site is ancient history. The brave defenders were decimated. And, the shrine is not guarded by troops."

"When did you start speaking Spanish?"

"I felt it was time we learn how to speak another language. It'd be helpful when we get down there. The periodic visits I made to our library to listen to *Spanish for Dummies* tapes will pay off big time."

"By the way, Rod, why don't the folks down there in the Alamo City refer to themselves as Mexican-Americans?"

"Maybe they do," he said. "Go ask one of their civic leaders for clarification on this point when we get there. I'm sure he or she will put you at ease."

"Oh, forget the whole issue," she forced a smile. "I'll refer to myself as a proud Swedish-American when we get settled!"

"You delicious Swedish meatball," he joked. "I'm going to pull over at the next rest area if you don't shut the hell up pretty soon. I'll sequester a secluded parking place and make mad and passionate love to you."

She tried to chuckle and then ignored him.

Larry had invited them to occupy their guest bedroom until they found a rental home. They planned to store their furniture and other household items. Their goal was to rent a home in Alamo Heights, an eclectic incorporated city just north of downtown San Antonio.

They celebrated Rod's fifty-first birthday on the second night of their journey. His energy and exuberance had returned. Hers didn't. They stopped to eat a late dinner at a trendy restaurant in Phoenix. Janice alerted the gregarious waiter to bring a piece of chocolate cake with one large candle after they finished the main course.

Janice was not feeling well. She felt hot and had an upset stomach. The bruises on her arms and legs were beginning to turn ugly colors. She put on her "happy face" to help Rod celebrate his birthday.

The third day of the road trip found them east of El Paso, Texas. Janice began to develop a high fever. Her forehead was burning up. She decided not to accompany Rod to dinner after they'd stopped at a motel in Fort Stockton for the evening. She complained a severe headache precluded any outside activity.

Janice again spiked a high fever as she went to bed later that evening. The fever caused excessive sweating and intermittent chills. Rod was fast asleep. She didn't want to awaken him. He'd be fretfully worried. She'd tough it out like a seasoned trooper. Larry had informed them long ago of the excellent medical resources in San Antonio. That brought her some solace.

She shared her major discomforts with him as they neared the outskirts of San Antonio.

"Rod, please forgive me. I haven't been feeling well this entire trip. I thought it was a minor stomach upset or the flu. Now I'm sure it's much more serious. I need to see a doctor when we get there."

The traffic on Interstate 10 was heavy. Rod was upset with a driver who'd just cut him off while he was weighing Janice's startling revelation.

He went ballistic. She hadn't informed him about her condition earlier. Rod finally cooled off, settled down, and then drove immediately to the emergency room at City Hospital. He notified Larry of the decision. Several hours passed before Janice was seen. The ER triage system had broken down. Three major car accident victims and one homicide case consumed the majority of the emergency room resources.

Screaming kids, three drunks accompanied by policemen, and several prone indigent old men were scattered in disarray. The waiting room resembled a fallout shelter after a major earthquake. The coffee and cold drink coin machine in the hallway displayed an "out of order" note taped to the glass front.

Rod gripped her shaking arm. "Please be a little more patient," he pleaded. "They're doing the best they can under the circumstances."

Soon she was ushered into a treatment room. The results of the blood tests came back after another excessive wait. Depressed red and white blood cell counts alarmed the ER physician. The staff hematologist on call was brought in.

Janice was admitted to the hospital and underwent a bone marrow biopsy. Meanwhile, additional blood cultures identified a raging infection that started to overwhelm her now ravaged body. Intravenous medicines were pumped into her body. She seemed to gain relief.

"I think the medicine is starting to work, Rod, keep your fingers crossed," she assured him.

The attending physician told Rod he should go home now and get some sleep. Janice was responding to the medications. Nothing more could be done. They'd wait and observe till morning and reevaluate. Rod, Larry, and his wife Pam were all exhausted and reluctantly left the hospital.

"We can kick off our shoes and stretch out for a while at home," Larry offered. "It'll do us good—we need it."

Rod was depressed. There was nothing he could do but pray and hope. Pam felt sorry for him. They tried their best to cheer him up.

"Okay, Larry, let's go."

CHAPTER 2

PAM went upstairs the next morning to tell Rod breakfast was ready. She knew he preferred breakfast to any other meal of the day. Pam had fixed his favorite dish–creamed beef on homemade biscuits.

He used to laugh and tell everyone that when he was in the Army, the cooks referred to that meal as SOS–loosely interpreted as "shit on a stick." The Navy guys allegedly called it "shit on a shingle." The Air Force flyboys always had steak. No matter, every GI was certain that it would play havoc with their lower intestinal tracts but worth the risk!

Rod and Larry returned to the hospital the next morning. They found Janice sitting up in bed eating a bowl of oatmeal. She had gained some of her colors back but wasn't her usual cheerful self. Son John in Green Bay had called her earlier in the morning and was encouraging. Janice knew she was racing against time. Her body ached, even though she was heavily sedated.

The biopsy results had come back with the depressing news. She was diagnosed with acute myelogenous leukemia. Larry and Pam had sat vigilantly with Rod the next few days offering him needed moral support.

"I vividly remember two friends who died in my blood-spattered arms in the steamy jungles of Vietnam," Rod reminded them. "I can't reconcile the fact that Janice is slowly losing her grasp on life."

Heroic attempts to stem the rampant infection were unsuccessful. Janice developed uncontrollable sepsis and then passed away on the seventh day of her hospital stay. She never got to see Larry's home in Leon Valley.

Rod had to be sedated. At first, he refused. Larry persisted. Rod gave in. He was a glorified mummy for several days, not able to make any meaningful decisions.

The family tried to convince Rod to return Janice's body to their native St. Louis for burial in the family plot. Her aged father and mother insisted she is brought home to her final resting place.

"Rodney, most of her grade school and high school friends are still living here," Janice's father said, still shaken from the series of events. "Several others are buried in nearby cemetery plots. She needs to be back here with them!"

Rod was still incapable of rational thinking. Larry took over and made all the final arrangements. He had met with their adult foster children to solicit their thoughts. All agreed with Janice's folks and allowed the remains to be consigned to a funeral home in St. Louis.

Their oldest son, John, supported the decision. At first, he pushed for a cremation to cut down the high costs associated with the more traditional interment. Rod was always against cremation strictly on religious beliefs. John had backed off.

"Rod, how about having dinner with us tomorrow night?" an old neighborhood friend asked him after the funeral. "We'll knock down a few brews like old times, hey!"

"Sorry, I'd love to," he lied. "The family has something else planned."

Several of Janice's old school chums stopped by and wanted Rod to join them for an old-fashioned cookout. Again, he couldn't relieve the stress of her loss. *Of course, I'm not ready to take up where Janice and I left off with the old crowd. I'm too damned depressed to share my feelings with them.*

CHAPTER 3

ROD decided he couldn't stay with Larry any longer after returning to San Antonio from the funeral services. He packed his bags and quietly snuck out of his son's home in the middle of his second week home from St. Louis. He had no intention of telling anyone why, or where he was going. He found one of the least expensive downtown motels not too far from the Alamo. He had to be alone.

Larry left home earlier that morning for a staff meeting. Like his father, he also enjoyed a hearty breakfast, but the staff meetings were held at seven o'clock on Monday mornings. He'd grab a couple of donuts and a large cup of coffee at Shipley's Donut shop later in the morning. The clinic chief wanted the meeting wrapped up before the staff was scheduled to see their first patients.

His wife Pam went upstairs later that morning to tell Rod breakfast was ready. She saw the made-up bed was left untouched and the room empty. Pam couldn't determine when or where he had ventured off to laces unknown. She checked the shower room down the hall. He wasn't there. She came back to the guest bedroom windows and ripped the drapes open. Pam noticed his little Honda wasn't parked in the driveway where it usually sat. The suitcases that were stacked in the far corner of the room were missing.

She began to panic, then shouted out in a shrilling voice, "Oh my God, what's happened to him?" She knew Rod was a different person when he got back from St. Louis, more depressed and on edge.

Pam called Larry but couldn't get through. Nobody was in the clinic to answer the telephones. Somebody forgot to switch on the answering machine. She needed to get a grip on herself.

She fed the kids in a hurry and hustled them off to school. She decided to drive over to Larry's office and interrupt him with the news of Rod's sudden and mysterious departure from their home. The clinic was located in an early German settlement south of downtown.

Pam hopped in her new Honda Odyssey and raced the van down Bandera Road to Loop 410, then on to busy Highway 28. She sighed when she arrived downtown. A Lexus SUV almost t-boned her crossing Durango at the Alamo Street light.

"Hey, jerkoff, watch where the hell you're going," she shouted at the top of her voice. The driver of the other car didn't hear her and sped away. She finally got to Larry's clinic, still in a frenzied emotional state of mind.

"Good God, Pam, you look like you've seen a ghost," Dr. Dean said, as he saw her running into the clinic. He was heading to the water cooler out front to fill his empty water bottle. There were several families with children sitting in the lobby waiting to be seen by their therapists. One of the kids was screaming and yelling out loud that he didn't want to see the doctor.

"I need to see Larry right away," she told Dean. "It's an emergency."

"I'll round him up for you, Pam. He's with his first patient. I can interrupt him." He ushered her into an empty office. "Is there a problem I can help you with?"

She noted the disgruntled kid in the lobby was still making a loud ruckus and threw a toy truck against the window. His mother looked on helplessly. An older man sitting nearby admonished the child for tossing the plaything. The little imp flipped him off!

Pam told Dr. Dean there was an emergency at home and needed to discuss it with Larry. She told him It couldn't wait. Pam hesitated to offer any details. She was afraid Dean would want to help. She didn't want or need his assistance. This was a confidential family matter.

Larry came hustling around the front lobby corner into the room where Dean left her. He cradled her hand and sat down next to her. She'd been crying.

"Larry, he's disappeared and must have left early this morning. I looked for a note. Nothing, no explanation."

"Oh damn!" Larry mumbled aloud. "I knew something like this might happen but didn't expect it to occur this soon. Dad has not been himself lately. I'm afraid he's gone off the deep end. Do you have any ideas where he might have gone, Pam?"

"I haven't the slightest clue, Larry. We've tried to give him everything he needed to get through his suffering. It wasn't enough. He can be an obstinate bastard. What are we going to do?"

"I'll cancel the remainder of my appointments after I finish with my patient. We'll get out of here and have breakfast. Together, we'll figure out the best way to get our arms around this problem."

CHAPTER 4

SOUTH-TOWN Psychiatric Services was owned by two prominent psychiatrists–Dr. Phillip Dean and Dr. Jim Smyth. George Martin Dean, a Child and Adolescent therapist was the third owner. Larry had gone to graduate school with George back in St. Louis. It was George who prompted Larry to relocate to San Antonio and join him in his thriving practice.

"How about leaving all that ungodly cold weather up there and experience the many wonders of the Southwest?" George would occasionally rant and rave at Larry over the phone.

Larry was always intrigued by the idea of leaving the Midwest and settling in a warmer climate. South Texas and its colorful history would satisfy this requirement. His wife argued they shouldn't leave their good friends and acquaintances simply to rush off to a "foreign land." Larry prevailed in the end. Pam soon made some new friends and adjusted to living in San Antonio.

Dr. Phillip Dean, young George's uncle, had practiced psychiatry in San Antonio for over thirty years. As the titular head of the clinic, he specialized in adult psychiatry. Dr. Jim Smyth, the other well-known psychiatrist had been with the group for five years and specialized in child psychiatry. They had met each other while serving at Brooke Army Medical Center in San Antonio while both were serving on active duty.

Larry had an opportunity to compete for a government contract after a few months of treating patients in the clinic. He obtained and then scrutinized a request for proposal (RFP) issued by the Department of Defense (DOD). The document was over three hundred pages of "governmentese." Thankfully, Larry received interpretive help from a retired federal worker who lived next door. The neighbor had years of experience with government contracting. They authored a competitive proposal using their combined skills and dogged perseverance.

"Why are you trying to work for the government?" Pam asked him one morning at breakfast after she'd scooted the kids off to school. "Wouldn't you prefer to spend more time and effort developing your practice with George Martin Dean? After all, that was the main reason he coerced you to move down here."

Larry smiled softly at her and ignored the question . . . convinced he could justify his pursuit of the government contract with her. He pulled his kitchen chair up closer to her. She was in the final stages of mixing a cake batter. The preheated oven was awaiting its assault.

"Honey, military dependents, especially children and their adolescent counterparts are faced with challenges that most other youngsters never experience in their lifetime. The frequent overseas deployment by either military parent places a heavy burden on the children. Peer pressure from other kids could be overwhelming at times for children of a single parent. With a deployed spouse, it remains difficult for the remaining one to obtain outside employment and still handle the responsibilities required at home."

Pam gave him a ho . . . hum shrug and walked over to pour herself another cup of coffee. She didn't offer to refill his cup. He shot up, grabbed his briefcase, and then hustled off to work. He was frustrated with her lack of concern for his new endeavor to secure the DOD contract.

Larry was notified by the post contracting officer several weeks after submitting his RFP that he'd be awarded the contract. The pact pertained to the behavioral health treatment of children and adolescents at the nearby military installation.

Two months into the contract, Larry was having a difficult time juggling hours between his private practice at South-Town Psychiatric Services and the government arrangement. He underestimated the number of referrals he'd get from the military care providers. Larry considered adding a therapist but decided to wait.

"Larry, be patient, things will slow down over there," one of his peers told him at a breakfast meeting.

Several other experienced clinicians had told him there was always an initial rush of patients referred at the beginning of such contracts. The cause was legitimate. The military system was rapidly reducing its in-house backlog to move on to other mandated initiatives. He hoped the patient volume would level off as the "newness" wore off.

CHAPTER 5

"**WHERE** the hell am I?" Rod muttered out loud. He rolled over in the king-sized bed, still confused. It was five in the morning. He had to get up and pee.

Lying next to him on her back was a good-looking, dark-haired lady. She was naked from the hips down and snoring loudly. The covers were tucked tightly around her lower hips. Rod glanced at a slim waist and rather hefty breasts heaving rhythmically up and down with each breath.

Reaching out at him was a coiled rattlesnake ready to strike. The serpent looked realistic with its protruding fangs dripping poisonous droplets. Whoever did the tattoo on her belly was a first-class artist.

What in God's name have I done now? Who the hell is this lady and how did she end up in the sack with me?

Rod stared at the bed stand next to him. He witnessed an empty bottle of Jack Daniels, an opened pack of Marlboros, three empty glasses–two of which had lipstick smeared on the top rims. An unopened package of Trojans sat innocently next to the table lamp base. The liquor bottle was tipped over on its side and balancing on the edge of the bed stand.

He slipped out of bed and stumbled his way to the bathroom, not wanting to wake her up. Rod was wearing only his baggy boxer shorts. His head throbbed like a freight train rumbling through the narrow track corridors of his brain. He was shaking with minor tremors.

She was sitting up in bed, wide awake when he returned from the john. Her opened eyes followed him back to the bed. "Good morning," she moaned to him in a soft voice. "Are you okay?"

"Who wants to know?" he replied sharply, as he approached her. He sat down on a chair next to the bed. "What the hell are you doing here?"

"Look, Rob Pritchard," she responded. "You of all people know what's going on here."

"My name is Rod Richards. Where did you cook up that other name you just called me?"

"Last evening at Teddy's Tavern."

Rod took several minutes to reflect on what had happened.

He loved Teddy's Tavern for several reason—more than the other watering holes in San Antonio he frequented while trying to rebound from his depression. Teddy's is located next to the Alamo. "The cradle of Texas history." The owner is número uno.

Rod was a military history buff. He envisioned himself fighting alongside Colonel Travis at the historic siege by General Santa Anna. He was heavily armed with a Kentucky long rifle hoisted to his shoulders and a Bowie knife strapped to his waist.

He also pictured himself downing a few brews when Teddy Roosevelt rode into the tavern to organize the Rough Riders. He saw himself riding alongside Teddy in the charge up San Juan Hill.

Lastly, and more importantly, he was completely enthralled with Charlene, the wispy black girl with the chiseled derrière who tended bar there on Fridays. He figured he might frequent the establishment more often.

"Wake up, wake up now," she ordered. "You were sitting up in the balcony area of the bar hugging a bottle of Jack. I was having a frozen margarita at the bar minding my own business. When that obnoxious cretin came up to me and started to harass me, I tried to get away from him. He was persistent. I screamed for help. You dashed down the stairs, grabbed his shirt, spun him around, and punched him in the face. He dropped to the floor like a sack of flour."

"Did someone call the cops?"

"Naw, the scumbag took off with his tail tucked tightly between the legs. You were my wonderful hero. Several of the other customers in the bar area clapped their hands in a loud crescendo. They had recognized your chivalry. Three of them bought several rounds of drinks."

"Well, what's your name, and how in the hell did you get into my bed?"

She jerked over and shook his hand. The bed cover skidded off the bed. Now she was naked as a jaybird!

"My name is Dalia Garza. I must've told you this at least ten times last night. We seemed to hit it off big time after you disposed of that creep. Plus, I was lonely. I've been divorced for six months and have been living like a cloistered nun. I didn't put up much resistance when you suggested we head to your hotel for a nightcap."

"Did I . . . did we do it?" he asked sheepishly, as he stared down at the floor. He was afraid to hear her answer.

"My new friend Rob Pritchard, Rod Richards or whatever your real name is . . . experienced a big-time flameout last night."

"It's Rod Richards. What the hell do you mean by that comment, Miss...?" He stared directly into those big brown eyes.

"Dalia Garza," she shot back. She was starting to get annoyed with him. She had already introduced herself. "You had too much booze last night, my friend. You couldn't even raise the almighty flagpole no matter how hard we tried to—oh, excuse the pun."

"Look over there on the bed stand," she continued. "You were so out of it that you couldn't even tear open that pack of condoms!"

Rod sheepishly glanced over at the bed stand with a quizzical look on his face. He looked at her and then took another long look at the stand. He didn't know for sure what to believe. He remembered one other time in his life when he got drunk out of his mind and swore it would never happen again.

"I know what's going through that quizzical male mind of yours right now," she giggled. "Why are there three partially empty glasses of booze sitting there?"

He shook his head, couldn't answer her.

She then proceeded to answer her question. "My girlfriend Juanita Comptos was with me at the tavern last night. We

16

normally go bar-hopping together. She helped me get you back to this stinking hotel room. It took two of us to engineer that feat. She stayed for one drink and then took off in a snit. She was angry that I wanted to stay with you to make sure you'd be okay, instead of going back home with her. I bet you thought you enjoyed a threesome last night." She laughed at the suggestion.

"Damn it," Rod uttered softly. "I was in no condition to even enjoy a two-some, or for that matter–even a one-some last night. I've got to fling off this self-destructive and demoralizing trip I'm on. I've been thrashing around like an uncontrollable maniac heading off in no particular direction."

She didn't respond to him.

"Dalia, I must apologize for my crudeness and inconsideration. This is not the real me. Trust me. How can I make it up to you?"

"Well," she paused for a long time. "We seem to like each other. Maybe you can take me out to dinner some night. We could get to know each other better."

Before Rod could reply, she looked at the bedside clock and gasped aloud. "My God, I have to be at work in ten minutes!"

"Where do you work?"

"I'm a staff nurse at Mission Oaks Mental Health Hospital. Thank God it's close by. You'll have to drive me over there. My girlfriend had the car last night."

She collected her clothes, grabbed her purse, hustled over to the bathroom, shut the door, and washed up, all in a record five minutes. Rod couldn't believe how good she looked after she came out of the bathroom. This quick transition always amazed him. He wondered how women could transform their appearance in only a few magic moments.

"Don't you have to wear a white uniform to work?" he asked.

"This is what we call *new age dress* now, Rod. Patients seem to respond better when caregivers don't look so sterile and therapeutic. At least this holds for our kind of patients. Please run me over there, now."

As they climbed into the little Honda, Rod asked her to write out her address and telephone number on a slip of paper he gave her. He wanted to make the best of this situation. "Maximization," he always referenced it. He would take her out to some neat restaurant for a relaxing dinner, and who knows what else?

Mission Oaks was only a five-minute drive from his motel. The downtown traffic was light. It was sprinkling, and the sun was trying to nudge aside the thin rain clouds.

Dalia smiled at him. "Be sure to call me now and slacken up on the booze, okay? You're going to drink yourself to death if you continue down that one-way road. Someday, I'd like to find out why you were trying to drown out your sorrows in a sea of alcohol."

She hopped out of his car at the front of the hospital and ran fifteen yards to the main entrance. She turned around and waved him a long goodbye before disappearing through the revolving doors. He rendered a sharp military salute back at her, wondering if he'd ever see her again. Rod was impressed with the inherent beauty of the Hispanic females. He'd been amazed with the beauty and graciousness of Vietnamese women during his rugged year fighting a war in their country. Dalia was certainly no exception.

CHAPTER 6

ROD returned to the motel, took a hot shower, and changed clothes. He was hungry and knew he had to get some honey, syrup, or jelly into his beat-up body. These were the only foodstuff that calmed his system after a night of excessive drinking. A stack of pancakes at IHOP was deemed his best friend on these occasions.

He'd yet to experience the magic of a big bowl of *menudo*– the morning after food that the locals refer to as *levanta muerto*. These words translate "to rouse from the dead."

Rod remembered this from his son who lived over in Leon Valley. Larry loved the breakfast tacos and occasionally the *Menudo* served at Tios on Bandera Road. Only on occasion, Rod suffered from a non-forgiving hangover. Estela and her staff there treat him well, even if he tends to be a little curt with them *on the morning after*.

There was an IHOP close to his motel. He headed there instead of driving out to Tios. He needed relief soon. Belgium waffles instead of pancakes. Rod had to make sure the maple syrup dispenser was full. He would consume every ounce of it. A side of bacon strips swimming in ketchup would chase the sugary syrup solution through his "begging" system.

He needed to make two telephone calls. First, he had to talk to Larry and Pam. An apology for sneaking out of their cozy house in the middle of the night. More importantly, he needed to ask their forgiveness for not letting them know his whereabouts. He knew they'd be concerned.

The second call was made to his old Army buddy who had retired in San Antonio. First Sergeant Howard I.M. Hill saved his young, inexperienced and overly confident rear-end in the jungles of Vietnam. Howard would offer a litany of sound advice for Rod one more time. Hill had been a heavy drinker. He almost got ushered out of the army at one point because of his alcohol addiction. Somehow, he was able to overcome his dependency and became a model leader, especially for the younger troops.

The phone call to Larry went better than expected. "Yes, I understand the weight of the depression you're wearing on your shoulders, Dad. It'll take time and a concerted effort on your part to overcome this heavy burden."

The loss of Janice had a life-changing impact on his Dad. Larry shared with Rod that losing his mother unexpectedly was also hard on him and his family. Larry offered Rod counseling services from Dr. Dean at his clinic.

Phil Dean had a wonderful track record for treating alcoholics. Rod denied that he was an alcoholic but knew he was heading in that direction. He preferred to maintain his distance from Larry and his family, at least regarding his drinking problems. Dr. Dean might be the answer. But after a quick assessment, Rod felt Larry was too close to the doctor.

Rod found Howard Hill after several attempts to determine his exact location and phone number. Of interest, he was working as a contract addiction counselor at a VA facility in San Antonio.

"Listen up, Top, this is your old radioman, Rod Richards," he excitedly reported over the telephone. "How the hell are you doing, old man?"

Hill paused for a moment or two to collect his thoughts, then he formulated his reply. "Why you three-legged anomaly, where the hell are you, and what in Christ's name do you want? I thought you died and went straight to hell!"

"Is that any way to talk to your favorite soldier, First Sergeant?"

"Favorite soldier my ass, you say, Richards. I damn near drummed your fat ass out of the army–and all by my lonesome. I'd never in my entire glorious life met such a know-it-all, hardheaded flimsy creature, until you presented yourself."

Rod remembered this was not true. Hill had recommended him for Officer Candidate School before he departed from 'Nam.' Rod had mulled the offer over for several weeks but declined it. The troops thought Hill's middle initials, I.M. stood for "I'm Mean." Nobody in their right mind dared to ask him about the initials without getting their ripe asses chewed out. Rod thought Hill once confided in him how those initials came about but couldn't remember the circumstances to save his life.

This friendly banter went on for some time. In reality, they respected each other. They had suffered, even cried, and almost died together in the quagmire known as Vietnam. Hill rotated from Hawaii with the 25th Infantry Division when President Johnson began the escalation of the war. His wife and the young boy stayed behind in military quarters at Schofield Barracks.

Hill re-upped for a second consecutive tour in the combat zone against his wife's wishes. His despondent wife sought the emotional refuge of a young Hawaiian who worked at the Non-Commissioned Officer's Club on base. In time, she sent her soldier husband a "Dear Howard" letter and left him for good.

The assigned radioman in Howard's squad was shot through the neck on a night patrol and was medically evacuated out of the jungle. Rod was an amateur ham radio operator. Hill knew about it and then assigned the radio duties to Rod. "What the hell," Rod would always opine to anyone who would listen. "It was better than running point on dangerous forays into the jungle. Point men were either suicidal or outright insane. They had to be if they'd volunteered for such missions."

"What can I do for you, Rodney, you old, no good, everlasting fuckup?" If another man ever used Rod's official name he would've decked him on the spot.

Hill hadn't changed one iota. He'd always injected a stream of bullshit a mile long in his everyday conversations. He retired from the army after twenty-five-hard-core years and took advantage of the GI Bill. He earned a degree in counseling after years of difficult adjustment to the civilian world. How he ended up in the medical field was beyond Rod's imagination. This man was compliant in dishing out tons of crap. There was no patience listening to anyone's screwed-up life experiences for most human beings.

Rod had an appointment with the addiction unit at the VA shortly after their telephone conversation. He drove past City Hospital where Janice had died. Rod started to shake all over and jerked his car toward the curb. His many happy years of fun-loving life with Janice raced through his mind. A cold sweat broke out. Cars following behind him began honking their horns. Finally, he composed himself enough to turn into the parking lot and head straight for the addiction unit.

Hill was masterful! Everyone he counseled had the highest respect and admiration for this man. In his line of business, success was measured by a term the mental health community calls "recidivism."

The VA facility maintained detailed records on how many addiction patients returned for additional treatment after they completed all phases of the initial program. Only five percent of Hill's patients required re-entry into the addiction program, a huge success when compared to other comparable programs across the country.

Rod was not a true alcoholic by definition. He was suffering from a severe case of depression. Hill had him evaluated by a staff psychologist who also felt Rod would benefit from undergoing Hill's addiction program. Severe depression is one of the underlying causes of alcohol addiction. Rod was more than willing to enroll.

"Attention here, you strait-laced old man," a young returnee from Iraq chided Rod. "I bet you drank nothing but cheap rotgut in Uncle Sam's old army." Another young addict weighed in. "What's up, pop, couldn't handle those Vietnam *mamasans* they issued you over there for, ah, physical relief?"

Rod could only remember the village drinking hole dancer the GIs called Salmonella Sal. She would trot over to the evacuation hospital and get her shots from Doctor Feelgood. It helped to maintain the VD rate under command-dictated control.

Rod Richards enjoyed the everyday bantering that took place under the watchful eye of Howard Hill. Embellishment was the name of the game. Rod was the oldest member of the group being treated. He enjoyed sharing war stories with the younger men. He was a decorated veteran. A few others had combat experience. Didn't matter, the fallout was predictable.

CHAPTER 7

ROD sailed through the treatment program in the same manner as in basic training years ago. While he was an honor graduate in his Army basic training, no such accolades were handed out in Hill's program. You either failed within days or hung on with both arms to achieve success. There were no in-between categories in Howard I.M. Hill's classification. It was up to you how you wanted the outcome of treatment recorded in your medical health records.

Larry was impressed with his father's clinical outcome. Rod never told him he was entering an addiction program, but Larry knew. It was a real joy being around his dad. He was doing a better job at Home Depot. The grandkids even took note. Rod started to participate in more activities with them, and they relished the time spent with him.

Hauling youngsters back and forth to their various playing fields infused a new sense of belonging for Rod. Pam made remarks to Larry about how his dad had changed. The upshot was a blessing for all concerned. She was elated to turn over the household taxi service to him whenever he was available.

"My dear Rod," Pam would kid him. "Isn't it about time you traded that little toy car in for a nice van like mine?"

"Well, Pam, it's paid for. You can't beat the gas mileage." Sure, he'd love a new and bigger car. That eventuality had to wait.

Rod moved from the motel and leased a small condo unit on Navarro Street that overlooked the Riverwalk. He relished jogging the winding walkway every morning. The location was far enough from "restaurant row" and the rowdy tourist gatherings associated with a popular Riverwalk location. His new digs were located near the main city public library.

He also bought a membership to the YMCA. It allowed him to swim and work out at the nearby location. He preferred to hit the pool at night to avoid the telephone company groupies from the neighborhood who crowded the facility during the noon hours.

Rod had become an avid reader. Howard Hill had introduced a form of bibliotherapy into his addiction program. It had a major impact on behavior modification. He ran over to the Leon Valley Public Library to pick up books recommended by the friendly staff. Hill even forced the patients to begin a jogging program which eventually led to 5k runs. At first, everyone had bitched at Howard.

"Look here, Top," they would gripe. "We've been through boot camp once, and we didn't enjoy it. What makes you think we'll enjoy your version of it now?"

"Listen up, my fairest of ladies," Howard would respond. "Only I, the benevolent one know what's good for you. Soon you will see, feel and touch the wonders of your newfound existence!"

This wasn't a problem or even a challenge for Rod. He had already adopted a vigorous running program. Only male addicts were required to participate in this strenuous activity as a matter of practice. Hill's supervisors felt he would be too intimidating for the few female alcoholics undergoing the treatment regimen. Howard objected based on equality of the sexes. Nothing changed.

Hill relished the thought of pushing basic trainees again back in the military boot camp model. That would never happen at the VA. His charges never stopped complaining to him about the running chore. Hill's constant prodding and colorful exhortations of "candy-assed crybabies" motivated them. Nevertheless, they didn't want to let Howard I.M. Hill down. Most of the patients were convinced that without this old soldier, they would bolo head-first out of the program.

Rod was more than ready to start a new life. He vowed to cut far back on his drinking and refocus on his everyday existence without Janice. He'd been through challenging phases of his life on several occasions. Combat duty in Vietnam didn't top the list.

He'd planned to follow-up with the attractive nurse, Dalia Garza. It didn't happen. Rod knew he'd revisit Teddy's Tavern in the future–loved the place. He'd approach things from a different perspective. There were greater priorities to address transitioning from Hill's program than seeking female companionship. Perhaps at another time or in another place opportunities would present themselves.

CHAPTER 8

ROD RICHARDS was extremely proud of his progress. Things were starting to fall into place for him. He loved his work helping customers at Home Depot. Rod knew more about lawn furniture, outside plants, and bug control remedies than he'd ever need to know in a lifetime. He refused a promotion to assistant manager because he had other pursuits on his mind. He was moving on. And up.

He returned to school on a full-time basis to complete a master's degree that he'd started years back. Many of the credit hours were still transferable. Juggling study hours with fun hours became a true art.

The annual San Antonio Fiesta celebration was just around the corner. It was time to have some fun. He didn't enjoy the last one because of Janice's illness, coupled with his gradual recovery from depression. It was hard to believe that he'd been in the Alamo City for a year. Party time would now take a degree of precedence over his schoolwork. At least he planned on it.

He devoted many grueling hours of classroom work, night-time, and weekend study marathons. Rod completed the didactic coursework in record time for a tough master's degree in management at Trinity University.

Rod was required to spend six months in a supervised residency with a local business. This demanding requirement to graduate with this advanced degree had to be approved by his Trinity faculty advisor. He had interviewed with a host of companies in the Greater San Antonio area but failed to get an appointment. He recalled one interview that went south in a hurry.

"Mr. Richards, your employment background and new tools garnered by your recent education are indeed commendable. However, you seem to move around more than the average person. If we train you, how can we be assured you'll stay long enough for us to recoup our investment in you?"

He also figured nobody selected him because they thought he was too old. Rod had heard of age discrimination in the marketplace before. Never in his wildest dreams did he think he'd be targeted at the ripe old age of fifty-two.

Larry was also pleased with Rod's accomplishment. He wondered how he could help him find a local business to complete the residency. Pam offered several suggestions. She had experience with temporary employment agencies in the past, feeling they'd be a valuable resource in placing Rod. She was helpful in other ways. Pam drove him to an upscale clothing store and suggested several new business suits for him to purchase.

"You need to look sharp when you walk through that interview door, Rod," she said one day. "You have to knock them off their feet! Get rid of those t-shirts and blue jeans."

"You're right, Pam. Janice loved my casual attire, and I sort of hung on to those things that pleased her. I guess it's time to move on with the wardrobe."

John Richards came to San Antonio for the weekend. His oldest son had been in the Dallas area to scout out a running back from Southern Methodist University. John worked as a college scout for the Green Bay Packer professional football organization. He was drafted by the team out of college but blew out a knee during his first training camp. He told Rod he'd never leave the Green Bay area because he thrived in cold climates.

"I love shoveling snow, ice fishing, and chasing around in those powerful snowmobiles, Dad," John chimed in whenever Rod questioned his sanity about living in a freezer.

Rod, John, and Larry had returned from a Spurs basketball game. The Spurs had wiped out the Boston Celtics. Everybody came home in a good mood. They all agreed that the Spur's overall defense was impressive when considering the high-scoring lineup of NBA teams.

"Boy, that Tim Duncan was great tonight," John said. "He hit the boards hard. The crowd appreciates a player who is willing to forfeit his body for the good of the team."

"Yeah," piped in Larry, "But you've got to score to get the win, and he managed to pump in twenty points for the cause."

Larry played college basketball but was not good enough to be drafted by an NBA team. He was almost 6-6 with a willowy body frame. He had the height and sleekness but lacked the aggressiveness to compete at the next level. The fact that both boys were excellent athletes could no doubt be attributed to their father's genetic makeup.

Rod had played minor league baseball. He pushed himself unmercifully to reach the big leagues but couldn't pull it off. He could hit the cover off the baseball but had difficulty snagging hard grounders coming at him from every direction. His manager praised his competitive drive. It couldn't mask his lack of requisite talent.

He enlisted in the U.S. Army. Marching twenty miles in one-hundred-degree heat with a seventy-pound rucksack on his back and parachuting from perfectly good airplanes were not considered athletic events by the army hierarchy. Rod pursued it for the extra money and the added prestige earned by his silver jump wings.

"Well, my dear father," John said after a few beers, "What are you going to do now that you own an advanced college degree? I'm so proud of how you've handled this past year since mom's been gone."

"I don't have it in my pocket yet, John. It's all mine when I complete a required residency." Rod was drinking his third glass of iced tea. Nobody commented about his beverage choice.

"Larry told me you were having a slight problem getting a company to hire you. He's a big shot now. Why can't he lead interference and find you a spot? You have tons of management experience and now have a mental health background."

"What the hell do you mean by that?" Rod responded too quickly. "Going through an alcohol addiction program doesn't qualify me for anything other than becoming the world's foremost gifted iced tea drinker. I will admit this. I've taken on a new respect for the medics and everything they do for healing people."

"Why don't you try to hook up with one of the mental health facilities around here?" John asked. "Good God, there are plenty of them to go around from what Larry told me. You'd think South Texas is one of the wackiest areas in the country. Maybe you tough Texans and your fellow Mexicans think you're immune to disorders of the head. Larry, get your dad and my dad a job, okay!"

"I never thought Dad would have the slightest interest in working in my field," Larry countered. "On second thought, there's always a great need for top-notch upper management working in our clinics and hospitals. You don't have to be a 'hands-on' clinician to succeed in our field. I'll talk to Dr. Dean at our clinic on Monday. We'll see if he has any thoughts on the subject. Dean's been around here a long time. The good doctor has many contacts in our field."

"Great going, little brother. Dad, toss me another can of beer."

"Will do, cheesehead."

Pam came into the room in a snit fit. Rod figured she was acting a bit out of character. She tried to warm up to him more often since Janice died. She was certainly not the kind-hearted, sweet lady-like person as Larry's first wife. That woman left him struggling with two kids—the results after being killed by a drunk driver.

"John," she exhorted, "Haven't you had enough of those Budweiser's by now? You shouldn't be drinking in front of your father after all he's gone through. Why don't you get off your butt and start the grill? We need to get those burgers on before we all starve to death. Larry, why don't you go out and help him? I'll round up the kids."

"Look, Pam, I appreciate your concern," Rod said after the brothers headed out to the patio. "I don't have a problem with other people drinking. That's their choice. You don't have to continue treating me like some street person trying to find his way around this convoluted world. I can handle it. That's the confidence my program instilled in me."

She stared him down.

Rod continued despite her mood. "Why don't you leave the boys alone? They're big guys now and are having lots of fun together. It's too bad they don't see each other often enough. They're not alcoholics by any stretch of the imagination."

Pam said nothing.

They reassembled to the kitchen when the burgers were placed on the table. Half were burned. Somehow the hot dogs survived. Larry's kids ate as though they hadn't been fed in a week. They were exhausted from playing kickball in the street.

"Brother Larry, how come you didn't cook up some bratwurst?" John chided him. "Johnsonville brats and a thick slab of sharp Wisconsin cheddar cheese make any bar-be-cue pit a royal throne."

Everybody ignored him. The fourth six-pack of Bud was retrieved from the cooler. Pam ate in a rush, gave everybody a disdainful stare of disgust, and then headed upstairs.

I find it difficult to understand why Larry adores this woman— for sure she's not my cup of tea or a shot of Jack Daniels. Screw it. I'm crashing in for the night.

CHAPTER 9

MISSION Oaks Mental Health Hospital was classified as a privately-owned corporation and a for-profit hospital. It was fully accredited by the Joint Commission on Accreditation of Hospitals (JCAH).

A certified public accountant owned fifty-five percent of the shares of the corporation. Doctors Phillip Dean and Jim Smyth were the other two owners. Each had equal shares in the corporation. Their ownership of South-Town Psychiatric Services facilitated admitting inpatients to Mission Oaks Mental Health Hospital.

Two other psychiatrists practicing in the clinic had expressed an interest to buy into the corporation. Phillip's nephew, George Dean was also part-owner of South-Town Psychiatric Services. He opted not to invest in the hospital. No reasons were cited.

Larry Richards offered to take Rod on a tour of the hospital. He obtained the necessary approval from Dr. Dean. The doctor notified the staff that Larry would be conducting a walk-through on the following Saturday. Rod became more interested in mental health operations after completing Howard Hill's addiction program. Hill had mentioned to Rod in an earlier discussion that he was a good friend of the owner.

"Looks like an old hotel building to me," Rod said to Larry. "How big is the place?"

"That's an interesting observation, father of mine. The hospital was a converted two-story hotel that went bankrupt. The former owners refused to affiliate with one of the major hotel chains. As you may know, it's difficult to compete against any national hotel organizations if you're not located on the popular Riverwalk."

"Larry, how many patients can they put in here?"

"The hospital was certified to operate fifty beds. You'll soon observe that twenty-five beds and a large dayroom are located on each floor. We try to keep our patients busy."

They toured the first floor. Something caught Rod's attention. He pointed across the hallway. "Is that a full kitchen operation over there?"

"Sure is. At first, the hotel offered full meals to its occupants. You'll note a nice patio area over there next to that outbuilding. The area handles the overflow from the tiny dining area. The hospital still provides a breakfast and lunch service to staff, visitors, neighbors, and even tourists who venture over this way. I'm told providing food-service operations is a positive revenue source for the facility."

Rod had more questions after they toured the second floor.

"I read in the brochure I picked up in the reception area that the hospital had a neat rooftop designed to challenge the athletic side of their patients."

"We won't go up there," Larry said. "The head nurse told me when we came in they were using the entire area this afternoon. That limits touring the area. We don't want to interfere. It's different. There's a unique swimming pool situated on one end of the roof and a portable basketball hoop anchoring the other end."

"Howard Hill emphasized the importance of integrating physical fitness into his program," Rod offered. "It seems to me that you psychologist-types have the same inclinations."

Larry nodded and continued his briefing. "The staff convinced ownership to import finely grained white sand from the West Coast to construct a beach volleyball court. The volleyball court is situated in the center of the roof. It gets a lot of play from female patients and staff members. These folks don't consider it as strenuous as basketball for some unknown reason."

Rod didn't accept the rationale but said nothing. The new-age female doesn't hold back.

They walked past several patient rooms. Rod noted the impenetrable glass windows in all the rooms and the padded walls in the middle room.

"Do they use the padded rooms often, Larry? Why do they have to clamp those ugly-looking restraints on people with all the wonder drugs available today? The room reminds me of a prisoner's cell. Yes, deep down in the dungeons of an old European castle."

Larry was amazed at his father's scope of operations. "I'm here to tell you that not every patient is a candidate for drug-induced suppression of their aggression and violence. You might save those questions for one of the staff members who work here. I'm sure they can clue you in."

"I've seen enough, Larry. How 'bout we hustle down the street to that Cantina Classica and get something cool to drink."

"Fine with me. I need to return to the parking lot first and retrieve something out of my car." He didn't elaborate.

The staff and visitor parking lot is located across the street from the hospital. The lot had a six-foot wooden fence separating the property from the surrounding neighborhood. It was lit at night to enhance the security for both the staff and their vehicles.

They started back to the hospital after enjoying a refreshing glass of iced tea and a snack of tortilla chips with salsa at Cantina Classica. A Metropolitan Police Department (MPD) cruiser was pulling away from the front entrance. Larry saw the chief of police sitting in the rear seat as the vehicle passed by them. He waved at the chief.

"Dr. Dean and Chief of Police Jesus Astrade were former high school classmates," Larry said after getting a prolonged stare from Rod. "They won numerous debates when competing against other school programs. Both could talk you out of a twenty-dollar bill in less than two minutes! Their teachers were sure that someday both would reach the pinnacle of nationally recognized trial lawyers. The two double-dated often. This cozy arrangement abruptly ended when the two were trying to woo the same young lady. She ended up ignoring the Romeos in favor of the class clown."

"You seem to know bundles about the head shrink and the top cop," Rod said with a smile as they walked through the front door of the facility.

The main entrance to the hospital was situated in the middle of the building on the first floor. There was a small reception area located behind a sliding glass window panel. All the administrative offices were located on the first floor of the building. Storage and utility rooms were located on the second floor above the offices.

Attractively decorated lobbies with expensive overstuffed leather chairs were located on each floor at the opposite ends of the administrative offices and the storage rooms.

"I like the ambiance here, Larry. It sure doesn't look or feel like a hospital to me."

The two lobbies were the only areas of the hospital that contained rugs. The remainder of the complex, including the administrative offices, had eighteen-inch square, colorful tiled floors. All the materials were manufactured in Mexico. Most of the hospital rooms were large private rooms. They had the capacity for configuration into a two-bed setup if needed.

"Does the hospital generate enough revenue to keep the place running efficiently?" Rod asked Larry. "I mean does it make money for the owners?"

"The majority of the patients admitted to the hospital are covered by third-party insurance programs," Larry responded. "The hospital does accept Medicare and state-regulated Medicaid patients. San Antonio is a military town because of several active military bases in the surrounding area. Active duty military dependents, retired service members, and their dependents are frequently referred to the Mission Oaks for mental health care."

"Can a military wife walk in here on her own accord and be admitted?" Rod asked.

"There are certain admission restrictions for active duty dependents because the military has 'in-house' mental health support. Referral to civilian hospitals can be made based on the non-availability of military beds."

"Do they accept charity cases, Larry? My thought is this. Because Mission Oaks is a private, for-profit hospital, these cases would be sent somewhere else."

"The hospital accepts a certain number of non-paying cases but has restrictive criteria for their admission. Such non-pay patients tend to require more extensive long-term therapy.

Mission Oaks is neither staffed nor equipped to handle more than one or two *freebee* cases at a time. Some folks have a hard time understanding our position."

Rod had a puzzled look on his face.

Larry clarified. "There is a state-owned and operated mental health hospital in the southern part of the city that handles state-sanctioned care such as Medicaid or court-ordered care, There are also several other non-governmental mental health hospitals and clinics in the surrounding suburbs and nearby cities and counties."

Larry suddenly looked at his watch and sighed. "Time to go, Dad. Pam asked me to run a few errands for her before suppertime. I sure don't want to disappoint her."

CHAPTER 10

THE police car arrived at Mission Oaks Mental Health Hospital ten minutes after the call from Enrique Salazar, the head of housekeeping. Lieutenant (Lt) Jesse Hagen of the MPD was accompanied by a young patrolman securing the butt of his service pistol.

Hagen had arranged for a squad of policemen to surround all outside doors leading from the hospital. The murderer might still be in the bowels of the complex and attempt to leave from one of the exits. This appeared over-cautionary. The murderer was probably long gone.

Boyd Bounder, the chief nurse of the hospital, met them in the front hallway. Mr. Clemens, the administrator was out sick for the day.

"Do you mind if I have some of the uniforms search your hospital?" Hagen asked Bounder.

"Look, Lieutenant, let me remind you this is a mental health facility," Bounder replied. "Our patients have spooked enough already. Word of the horrific murder spread like wildfire throughout the patient rooms and hallways. Even the staff is on edge. Can you have some plain-clothed officers search? I think that would be less traumatic to all concerned."

Hagen sighed out loud with his disgust at Bounder's suggestion. He told the officers who'd arrived with him to stand down. He then radioed the request back to headquarters. Soon, five officers dressed in various civilian garb reported to him. Bounder gave Hagen a schematic of the hospital engineering plan. Hagen's group made a quick assessment of the two-story hospital configuration. They were given their assignments and took off on the run.

"Slow down you damn idiots!" Hagen shouted. "You're too energetic and eager. You're going to alarm everybody in this mysterious place. More than likely the murderer is gone by now. At the same time, stay alert."

"Don't you therapists have some kind of emergency lockdown system here?" Hagen asked Bounder.

"No!" Bounder replied with an empathic voice. "Why would a hospital need such an exigency plan? We're a peaceful community."

"Haven't you ever heard of terrorists storming public facilities—either blowing them up or creating hostage situations?" Hagen fired back at him in disgust. "You sure as hell better get such a plan developed and get it done soon. I'm going to report your lack of concern to the chief. He'll be on your case quicker than greased lightning to get it done."

"This isn't a public facility, Lieutenant," Bounder said in a harsh tone of voice.

"Tough shit. Just get it done." Hagen exhorted.

The search was conducted in an orderly fashion. Each patient room, all the storage rooms, the day rooms, and all the utility closets were checked out. Even the administrative offices were searched. Any person visiting a patient was interviewed. Personal information was written in the officers' logbooks.

"Ouch! Hold on, officer," one patient visitor shouted. "You have no right to do that to me. I'm going to call my lawyer and sue you for excessive and unwarranted force."

The officer ignored the warning and spread-eagled her against the wall. A second police officer read the Miranda rights to her. They suspected the lady was going for a gun. She was concealing a canister of mace and decided to show it to the officers. Everybody seemed to have a legitimate reason for being in the building. There were no suspicious persons believed to be the killer. The search was completed in two hours.

"Take me up to the murder scene," Hagen directed Bounder after he dispatched the plain-clothed officers. "I have a team of forensics on their way over as we speak. The medical examiner is with them. I'm glad you had the foresight to partition off the area and place a guard there to prevent entry by any unauthorized personnel. You've got a lot of weirdos running around this place. God only knows what would've happened if one of them messed with the dead body."

"We'll wait until everyone is here," Bounder said. Hagen was about to object, then fell silent.

In a short time, the assembled group of investigators headed to the elevator for a tour of the murder scene. They found the victim partially covered with a hospital blanket when they entered the second-floor dayroom. It was a gruesome sight. Even Hagen emitted a long, deep audible breath.

The forensic team went to work. Behind them was an overweight man dressed in a black sweater, black pants, and wearing dark wire miniature glasses. He ignored the busy cops and went to work. If anyone hadn't figured it out by now, Hagen introduced him as the coroner. He didn't refer to the man's official title–medical examiner.

"She died roughly nine hours ago," Dr. Juan Pena reported to nobody in particular. "That would have put the time of her death at around, let's see, it's eight now. She probably died sometime near eleven o'clock last night."

"What time is 'lights out' around here?" Hagen asked Bounder.

"We try to shut down the dayrooms by ten o'clock and get the patients back to their rooms. We conduct an informal bed check at nine. Sometimes our evening routines are preempted by unplanned disruptions. We have to delay our usual process when this occurs."

"I can't believe that nobody heard any screams for help or shuffling around in the hallway," Hagen said. "A stabbing victim has enough time and physical wherewithal to shout for help. There had to be a major struggle. Maybe the sounds were masked by some outside ruckus. We dispatched a unit last night in response to a 911 call about a three-car accident near this building. Ten-to-one we'll find that murderer soon."

Hagen received a text message on his cell phone from the supervisor of the plain-clothed officer detail that searched the inside of the hospital. He let out a big sigh of relief when given the "all clear" report.

"The building has also been declared safe from any intruders by the search team deployed outside the hospital," Hagen reported. "We'll come back later and do a more detailed interrogation of everybody here. We'll include the patients and the entire staff. I trust you can arrange that for us, Nurse Bounder?"

Bounder replied in the affirmative.

"I also think it's weird that the body wasn't discovered until this morning," Hagen continued. "Didn't anyone go up and check out the dayroom in the course of late-night rounds? Not," he gruffly answered his question. "I hate dealing with hospitals. This one is worse than the others."

"Make sure that photographer takes close-ups of those etchings in the pooled blood," Hagen kept on ordering. "She might've been trying to leave a message before she died. Why else would scribblings be depicting a series of nine or possibly ten numbers? Be extra careful about not touching the scissors."

Hagen commented to the investigators, "This weapon is too big to come from somebody's office desk drawer in the hospital. In my opinion, the scissors could be from the hospital kitchen. Make sure you're gloved. Don't pull the damn thing out of her chest, either. We'll find a set of fingerprints on the scissors if we're lucky. Make sure you dust everywhere that a person could touch while committing the act."

The Lieutenant turned to Pena and told him, "When you get her body back to the morgue, make sure you scrape under her fingernails to check for skin samples. She may have clawed the murderer with those long fingernails. Also, check to see if there is evidence if the perp fucked her. We need as much DNA evidence that we're able to collect around here."

The medical examiner shot a glare at Hagen.

"Anything else I can do for you, your majesty?" Pena shouted back at Hagen. "Shall I wipe her ass also? I've been in this business for thirty-some-odd years. This isn't the first murder case I've been involved with. For your highnesses' information, we have a specific protocol to follow on cases such as this one."

"Who is this woman anyway?" Hagen questioned as he looked at Bounder.

"Her name is Elsie Turk," Bounder replied. "She was a patient on the first floor. Been here three weeks. I've got to notify her doctor right away. He'll notify the next of kin."

"What's she been treated for? Give me a diagnosis?" Hagen demanded. *I can't take these shrinks anymore.*

"Sorry, we can't release privileged medical information at this time. It's a legal issue."

Hagen was getting upset with Bounder. "How in the hell are we going to investigate the facts surrounding this murder if we don't know what was wrong with her? Do you hapless shrinks think we have some kind of a magic box we dial into that spits out all the answers?"

"Well, don't you?" Bounder smirked. "Anyway, you'll get it at the appropriate time. Dr. Dean is the attending physician. He'll meet with you and discuss whatever information he's allowed to release. Legal issues take precedence."

"I'll slap a damn subpoena on this place faster than the blink of a camel's eye," Hagen shouted back at Bounder. "You medics think you got the world snookered and can do whatever you damn well please! Does that Hypercritical Oath you took make you stand taller than the rest of us mortal human beings? Well, there are laws, you know, and definite procedures that must be followed if we're going to crack open this case."

Bounder was beginning to wonder if Hagen could benefit from therapy himself! I should send him a copy of the Hippocratic Oath. If he took the time to read the oath maybe he could influence the chief to mandate all the detectives to pledge ethical behavior in the performance of their duties.

The initial murder investigation was conducted down to the tiniest detail. A separate team of three plain-clothed police officers returned the next day to continue the investigation. They interviewed every patient in the hospital and all the staff members. They called in those who were not on duty that night. The group identified four "patients of interest" who would undergo more extensive questioning and evaluation. Their attending physicians might be hesitant or resistant. The next step would result in additional pressure on the already fragile individuals. They also felt two hospital staff personnel should undergo more intensive interrogation.

The team reviewed the photos taken at the crime scene before they had arrived at the hospital. They were stymied about the numbers that were written in Elsie Turk's pooled blood. Nothing made sense. The team planned to bring in a highly skilled, interpretive criminal analyst from Chicago to help them unravel that part of the mystery.

One of the team members asked Bounder, "What can you tell us about the victim that's legal to release?"

"Elsie Turk was a forty-five-year-old female Anglo of German descent according to our records," Bounder offered. "She didn't have any recorded or known next of kin, nor did she have a local address. It was common knowledge that she was one of the few charity cases that Dr. Dean would agree to admit to the hospital."

Bounder hesitated to tell them more. The word in the clinic was that her mental health history was so intriguing that Dean felt compelled to further investigate. He was in the process of writing an article to be presented at the annual American Psychiatric Association meeting the following month. There wasn't a record indicating the person or agency that referred Elsie Turk to Dr. Dean's care.

The local newspaper was uncomplimentary about the lack of security for mental health patients at Mission Oaks Mental Health Hospital. The reporters were stymied about the circumstances surrounding the murder and the investigation that followed. The administrator was defensive and outright rude with the reporters when they sought more definitive information. The murder happening in a downtown hospital was ruthlessly played out by the press. After all, it was a tight-knit mental health facility.

The hospital ownership group shifted into high gear when things began to settle down after the gruesome murder. They questioned the leadership abilities of Mr. Clemens in his capacity as a hospital administrator. The entire staff seemed to be coming apart at the seams. Clemens was fired after he was cleared by law enforcement from any involvement in the murder.

The owners felt strongly they could defend their action if confronted by a formal complaint, or lawsuit initiated by the disgruntled Mister Clemens. Boyd Bounder was appointed the interim hospital administrator.

An unannounced event took place five days after Turk's murder. Lt. Hagen brought in a man wearing a custom-tailored pinstripe suit. He was accompanied by a woman dressed in an expensive, two-piece light blue Armani outfit. The lady was wearing attractive spiked Prada's on her small feet. They assembled in Boyd Bounder's office on the first floor. Boyd eased the door shut.

Hagen asked Bounder if his office was wired.

"Wired for what?" Bounder replied. "This is a hospital, not some type of high-flying secretive research laboratory."

Hagen addressed the assembled group. "The following discussion is highly confidential. Only Bounder–nobody else in the hospital or community needs to know the specifics."

Everybody listened with interest.

Hagen went on to say that, "Marie Martini here is a CIA operative from Langley, VA. Jorge Vasquez is a special agent from our local FBI office. They will be taking over the investigation of Elsie Turk's murder. The MPD is finished with the investigation from this point forward. We got other things to do."

"So, we won't be seeing you anymore," Bounder said.

"We'll provide any liaison or other assistance if duly requested by either of the federal agencies. I trust everybody was impressed with the MPD. We pride ourselves on a quick and effective response to disasters of this nature."

Bounder said nothing.

Lt. Hagen saluted the group, did a sharp about-face, and marched out of Bounder's office.

What an imbecile, Bounder thought. He thinks he's still in the fucking military. Why the FBI? How come the CIA is interested? Why in God's name did I ever agree to become the acting hospital administrator when they fired that worthless Clemens?

MURDER IN A SAN ANTONIO PSYCH HOSPITAL

The agents talked briefly to Bounder about how they would conduct the investigation. They apologized for having to leave the hospital so soon. They had to return to Vasquez's office ASAP for an important conference call from Washington.

"I'll call you the next day or so, Mr. Bounder," Marie said. "We'll set up our next meeting when convenient for both parties. Thank you for your courtesies."

The investigators departed the hospital. Boyd wondered why they didn't start digging into the case as soon as they'd arrived. After all, murders are not daily events in psychiatric hospitals. He rationalized. *Oh well, I'm just a plain old clinician. I'm sure they know what the hell they're doing. I sure wasn't aware government officials from Washington could afford the expensive attires they flaunt around us normal people logging duty in the trenches.*

CHAPTER 11

"**WHAT** makes you think he's qualified?" Dr. Dean asked when Larry presented his case for Rod to complete his residency at Mission Oaks. Dean also served as chief of the medical staff at the hospital in addition to being one of the primary owners.

"He doesn't have any formal mental health service background. And you're proposing that I toss him to the wolves. C'mon Larry, think about it."

"Look, Phil," Larry countered. "He's not being asked to treat patients here but only rotates between the administrative departments of the hospital."

"You'd blow a fuse, Phil if any administrative types even hinted that they could help some of the patients by interfacing with their treatment. Rod has managed multi-million-dollar properties in the past and has extensive people management experience to boot. He's not one of those twenty-two-year-old, wet behind the ears graduate students from Trinity University with a recent Hospital Administration Degree. The only experience these young men and women possess is their magical kingdom of academia. Furthermore, there's no conflict of interest involved if you're worried about that. I don't treat patients at this hospital."

"Let me sleep on it, Larry. I'll have to run this past the other owners to get their concurrences. You know Smyth will follow suit if I end up agreeing. Let me remind you that CPA Mooney is an obstructionist. He is the majority owner. He's ornery. On top of that, the man thinks he's God's gift to mankind."

"Fair enough, Phil, but please don't take long. Dad is sending out numerous resumes. He's starting to become a little disappointed about not hooking up anywhere. Dad's of the opinion that prospective bosses think he's too old to jump headfirst into something new and different. My father thrives on new challenges. He always has, believe me!"

Several days had passed when a telephone call in the early evening jolted Phil Dean away from his favorite TV program– "Dancing with the Stars." His wife was out with the girl-groupies at the Olive Garden Restaurant. It was one of their monthly get-togethers after playing bridge. He savored a night of uninterrupted space.

The wife was a marathon talker. She was convinced everybody was in awe at her every word whenever she engaged in a conversation. Phil had one of the other staff psychiatrists cover for him tonight. He snatched the phone off the hook in anger and was ready to berate the caller.

"Doctor Phil, this is Howard I.M. Hill. How the hell are they hanging, old man?"

"You first-class jerk, Howard, I was about to watch a world-class athlete win the whole shebang on the 'Dancing with the Stars' program. Why have I been bestowed the great honor of receiving a telephone call from the humblest Howard Hill, sanctioned and famed leader of the Army of Local Addicts?"

Hill and Dean went back a long way. Dean headed up a community drug and alcohol program when Hill was brought in by two cops late one afternoon in a drunken stupor. They'd asked Dean to take him under his wings as a favor to Jesus Astrade, their chief of police. Hill and Astrade served together as young teenagers after the Korean conflict. They became great friends over the ensuing years. This was an unusual trio . . . if there ever was one that walked the local streets–Astrade, Dean and Hill.

Dean was hesitant to treat Hill at first because of his friendship with Astrade but soon acquiesced. Howard became his favorite patient of all time in the short time he underwent treatment. Hill's witty humor and dingbat antics drove Dean out of his mind. They formed a unique relationship over time. It was Phil Dean who was instrumental in convincing Hill to return to school and turn his convoluted life around. The rest is history.

Howard Hill was now considered one of the leading addiction counselors in the State of Texas. He didn't use his middle initials anymore. Ignatius and Matthew were two of his young mother's favorite saints. She felt heavenly blessed to bestow their biblical names on her first-born son.

"Phillip, very kind soul and revered psychic healer of those mentally challenged, I need a big favor from you," Howard began. "One of my best people out there needs a short-term residency to fulfill his graduate program requirements. I can't think of a better place for him to make his mark than at Mission Oaks. I need your firepower to make that happen."

Howard Hill wasn't one to mince words when he wanted something done, no matter who he was talking to.

"Howard, how long have you been acquainted with this Rod Richards?" Dean asked.

"I've known Richards for years, even graduated number one in my addiction program a short time ago. He wasn't an alcoholic, clinically speaking, but suffered from a case of severe depression. His wife died unexpectedly."

"Yes, Howard, I know about her untimely death."

Hill wasn't through yet. "On top of that, he saved this over-aggressive idiot on two occasions in Vietnam. One time I got all boozed up and ventured out with a .50 caliber machine gun mounted on my jeep. I was hunting for those pajama-clad, sons-of-bitch Viet Cong. I boldly ventured across the Laotian border for some big-time killing action but never found the goddamn enemy."

Phil said nothing.

"I didn't get caught, Phil. Richards covered for me when I returned. Our combat, inexperienced and godforsaken colonel was a lulu. You don't want to know about the second time Richards bailed my thick-skinned hinder out of trouble. War is a living hell, brother Phillip!"

"Funny thing happened on the way to the forum, Howard," Dean laughed at him. "His son approached me the other day with the same request. I've already interviewed him and decided to bring him aboard. It's contingent on the approval of the rest of the ownership."

"Hooah," Hill shouted.

"What can we lose, Howard? The guy seems to have his act together. His unique experience is hard to find on the open market. I'm expecting great things from him, believe me. I'm for hiring him permanently if he does well. Be assured though, I'll hang all the goddamn blame on you if he flunks the test–you no good son of a bitch!"

They laughed and continued to joke around and hassle each other. Dean missed the entire winning dancing performance. The nimble, former professional athlete and his skilled dancing partner surfaced as winners. One other team consisting of a handsome Hollywood actor and his strikingly beautiful partner were the odds-on favorites to win. They were gracious in defeat.

Dean was always happy to talk to Hill on any subject of which Hill always professed to be the expert. Dean knew enough to let Howard inflate his ego at will. He found it senseless to attempt to deflate him.

CHAPTER 12

ROD Richards left Navarro Street in plenty of time for his scheduled appointment at the hospital. Fiesta party time was long gone. He thought it was hard to believe he'd been in the Alamo City for a year and a half. He loved the short drive past Frost Bank with the little park across the street. He occasionally walked this same route at night from his condo when he preferred a leisurely walk in the early evening. It was quality time to reflect on the happenings of the day.

He even enjoyed running again, thanks to Howard Hill's program. Jogging the Riverwalk often encountered too many tourists. He put up with it. The exercise generated enough endorphins to satisfy him. Rod swung into the hospital parking lot, locked the Honda, and crossed the street to the hospital entrance.

It was mid-morning on Tuesday. Rod was scheduled to meet Harry Mooney, the CPA majority shareholder of the corporation that owned the hospital. Mooney was curious why Dr. Dean consented to the short-term residency. He wanted to see for himself what this Rod Richards was like in person and under stress. Upfront, he'd advised Dean he was against the decision. Mooney was unable to come up with any valid reasons when pressed for his dissent.

It was well known by most senior hospital staff that Dean had a way of getting what he wanted. Mooney was aware of this fact. He was often quoted by the administrative staff expounding that "those physicians think they inherited mother earth and have clear title to the entire world."

Dean and the other physicians were convinced Mooney could benefit by spending more time in his treatment facility. The only undeniable fact that assured his constant presence on top was his majority ownership in the place.

Peppi Perez is a friendly middle-aged outgoing receptionist. She greeted Rod when he came into the hospital lobby. Peppi was an old-timer at Mission Oaks. She'd worked as a front desk clerk when the building was a hotel. Peppi stayed on with the new ownership at the time the building was converted to a hospital.

Peppi was short, overweight, and wore drab, unattractive clothing. Her bubbling personality masked her other shortcomings. The hospital staff loved her. Mooney all-out trusted her, often telling her stories he wouldn't share with his peers. Somehow, Peppi engineered the recovery of his lost watch when he stayed in the hotel one weekend before it went bankrupt and later became a hospital.

Rod felt comfortable with the atmosphere of the hospital. He judged it not intimidating, but friendly. The place resembled a western museum. Paintings depicting the siege of the Alamo hung throughout the lobby area. A large picture of the defeated Mexican General Santa Anna was draped above the outside lobby entrance. Davy Crockett and Lieutenant Colonel Travis would soon displace the Mexican dictator.

"He's expecting you," Peppi said as she led him to Mooney's office behind the main reception area. "Have fun," she said with a huge grin. *This ought to be good.*

Rod wondered what the hell she meant by that comment. He observed a huge mahogany desk stationed near an opened window upon entering the big office. The entire room was paneled in dark pecan robbing the area of much-needed light. Two huge, mounted elk heads hung on opposite sides of the wall. One elk head had an eye sewn shut. Rod thought there had to be an interesting story begging to be told.

Below the one-eyed animal was a wet bar containing several bottles of gin and vodka lining the shelves. No evidence of any mixes or soft drinks. Rod questioned why but wasn't about to pursue an answer.

Three large leather, overstuffed chairs surrounded a gigantic redwood stump that served as a handy coffee table. An assortment of cookies and a carafe of coffee were placed in the center of the coffee table. Two porcelain cups, an arrangement of silverware, and embroidered napkins with the initials H.M. sat next to the coffee container. The room lacked expensive wall-to-wall carpeting. A shiny black bearskin throw rug was situated between the chair arrangement and the big desk. The bear's head was still intact, and a vicious-looking set of teeth protruded from the opened mouth. The room reeked of cigar smoke. Mooney was standing by the window gazing out at the parking lot in deep thought.

"Welcome aboard, Rod," he said as he turned around and reached out to shake his hand. "We're happy to have you aboard," he lied. "I hope you like my little office here. It brings out the sporting mania in me. Rather unusual for a hospital, don't you think? It was the main reception room of the old hotel that we bought and converted into this fine hospital."

Harry Mooney was overweight. A ballooned belly hung over his suspendered trousers. His pant legs were tucked into ostrich cowboy boots. Liver spots adorned his cheeks and the back of his hands. His bulgy nose looked like a Texas road map with numerous red stretches of highway. A monk's short haircut accentuated his receding bald head. Mooney's fleshy neck was jammed into a starched collar.

He didn't fit the image of a CPA with the green visor, thick glasses, and outdated clothing. Rod wondered how he ever accumulated enough wealth to buy a hotel. This guy was not impressive by any stretch of his imagination.

"I've arranged a schedule for you to spend the majority of your time in most of the administrative areas," Mooney continued his earlier welcoming. "The six months will speed by for you. I'm sure of it."

I wonder how happy this guy is with having me here, Rod reflected. From everything I've heard about Mooney, he's a big jerk. Just because he's a glorified CPA and owns the majority of this place doesn't automatically get him etched in my book of valued acquaintances.

"I appreciate your kind words of confidence and allowing me residency training at Mission Oaks. I'm sure you'll be pleased with my performance. I've always tried to improve things wherever I've worked. You'll be delighted you brought me on board."

"Fine, let's go meet some of the main people you'll be working with," Mooney said. *This guy is trouble. I sense it. Too proud and confident.*

They headed down the hall to Boyd Bounder's office. Voices could be heard behind the door. Mooney barged in without knocking. Bounder was chewing out a male orderly who failed to check out one of the secured hospital areas last night. Boyd was pointing both index fingers at the guy's chest. The poor lad was reduced to tears.

"Morning, Boyd," Mooney said. "I thought you were alone in there." Rod noted the man was deaf and outright rude.

Mooney had no intention to apologize for the interruption. The four men stood in silence for a moment while the orderly dabbed a handkerchief to each swollen eye. The young man was starting to shake. He stared at Mooney and began to cower.

"Could you do this chit-chat at another time, Boyd?" Mooney asked. "I have someone important here I want you to meet. Sorry, I can't wait. I gotta head out right away."

Rod thought the man was an idiot. *The human being this guy loved the dearest was the person in the bathroom mirror looking back at him each morning when he brushed his teeth.*

Bounder hesitated while he searched for a sharp reply to fire back at Mooney. He decided against it and then turned to the orderly and excused him.

"This here is Rod Richards," Mooney said with pride as if the newcomer were his long-lost prodigal son. "He's going to spend six months with us. He's performing a required short-term residency for his master's degree. I expect him to jump into every nook and cranny of the hospital. He has loads of management experience. We're happy to have him join us. Maybe he can shake up the organization and make it more efficient." Mooney was on a roll, never for a loss of words.

Boyd nodded.

Mooney continued. "Boyd, I believe I sent you a dossier about Mr. Richards last week. I hope you read it over in great detail. Dr. Dean was hesitant in bringing Rod in here, but I convinced him that we had nothing to lose and everything to gain. I trust you agree, Boyd."

Bounder ignored Mooney and then faced Rod.

"Very pleased to meet you, Mr. Richards." He extended his right hand. "I took the liberty of scheduling your residency program because I'm the acting administrator. It's divided into six, one-month segments. I skewed the training plan both to your documented strengths and to our own needs at this time. You'll meet a dedicated staff. I hope you'll be pleased with the arrangement."

Mooney clapped his hands and interrupted. A practice he'd perfected over the years of mismanaging his staff. "I've got a meeting with the esteemed Captain Jesus Astrade at the police station requiring me to leave you boys to your duties. They're in the early planning stages of developing some sort of program to provide mental health care to adolescent inmates. An outside, contracted researcher found about seventy percent of the incarcerated deadbeats need our type of support. Astrade feels the percentage is even higher in our county. Maybe Mission Oaks can help them. I'll see you, fine folks, later."

Mooney hitched up his suspenders a notch and pranced graciously out of Bounder's office as though resembling one of the famed Budweiser Clydesdales.

CHAPTER 13

BOUNDER signaled for Rod to take a seat. "I've heard nothing but good things about you. I golf with George Dean, one of the therapists at South Town Psychiatric Services. He's Dr. Dean's nephew and followed with interest the heated discussions about you. Seems your proposed residency wasn't a hit with everybody. Mooney fired the old hospital administrator. The hospital board felt I could hold the fort down until they hired a replacement."

Rod smiled, enjoying the dramatics.

"Things have been hectic around here," Boyd continued. "You may've heard we had a murder take place in our upstairs dayroom. An extensive investigation has already begun. I won't get you involved in that mess because it would interfere with the purpose of your residency."

"I appreciate your comments, Mr. Bounder," Rod responded.

"Stop, hold it right there. I'd be upset if you didn't call me Boyd, okay? And none of that 'yes sir'–'no sir' business either. I do know you were an army man with responsible positions. A person's rank doesn't mean a thing in this environment. Our philosophy is to treat everyone as dedicated professionals. There is no caste system at Mission Oaks."

"Thanks," Rod said. "And please call me Rod." He liked informality.

"Mooney would love it if everyone genuflected at the mere mention of his exalted name," Bounder laughed. "As far as I'm concerned, and don't you dare quote me on this, he's a glorified bean counter who happens to own a big piece of this pie. He's rarely seen by anyone with a client in his office. I don't like chin-wagging out of school, but Mooney is the one exception. The character is in a world of his own. I'm sure you've already witnessed the fact."

"Got it, Boyd," he said and smiled back at him. "By the way, do you have a relative that lives in San Francisco? There was a Brahm Bounder who lived in the apartment we managed. He's a big dude, a redheaded Texan from down in the Rio Grande Valley. You two seem to have many of the same characteristics and mannerisms, although I've only known you for a few minutes."

"I bet Brahm is my long-lost uncle. Dad told me that he had a brother who left home at a young age and headed west. I still hear stories about him every time I meander back home. I'm from Harlingen, Texas. Brahm's family ranch is up the road near Raymondville. It's a short drive from our homestead. I'm sure he's getting on in age."

"He's had a little heart trouble," Rod informed him, "But I guess that comes with getting older. He sure helped us out when we took the manager's position. I'll drop him a note and tell him I landed in your lap. I'm sure that he'd appreciate knowing that."

"Do that. Let me gather some hospital policies and operating procedures requested by the investigators for their review when they return. Sit tight, Rod. Then we'll head down to the dining room for lunch. We can continue our discussion there and maybe meet some of the key hospital staff."

Rod didn't pursue Boyd's comment about the murder situation. He had enough on his plate for the time being. He'd caught some of the earlier media reports on the murder. That was before he knew his destiny would be tied to Mission Oaks Hospital.

"Most of the department heads are brown-baggers but smart enough to read the weekly dining hall menu," Boyd offered. "They like to pick out the special days they prefer to eat here. There seems to be a routine. Mexican food is served on Monday, steak on Wednesday, and fish or some other type of seafood on Friday. It's anybody's guess what we'll get in between those featured days. Our kitchen and dining room are unique."

"Agreed, Boyd. My son Larry filled me in about the kitchen. He led me on a *cook's tour* through the hospital when we first talked about future employment opportunities. He implied the dining room was a profitable venture. Foodservice operations are seldom money-makers from my experience but provide a needed service."

"You hit the nail on the head. Dr. Dean thinks it's profitable. He forced Mooney to hire an experienced chef from one of the Riverwalk hotels. Too bad we can't charge the customers the going rate they get over at the Marriott. This could be an area for you to check out during your residency."

"Why have you restricted patients eating here?" Rod continued with the questioning. "I would think if the patients ate here it would represent a healthy diversion from sitting in their rooms all day. A little extra exercise walking the stairs and the long hallways would do them some good."

"Rod, we can't get a staff consensus on your opinion. The therapists feel like they need a break from the patients. The gathering here allows them to share ideas and build relationships with each other. It fosters *esprit de corps* in your military lingo."

He took an immediate liking to the big Texan. Boyd wasn't a day over thirty-five in his assessment. Bounder wore a buzz cut which accentuated his bright red hair. He was muscular as evidenced by the bulging arms that crawled out from a short-sleeved shirt. He was also wearing cowboy boots, but not of the ostrich variety. Rod didn't notice a wedding ring on his left ring finger nor pictures of cute, little ankle-biters adorning his desk.

There was a huge plastic longhorn mounted on the wall opposite Bounder's desk. A picture of him decked out in a burnt orange football uniform hung next to it. A "hook-em horns" logo was affixed to the bottom of the frame. Boyd told everyone who saw the photo that he was a heavily recruited, third-string blocking dummy at the University of Texas. He joked and expounded that he was known by the first and second-string gridders as a lover, not a fighter.

Rod was nearly knocked over by a speeding four-wheeled scooter as they stepped out of Boyd's office. The enormous guy driving the machine was decked-out like Santa Claus and singing "Jingle Bells." He had a set of copper bells he clanged after each verse of the Yule song. His flowing white beard swung back and forth with each refrain. *Strange, Rod thought. It's only the first of March. What's with this guy?*

"Watch out where you're going mister," Rod shouted as the carriage sped past them and screeched around the corner of the hallway.

Boyd laughed out loud, bending over in near hysteria. He had a hard time containing himself. Rod stared back at him, wondering what in the hell was so funny.

"That's Eduardo Munez, Rod," he said. "Eduardo is a man of all seasons, not necessarily in the order which they appear on the calendar. Where he gets those colorful outfits is anyone's guess. He must have an outside supplier. However, we do have some ingenious people in this building. Yes, staff members or simply patients receiving treatment who could have provided the Santa Claus outfit. We're not sure." Rod shrugged.

"He's been with us for an extended period now," Boyd continued. "The VA is paying for his care. Munoz was awarded a Bronze Star with Valor for his actions at the close of the Korean War. It stipulated gallantry above and beyond the call of duty. He singlehandedly wiped out twelve North Korean soldiers who tried to ambush his squad's position."

"What's his mental health problem?" Rod asked. *This guy must be some kind of super dare-devil.*

He's being tre

"Eduardo is being treated for delusions of grandeur. Sometimes he thinks he's Napoleon Bonaparte and dresses up in royalty attire. He can't carry a sword, though he has asked us to provide him one. Now and then he supposes he's Adolph Hitler. He submitted a letter to the administrator asking for a list of the Jewish patients hospitalized here. Eduardo is harmless. All the patients enjoy his antics and outlandish sense of humor. The nurses don't."

"I would think the VA would take care of disabled veterans within their system," Rod replied. "That's what Congress intended, and we're paying plenty of taxes for these former members to have access to quality care. They deserve only the best for their dedicated years of service. Why did they send him to us?"

"They tend to be overwhelmed with mental health patients most of the time and have to farm out a certain amount of their beneficiaries. We never complain. The reimbursement for our services helps cash flow. Our official position is accepted by the staff. We will provide the needed care and help the VA to the extent of our capabilities. Sure, we've turned down some of their referrals. We can't handle violent cases that require extensive and expensive medication. They'd walk around here like zombies from outer space."

"Then why is that patient riding around in that annoying power cart?" Rod asked.

Boyd was quick to justify. "He was also wounded in action north of Seoul. A low-velocity pistol round nicked his back near the lower spine. He believes he's unable to walk. Yet, I saw him on two occasions get out of bed and head to the bathroom, marching like a strait-laced soldier. We think it's psychosomatic, but he's convinced he'll never walk again. He harangued or twisted somebody's arm in the VA system to issue him the motorized cart."

As he swung around the corner, Eduardo wondered who the new guy was talking with Bounder. He had to know everyone associated with the staff because he hated outsiders. This guy looked and acted like a federal agent.

Any outsider was considered a threat to Eduardo and his loyal associates. He didn't need another anonymous person running around the hallways at this particular time. He had an important mission to accomplish. Anyone or anything that threatened his assigned task had to be dealt under his scripted protocol.

"Not bad at all for hospital chow," Rod said as they headed back to Bounder's office after eating lunch. He was relieved he didn't run into the nurse he'd shacked up with several long months ago. He half-hoped that she'd quit her job here and went somewhere else. It'd be better for both of them if that situation happened. Anyway, he wasn't about to pursue that avenue on the front end of his residency. Maybe later.

"Well, as I told you," Boyd said, "We never know for sure what's going to be tossed on our plates on Tuesdays or Thursdays. The Swedish meat- balls and pasta were filling. We're proud of our chef. He turned down the opportunity to return to work at a Riverwalk hotel. He loves the freedom of operation and outstanding atmosphere we offer at Mission Oaks. We encourage his culinary creativity."

"I see, but at what expense to the hospital? Do we have a centralized system for purchasing our food supplies?"

"I have no clue, Rod. Good question. As I said before, you might look into the entire foodservice operation as you get settled into your residency. Needless to say, many important issues must be prioritized before heading off in that direction."

Rod was despondent when they served him the Swedish meatballs. *He thought again about his Swedish wife, Janice, and the wonderful life they had together until her death. Nobody could prepare those meatballs like her! Time for another major life adjustment.*

"I've converted one of the patient rooms on the first floor for your temporary office," Boyd broke his silence and chuckled. "Not every employee has their private bathroom. Let's head over there, and you can spend several hours reviewing the stacks of documents I put on your desk. I'll drop by this afternoon to see where you're at in the process. I'm sure I can answer any questions you will have jotted down."

Bounder left with a wave of a hand. Rod hunkered down in his desk chair and scanned the pile of paperwork staring him in the face. He brought both arms and hands up to the back of his neck and joined the fingers together. Maybe a little too tight. He took a deep breath, smiled widely, and then went to work. Soon he hoped to understand the onerous and intricate duties of a hospital administrator.

CHAPTER 14

TWO federal agents arrived at Mission Oaks Mental Health Hospital early one morning and asked to speak with Dr. Phillip Dean. They presented their credentials to the receptionist, Peppi Perez. She politely told them that Dr. Dean wasn't in the hospital, but they could speak with the acting administrator. She called Boyd Bounder and asked him to come up front to the reception area.

"Nice to see you again, agents Martini and Vasquez," Boyd said as he met up with them. "I've been expecting you for some time. It's been a week or so since we've seen each other. Our entire staff has been briefed about the purpose of your investigation. We haven't notified the patients. They are still walking on eggshells since they heard about the murder. There's no sense magnifying their apprehensions. We know that you'll talk to some of them as you conduct your investigation. Let's go down to my office where we can sit and discuss the ground rules for your interrogations."

He turned to Peppi and asked her to contact the dining hall to bring a pot of coffee and some sweet rolls to his office. She nodded an affirmative to Bounder, smiled warmly at the group, and returned to her cubicle. The other three then proceeded to Bounder's office.

"Do you mind if we call you Boyd?" Marie Martini asked. It now appeared to Bounder that the lady from the CIA was in charge of this threesome. Vasquez shrugged his shoulders as he stared back at her.

"Not at all," Bounder said. "I trust I can call you Marie."

"Of course. Where's Dr. Dean? We were specific when we asked he be here today to join us for the opening briefing."

"He's tied up at his clinic with an emergency," Bounder replied. "He told me that he'd get over here as soon as possible. Some lady walked unannounced into his clinic first thing this morning. She told him she was going to kill her therapist, her husband, and then herself. She was waving a Colt .45 at the young associate who tried to approach her. Dean intervened. We shouldn't wait for him. As a routine, these situations are usually drawn out and time-consuming. Let's hope the confrontation is resolved without anybody getting hurt. I pray it doesn't turn into one of those nasty hostage scenarios."

"Alright Bounder," a disgusted Martini sighed. "I guess that takes precedence over our little confab for now. We've seen too many of these disgruntled idiots running around in public making ridiculous demands. Some of them turn the gun on themselves and end up with a bullet hole in their temple. It's vital we get him in here on the front end of our investigation. He was the doctor treating Elsie Turk. I guess we'll have to proceed without him and hope he gets here soon."

Bounder gave a thumbs up.

"Mr. Vasquez will be here for a short time today," Marie proceeded. "His presence is more of a courtesy call, or I should say formality. The FBI has deferred this investigation to us for several reasons. Right, Jorge?" she said as she turned and faced him.

"That's correct, Marie. This is your problem. The deceased was working for your agency at the time of her death. To top that off, she was murdered in a privately-owned facility. The FBI has enough other important things on their platter to deal with at this time."

"What the hell are you talking about?" Bounder asked in a surprised manner. "What's this 'working for your agency' business all about? Our Dr. Dean took her on as a charity case. She had an unusual mental health disorder, one not often seen by anyone in our clinical communities."

"The whole scenario you described is false, Boyd," she said, "A total fabrication by us and the good Doctor Dean. Elsie Turk was one of our more accomplished field agents. She worked in our Counter Terrorism Unit for many years. The agency brought her back from Qatar in the Middle East for a specific mission in San Antonio. I'm not sure I can share the entire game plan with you at this time."

"Good Lord," Bounder said. "How serious is this thing and why us? Give me something tangible. I gotta make some element of common sense out of this drama."

Marie responded. "our folks had help from your local FBI office. We learned there might be an al-Qaeda for United Liberty cell being formed in your city. Al-Jazeera posted some interesting and threatening information on their website. They inferred that the so-called *Cradle of Texas Liberty* could disappear overnight. We think they were referring to the Alamo. Other historic monuments and well-known sites like NASA in Houston could also be targeted. We can't afford to take any chances."

"I can't believe they'd target the Alamo," Bounder said. "I learned about terrorist organizations. They want to kill a lot of people when they strike. That wouldn't be the case here. A large crowd at the Alamo is not an everyday event. I don't buy it!"

Marie interrupted Boyd's assumptions. "An active companion cell was also identified in a Detroit, Michigan suburb. Elsie Turk was instrumental in ferreting out this information before she was placed here at Mission Oaks Hospital. That location is many miles distant from here. We think there's a tie-in with some radical elements operating in San Antonio. I want to be more specific here. We suspect the principal terrorist involved with this local cell works in your hospital. That, or one of your patients."

"I have a hard time believing that," Boyd said. Marie ignored his comment and continued.

"We even think that person might be a relative of either a staff member or the patient. It's too early to rule out any of these individuals as possible suspects. Lt. Hagen's investigators identified several persons of considerable interest that need our immediate attention."

"We were brought in by the Metro PD," Jorge Vasquez jumped in. "They're not sure what to conclude about Elsie Turk. Her actions are a big mystery to every one of their investigators. There was a complete absence of any background information on her to help them out. There preferred to display caution and asked for our help. The Metro PD reported Dr. Dean wasn't the least bit helpful. They thought we should lean on him a little bit. He has to know more. Maybe he's trying to cover up something."

Bounder walked over and poked him on the shoulder. "Bullshit. Don't you dare question his ethics."

Vasquez stepped back. "Say what you think. We've been monitoring some internet chatter that *raised the red flag . . .* so to speak. One of our more astute agents on the ground was opportunistic enough to snatch some credit card intercepts. His action heightened our realization we have a major problem brewing right here under our collective noses. The big FBI boss decided to contact the CIA because of potential international terrorist implications."

"I've got a list of the six people I want to talk to right away," Marie Martini said. "Jorge, you don't need to hang around here any longer. I'll call you if I need you FBI guys to squeeze in at some point. Thanks again for working with us. Goodbye." She brushed him off as though she was swatting away an annoying mosquito.

"Sounds good to me," Vasquez said. He finished his coffee and stuffed down the remaining two sweet rolls as though he hadn't eaten all day. He stared at Bounder, left the room, and mumbled under his breath. *Let that overbearing she-cat take charge. The head shrink thinks he knows it all. Good riddance!*

Bounder stepped closer to the CIA agent after Vasquez left. He checked her waist, then up to her bright eyes.

"Marie, you haven't done a good job of concealing the weapon that's bulging out of your hip like an unwanted appendage. I can't allow you to be armed while roaming around in my hospital. We have some patients here who could become disturbed and create a problem if they knew you carry a gun on your person. It's dangerous. Please give it to me. I'll have it secured while you conduct your interviews. It's best for all of us, Marie."

"I suppose you're right, Boyd," she said with reluctance.

Marie was wearing clothing which to Bounder seemed at least one size too small for her little body. She unbuttoned her outer jacket and reached around her waist for the weapon. It was a Sig Sauer 9 MM handgun. She left the outer jacket unbuttoned. Marie was quick to catch his prolonged stare at her chest.

Boyd remembered his dad's favorite expression whenever he pulled out an unfiltered Camel cigarette. He would always tamp it down on the fender of his pickup truck or a nearby fence post. "Round, firm, and fully packed," his dad would laugh at any cowhand standing nearby.

That's what Boyd was thinking as he continued his visual assessment of her body.

"Now that I have your complete attention," she said as she buttoned her jacket and started to hand over the weapon. "What's next on the docket, Mr. Bounder?"

"Huh, oh, I was looking at the gigantic pistol you were giving me. The damn canon is almost as big as you are, Marie. I thought you agents all carried Glocks. How can you handle that big gun when you're confronted by the bad guys?"

Bounder's canon was beginning to stir. Marie shot a glance down at his crotch and confirmed the inevitable with a slight grin on her pretty face. She knew she had him in her crosshairs. She'd make him squirm.

"Mr. Bounder," she said with a slight grin, "Let me clarify the issue about Glocks if you have to know about handguns. Many metropolitan police departments carry a standard-issue Glock 17 or even a Glock 26. Both are nine-millimeter weapons. There's also a Glock 37 which packs a heavy- duty .45 caliber round that can knock down a giant at close range. That's my spiel on handguns."

Marie was a good-looking woman. He later learned she was a hundred- percent Italian. Both sets of grandparents came to the United States from a small village outside of Naples when they were still children. This striking beauty wasn't much over five feet tall. It was obvious to him she spent off-duty time working out in the gym.

She allowed him time to collect and summarize his thoughts.

Her physique was the envy of every female employed by the CIA. Marie's dark black hair was cut short, much like a businessman's. It was beginning to show hints of gray around the temple. She wore a neat tan. Her darkened skin emitted a beautiful bronze glow. Bounder estimated her age at forty. He had never been in the presence of a woman quite like this one.

Boyd suggested they take a short break before the interviews. She agreed. He showed her where the restrooms were located and the area where the overstuffed chairs hugged the walls opposite the reception area. Peppi was quick to offer her a chair. He then returned to his office and swung his long legs and feet up on the side of the desk.

"May I get you a glass of water or a cup of coffee?" Peppi asked Marie. She liked the cute government agent right away when she first met her several days ago. *Reminds me of myself when I was that age. Thought I had it all. Well, I did but times change.*

"No thanks, I'm fine, I'll just take advantage of the restroom." She surveyed the colorful paintings on the wall. *How gaudy for a hospital lobby. Cowboy town. What the hell.*

Peppi opened the morning newspaper and started to read the comics. She giggled several times, loud enough for Marie to hear. Peppi scanned the *Hints from Heloise* section and then tossed the paper in the trash can.

Bounder went back to his office with a thousand thoughts. He was interested in this woman's background. Where did she come from? Was she married? He wondered how such a beauty could be so successful in a government agency dominated by thrill-seeking male operatives. Perhaps he missed the 'glass ceiling' implications taking place behind his back in modern society. *I'm sure she's seen the world, witnessed human beings doing unforgivable acts. Without a doubt, this beauty had her share of suitors.*

CHAPTER 15

AGENT Martini didn't miss a beat. She graduated with honors from the University of California, Berkeley, with a degree in criminology. Instead of pursuing criminal justice work, she was paid well to model for a local firm that specialized in high-end formal wear. Her manager was astounded by the poise with which Marie carried herself. She seemed to be on the super-model fast track when recruited by the CIA.

They were looking for a "stunner" who'd be willing to train for some risqué assignments in the Middle East. She impressed her handlers with extraordinary results on her first three case assignments in the states. She was now deemed ready by her supervisors for a major assignment overseas.

She arrived in Qatar posing as an archeological doctoral candidate from UCLA. The last requirement for her dissertation was to complete a "dig" near Doha on the eastern seaboard of Qatar. She acted out her cover in an enthusiastic and convincing manner. Marie relocated to Bahrain to document her findings after the dig. It was here that her sensitive and secretive mission began.

A convenient arrangement was made by a third-party local bigwig to place Marie at a reception. There, she'd have the opportunity to meet Sheik Abdullah Salamah, a prominent local businessman.

The sheik was born a Sunni Muslim in Jeddah, Kingdom of Saudi Arabia, and established a thriving import-export business. It operated out of Bahrain. His family was one of the wealthiest in Saudi. Being the firstborn and only legitimate child, he had the great wealth bestowed on him at a young age. Both parents were killed in a plane crash. Abdullah soon became a fanatical follower of the Wahhabi ideology. He was encouraged by a radical uncle who guided him into adulthood.

"Good evening, my lady," a uniformed valet impeccably dressed in white acknowledged Marie. "May I show you the way to the cloakroom?"

"That would be fine," Marie said. She detoured to the ladies' room to refresh her makeup after he led her there. She headed down the long hallway to the reception area when she finished touching up.

Marie was stunning and gracious as she moved around the reception hall from one influential guest to another. She caught the eye of the handsome sheik. He cornered one of his western associates to introduce them before the guests sat down for the extravagant banquet. They were placed diagonally across from each other by the host's valet. The sheik tracked Marie down after the guests began to bid their farewells to the host. He was smitten with her on the first contact.

"Would you be available for a tour of our beautiful Bahrain tomorrow?" he asked her.

Marie didn't want to appear too eager on first meeting her target. She hesitated for a few moments and then responded to him. "I'm so sorry, Sheik Salamah, but I've made commitments that I cannot cancel at this late notice." She then begged off until the following week.

She and the sheik began seeing each other often. Soon they became intimate. Their lovemaking was so sensual and extraordinary she had to keep reminding herself she was a CIA agent sent there for a specific mission. He was so experienced in the ancient art of love-making she had a difficult but enjoyable time keeping up with him.

Marie was no amateur at love-making either. She was promiscuous in college, having bedded the All-American quarterback and the captain of the debate team on alternate weekends. She got bored with both guys after several weeks and decided to concentrate on her studies.

"You are a beautiful princess, Marifta. I've seen none other like you in this fine city." Whenever they met he'd call her by the pet name he'd given her.

They would join each other in the lounge at the Ramee Baisan Hotel Bahrain, near the center of the Manama section of busy Bahrain. The smooth-talking Salamah decided to move their afternoon trysts to the Ramee Palace Hotel. It provided a more remote location from the sheik's operating base.

"I would be honored if you became my mistress, Marifta," he whispered in her ear one evening after they'd made love.

"Please, Salamah, let's take it a little slower for now," she stalled him. "We barely know each other."

Marie's CIA handler also kept pushing her to gather more information on his suspected arms shipments to certain third-world countries. Normally, this type of gun-running activity wouldn't be given a high priority by U.S. enforcement authorities. They suspected certain lethal biologic agents were also included with the shipments to one of the countries allied with the United States.

Islamic researchers, funded by one of the sheik's unlisted shadow companies, developed a stable form of the amoeba *naegleria fowleri*. When infused in freshwater ponds, lakes, and rivers, the water-borne disease caused by its pathogens could produce a fulminating, rapidly fatal outcome. The sheik was thought to be the mastermind and financier of the entire operation.

He was so entrenched with their intimacies he didn't want to lose her. She'd refused his request to become his "one and only" mistress. The man suspicioned Marie might not be that sweet graduate student from UCLA– but perhaps a foreign operative.

Regardless, the sheik would try to sway her one last time. "Marifta, my sweet one, you are a stubborn woman. I want to share my love and successes with you and only you, my dear little one."

Marie again refused, telling him that she just wasn't ready for a serious commitment but didn't want to break off their relationship.

He was concerned she knew too much about his business operations. That could cause his downfall. It was time to take drastic action to protect his vast financial interests. A specific time and discrete place were arranged by Salamah to have her murdered, but the kill had to be delayed. The only hitman he knew and trusted was unavailable. The gunman was recovering from a deep knife wound to his shoulder while on an earlier assignment for one of the sheik's business partners.

The CIA pulled her out of Bahrain. They suspected Marie was in imminent danger. They contrived a believable scenario to mask her disappearance. She returned to the United States without the sheik's inability to detain her.

At the same time, the CIA had considered moving Elsie Turk, Marie's handler, to Qatar for another assignment. It didn't materialize.

The operatives in Langley were tracking some reports about new terrorist activities in the United States. They needed Elsie to do some background work on possible connections to the Middle East. They wanted this completed before they moved her to Qatar. In the interim, they decided to place her in San Antonio while Marie underwent additional counter-intelligence training at Langley. The powers-to-be felt they should allow things to cool off before assigning another team to expose and capture the sheik.

Meanwhile, Salamah had hired a former bodyguard to find out more about Marie's sudden disappearance. The bodyguard reported back that local authorities had determined Marie was kidnapped. They had no material leads and closed the case.

The sheik finally shrugged it off. He had already found another beautiful and willing woman to share his bed. It was never a problem, or challenge for the handsome Arab to collect a string of beautiful women whenever and wherever he desired heightened self-indulgences.

CHAPTER 16

MARIE finished her business in the restroom and returned to the front lobby. She had a brief chat with Peppi before she headed back to Boyd's office. Peppi told her Boyd Bounder was a wonderful man. Everybody in the hospital loved him. Marie wondered if Peppi was speaking the truth or just trying to impress her.

She returned to Boyd's office. They stared at each other for a few moments, not knowing where the body language and conversation would lead them. There was a surge of electricity flowing between them. The fine hair lining her arms spiked up. She wondered if all Texans were tall and this good-looking. The room fell silent.

"Here are the people I need to talk to," she told Bounder, reverting to a more formal approach. She handed him the list.

He took the document and scanned over the names spelled out alphabetically on the typewritten sheet. The two hospital employees were identified first, followed by the names of the four patients.

"Good God," Bounder uttered. "I can't believe you categorized these two staff personnel."

Marie was surprised at his reaction. Murder cases have no "out-of-bounds" when investigations begin.

"Dalia Garza is the head nurse on the first floor. She's worked here for years. Miss Garza is the most effective nurse we have on staff. Her patients all love her."

Marie sat bored. *Is this going to be like pulling rotten teeth in the dental office?*

"I see Amfi Aziz is also on your list," Boyd smiled. "I think she's some kind of Saudi princess. This whole scenario is strange. Her husband is a Lieutenant in the Saudi Air National Guard. He's at Randolph AFB undergoing training to become a navigator. Jesus H. Christ . . . they both came highly recommended by political bigwigs over there. I'm sure DOD vetted him to the nth degree."

"Mr. Bounder," Marie became more assertive. She thought he was coming unglued. "I'm not at liberty to tell you why the MPD investigators identified these two staff members as persons of interest. It won't take me long to determine the validity of their report. As you know, many factors go into ascertaining why some people seem to draw more attention from the investigators than others."

Bounder disregarded her comments. He scanned down the list of patients that were on the list. He wasn't shocked at any of the other names. Boyd knew most of them. He sat in on the daily reports given by the nursing heads as work shifts changed. Their mental health disorders were complicated and required several weeks of treatment.

The average patient admitted to Mission Oaks required a stay of about eleven days, then followed-up by periodic outpatient treatments. All four of the patients had unusual backgrounds requiring longer inpatient stays. Bounder understood why the MPD investigators fingered these specific four people for follow-up interviews.

"I need you to get me the complete personnel files on the two employees," Marie instructed.

"No problem." He seemed more cooperative.

Marie stood up. "Be sure to include all the demographics and any background information vital to our needs. Make sure I'm given all the confidential information. I want results of psychological testing performed here or elsewhere, drug screens, and any police records that might be addressed in their files. Also, list their mental health problems in lay terminology. I need to understand what's wrong with them. I need it right away, Mr. Bounder—not tomorrow or the next day."

Boyd was concerned. "We may have a hard time gathering any information about Nurse Amfi Aziz. The DOD has pigeon-holed most of the demographics on her. We do have written evidence of her nursing credentials. She had been working at King Fahad Medical Center in Riyadh, Saudi Arabia. She was a med-surg nurse over there and had extra training in the mental health disciplines. The Saudi officials asked us to expand her expertise in psychiatric medicine. I'll round up what I can for you."

"I can live with that, Boyd."

"Why don't you go over to Cantina Classica down the street for an early lunch," Bounder suggested. "Their enchiladas are out of this world, and they serve the best homemade corn tortillas in the city. I should have the majority of the information you asked for by the time you get back."

Marie agreed, she was hungry. She sat down, bent over, and tightened an ankle strap on one of her high heels. She wore three-inch heels that gave her extra height. Both big toes protruded out of the footwear. They were painted a pretty rose color.

It took her several minutes to adjust and readjust the strap. Bounder was writhing in agony. He saw an expanse of cleavage that excited him. *What the hell. Is she doing this to me on purpose? I like what I see! Where do we go from here?*

She pulled herself up off the chair and sauntered to the door. Marie turned back and looked at him as she opened the door to let herself out. Boyd picked up a slight, but a noticeable wink of her eye.

"Better get that pistol locked up before the weapon grows legs and disappears, Boyd. I feel naked without it," she said with a devilish grin.

I wish you were, he imagined . . . round and firm and fully packed!

"Bon appétit," Bounder called meekly as she gently closed the office door behind her. He had never experienced flirtations from a woman the caliber of Marie. Boyd wondered if she might have a sincere hankering for him. Only time would tell. He'd let the proverbial clock run on to see when and where the small and big hands elected to stop.

CHAPTER 17

BOYD was in his office when Marie Martini returned from her lunch down the street. She opened his office door and went in without knocking. Boyd conjured up the thought that his office had become a public domain. Every Tom, Dick, and Harry had immediate access to it.

"I hope you had some of their out-of-this-world enchiladas," Boyd said as she sat down across from him. She smiled back at him, then framed her reply.

"Nope, I tried the puffy tacos. They were too greasy for me. I guess it'll take time for me to get used to the well-known Tex-Mex food served in these parts. I was in luck, though. They fixed me a good healthy salad, and I survived. Several of the Spurs basketball players were also eating there. I don't know when I last saw human skyscrapers like that, she laughed. Do they play tonight?"

"Not that I know of Marie. I prefer to attend football games. Love the violence!"

"Do you have the list I asked you to prepare for me?"

Boyd was hoping for a little chit-chat with her before she jumped into the more serious business at hand. He got up, unlocked a filing cabinet drawer, and pulled out a red-colored manila folder. Boyd gathered and categorized the patient data after their last meeting. He had help from an administrative assistant. Peppi was on a prolonged break.

"Here's everything you asked for, plus some additional information I scrounged up. I thought the more the merrier."

She ignored the comment. There was no merriment inherent in her line of work.

Boyd handed her the folder and sat back down in his chair. She opened the binder and glanced at the contents. For some unknown reason, Boyd had decided to include several standing operating procedures for hospital personnel, new hire protocols, and various work schedules.

Marie zeroed in on the list of people she wanted to contact. The typewritten document was not informative. She needed to review individual personnel files of the employees and the complete medical records of the patients. The former should be no problem, but she knew doctors felt uncomfortable when non-physicians reviewed patient medical records. The one-page document was brief and descriptive.

TO MARIE MARTINI, CIA - FOR YOUR EYES ONLY! CLASSIFIED SENSITIVE MATERIAL

Employees: 1) Dalia Garza. Mexican-American, age 38, unmarried. Born in Matamoros, Mexico but naturalized U.S. citizen. Head Nurse, First Floor. Graduated Nursing School at Incarnate Word College, San Antonio. Employed at Mission Oaks for over four years. Excellent performance reports.

2) Amfi bin Aziz. Saudi National, age 28, married. Born in Taif, Kingdom of Saudi Arabia. Shift Leader, Second Floor. Graduated from King Saud University, Riyadh, Kingdom of Saudi Arabia. Work permit and temporary visa arranged by the U.S. State Department.

Patients: 1) Cook, Norman. Male Caucasian, age 41, divorced, was admitted almost two weeks ago for guilt and worthlessness. Treated for a major depressive disorder, moderate.

2) Hanson, Clark. Male Caucasian, age 55, widowed, was admitted three weeks ago. Treated for a major depressive disorder, severe.

3) Munoz, Eduardo. Mexican-American. Age 72, married with 3 grown children, was admitted five weeks ago. Treated for delusions of grandeur.

4) Peck, Roberta. African-American, age 28, single, was admitted four weeks ago, thinks she's the Blessed Virgin Mary. She is now being treated for paranoid schizophrenia.

"Thank you, Mr. Bounder," she said in a formal voice as she flipped the file into a locked briefcase. She then sat back, took a deep breath, and stared into his eyes.

He wondered what was coming next. *Subpoenas? Arrest warrants? A date for tonight? A flop in the sack?*

"Sorry for the short notice," Marie apologized. "I've got to catch a plane. Yours truly has been called back to Langley by the big bosses in the sky for a few days. Something came up about my last assignment overseas. We'll hit the road running when I get back to San Antonio, okay with you?"

"Of course. Is there anything you want me to do while you're tending to CIA business?"

"Please make sure that none of the patients on the list are discharged from the hospital. I wouldn't let the two employees take any of their vacations either. I want them here in town, accessible at all times when I return."

"Have a good trip," Boyd said cheerfully as Marie hurried out of his office.

He wondered why she became so cold and officious. Did he turn her off? It's just as well. We shouldn't let our hormones go berserk during a murder investigation. The deceased agent shouldn't become a secondary interest to either of them. She was murdered in the line of duty. That horrible event took place right underneath our noses. The dead Elsie Turk deserves more from us, a lot more.

CHAPTER 18

DALIA Garza enjoyed her work at Mission Oaks Hospital. She loved her co-workers and felt she was instrumental in helping so many mentally challenged people cope with their illnesses. Her background was a guarded secret. She refused to share the dramatics with anyone except her best friend since childhood.

She'd reflect on her youth on numerous occasions when alone at night, revisiting several situations that impacted her life. Then shake her head in utter dismay. Tonight was no exception.

How could it ever have happened to me, she kept asking herself, time after time? She remembered vividly those early days of her life.

Dalia was born in Mexico in the northern section of Matamoros, across the U.S. border town of Brownsville, Texas. Her home was located near the site where U.S. Highway 77 becomes 5 de Mayo across the Rio Grande and into Mexico. She had a brother who was five years older than her. Her folks were transient workers who traveled wherever they could find the work to pick crops. It took them a long time to obtain the necessary permits to enter the U.S. for seasonal work.

There are thousands of Garza's in Mexico applying for temporary work in the United States. This number is in addition to the hundreds of Garza's that cross the Rio Grande illegally. Seasonal workers would be absent for several weeks at a time following the migrant path to the north. Her parents earned enough money on these long trips to carry them through the winter and early spring. On several occasions, they'd grab a bus and head to South Texas to pick locally grown crops. They never had a problem finding work.

Dalia's aunt lived a few houses down the street. The aunt and uncle would take the kids in their home for the period Dalia's parents were working in the fields. This convenient arrangement worked for the aunt. She'd receive her pay in U.S. dollars.

"Where are your parents going to work this year?" Dalia's aunt asked her one day.

"I'm not sure," Dalia said. "I guess I'm too young to be consulted on their travel plans. They seem to go someplace different each year. Why don't you ask my brother?"

"Just curious, your mama will let me know soon enough."

Dalia's parents decided to follow the migrant trail that year to far away Wisconsin. They were contracted by an agency to pick apples in Door County. This county's landmass juts out from Green Bay like the gloved- left thumb of a right-handed baseball player. The nights were cooled by breezes off Lake Michigan. Her parents loved the area from their previous stint up north. However, their work kept them away from the children for too long.

"I can't tend to your children anymore when you're gone for such a long time," her aunt informed Dalia's mother. "It's become too hard on me and my husband."

At least when they worked in South Texas, her parents were able to get home periodically to take some of the pressure off the aunt and her husband. The older boy was becoming more and more of a management problem for them as he got older. He would often be gone for one or two days with no plausible explanation that would justify his absences.

Angel Garza was born with a club foot on his right leg and a shortened left arm. This arm had the same degree of curl as his foot. The shriveled arm resembled a fishhook from a distance. Besides being physically challenged, Angel had flaming red hair— somewhat unusual for a Mexican. The doctor who delivered him at home told his mother he had malformed in her womb.

"I'm sorry, Mrs. Garza," the doctor said, "But there's nothing we can do for your child. He'll have to live with the deformity. Your family must love and support him as much as possible."

Angel was mocked by all the children in the neighborhood as he grew older. He couldn't walk or run as well as them. The taunting became more severe when he was in elementary school. Angel became a despondent loner.

"Hello there, gimp," or "hey there crip" were unwelcome jibes that brought shame and degradation on him. He wouldn't eat or play with other kids. Angel became more withdrawn and depressed. His parents were worried about him whenever they left him alone. One summer he tried to hang himself from a rafter in the outbuilding behind the house. Luck prevailed. A neighbor walking by the rear of the property saw him and raced to cut him down.

Dalia's parents couldn't afford to seek medical intervention. They took emotional refuge in their Catholic Church near the main downtown plaza. The parents prayed for hours asking for God's help. They ignored Angel in the process.

"But why us, Father?" they asked. "What have we done in our lives for the Lord to punish us like this? We've always lived and practiced good Christian values."

The humble priest assured them it was a privilege—an act of God's benevolence. After all, they were chosen among all the other town families to live with this burden. They should be honored and accept His will.

Angel avoided all things religious, blaming God for his crippled body. He refused to go to church on Sundays and skipped out on the religious education programs the pastor organized for the parish youngsters.

He was rapidly maturing as a young man. Against his parents' wishes, he quit school and crossed the border in an attempt to join the U.S. Army. The recruiter laughed at him.

"Go back home where you came from, young man or I'll have you arrested as an illegal and thrown in jail."

Angel began to hate all things American. Dalia was always there to comfort him whenever he returned home from any demoralizing confrontation. He often confided in her, though she was much younger.

Dalia could never understand her parents. She always thought they hated him because they never showed him any love. The support system at home was left to her. She loved her brother, that is until the tragic event occurred that would drastically change her life.

CHAPTER 19

DALIA was awakened from her dreams of childhood happiness by an outside noise that sounded like a car had backfired. She was cold and clammy with perspiration soaking her nightgown. She dozed off again but was haunted by the nightmarish illusions of her early childhood growth.

She relived every detail of that terrible night. There was no way she would ever forget what her brother Angel did to her. He'd burn in hell.

Dalia was thirteen when her brother sexually abused her. They were home alone one steamy summer night. Their parents hadn't left yet for their trip up north and were visiting far across town at Dalia's grandparents.

Angel was gone most of the day drinking and smoking pot with some of the older kids in the neighborhood. The small selection of friends he'd become acquainted with no longer mocked him. They encouraged him to steal cars. The gang sold the stripped-down parts on the black market.

"Angel," one of the gang members shouted out to him. "Tonight we're going to break into that grocery store next to the downtown chapel and steal cigarettes and canned goods. Wanna join us?"

He was the one who tossed the large rock through the front door window of the store to gain entry. They followed him in after the gang assured themselves nobody had heard the breaking glass. They helped themselves to the meager inventory.

The older boys pooled their reward money and hustled him over to Papagayo's for a little fun. They knew he was still a virgin.

"Angel," one of the older members of the gang bragged, "You're in for a real treat tonight."

Papagayo's was a favorite getaway for the Matamoros *senors*. Texacans from Brownsville also headed across the border for a night of debauchery. The brothel was formerly a run-down motel several kilometers south of town on Mexico Route 101. It was the only building in the general area. One sign was barely visible. The beer sign read *Corona cerveza aqui.*

Angel had the time of his young life with a willing, straw-haired and buxom accomplice. She was close to his mother's age and dumpy in stature. The prostitute had an ugly tattoo depicting two armadillos humping each other on the right flabby upper arm. On the upper left arm were the letters *gracias amigos.*

He could care less about her age and so-so appearance because she assured him that the "stump" between his legs was far more impressive than his hooked arm and deranged foot. Earlier in the afternoon and before entering the whorehouse, his friends had pumped him up with peyote. It's a mescaline soft drug similar to LSD but with a lesser edgy effect for the user. The cactus product was available in Northern Mexico.

Dalia had gone to bed earlier than usual several weeks after Angel's "coming out" foray with his friends. She was feeling weak and tired but had enough energy to take a warm bath before retiring. She was in her hated monthly female plague. Abdominal cramping always accompanied her period. She heard the front door slam downstairs. It had to be Angel because the folks were gone.

"Where are you, my little urchin,?" he cried out. "Big brother wants to see you."

Angel was horny after smoking pot and drinking cheap tequila the older boys stole from their homes. He was unsteady when his friends "poured" him out of their car in front of his home. They laughed when they pulled away in their souped-up pickup truck after watching him trip on the first tier of stairs leading to the front porch.

"*Buenas noches, amigo,*" they laughed in mock at him.

He'd noticed how his little sister had grown over the past several years. Her breasts were big for a girl her age. His close friends had teased him about her sexy physical appearance. Angel began visualizing Dalia in the dirty magazines he read that were hidden under his bed. He collected as much porn as he could get his hands on.

Angel climbed the stairs to her bedroom in a clumsy manner while whistling a soft tune but loud enough for her to hear. He threw open the bedroom door and staggered over to her bed. He laughed when he noticed she was sitting up in bed staring at him.

"What do you want, Angel?" she cried out.

"I think it's time you and big brother have a little sex talk," he murmured to her. He was breathing in heavy snorts now but not from climbing the long stairwell to her room.

"Come, get out of bed! Give big brother a warm hug."

Dalia was frightened. She figured he'd either been drinking too much or was high on mescaline . . . whatever the stuff is called. She hunkered down in bed and took a defensive posture, pulling the blanket up to and around her neck.

"No fair hiding that voluptuous body from these big round eyes of mine," he said, ripping the blanket from her.

"Angel, get away from me, you're scaring me. Go away! What do you want from me? Mom and dad are on their way home," she lied.

"Give me a taste of that intoxicating sweetness that oozes from your lovely, young body. I want a bite of that apple from the *no-no tree,* and I want it now!" He opened his mouth and curled his tongue around his lips several times and smiled back at her.

"It's time you experience what a real man can do for you." His breathing was accelerating out of control. He was as hard as a rock.

Angel ripped her clothes off and climbed into her bed. Dalia tried to fend off his advances. He was too strong for her. He spread-eagled her sideways across the bed. Rough, anxious, and out of control.

She screamed out, "AAAAH! No Angel, no Angel, please don't do this, I–"

It was over in two minutes. Angel jerked his trousers up, picked up her crumpled underclothing from the floor, and forcibly tossed the items at her head. He left the bedroom without saying a word.

She cuddled up into the fetal position and sobbed. "Why would Angel do this? Was it my fault that he did this to me? I feel guilt."

Her entire body was writhing in pain. She had to rid herself of the mess from his excitement causing her lost innocence. She tore the sheets off the bed and threw them in the trash, then filled the bathtub with scalding hot water.

She eased her bruised body into the tub and gritted her teeth. The water was so hot it numbed her entire bottom. It felt like a thousand needles pricking her. It was painful. She was eager to wash away the entire horrible experience, regardless of the scalding bathwater and the intermittent aching.

Dalia couldn't tell anyone. Her mother wouldn't believe her. The father would want to kill Angel if he thought it was true. She would avoid Angel at all costs. He left home that night and was never seen, nor heard from again.

Juanita Comptos was a year older than Dalia but in the same grade at school. They had been close friends for years and were confidants to each other on every issue that challenged young females. They were deemed "inseparable" by their young peers. Juanita could not believe the gruesome story Dalia shared with her after Angel had disappeared.

"I'll kill that crippled bastard of a brother for what he did to you if I ever see him again!" she said to her friend in deep anger.

"Please, Juanita, let's forget the whole thing ever happened to me, okay? I don't want you to get in trouble on my behalf, and I don't want our other friends telling bad stories about me."

I wonder if Juanita will arrange to have my father murdered. I had learned at an early age he is one of the "darker" members of the Mexican Mafioso and reputed a paid assassin by some distant relatives.

Was Angel so overcome by guilt and remorse he ran off and killed himself, rather than face the scourges of my father? I've got to live my own life now with this terrible burden haunting me forever!

Dalia knew she could never put the violent intrusion to rest. Days and months passed by, and her life gradually returned to normal.

CHAPTER 20

LIEUTENANT Hagen brought the long-awaited interpretive criminal analyst to Mission Oaks Hospital after getting CIA concurrence. Irene Finerty had flown in from O'Hare late the previous evening and checked into the St. Anthony Hotel on Travis Street.

They proceeded past the receptionist to Boyd Bounder's office once inside the hospital. Peppi tried to stop them. They pushed past her. She gave Hagen a look of utter disgust. He either didn't pick it up or ignored her.

"We got word that agent Martini was called back to Langley and the investigation of Elsie Turk's murder had been placed on the back burner," Hagen informed Bounder.

Boyd was aware of that fact. She kept him informed.

"The chief told me he was upset with the delay," Hagen expounded. "To our good fortune, we're not being hounded by her family or a friend. Elsie was a real lone ranger. The press has backed off, realizing the ball was in the CIA court. We were non-paying spectators at this point. It pisses me off, though. We owe it to Turk to get this thing moving off-center."

"Boyd Bounder, meet Irene Finerty, one of Chicago's finest investigators," he said with pride as he turned to Finerty. "Five to one she'll figure out the meaning of those numbers we found etched in Turk's dried blood splatter. Finerty is nationally known and respected for her work in our field. Even though she's a woman, Bounder," he smirked.

"Pleased to meet you, ma'am," Boyd said warmly, ignoring the sexist putdown. Finerty stood with her fists tightly cuffed. Bounder was afraid she was going to take a swing at Hagen. He'd earned it.

"Lt. Hagen and Miss Finerty, I am no longer the acting administrator here. I need to back-peddle from the Turk murder investigation. I'll bring you to Rod Richards' office. He replaced me last week. I'm no longer the acting administrator."

Rod had impressed the hospital ownership midway through his residency. They persuaded him to be named the acting administrator in addition to fulfilling his mandatory residency requirements. Dr. Dean told Rod he'd certify the completion of the residency, regardless of what happened during the ensuing months. Rod was hesitant but looked forward to the new challenge.

"I've reverted to psychiatric nursing again—my first true love and the reason for my existence," Boyd said with a big smile. "Just the same, please let me know if I can help in any way down the road."

A heavyset black lady in hospital clothing blocked their pathway as they walked further down the hallway to the administrator's office. Behind her was another patient bobbing and weaving as though he was sparing with an invisible boxer. He flicked a quick right cross to a picture of an American eagle hanging on the hallway wall. He missed the big bird's beak by at least a foot. He spun around and jogged back to the ward when he recognized Bounder. The black lady approached Hagen and got in his face.

"How 'bout fetching me an ashtray, little man?" she pleaded while a half-smoked cigarillo dangled from her wet lips. The ashes were looking for a place to land. She cupped her right hand and held it out in front of her in case the ashes elected to bail out.

"Who the hell are you?" Hagen asked in a gruff manner. "You shouldn't be smoking in a hospital, for Christ's sake. Don't you know it's dangerous with all the oxygen equipment around here? We could all be blown to smithereens!"

Boyd did a quick assessment. There wasn't any oxygen in use by any patients in the hospital as far as he knew. There are numerous "no smoking" signs strewn throughout the hospital. Patients surrender individualism and certain freedoms when they're admitted to a hospital, but their "smokes" are deemed a constitutional right, not just a privilege. Boyd felt he needed to stress the "no smoking" restrictions again at the next staff meeting.

"Excuse me!" Roberta replied in shock at Hagen's comment. "I'm the Virgin Mary, and I have been blessed by God and given the right to do most anything I darn well please to do, whenever and wherever I want to do it. So get out of my life!"

All of a sudden a tall, smartly dressed lady came out of a nearby office. She pointed directly at the patient as she approached the group.

"Roberta Peck, you know better than that!" she reprimanded the black lady as she confronted her. "The good Lord wants you to return to your room right this minute. Go there and kneel in prayer. Beg for repentance."

The patient did an about-face and headed back down the long corridor toward her room. She was in no hurry. Didn't utter a sound. The unlit cigarillo found refuge on the hallway floor. Hagen rushed to stomp on it.

"Sorry about that," she smiled at Boyd and looked at the other two. "They're supposed to keep the corridor doors locked from inside the patient wings. I'm Lucie Guerra, the high-priced hall monitor around here, folks. How can I help you?"

Lucie was the first hire Rod made at the hospital. The previous secretary was married to an active duty service member and had accompanied her husband on an overseas assignment. Rod interviewed twenty candidates before he decided on Lucie.

She was bred into the upper crust of San Antonio society. Lucie had been a loan officer at a local national bank but got tired of making new car loans. She wanted a simple job not involving credit reports and character assessment. Lucie loved her new job and was attracted to her new boss. She liked his candidness. Besides that, he was handsome and single.

Bounder left the group and returned to his office.

"I need to talk to your administrator right away, Miss Guerra," Hagen said in a ruffled, matter- of-fact tone. "We have important police business to discuss." He was starting to become impatient with the unexpected delays taking place. Hagen had a one o'clock tee time at Brackenridge. This was his day off. That was . . . until Chief Astrade called him in.

"I'll let him know you're here," she said.

Rod came out of his office after what appeared to Hagen—twenty exceptionally long minutes. He smiled at everyone as he politely introduced himself.

"Pleased to meet you, Lt. Hagen," he lied. "I've heard a lot about you from my associate, Boyd Bounder." *All negative, a real horse's behind with a gold-plated badge!*

"Look, Richards," Hagen said, "I got some heavy-duty police business awaiting me. Let's get this thing over with as soon as possible, okay?"

Rod nodded his head in agreement.

"This here lady standing next to me is from Chicago. She was brought in to help solve the Turk murder. I hope that someone briefed you on the case." He concluded in a dour and condescending manner.

Rod didn't say anything. He glanced over at the Chicago cop.

"Miss Finerty, meet the new hospital boss," Hagen said. "I'll leave you, two fine people, alone now. I gotta run."

He raced from Rod's office and bumped into Eduardo Munoz in his motorized vehicle. Munoz was dressed in a German Third Reich military uniform wearing a pistol belt with a plastic water bottle crammed into the holster.

"God be damned you—you fruitcake!" Hagen shouted at him. "Watch where you're driving that obnoxious machine. I should ticket you and haul your big ass in." He twisted around Munoz and shot out the front door of the hospital.

Munoz wasn't surprised by the cop's harping at him. *I wonder why that uniformed jerk is still around here. Not good.* He raced his mini-vehicle back down the corridor through the double doors and into the ward area. *Who the hell is that kooky black lady I almost ran over back there?*

Rod almost hoped that Munoz had rammed into the stupid detective. It would have been an interesting scene. He was sure Eduardo lived in another world and divorced from his own.

"I sympathize with you for having to put up with that dunderhead Hagen," Finerty said to Rod. "I've only known him for a short time. My uniformed buddies back in the Windy City would skin him alive and feed him to the hungry crabs in the Chicago River."

Irene Finerty was a tall, fair-skinned redhead with flowing long hair. She was born on the south side of Chicago near Ashland and 95th Street where several Irish cops lived. Finerty was groomed to become a police investigator by her cadre after graduating at the top of her police academy class. She had advanced degrees in both microbiology and kinetics from downtown Loyola University.

Rod guessed her age to be around forty. Her green horned-rim glasses sat precariously on the edge of a sharp nose. She was flat as an ironing board from stem to stern and not pretty—probably labeled by her male counterparts as a true academic. Finerty stood in a rigid stance, leading Rod to believe she wanted to be in control of the situation.

"I don't know why Hagen brought you over to our hospital," he said. "Perhaps you want to see the exact location where Turk was found dead. The entire area has been cleaned and sanitized after they released the crime scene. His investigative staff has numerous pictures of the congealed bloodstains with the numbers etched-in."

"All I want here and now is a quick walk-through of the crime area. Then I'll meet with the investigators and review the photographs."

"Fine with me," He was eager to return to a hospital incident report he was reviewing before the interruption. A visitor filled out a written complaint about Peppi Perez's confrontational attitude. The complaint was centered on a shortage of available parking spaces in the hospital lot. The receptionist asked her what type of vehicle she was driving. The visitor told her that it was a motor home with an SUV in tow. Peppi chewed her out about parking there "with that monstrosity."

Rod led Finerty upstairs and showed her the dayroom where Turk was found dead. The ping-pong table had been folded upright and stored in a corner. He rolled the table over to the exact position on the floor where Turk was discovered and opened it up. He then excused himself and left the area. He left instructions with the ward attendant to escort Finerty out of the building when she finished.

Rod returned to his office. Lucie told him she received a call from Langley that Marie Martini would be back in town next week. She said the caller informed her Martini wanted to wrap up the investigation as soon as possible.

"We're supposed to ensure that all the people she wants to interview are standing by in tall order," Lucie told him. "Boyd did a nice job on his end. He disapproved of a request from the Saudi nurse to take a few days off. She was upset and told Boyd it was a religious holiday."

Lucie was perceptive. Rod was learning more about his staff.

This is wonderful, absolutely wonderful, right in the middle of our staff planning for the upcoming accreditation visit by the Joint Commission on Accreditation of Hospitals. Now we're saddled with investigators poking around our facility. The patients are wondering what the hell is going on. Staff members are beginning to react like deer, frozen spellbound in the headlights of an oncoming automobile.

CHAPTER 21

ROD gingerly lifted two bras and three pairs of panties from the dryer. He stared in awe at the colorful patterns of assorted animals embroidered on each item. *Looks like we have an animal lover living here.*

The condo where Rod lived had a laundry room at the end of each floor, and the machines were free to the user. He had returned from the nearby Hobby Center after having a light lunch and nearly got smashed by a car speeding the wrong way down the marked one-way street.

"These overzealous tourists get to me," he complained to a homeless guy wheeling an empty grocery cart down St. Mary's Street. "They need to construct all bi-lingual signage in San Antonio."

"Yo, man," the indigent said, "I agree with you. But remember, kind sir, their money spends with ease in our town. We have to find ways to accommodate them."

Rod's new job at the hospital required a complete wardrobe overhaul. Pam helped him in an earlier shopping spree. His old denim cutoffs and golf t-shirts wouldn't cut it now. Rod returned to the condo after he visited the Hobby Center. He jerked his bedroom closet door open to inventory his stash of clothing. He discovered to his great dismay the only shirts and slacks he owned were sitting helplessly in the laundry basket.

The stinky jogging outfit tossed over his tennis shoes was pleading for help and a dose of fresh air. Now he needed to remedy the situation. Larry's wife helped him update a few clothing items but not enough for his present job. *When was the last time I washed and ironed?* He tried hard to remember.

"Hey buddy, get your grimy mitts off my undies!" The tall, good-looking brunette standing in the hallway door was beyond upset. Her legs were crossed and her hands firmly secured to the hips. "Are you some kind of pervert or what?" She was wearing a tight green polo shirt and baggy black Nike shorts. She stood in her bare feet holding a duffle bag.

"Sorry, Miss, or Mrs.," he said, "But I was about to toss my washed clothes into the dryer and was shocked to find these dainty things glaring up at me. I guess they're yours, huh?"

The young lady came over and snatched her bras and panties away from him like some hawk tearing flesh from a downed prey. She felt no need to answer his obvious stupid question and shoved the underwear into the duffle bag.

"You new here?" she asked. "I haven't seen you around the building. When did you move in? What floor are you on?" She drilled him with these questions while her eyes roved up and down his lithe body. *Not bad, at least compared to the older duffers who live here.*

"Hold on, Miss. Allow me to answer your questions one at a time. Please give me a minute, okay?"

She allowed him to continue.

"I leased a unit at the end of the second floor and moved in a month ago. My name is Rod Richards. I'm the acting administrator at Mission Oaks Mental Health Hospital. I'm an unmarried heterosexual and don't drink much anymore. I drive a little beat-up Honda on its last leg. That's my summary. How about telling me a little something about you?"

"Oh, sure can. I'm Keena Simpkins, glad to meet you," she said as she thrust out her long tanned arm. They shook hands firmly. *It might have been my imagination, but she held on to my hand for a bit too long.*

"I'm twenty-eight, never hitched, and I like virile men," she said proudly. "I have some Indian blood flowing through my little veins. My grandmother was a proud Kiowa, snatched off her reservation one night by a brave but stupid Texas Ranger. The dude had ambled across the Texas border into Oklahoma by mistake."

He had read somewhere the Rangers lived by a written rule not to cross any state lines, regardless of the situation.

"The Texas Ranger had been pursuing a young brave. He allegedly killed a landowner in a northern town in Texas. The ranger took ole grandma as a hostage and rode off–damned near got shot to death. They got along with each other, believe it or not. Marriage soon followed."

"I like the narrative," Rod smiled, feeling more relaxed with this interesting woman.

"Oh, I apologize for getting off the track," she went on. "I live in a unit down the hall. I'm a marketing consultant and on vacation for four days." Keena felt a shiver running through her body. *This guy is trim, good-looking, and has a cute scar on his left cheek. He must not be a day over forty. I like men with a little wear and tear on them.*

'Sorry for being so unfriendly and obnoxious like that," she was on a roll now. "You may be aware there are many weirdos running around this city. A girl has to protect herself."

He loved every minute of her ramblings. *I need to know her a lot better.*

"Why don't you come to my unit and have a glass of wine, er, I mean iced tea," she said. "I'm down the hallway from you next to the elevator. It's the least I can offer for jumping your frame as I did."

Rod would've preferred her to jump his frame. She was beautiful, perky, and outright friendly. *Some guy missed the boat along the way for not taking this young lady off the open market!*

"Thanks, Keena, but I'd like to take a rain check on your offer," Rod smiled back at her. "I got to get these clothes in the dryer and head back to the hospital." *What a crock of bullshit. Don't want to seem too eager. Let her think about that for a while.*

Rod hurried out of the laundry room. He left her swinging the duffle bag back and forth–hand to hand as though it were a hot potato readying to be cooled off.

He dumped his clean clothes on the couch and headed back to the hospital. Rod took a short detour and motored down Navarro Street to the "big enchilada," better known as the main San Antonio City Public Library. He dropped off two Vince Flynn books that were overdue.

It was Saturday afternoon. He didn't expect to run into many staff members at the hospital. The annual San Antonio

Fiesta celebration was in full swing. Everybody was in a party mood. *I've been here for almost two years and so much has happened to me. Events in my life have gone from the absolute nadir, upward in a promising direction. I better not screw up.*

CHAPTER 22

ROD noticed a lady reaching into the trunk of her car for a bag or a box as he entered the parking lot. It looked as though she was having a problem extracting it from the trunk. He swung in next to her. He wondered if his sudden appearance startled her. She recovered after staring at him for a long time before he hopped from his car.

"I heard you were the new administrator at Mission Oaks," she said to him in a cheerful voice. He approached her car. "How in the world did that ever come about? Whatever happened to that old fart, Clemens?"

This lady caught Rod off guard with her string of pointed questions. He stared at that face. He kept checking her out, thinking he knew her. But where?

"Clemens was let go," he answered. "I guess the board of directors had reason to jettison him. I wasn't here then. Boyd Bounder was in charge when I came aboard. By the way, do I know you?"

"Silly man, how can you forget that fantastic night we had together several months ago? I had met you at that hotel bar and–"

"Holy shit! You're Miss Garza! Excuse my quick tongue. Sorry I didn't recognize you. Why haven't I run into you at the hospital? I recall now. You're a head nurse on one of our floors."

She approached him with a warm smile and extended her hand out to his. "You're correct. I'm Dalia Garza. I believe you're Rod Pritchard."

Rod shook her soft hand and corrected her on his last name.

"Today is my first day back to work in some time," she said. "I just finished an active duty stint with the Army Nurse Corps. It was my turn to fulfill the obligation I agreed to when I joined the Reserves. Yours truly is affiliated with the Burn Unit at Brooke Army Medical Center at Ft. Sam Houston. The highly specialized unit gets called upon for humanitarian purposes to support some catastrophe in the world. We flew to Chile to help that nation provide care to burn casualties from a major earthquake. Behavioral health nurses are in short supply in the burn unit. They keep us busy."

"Dalia, my recent history is complicated. To set the record straight, I'm only the acting administrator at Mission Oaks. Perhaps I can bring you up to date one of these evenings, that is, if you're available and willing to listen to my sad story of woe."

"Rod Richards, I would be happy to take you up on your proposal. Let me know when and where."

He grabbed the small heavy box hooked on some webbing in her trunk. Together they walked across the street to the hospital. Several tourists were wending their way down the sidewalk on matching red Segways. They were heading for the Cantina Classica further down the block. *Dunderheads. Why the hell aren't they out on the road? Where is that clown Hagen when you need him? On the golf course?*

"Hi, Rod, what's going on?" Harry Mooney asked when they entered the hospital. He was puffing on a stinky cigar in the front lobby. "And, hello to you, Miss Garza. How was your vacation?"

Rod's ears popped at the word "vacation," but he hesitated to lecture Mooney about the difficulties facing people who fulfill military obligations. The CPA had no clue. He speculated the joker somehow dodged Uncle Sam's call to arms at a younger age.

Dalia nodded a quick "howdy" and continued down the hallway. She didn't care for the principal owner of the hospital, nor did she intend to get into any conversation with him. Mooney tried to hit on her one night in the first-floor dayroom. It took every ounce of effort to fend off the fat bastard.

"George Gay in the business office told me about some changes you convinced him to make to our billing system," Mooney reported. "Tell me the details about the modifications."

"Sure, Harry. Let's go to my office. I'd appreciate it if you'd kill that cigar."

Mooney gave him a disgruntled look, hesitated, and then snubbed it out in his chubby palm. His mitt must have been on life support, otherwise, he'd have howled like a wounded moose.

Rod asked Peppi to send for some coffee. She smiled at him and picked up the phone to call the dining hall. She envied Lucie working next to him every day. *If only he'd–*

"Here's the story, Harry. I reviewed the account receivables with George. There were some problems in the procedures for 'aging' the accounts in his monthly A/R reports. I felt he should separate those receivables on patient cost shares from those of the third-party payer groupings."

"Why, Rod? We've done it that way for years. Most of our patients are covered by reputable insurance carriers. The few Medicaid patients we admit here present no problems. We figured if the amounts were lumped together, it would present a better overall picture of the aggregate monies owed us."

"We're talking apples and oranges here, Harry. We know the third-party payer insurance companies take anywhere from two to four months to process our claims. They pay about seventy-five percent of the claims during that time frame. They either request further information on the rest of the claims or simply deny them."

"What's new about that?" Harry was intrigued. "All insurance companies attempt to hold off paying claims as long as possible. Remember, it's money in their till and not in our pockets. The bastards earn interest on our money! They need to be investigated by the state insurance commissioner!"

"Nothing new here, Harry. It's how we go after the patient cost shares that bothered me. We keep them on the books forever, even if they haven't paid any amount toward their bill. This skews our receivables unrealistically upwards. They need to be written off as non-collectibles after a reasonable period. Let's say one year."

"It pisses me off," Mooney frowned. "These people seek our care, get treated by skilled professionals, then ignore us once they leave the hospital."

"It's human nature," Rod offered. "Folks will do anything to alleviate their immediate problem. Then, once the crisis is over, they tend to revert to their old habits. They either forget about their cost-share liabilities or ignore them."

"So, what did you suggest that we do?" Mooney queried.

"I had George change the pre-admission process. Almost ninety percent of our patients have some amount of cost-share with their insurance companies. We ask them to acknowledge this requirement in writing on our printed pre-admission form. Then we attempt to obtain their credit card data. We can process the cost-share at the time of their discharge."

"Brilliant idea, Rod, but what if they refuse to give us their credit card information?" Mooney asked. "Is it legal to demand the card?"

"Not sure–don't care. We found only three patients in a two-week test period refused to give us this information. Two had stated they don't use credit cards and always pay cash instead of using those 'plastic devils.' The third patient told us in no uncertain terms . . . to go to hell!"

"I could give you a big wet kiss. What a great idea!"

Ugh, please dear Lord, no thanks, have 'em offer another "Good Ole Boy."

"Cash is king around here," Mooney said with pride. "Cash flow in our line of business is truly God-like. I knew your extensive experience would serve as an asset to our little hospital. Thanks a lot, Rod Richards."

The coffee arrived as Mooney got up to leave. He looked at the tray placed on the coffee table, shrugged, and re-lit his stogie.

"Suggest you jack up our chef, Rod. Better yet, I should go down there and do it myself. The goodies should've been here twenty minutes ago. Maybe you also need to light a fire under our receptionist's behind. She was reading a newspaper when I came in, oblivious of my presence. I'm beginning to believe she's outlived her usefulness around this place."

Rod was curious. He thought Mooney adored Peppi. Something must have come up causing him to distance himself from her. Maybe Peppi told him to stop smoking those terrible triple-cancer sticks. He wouldn't doubt it. He had observed she had a hard time holding her tongue. Longevity in a job can do that.

Mooney headed to the front door of the hospital, shaking his head in disgust. He shot a murderous stare at Peppi. He flipped off a few ashes from his cigar on the floor as he passed her location.

She still ignored him, arranging and rearranging several hospital brochures in the magazine rack.

Rod sat down and took his time relishing the two hot cups of coffee and the heated cinnamon-pecan rolls. It didn't hurt they were swarming in butter. He missed lunch and was hungry. *This is pretty damn good. I got the goodies all to myself. Maybe I should give the chef a bump in salary.*

CHAPTER 23

MARIE Martini called Boyd from Dulles International Airport before boarding her direct flight to San Antonio. It was Monday morning in the Alamo City. They'd developed a tighter relationship during her previous visit, supplemented by a few telephone conversations while she was away at Langley.

"Good morning, Boyd," she said, eager to hear his voice. "Would you be a dear and pick me up at the airport this afternoon? My ETA is 1430 hours on Delta 406. I don't want to rent a car. Your compatriots down their drive like they're competing in a high-stake bumper car contest."

"Hey, don't fret about that, Marie. Us Texans are brought up to drive that way."

"You don't have to convince me, Tex. I'm booked at the Haxton Hotel. You know, the one that overlooks the river. It's a short walk to Mission Oaks from there. I enjoy staying on the Riverwalk. The tourists don't bother me like they do some old codgers. I enjoy watching them joust with each other tossing breadcrumbs to the waiting ducks. They shouldn't be feeding them."

"Sure enough Marie. Look for me in the baggage pickup area. I'll be there with bells on." He almost said, *with balls on* but first needed to know which Marie Martini was coming to town—the teaser or the prude!

He called Rod and told him of Martini's forthcoming arrival this afternoon. Rod, in turn, notified Lt. Hagen at MPD. He asked him to alert the sleuth Finerty from Chicago.

"The two investigators need to get their heads together as soon as possible," he told Hagen. "This inquiry is getting stagnant—gotta be solved post haste."

Irene Finerty left the St. Anthony Hotel and headed to the police station. She fought through a mob of homeless people lining up to get fed by a local charitable organization. She enjoyed the brisk morning walk to the MPD if it wasn't too humid outside. She had arranged to meet Dr. Juan Pena in Lt. Hagen's office. Finerty had already spent considerable time with the medical examiner reviewing the photographs of the blood-stained floor with the scratched numbers.

"Where's the woman from the CIA?" Hagen snarled at her with his hands glued to his hips. "She's supposed to be here with you, so we only stage this matinee one time."

Pena looked at Hagen and then shrugged his shoulders.

"Look, *dickhead*, you are the head *dick* in the investigative squad, aren't you?" Finerty shot back at Hagen with visual daggers shooting at him from both her enlarged pupils.

Hagen stared at her and said nothing.

She continued. "For your information, Hagen, she called me from Dulles International and said her flight would be delayed several hours. Bounder, over at the hospital is picking her up when she lands. I have to leave San Antonio later this evening."

"Why so soon, Finerty, ya just got here?"

"Some junkie thought he was the second coming of Clark Kent and swan-dived off the Hancock Building in downtown Chicago," Irene explained. "They had to gather up his body parts with brooms and shovels. My team wants me back right away to assist in the investigation."

"Okay, I guess you can brief agent Martini on your way out of town," Hagen said with a deep sigh and noticeable groan.

"What do you make of those numbers?" he asked after they both cooled off and settled down.

Poor Doctor Pena stared in awe at both of them, not saying a word for fear of getting his head ripped off and shoved down his abundant neck.

"I can't differentiate between nine or ten digits," she said. "Three numbers were overlapping with each other. I figure she was trying to depict the murderer's social security number–if I stay with nine. Ten numbers could represent a person's telephone number. It's beyond me how she could've recalled anything and still be lucid enough before dying to scribble numbers out in any meaningful manner."

"So, where do we go from here?" Hagen asked.

Dr. Pena continued to remain silent, looking at each of them as they bantered back and forth. He enjoyed their competitive natures.

"First of all, Lt. Hagen, your department is not doing the investigation," she said, "The CIA is conducting it, remember the arrangement?"

"Give me some professional courtesy, lady," Hagen shot back. "Tell me what you're going to do with these numbers, for Christ's sake! We're all on edge. Our brave boys in blue have a bet on the outcome."

"Fair enough," she said. "I'll run them through some sophisticated database programs when I return to my office in Chicago. I've spent years designing and refining the software. My program has proven successful in the past."

"That's neat as pie," Hagen said with a sarcastic tone of voice.

Pena snickered.

She ignored Hagen and then continued her dissertation.

"The San Francisco Police Department told me something interesting at a recent international conference of criminologists. If they had access to my system when that loony Zodiac killer was running loose in the late 60s, they would've nailed him. However, there are millions and millions of possibilities. I'll let Marie Martini know if I can find one SSN or telephone number that can be traced back to Texas. She'll have the tools to proceed with follow-up action."

"Doctor Pena, did you find out anything interesting in your autopsy or examination of the deceased's fingernails?" she queried the medical examiner.

"I never thought you'd ask me," he responded with a wide grin. "We haven't released our findings to the MPD. They're not the lead investigators in the murder case."

"Yeah, and Chief Astrade is pissed," Hagen said. "He wants to keep abreast of the investigation for his own and the department's benefit. You all best get it."

Doctor Pena stiff-armed him, reiterating he works for the county and not the city. He could only release his findings to the CIA.

"Doctor, we're on pins and needles to learn what you found," she said. "Please tell us so I can get on my way."

"Sure will. The primary cause of death was due to massive hemorrhaging from a severed aorta extending from the left ventricle of her heart. The left ventricle is much thicker than the right one. It pumps blood into the systemic circulation through the aorta. The right ventricle pumps the blood to the pulmonary circulation system. It has a shorter haul, so to speak."

"Jesus Christ!" Lt. Hagen shouted, "We're not second-year medical students, Pena! Can't you talk in more simple terms?"

"Sorry about the anatomy lesson," Pena apologized, and then hurried on with his explanation in plain talk.

"Our experts found scrapings of hair from beneath her fingernails. We've determined the strands of hair came from a person with red hair by microscopic examination. We're running further DNA analyses. I detected several old, scarred injection sites between the ring fingers of both hands."

"What the hell!" Finerty said, "I never heard of that before."

"These are not normal findings," Pena went on. "It's hard for me to tell what she may have been shooting up if anything. We'll for sure never know. One of my far-out colleagues believes she engaged in a spiritualistic practice interpreted from the old Sanskrit language of India. I'm not sure where the colleague learned about ancient ceremonies of any type. I'm not versed in those kinds of things. I'll let the CIA agent know later about the DNA findings."

"Sounds like a plan," Finerty said.

"There's one more interesting fact here." Pena was ramping out a big-time narrative. He had both their undivided attention.

"She was legally drunk based on the blood alcohol tests we ran. The levels were so high she wouldn't be capable of riding a kid's tricycle on the sidewalk without crashing into a tree. The alcohol poisoning in her system would've killed her if she hadn't been stabbed to death in the heart."

"Well, son of a bitch!" Hagen cried out. "Do the patients over at Mission Oaks have a hidden distillery on the ward? I'll visit Bounder tomorrow and hound him to death until we find it. Good luck on your end of the investigation, Finerty. That CIA woman certainly has her work cut out for her. Make sure you brief Martini before you leave San Antonio."

"By the way Dr. Pena, you never said whether or not she was sexually molested," Hagen commented. "Did the murderer screw her?"

"Oh, oh, sorry I failed to mention that part. There was no evidence of physical abrasions or semen in or around her vagina. One would conclude the murder was an act of revenge or uncontrolled anger on the part of the perpetrator."

"Are you going to tell us anything about the fingerprints?" Hagen asked. "What did you get from the forensic team?"

"No prints according to their report," Pena replied. "We thought we had identified some prints on the fire alarm box. It turned out they were old smudge marks, probably from when the unit was mounted on the wall. One of the investigators suggested we check it out. He thought the killer might have yanked it to cover his escape. The perp didn't consider it or changed his mind at the last minute based on our tests."

With that being said, Hagen hurried out of the room to make a call to Astrade. He had to bring him up to date concerning the latest information on the case. His head was swarming with bits and pieces of fact versus supposition.

"Thank you, Dr. Pena," Finerty said. "You don't need to send me any documentation on this case. Please be sure to label your package 'confidential' when you prepare it for Marie Martini. As usual, the fewer people who know about these circumstances, especially that dumbbell Hagen, the better off we are on all counts. Thanks for your interesting report. Goodbye."

"Have a safe flight back to O'Hare," Pena said, "And please let me know if that jumper from the Hancock building was Clark Kent."

They both chuckled. She let herself out of the office.

CHAPTER 24

A pleasant surprise was awaiting Rod when he returned to the condo after being gone most of the past two days.

He pulled the Honda into the parking lot to his assigned space and heard coughing and choking through his opened car windows. *What in the hell was that? Some old fart might need the Heimlich maneuver performed on him.* He jumped out of the car and sprinted toward the sounds.

He peered through the wrought iron fence into the pool area. Keena was lying on a recliner sunning herself. The pool structure extended over the edge of the property and looked straight down on the Riverwalk pathway. *How weird, he observed. Sunbathing? The sun was long gone, already hidden by the adjoining building.*

She was wearing a skimpy, fire-red bikini. The top part of the bikini had been thrown over the back of the recliner. She was alone and listening to some obnoxious rap music on her portable radio. He decided to amble over to determine the cause of the choking spell.

"Hi there, Rod," she said in a sexy tone. She slowly sat up, not concerned about covering herself. "I damn neared choked on these salted peanuts I've been nibbling on. There must've been some shells in the bag, or I swallowed the wrong way."

Rod smiled and said with a smile, "Keena, remember you told me a girl had to watch out for herself because of the weirdos running around here. What gives with the upper body display?"

"I knew that was you, Rod. I heard that noisy piece of crap you call a car chug into the garage. The jazzy music caressing my ears didn't have a chance in the world to drown out the ruckus of your little Honda. Why in the hell don't you splurge and get a real man's automobile?"

"I've had these wheels for a long time. I like to announce my arrival. Nobody gets alarmed when I pull up. It doesn't pay to scare anybody out of their wits these days. One could be sued for causing a heart attack."

"I'm finishing up here, had enough sun." She grabbed her bikini top and radio and looked at him. "Do you want to take me up on that drink I offered? Remember when we first met in the laundry room?"

"Keena, I think that'd be a great idea. I'm about to die of thirst." He scanned her entire body with much delight. It's been a long time since he'd spent time with a woman, in particular, one as striking as Keena.

She flipped a colorful beach towel over her shoulders and chunked the remaining bag of peanuts over the railing and onto the pathway below. She grabbed her bikini top off the recliner. They proceeded to the main hallway entrance and took the elevator up to her condo unit.

Keena's place was an absolute mess! Papers were strewn all over the floor. Dirty dishes were haphazardly stacked in the sink and along the kitchen counter. Drapes covering the window were drawn closed. Several new items of clothing, evidenced by the protruding price tags were draped over the sofa. He was afraid to peek into her bedroom for fear of finding someone dead, drunk, or decapitated in her bed.

"Excuse the appearance, Rod. I had planned to tackle my housecleaning chores later this evening. Have a seat while I get changed."

Sauntering toward her bedroom, she slipped down the bottom of her bikini and pirouetted out of it like a skilled ballet dancer. She left it lying on the floor. He couldn't help but stare at the perfectly rounded, tanned behind that wagged back and forth like a hound dog's tail. She smiled back at him while turning the hallway corner and entered her bedroom. Rod wondered how her entire body got so evenly tanned. Normally sun worshippers have well-defined tan lines with a distinct whiteness covering their private parts. Not this Indian maiden!

Five minutes later she came out of the bedroom dressed in tight blue shorts with faded rectangular patches sewn to each thigh. She wore a short pink, halter top leaving her midriff exposed. White tennis shoes without socks adorned her feet.

"What'll it be, Rod—coffee, tea, or some chilled white wine?" She sat down next to him on the sofa, not caring the least about the new clothes scattered on it and the crumbled bikini on the floor.

"I'll have some iced tea if it's handy," he replied.

"Got it. I made it last week so should still be okay. I'll have some wine. Hope you don't mind. I don't drink in the afternoon as a habit, but hey, rules are made to be broken, righto? Must be five bells somewhere in the world."

He winked his approval.

"I have some super good marijuana an associate at work gave me," she said. "He just got back from a meeting in San Francisco and bought some from a reputable dealer there. He said there's a strong movement in California to legalize the use of marijuana for medicinal purposes. Look at me, man, I got a few aches and pains that could benefit from the magical plant."

"What else would you expect from those wonderful Californians?" he said with a smile. "It's no mystery to me."

"Believe it or not," she said. "I have my *pot* growing in a small planter tucked in the west corner of the parking lot. Nobody, but mother sun could get to it. How about some weed?"

"No thanks, I haven't had a joint in years. From a medical standpoint, I'm as hale and hearty as they come."

Keena nodded in agreement. There wasn't an ounce of fat on his trim body that she could detect. She felt a tiny shiver race up her spine. *Humm, good.*

He picked it up but said nothing.

She sprung up and headed to one of the kitchen cabinets, fixed the iced tea, and poured a glass of wine. Then she reached back in the rear of the cabinet and withdrew a bong, filled the water chamber, and grabbed some other paraphernalia. Keena sat down again and placed the marijuana in its place of duty and stoked up.

"Now, where were we?" she asked in a soft voice snuggling next to him.

"We're getting to know each other better," he stuttered, wondering what he was getting into here. "What company do you work for, and who do you market to?" *Best slow her down some.*

"I work for one of the local lobbying organizations. My job is to solicit out-of-town businesses to relocate to our great city. This requires me to travel on occasion, although we work the many conferences that convene here. I spend a lot of time on the Riverwalk selling the merits of living here and doing business in our wonderful town. I have a pretty darn good track record if I say so myself!"

"So, you are a solicitor of sorts," he interjected with a grin.

She edged closer to him. By now the soothing effects of the marijuana seemed to have penetrated her entire body. The tingle that embraced her backbone now enveloped her entire body. She placed her hot hand on his left thigh and began squeezing it gently, as though she was kneading a lump of bread dough.

Rod was beginning to swell, *but not with pride!* All of a sudden the cell phone on his belt buckle buzzed. He glanced at the digits. It was Dr. Dean's hospital number.

He disengaged Keena's hand which had already slid up to the golden spike. He was no longer at half-mast.

"Keena, there seems to be some kind of problem at the hospital. I have to put in a call to the medical director right away. I'm sorry, but I've got to run. Will you be home later tonight?"

"Sure," she said. "Knock three times and whisper low." She laughed and hugged him.

He limped bowlegged back to his apartment and called Dean.

"What's up?" he asked when Dean came on the line.

"I'm sitting here with Marie Martini from the CIA. She wants to talk to me about interviewing the people Boyd Bounder has standing by. She got in late. Her flight from Dulles was delayed for several hours. Bounder said he had another commitment and couldn't stick around. I think you should be here to run interference."

"I'll be right over, Phil."

Rod had a hard time finding a space when he arrived at the hospital parking lot. There was a big function underway at an open theatre on the Riverwalk. Fiesta was in full swing. Dedicated partygoers knew where to find free parking. He made a mental note to have housekeeping place the red cones in the parking lot when big events were planned for downtown. He wrestled with the thought of generating some additional revenue by contracting a downtown parking company to manage his parking lot.

He went into the hospital and saw Dean with an attractive woman sitting with him in the front lounge area. He hadn't met the lady before. From Bounder's earlier description of the CIA agent, he knew it was Marie Martini with the doctor. Boyd had told him to be careful. She was a *live pistol*, whatever that meant.

"Hi, Phil, and hello Miss Martini, I'm Rod Richards. Boyd Bounder told me about you last week and what was happening with the investigation."

"Pleased to meet you also," she said extending a warm hand to him. "I hope his report was positive. Boyd is a first-class gentleman."

Dean told her several patients she wanted to interview were ready to be discharged from the hospital. She should talk with them first. He told her she would have plenty of time to interview the two employees–Dalia Garza and Amfi bin Aziz. They weren't going anywhere soon. He wanted her to have background information on the two nurses before she engaged in conversation with them. She knew from experience it would help her when she interviews them and also the patients.

Marie agreed that might be helpful to flush out nurse-patient relationships. It'd give her a better insight into any potential conflicts.

"How do you suggest we proceed?" she asked Dr. Dean. "Do you want to bring them to the conference room? Maybe we should talk to them in their hospital room?"

He thought for a moment. "I think it'd be better to talk to them in a neutral setting like this conference room. The rest of the patients on the ward would be less suspicious of what's going on."

"What do you think Rod?" Dean asked. Before he could answer him, Dean went on to say, "By the way, I would like you or Boyd to be present with Marie when she interviews the patients. I think a hospital representative known by the patients would tend to put them further at ease. I have to leave the facility after I brief agent Martini on their medical conditions. My wife and I have tickets to the theater. Some hot-shot comedian is in town. The wife enjoys these kinds of performances. I prefer the symphony."

"Phil, I think it'd be better if a clinical person were present during the interviews," Rod suggested. "The staff member could interpret any medical diagnostic information that might confuse Marie. I'm sure the patients don't know me well enough to be comfortable in that personal setting."

"That's a good idea," Dean agreed "See if you can run down Bounder at home. I'll start my part now with agent Martini. Is that okay with you, Marie?"

"Got it. We can always interrupt the good doctor later at the theater if we need him to further *clarify* Boyd's clarifications." She looked at Rod and laughed.

Rod left the room to call Bounder. He hoped Boyd wasn't out partying tonight. Boyd had a friend from Corpus Christi visiting the city. He insisted they'd have dinner on the Riverwalk. He'd never be able to extract him from the mob of folks flooding the downtown area.

CHAPTER 25

MARIO Caseres, chief of maintenance, came through the front door of the hospital while Rod was on the way to call Bounder.

"What's up?" Rod asked when he spotted him. Caseres looked fit to kill. Sweat was dripping from his forehead.

"I'd like to put a bomb in the laundry room and blow up those lousy washers and dryers. They're always breaking down. I want to replace the entire lot of them. Housekeeping doesn't give a rat's ass what time of the day or night they call me, or what I might be doing at the time. You'd think WWIII was about to begin whenever they call and demand action!"

"Mario, I've reviewed the maintenance logs when I rotated through your department. I meant to discuss some things with you but got jerked up to the front office. I think we spend too much money running our laundry operation on site. I noticed some of your staff bringing in clothes from home, and I don't simply mean one laundry bag either."

"Sure enough," Mario said. "They feel it's a benefit that comes with low-paying jobs. I'm not sure when that practice started. I sure enjoy supervising workers who care for me and are happy with their work. I turn the other cheek."

"I want you to conduct some research for me," Rod said.

"What do you mean by that?"

"Get together with your counterparts at the three medical centers downtown. See what they're doing with their hospital laundries. If I'm not mistaken, they've formed a consortium allowing them to outsource their laundry requirements to a private vendor in town. The arrangement could work best for us in several ways if we join them."

"How do you figure that?" Mario asked.

"Simple, Mr. Caseres. First, it might drive down the overall costs of the participating hospitals because of increased volume. Second, it would free up our outbuilding to be used for another revenue-producing activity. I have some ideas. It's too premature to discuss them. And the last thought . . . it'd make your job easier."

"Hey, will do, boss," Mario smiled at the job inference. "I'm playing Mexican Train with two of them tomorrow night. I'll pick their brains, see what's going on."

Rod looked confused. "I don't understand what this Mexican Train is all about. How do you get into brain-picking while playing it?" *These Hispanic folks have some weird after-hour activities.*

"It's a form of dominos people around these parts have fun playing. The brain-picking session has nothing to do with the dominos game. It could allow me to determine how other hospitals handle their laundry business."

"Fine," Rod said. "Get back to me next week. We'll compare notes. I'm having lunch with the All Saints Medical Center Assistant Administrator. I'll query him on the matter. Meanwhile, hold off on changing out any of the equipment. We don't have any new line-item purchases in our operating budget for the hospital laundry, Mario."

Caseres took off for the outbuilding. Rod continued down to his office to call Boyd. Peppi gave him a *high five* as he passed her in the hallway.

"I guess I can put off running some chores for the hospital," Bounder said when he picked up his phone. "One of the charge nurses asked me to buy some supplies for the ward. That can wait. My buddy from Corpus called and canceled out on me. I'll head over there right now if you and Phil Dean think it's imperative. I reckon I should sit with Martini while she grills the patients."

"You sure know one hell of a lot more about patients than I do," Rod responded. "You have the tools to handle them if they got upset or violent. I'd probably cold-cock 'em. We'd be facing a major lawsuit."

"You've got that right," he laughed. "At least Marie wouldn't shoot them. I have her big gun locked up in our safe."

"Get here when you can, Boyd. I'll cover for you until you arrive. Watch out for those wild drivers out there. You know how they party during Fiesta. I think all the local cab companies run their drivers through a special confidence course to handle these raucous crowds."

"Hey, man, I tend to drive the same way."

Rod left his office and started to head back to the conference room. Dr. Dean and Marie Martini were reviewing the list of patients. He decided to swing by the kitchen and get a pot of freshly brewed coffee. Everyone would appreciate some hot java and some chocolate chip cookies to munch on.

He heard a woman crying in the hallway while going to the dining room.

Peppi Perez was trying to comfort one of the patients. She was glad to see reinforcements coming to her aid.

"Can I help here?" Rod asked when he approached them.

"Sure can, Mister Rod," the relieved Peppi said when she saw him. "I'm not too good at helping confused patients." She left him to the challenge then headed back to the safety of her receptionist area.

"What is your name, please?" he asked the patient.

The poor woman seemed frightened. She cringed and cinched her hospital gown tighter. "Don't get near me, you hear. Don't touch me either! I've had enough of this crappy treatment around this institution. I'm going home."

"Look, Miss–"

"Cecilia Reyes, if you need to know, good sir," she interrupted him. "I'm a hopeless case, no good to anyone. I'm going to kill myself."

She started crying again, began to hyperventilate, and then screamed her bloody lungs out. GAAAH! She started to shake out of control. He thought she was going to burst at the seams.

Rod had no clue how to intervene in this crisis. Such action was above his pay grade. He could handle a drunken soldier tearing up the barracks–not a lady crying helplessly.

He was groping for a plan of action to stabilize the situation. A female ward attendant intervened after witnessing his dilemma in the hallway. He gladly stepped to the side.

"Cici, Cici, we need to return to the ward right away," the attendant told her. She put her arms around the distressed woman. "Someone is here to visit with you."

The patient stopped crying and began returning to normal breathing. She was still distraught.

"Is it my Uncle Sam?" She asked.

"No, silly, it is your *tio* Carlos from Seguin. He's anxious to sit with you again. Let's go back and leave this gentleman alone. Your uncle Carlos has a surprise gift for you."

"Sorry about that, sir," the attendant apologized. "Cici said she was going to the bathroom and then slipped out the corridor door on us."

She told him in a low whisper Cecilia Reyes was extremely depressed, They need to take more restrictive action. She hadn't received her medications today to complicate things further.

Even he knew patients wanting to kill themselves need close supervision. Rod made a mental note to discuss security precautions with Bounder.

He remembered something his son Larry told him some time back. Suicidal tendencies can surface among people with mental health conditions other than depression.

Rod didn't know at the time whether Larry was trying to subconsciously steer him away from considering suicide after Janice's death. He was on the cusp of such action after her illness and untimely death. Now he had more reasons to live a productive life.

CHAPTER 26

"LET'S get started," Dean said to Martini. "Would you please hand me the list?" He scanned the paper that Bounder had prepared for her. "I know all the patients on our wards except for the few hospitalized adolescents. I wouldn't think there'd be any teens on the interview list."

"I trust your opinion," Marie smiled

"Marie, Rod is gone. Bounder is not here yet. I want to discuss in confidence our two employees listed here. What I'm about to tell you is for your ears only. Got it? Nothing, absolutely nothing can be shared with any of our people, even those who you feel can be trusted. The mental health business is complicated and tends to take many twists and turns. These gyrations can be harmful to the patient or the patient's family. We see it often."

Marie looked on with intensity.

"I've been treating Dalia Garza for over five years, even before she began employment here. She was sexually abused by an older brother when a young adolescent. It was devastating for her, as you might expect. Childhood trauma can lead to severe social and interpersonal relationships in adulthood. One day you can be her close friend. The next day she might ignore you and her other good friends."

I had two friends like that in Chicago," she said.

The doctor continued the story. "She began an intimate relationship with her childhood friend, Juanita Comptos. They left Mexico and earned undergraduate degrees from a school in Kingsville, Texas. They both received nursing degrees at Incarnate Word College here in town. She lives with Comptos in a rental house, not far from our hospital. Juanita is a school nurse at one of the local schools."

"I have two questions for you," Martini said. "Is their intimate relationship sexual, and why did you hire her to work at a mental health hospital, of all places?"

"Yes, it is sexual," he admitted. "Dalia told me she hasn't been with any man since her brother abused her years ago. She is more comfortable having sex with another woman."

Dean elected to put off answering her second question.

"I thought her employment record indicated that she was recently divorced from a husband," Martini stated.

"Just a smokescreen, so to say," Dean offered. "I had the personnel director alter her records. I hired Dalia four years ago—she overwhelmed the entire interview team. Her grades in nursing school were exceptional, as were her letters of reference. She felt comfortable and supportive with the environment at Mission Oaks."

"I always thought people with mental health problems tried to surround themselves with psychiatry types," Marie said.

"That's a common belief. She tried to join the Army Reserves. I couldn't justify recommending her. The possibility of dangerous deployments here and abroad dictate caution on all fronts."

"I support that theory," Marie said.

Dean brought her up to date. "Dalia had returned from a short leave of absence from the hospital. She went back home to Mexico to tend to her aged father. He suffered a severe stroke, and he's living by himself. The father didn't have a family nearby to help out. Dalia felt she could get him back on his feet in a short time. We were in a staffing crunch but managed to cover for her. Our Boyd pitched in and worked a lot of overtime. The man didn't charge the hospital. That's the type of guy he is—strong and mission-oriented!"

Marie was quick to develop a warm fuzzy feeling about the big redhead. She missed him when she was recalled to Langley.

"Dalia needs a strong support system near her, Marie, as you surmised. One of our therapists has experience with dance therapy and found success in this treatment modality. The literature has proved dancing as an exceptional venue for persons with a history of sexual abuse."

"Oh, um, is that right, Dr. Phil?" She chuckled—Dean was much too serious.

"Yes indeed. It allows them to express themselves outwardly and at the same time, feel good about their bodies. Dalia thrived on it. She has performed her duties at the hospital far beyond our expectations. The patients trust her. She has vastly improved her interpersonal skills over the last few years. I have to admit though, she's still guarded and avoids attachment with anyone other than Juanita Comptos."

"Are you treating her friend Juanita?"

"No. I witnessed a positive and strong-willed individual the few times I've been in contact with her. I hesitate to admit it, but I think Dalia needs her more than she needs Dalia. I was informed the MPD folks were aware of the relationship between Juanita and Dalia."

Marie was taking more notes than usual.

"She's a free spirit and can be controversial at times," Dean said. "Juanita participated in several street protests and was hauled in one time for obstructing justice. The cops knew both women were raised in Mexico, and Juanita's father was incarcerated in a Mexico City prison. He ran with the wrong crowd and ended up serving twenty years. I think either they or the FBI are keeping close tabs on Juanita."

It wasn't known by law enforcement that Juanita had converted to radical Islamic beliefs. She joined their worldwide crusade and underwent training to destroy America and her allied countries.

"Hmm, I wonder if I need to bring Juanita in for questioning," Marie commented. "Better yet, I'll talk to that local FBI agent Jorge Vasquez. I can share some of this information with him. He might be read in on the facts. It won't hurt to cover that base. I think the man is a little slow on the take."

"I agree we can't let anything of importance slip through the cracks. But you have to keep in mind the confidentiality issue."

She ignored his comment. There were no strict firewalls in dealing with a serious crime in her line of business. "Doctor, do you think Dalia was involved in any way with the murder of Elsie Turk? Is she capable of performing such a violent act? Why do you think the MPD investigators labeled her as a person of interest?"

He thought long and hard about the pointed questions. "I don't think she would kill another human being for any reason. She is understanding and compassionate. I think she and Turk were developing a close professional relationship. I'd agreed with your CIA friends to put Turk here. They were aware I'd be challenged to convince the treatment team she had a mental health problem."

"Don't be so humble. They knew you were the best."

"Thanks. We used an experimental drug with her and the CIA's approval. I put her into a reversible, pseudo-paranoiac stage. At first, Elsie told me she could play a convincing role without the need for any mind-altering drugs. I convinced her otherwise because our team would discover the hoax."

"Well, how'd that go, doctor?"

"Okay. Dalia felt Elsie had progressed enough to be discharged. So did other team members. I was afraid our game plan for Elsie was falling apart when she was murdered."

"I know you cautioned me earlier, Dr. Dean, about sharing this sensitive information. It'll be held in strict confidence . . . to the degree we can control it without tying up our hands in the investigative process. I think you understand."

Dean didn't like her response. She saw him squirm.

Rod walked in with a carafe of coffee and a plate of chocolate chip cookies. They were still hot. The aroma drove everyone bonkers. Peppi had swiped two of them when Rod passed her in the hallway on his way to the meeting.

"How's it going here?" he asked. "Bounder should be in soon. I thought you'd enjoy a refreshment break." He placed the goodies on a nearby table and grabbed one of them before returning to his office.

"To be frank with you, I don't need to waste your valuable time talking about nurse Amfi bin Aziz," Marie told Dean.

"Why is that?" *She must have psychic abilities.*

"I checked up on her when I was back at Langley. They had tons of information about her from the application requesting

116

permission to come to the U.S. for further medical training. It's alleged she's related to a Sheik Salamah back in Bahrain. I had the misfortune of knowing the man. The CIA folks are checking out the extent of the relationship. It would be an absolute nightmare for me if she turns out to be one of his former mistresses!"

Dean forced a quizzical look on his face.

She didn't offer to explain.

"I'm more concerned about her husband who is training at Randolph Air Force Base," Marie continued. "He was screened to the nth degree before the CIA and State Department signed off on the Saudi application for navigation training. I think we can move on to the patients at this time if you folks are fine with the Amfi's professional capability."

Bounder showed up as Phil was bidding goodbye to Marie. She put aside her coffee cup, got out of her chair, and then gave Boyd a warm hug.

Dr. Dean glanced at them but didn't say anything.

"I need to head out," Dean said, "Or we'll be late for the performance at the theatre. *Adios amigos!*"

Meanwhile, Rod was back in his office reviewing some Standing Operating Procedures (SOPs) that needed updating. His mind began to wander off.

I wonder what Keena has planned for us tonight. It should be interesting, to say the least. Maybe we'll discuss life, liberty, and the pursuit of my happiness.

CHAPTER 27

IRENE Finerty had caught up with Marie the day before she flew out of San Antonio. Irene told her about Dr. Pena's findings and the strands of red hair that were caked underneath Elsie Turk's fingernails.

Marie wondered how she would broach this fact with Boyd. She liked him, even on the verge of loving him. She wouldn't object if a steamy relationship developed while she was deployed in the city.

Boyd was handsome, polite, and would make a good bed partner. She was disappointed when he dropped her off at the hotel after she'd landed. The delayed incoming excursion from Dulles International gave her more time to dwell on the subject—even fantasize about the amoral possibilities. She had invited him up to her room for a "thank you" drink. He said he had some other pressing business matters to address.

"Let's go over the list of patients," Boyd suggested. "I know all of them and can offer some meaningful input for you."

"Okay, let's start with Norm Cook. From your notes here he's a forty-one-year-old, divorced white male being treated for guilt and worthlessness. You've had him here for a while."

Boyd called the ward and soon an attendant entered the room with Cook. The patient was short and thin, with big ears and prematurely graying hair. He sat down next to Bounder and folded his hands in front of him. Boyd told the male attendant to find a chair outside the conference room. He would call him when it was time to return Cook to the ward. He then introduced Norm to Marie.

"I know why you want to talk to me," Cook said with dejection. "Me, I was nothing. I repeat, nothing but a real first-class nobody. That is until I met Elsie Turk. She was so nice to me, encouraging me to face reality and get on with my life. My eight-year-old son Pete died because I neglected him. He walked home from school one day and got hit by a drunk driver. He'd still be here with me if I'd picked Pete up from school that day. I'm no good to anyone anymore. My wife left me after the funeral. She accused me of neglecting my son and even her, most of the time. Damn, a man has to move on and earn a living!"

"Why do you think Turk spent so much time with you?" Marie asked, ignoring his last reference to earning a living. The statement made no sense to her.

"I think she saw a future for old Norm Cook. She convinced me it could be obtained. She got tired of hearing me despair about my ruined life. The wife told me I was the best ping-pong player she'd ever faced. Her words of praise made me feel good. I miss her. I hope you get the guy who murdered Elsie Turk real soon." He then slouched over and started to go to sleep.

Boyd signaled for the attendant to come back and return Cook to the ward. Marie scribbled a page of notes when they were alone again in the room. She shoved the spiral notebook back in her briefcase.

"What do you think, Boyd? I can't picture that weasel being involved with the murder. He seemed defenseless and feeble. Isn't he on medications right now?"

"No, none that I know of. Cook is a typical case of a moderate depressive disorder. He was a basket case when he was admitted but is almost ready to go home now. They tell me he only sleeps an hour each night. The therapist is addressing that problem before they let him go. He might have some form of sleep apnea. We've requested a consult from a respiratory therapist to run some tests on him. He might even have to undergo one of those obnoxious sleep studies."

"A fellow agent friend of mine had to undergo one of them. He sleeps with a mask now. His wife told me he looks like that killer in the movie *Silence of the Lambs*."

"Cook's psychiatrist tried to get another week for him in the hospital," Boyd continued. "The insurance case manager wouldn't approve the additional stay. I also think Elsie Turk contributed to his recovery. They seemed inseparable. He respected her . . . almost went catatonic when he heard she was murdered in the day room."

"I'm not sure why he was identified as a person of interest," Martini said. "Perhaps the investigative team felt the relationship with Turk was too personal and could result in a major fallout between them."

Boyd nodded.

She continued. "Clark Hanson is up next. You wrote that the fifty-five-year-old Hanson is widowed and suffering from severe depression. That's in contrast to Cook's more moderate disorder. He's been hospitalized about the same number of days as Cook. Would you bring Hanson down now so we can get one more out of the way?"

The same ward attendant reappeared with Clark Hanson and was familiar with the questioning protocol.

Introductions were made. Hanson settled in next to Martini. He was overweight and visibly nervous. He wore long ponytails that befit his elongated horse face.

"Do you know why you're here today?" Marie asked as she stood to face Hanson.

"Sure do," the patient replied with an intensity that alarmed Boyd. "You think I killed that lady upstairs, don't you? I got some problems, otherwise, I wouldn't be here. Whacking somebody to death is not my thing. She deserved to die for all I know. The street lady forced herself on everyone around here. She tried to encourage me to have sex with her. On top of that, she was always asking me stupid questions. She got pissed at me when I ignored her advances."

Marie wondered how any female could be physically attracted to this obese, foul-mouthed idiot.

"She seemed to get along better with that wimp, Cook," Hanson continued. "Maybe they did it in the closet after the goddamn bed check. Who knows, wouldn't put it past either of them."

"Why do you think the investigators identified you as someone who might know about the murder?" Marie asked him bluntly.

"Beats the hell out of me. I suppose they need to pin it on somebody in the hospital. That Turk lady thought she was the reigning queen around here. She dressed like royalty. The rest of us have to wear these stupid, bright yellow hospital gowns. We look like spaced-out fucking canaries."

Marie didn't say anything for a moment. *That's weird. Elsie Turk was found in the same yellow pajamas worn by the rest of the patients. I wonder if he's also colorblind.*

"Did you shove her away from you whenever she came on to you?" Martini snapped out of her thoughts.

"Damn right I did! I couldn't stand her. One time I popped her with the back of my hand. She laughed at me and walked away. That stupid bitch ward attendant saw me and wrote me up. Would you let me go back to my room now, please?"

"Sure," Marie said and nodded to Boyd to get the ward attendant.

When Hanson and the attendant left, Marie made some more notes in her spiral pad and slammed it closed.

"What a flake, Boyd. Is this guy for real?"

"He's being treated for severe depression. Depression is accompanied by thought patterns that are rife with distorted perceptions, maybe even faulty logic. We had to put him in restraints several times when he first got in here. His therapist has him dosed up on some heavy-duty medications."

Marie made more notations.

"I'm not sure when he'll be discharged, Marie. He has a female psychiatrist and is pretty smitten with her for some unknown reason. He announced in a loud voice to anyone who'd listen to him chitchat that he hated females of all ages, colors, and creeds. I can see why Lt. Hagen's crew fingered him."

"Let's get out of here," she half-pleaded. "I've had it for today. Let's go somewhere and get a drink."

Boyd agreed. "How about hitting that fun bar down on the Riverwalk level at your hotel? I don't think you've had the luxury of tipping one there. They never seem to run out of shelled peanuts, and you get to toss the shelled skins at each other or the musicians."

"Great idea, get me there soonest!" Marie ignored the red hair implications that this big Texan might be the killer. Naughty ideas began racing through her mind.

CHAPTER 28

ROD knocked the required three times and whispered low. "Are you in there, Keena?"

Some shuffling could be heard inside when she got to the door and sprung it open. He reeled back from the sweet odor of the marijuana creeping out the door and grabbing his unsuspecting nose. She had shifted from the ceramic bong to the more transportable rolled weed.

He remembered the ever-present sweet smell that permeated most of the barracks back in Vietnam. He hated the aroma. Trouble was never far away.

"Hi there, my hard-working fellow condo-mate. About time you got back," she said as she welcomed him into her unit. She had changed into a dark blue dress that didn't look as though it was painted on her. It surprised him. She had matching blue flats on her feet.

Rod was impressed. He was shocked when he noticed the dirty dishes were washed, dried, and stowed. The new clothes tossed around in the living room were hung up in the bedroom closet. Several small reds, white, and blue candles were lit and placed in neat arrangements around the apartment. They gave off a pleasant lilac bouquet that competed with the marijuana fragrance. The whole place looked pleasant, different.

Where was the mood music? Maybe that comes next! Wow, maybe the weed was good for something meaningful and constructive after all! Need I take a hard look at giving it a shot?

"Have you had dinner yet, Rod? I put some chicken pot pies in the oven but forgot to turn the damn thing on. I figured I could do that afterward. Come into the kitchen and have a drink with me."

He complied, anxious for the next step.

She poured three fingers of Bombay Sapphire gin into a glass with a lemon peel hugging the lone ice cube drifting on the surface. Keena then went to the refrigerator and brought out a cold glass of iced tea. She gave him the gin. She began to sip the tea.

"Whoops, switcheroo-switcheroo," she laughed. "Just kidding, Rod." She quickly swapped glasses with him. "Let's go stretch out on the couch. You can tell little ole me about your day at the funny farm."

"Look, Keena, I'd appreciate it if you got more serious about the mentally incapacitated people that need our treatment. We all can't be as sound in mind and spirit as you seem to possess. Our therapists would have nothing to do, right, gal?"

"Sorry about that," she said *tongue in cheek*. "I was just trying to throw in a little levity. It backfired on me. Let's take a timeout and get to know each other better. I know you told me you were single. Were you ever married?"

"Yes, once." He wasn't about to get into great detail about Janice. "We met in St. Louis and got married after a reasonable courtship period. She was born to Swedish parents and a wonderful lady. My wife was athletic and beautiful. We have one son living here who works at a mental health clinic south of downtown. Another son lives in Green Bay, Wisconsin. We were also fortunate enough to raise three foster children."

"What happened?" she asked. "I mean with the marriage."

Rod explained about their sojourn in San Francisco managing an apartment complex and the move to San Antonio. He couldn't go any further. Tears began to seek the corner of his eyes and began to drip down his cheeks.

She noticed but said nothing.

"I'm sorry to get all emotional like this, Keena, but she's gone, died unexpectedly."

"You poor soul," Keena said putting her arms around him. "We'll have something to eat. I'll put some flame under those delicious chicken pot pies."

"Keena, I'm not hungry." He glanced down at his watch. "I think I should go now. It's getting late, and I have some reports to review tonight if it's alright with you." He got up to leave and headed for her front door.

"Goodnight, my poor lonely Rod," she cooed. "I've got an important early meeting tomorrow at work," she lied. "Let's get together soon, okay?"

He left without saying another word.

Keena was a little confused with this man. He still had deep feelings for his departed spouse. She was attracted to him, wondering if she was wasting her time pursuing him.

Rod got back to his condo and took their wedding picture out of the scrapbook, studying it for a long time. More tears trickled down the tip of his nose and splattered on his arm. *What a wonderful life we had together. Why did you have to go and leave me all alone?*

Rod went to bed, able to control his crying jag. He clutched the wedding picture to his chest and drifted off to sleep.

CHAPTER 29

ANGEL Garza lived a twisted life in Mexico. He joined a gang of other young men in Mexico City hell-bent to buck the rules and mandates of their society. He severed all ties with his family and local friends he'd hung out with. Brief imprisonment in Saltillo for selling street dope to minors didn't alter his negative feelings. He was still a criminal in his mind. The interment only hardened his resolve.

The Mexican cartels operating in the northern part of the country wouldn't open up their arms to him because of his criminal background. They ascertained he'd be an unwelcome liability rather than a proven asset. Criminals had to watch their backs.

Garza illegally, and under a veil of secrecy crossed the border one dark and stormy night. He didn't stop running until he arrived in a small suburb outside of Detroit, Michigan, stealing and foraging for food along the way.

He only finds menial garden work because of his shriveled arm and club foot. A higher paying job became available hauling garbage for a local disposal company. He was homeless, begging on the streets like other indigents. One day a stranger approached him. He had been observing Angel for several days and was curious about the handicapped youngster.

"Hello young man," he said to Angel. "I've noticed that you like to frequent this street corner. Do you live nearby?"

Angel hesitated, then replied. "I'm new in the area and just checking out the neighborhood for a place to live."

After several weeks of *accidentally* running into Angel, the bearded man soon swayed him to attend a special meeting with a group of individuals of like interests. Angel found a new calling.

Radical Islamic extremists were not prevalent in the area. He read everything he could get his hands on that addressed their religious movement. Angel was disappointed with the western civilization that embodied the material, rather than the spiritual way of life. His physical condition precluded him from enjoying the fruits of mainstream America. There was a strong and overriding emphasis on capitalism and of course, sports and athletics.

The radicals were preparing for war, a different kind of war against those who opposed their idealism. Angel was convinced and accepted Jihad fanaticism as the answer to his frustrations and shortcomings. He had no choice.

He was on his way to undergo training in the faraway land of Afghanistan five months after the first meeting. The new follower traveled by way of Yemen and Sudan.

CHAPTER 30

ROD was busy reviewing a report from the business office. His door was wide open. He heard Boyd Bounder and Marie Martini come laughing down the hallway toward Boyd's office. It was Tuesday morning, and he had just completed a telephone call with the JCAH.

He asked them if they would postpone their re-accreditation survey of Mission Oaks Mental Health Hospital for four months. He explained the ongoing CIA investigation to justify his request. Rod assured them a delay would be in the best interests of both parties.

The JCAH official agreed. They rescheduled their visit four months out. The commission had other commitments lined up and couldn't conduct the survey earlier. That situation was fine with Rod.

"Hi, guys, what's going on?" Rod asked the two characters as he stuck his head out the door. "Are you adults still in the jovial Fiesta party mood, or what?"

"I think we've recovered a little bit from all those excesses," Boyd replied. "Marie is anxious to speak with the other two patients on her list. We're heading to the conference room to get that done."

"Boyd, hold on a sec. I have an important matter for your information and planning purposes. I spoke with the JCAH. They are delaying their visit here for four months. By then Marie will have found Turk's killer, and we'll be prepared for their inspection. I plan to meet with department heads next week and game plan our preparations."

"What great news about the delay, my friend. I'm sure Marie will have things well in hand soon. We can all go back to living and working a normal life. Of course, we never experience the normal around this place."

Rod thought he noticed more bounce-to-the-ounce and excitement in Boyd's demeanor. Marie also had a special ambiance about her, even though she didn't say a word. Something was going on between them and that *something* had to be good.

Lucie poked her head into Rod's office and told him Phil Dean was on the telephone. She said he sounded angry. Rod appreciated the fact Lucie was an expert on reading people. He wondered what was up with Phil and picked up his phone.

"What do you mean you're cutting off our treatment drugs of choice, Rod?" Dean shouted into the telephone. "I spoke with Tom Lubay in the pharmacy. He said you were altering the hospital formulary. Is that correct?"

"Hold on, Phil. I told Tom I wanted him to study which generic drugs we could substitute for the higher cost, brand name drugs. I pulled the pharmacy records and studied our drug costs over the last three years. Most interesting."

He could hear Phil breathing heavily on the other end of the telephone. The doctor said nothing.

"The status quo is not acceptable," Rod broke the silence. "Drug expenditures are rising about twenty percent per year. Our pharmacy costs are off the roof. They'll exceed our payroll liability costs if we don't monitor them closely."

Dean remained quiet. Rod knew the good doctor didn't mince words with him. *He must be loading up for the big blast to follow.*

"When he completes his study," Rod continued before Dean threw the next verbal punch at him. "I'll get together with you first, the medical staff, and then discuss his findings. I am by no means cutting off anyone or anything until viable alternatives have been addressed. I also told Tom I wanted the study conducted by him only. Transparency to any medical staff member was to be avoided."

"You know what young man?" Dean jumped in. "That formulary hasn't been changed in years. Everyone is happy with the present content. The insurance companies include our cost of drugs when adjudicating our claims. Don't they?"

"No, they don't," Rod shot back. He now had some unsolicited ammunition to use to his advantage. "Most of them pay our invoices on a daily per diem charge. This includes everything involved in the treatment of the given diagnoses. We tried to 'unbundle' the charges and list each item separately. It didn't work. We got letters back from the third-party payers saying they wouldn't accept the unbundling. Most of them pay claims on a Diagnosis Related Grouping, more commonly referred to as a DRG. They'll consider that fact and pay us more when we provide a certain service above and beyond that preordained by the diagnosis. At least that's what we expect to happen."

Doctor Phil seemed to be impressed with Rod's grasp of the situation. Rod took a deep breath and continued his rationale for the transformation. Change is inevitable.

"I understand your comment that our practitioners are comfortable with the formulary. That's exactly my point. It's the reason why I want it reviewed. Everyone doesn't have to approve and pay the bills. That's my job. Right, Phil?"

"Okay, okay, ride on cowboy, use the sharp spurs strapped to those big boots of yours to right this wayward ship!" Phil said laughing.

Rod took a moment to reflect. *Riding a horse and righting a ship doesn't make much sense to me. He knew what Phil was trying to say. He sounds a little bit like my good friend Howard I.M. Hill. I wonder if they're related!*

Dean continued after a brief pause to catch his breath. "That's why we hired you, Rod. We need someone to tell us physician know-it-alls can't always do what our little hearts desire. We're stubborn but not unreasonable. Good move! Let me know when Tom has his facts and figures finalized. We'll go from there." He hung up.

Rod didn't mention any of this to Dr. Dean. He suspicioned Tom might have some kind of deal going on with the pharmacy detail reps. They visit Mission Oaks and pass out healthy amounts of drug samples. Who used the samples was the big question in his mind.

It became obvious to him the reps push the drugs with the highest margins of profit–those that favor the pharmaceutical company, not the hospital. It may be unfair to the detail folks to think they're not willing to discuss generic alternatives. Facts are indeed facts. They can't be denied.

Rod picked up the telephone and called Enrique Salazar in housekeeping. He was getting ready to do battle again. He never cared for Salazar. The man was an inadequate supervisor.

"Enrique," Rod said when Salazar finally picked up the telephone. "I spent time around the hospital last weekend and wasn't happy with the cleanliness of the floors on the second floor. You need to light a fire under your people and hold them to a higher standard of work."

"Mr. Rod," he said solemnly. "I gave my people extra time off to enjoy Fiesta. You know it only comes once a year in San Antonio. Families rally around all the activities going on during the celebration."

Rod was getting pissed off at Salazar's jovial response to the subject. He hated it when supervisors soft-peddled their responsibilities. This wasn't the first time he spoke with Salazar about shortcomings in housekeeping.

"Then I suggest you get in here and do the floors yourself whenever you release your people to have a good time at my expense," he shouted into the phone. *Got to get a better hold of myself. Maybe Salazar is short-staffed and hasn't asked for more help.*

Salazar soft-peddled Rod's outburst as if they were talking about yesterday's old news.

"I need newer equipment to do the job right, boss. We've been babying these pathetic scrubbers for years. Even Mario Caseres in maintenance told me he's tired of fixing them. Someone is going to get electrocuted if they come in contact with the frayed wiring."

"Well, Enrique, that's why they invented electrical tape. We're going to have to babysit them a little longer. I've had my sights on some of the newer equipment designs available for our floor maintenance. Hang in there and do the best you can with what we have on hand, alright?"

Salazar agreed to hold off. *Bastard. The big new gun is causing a ruckus he'll regret.*

Rod placed the phone back in its cradle with a gentle touch.

What he didn't share with Salazar was his research about outsourcing most of the areas of housekeeping. He read the advertisements in the hospital journals about several major hotel chains offering contracted housekeeping services. He also learned from another hospital administrator other companies also provided such services. He had scheduled an appointment to meet with one of the company representatives but had to cancel it.

The murder investigation had taken front and center stage. The replacement of hospital equipment that didn't directly affect patient care would have to wait. He'll re-surface that notion soon. His to-do list was growing by leaps and bounds.

CHAPTER 31

BOYD and Marie were settled in the conference room. They were ready to resume questioning the last two patients. They had spent the past two days and nights in a rambunctious sexual marathon in her hotel room. Both were exhausted but satisfied with each other's contribution to the revelry.

He couldn't believe Marie's proficiency in all matters related to satisfying her bed partner. She introduced some foreplay games she learned in Bahrain from Sheik Salamah. Boyd didn't have as much *mileage* as her, but he seemed to hold his own in the love-making department.

"I need to ask you a question, Marie before we begin the interrogation. Where in the world did you learn those erotic gymnastics forms you put on me last night?"

"I don't believe in show-and-tell about past sex activities as a matter of practice. You might be my one exception. I think we know each other well enough now for candid talk. An attractive Arab Sheik I met on my last assignment overseas taught me a few new things about making love. Let's leave it at that."

The *Bedouin Barrage* was her favorite arousal method. Boyd had gone ballistics when she pulled it off on him. He was at a loss how to reciprocate. However, it was time to get down to business for both of them. She needed to wrap up this investigation and move on.

"How about bringing down Eduardo Munoz?" she suggested as she yanked the list out from her briefcase.

"The man's been here over a month being treated for delusions of grandeur according to your records."

Boyd nodded in agreement and called the ward. Munoz motored into the conference room in ten minutes, almost taking the door down when he entered. He was dressed in worn-out camouflaged fatigues purchased at an Army-Navy used sales store downtown. A green plastic helmet liner sat far back on his head, clinging on for life.

"I've been called back to active duty, you see," Munoz reported to Boyd. He didn't like this government "plant" woman and decided only to respond to Bounder's questions.

"How well did you know Elsie Turk?" Marie asked him.

Munoz fidgeted for a few moments and then disregarded her question.

"I will ask you one more time, Mr. Munoz. How well did you know Elsie Turk?"

All of a sudden Boyd grabbed Eduardo's arm and gave it a jerk. Munoz shifted back on the scooter seat, reeling back in utter surprise at the unplanned counterattack.

"Excuse me, Nurse Bounder, but I would appreciate it if you'd unhand me and do it right away! You do not need to get physical with me. I'm defenseless. Even a blind man could see that."

Boyd thought. *I wonder how the blind person could see this happening. This patient is something else.*

"However," continued Eduardo, "I've got a platoon of Army Rangers waiting in the hallway. They'll march in here and kill you both with their bare hands if I blow the whistle." He extracted a large silver referee's whistle from his pajama pocket and shoved it in his fat mouth.

Boyd released his arm and smiled back at him. Marie had no idea what was coming down next in this *mano-a-mano* confrontation.

"Eduardo, I think it'd be in the best interests of all of us if you'd cooperate with Miss Martini. Look at it this way. You'll be able to take your Rangers to the circus and let them engage in some big-time fun the sooner you answer her questions."

"I didn't know Ringling, Barnum, and Bailey had their company of outstanding performers here in town," Munoz replied. "I love the way those big elephants wiggle their way around the floor without a care in the world."

Marie shrugged. Bounder smiled.

"See here, people," Munoz continued his charade. "Nobody on the ward told me the circus is here, and I didn't get a written memo from my chief of staff. I've needed to get those warriors over there. They have to lighten up a little and let off some steam. They just returned from a demanding mission in South America."

Eduardo shoved the whistle back in his pocket and steered his machine toward the conference room door. He was done with this diversion and ready to execute his next assignment.

"Hang on there," Boyd shouted. "Let's get these few questions answered right away, then you can rejoin your troops."

"Yes sir, Colonel Bounder," he replied with enthusiasm, saluted sharply, and then turned his motorized cart back around to face Marie.

"How well did you know Elsie Turk?" she repeated for the third time. *Is this guy deaf or dumb?*

"I didn't know her at all, ma'am. Didn't anybody around the Fort take the time to inform you that we avoided each other? I could smell trouble the minute I saw her on the ward and steered clear of her. She had that certain look about her."

"And what look was that?" Marie asked with patience.

"It was that look of privilege . . . that look of a woman who would stare in contempt at us commoners on the ward. Yes, sir, she wanted to avoid us, especially me. She knew I came from sovereignty. She had no desire to challenge me when I had my big sword strapped to the waist."

Marie looked over at Boyd with a quizzical look on her face. She almost burst into laughter. She hadn't paid a dime for this entertainment. Would've spent a dollar.

"Do you mean that paper machete you made in the arts and craft room, Eduardo?" Boyd asked.

"Yes, sir! It's a lethal weapon, but I have a permit to carry it."

"Did you kill her, Eduardo?" Martini asked in a more serious manner trying hard to shake an admission of guilt from the batty man.

Eduardo stared at her and said nothing.

"You hated Elsie Turk for scorning you," Marie hammered away at Eduardo. "This inflamed you so much you swore you'd murder her. Isn't that right?"

Munoz almost fainted and pulled the helmet liner over his face. "God forbid. No . . . no . . . no way I'd ever do such a cowardly act like that." He began to shake, and sob, then cried aloud in a crescendo of "oh-my-gods!"

"I think you can go back and rejoin your troops now, Mr. Munoz," Marie said with a slight grin. "Have fun at the circus."

"Yes ma'am, yes sir," Eduardo responded and became animated again. His feigned sorrow had disappeared. He saluted each and took off in a hurry.

"You can scratch that poor excuse of a person off my list," Marie said. "I've seen some real loony tunes in my day, but that guy tops the list. I don't think he's even capable of lifting one fat finger against anyone. By the way, Boyd, did you smell alcohol on his breath?"

"Yes, that was alcohol I detected. One of his Ranger buddies must be smuggling booze to his royal highness. I also smelled onions. The kitchen served hamburgers today. I'll bet one spicy taco he piled those babies on his bun."

"Get serious, Bounder. Let's get Roberta Peck down here and be done with it."

She shifted down a gear and fashioned a softer approach with the man. "By the way, how are you feeling, my big redheaded cowboy? Are you having fun yet?"

Boyd smiled too long at her, then picked up the telephone and called the ward.

CHAPTER 32

MARIE extracted her files again and reviewed the notes she had on Peck. The typewritten report read: *she was a twenty-eight-year-old, single African-American woman admitted with severe paranoid schizophrenia. She thinks she's the Blessed Virgin Mary.*

A female attendant brought Roberta Peck to the conference room. "Here's the savior of the modern world," the attendant said with a slight smile. "Call me when you're finished, and I'll get back down here." She was then dismissed by Boyd and left the room with long strides. She wanted nothing to do with the action unfolding in the conference room.

"Hello, Miss Peck," Marie said. "I trust you know why we brought you down here."

"I haven't the slightest clue. It is both an honor, and at the same time, a disgrace to meet you. The scuttlebutt up on the wards is that you're trying to pin the murder of that Turk woman on one of us patients here. Isn't that right?"

"The honor is mine, Roberta," said Marie. "I'll forget the 'disgrace part' if that's okay with you."

"Let's get this over quicker than greased lightning. I have a prayer meeting starting upstairs in ten minutes. If I'm not there, nobody else knows how to conduct it. Why my precious son Jesus Christ ever allowed some of these stupid incompetents around this place to be born into my earthly kingdom is far beyond me."

"How well did you know Elsie Turk?" Marie asked. She was also in a hurry to get this over. She was getting more and more confused with the whole lot of them.

"We were good friends," Roberta responded in an earnest manner. "God answered my prayers by sending the Turk lady to me. We spent hours in the arts and crafts room doing scrapbooking. A fellow patient upstairs named Nick Ryan would give us all his magazines and papers after he read them. Elsie and

I would cut up pictures of anything related to the current fashion industry and pretend the clothes were made for us."

"I guess you used the J.C. Penney catalog to help you determine which clothing you would make," Marie stated. *I can't wait to get out of here. This woman is driving me nuts!*

"Naw, we had our creative ideas," a proud Roberta Peck said.

Bounder wished he could've taken a nap during the entire saga.

"Elsie was a real whiz at it, too. She taught me so much. I guess she traveled all over this world of ours searching for fashion shows. She told me her favorite place was the Middle East. The local women fight with each other to model the latest Western fashions."

Marie said nothing. *What a gigantic crock of bull. If those women over there were ever caught wearing western clothing and exposing a lot of their flesh in most public places, they'd get stoned to death!*

"Where did you get the pair of scissors to cut out the magazine and newspaper items?" Marie probed.

"My nephew owns a wallpaper shop on San Pedro near the North Star Mall—real success story, too. He brought them in one day when he visited me. That way we could cut better and clearer images. They were sharper than those kindergarten cutters the ward attendant gave us. Those neat blades had to be locked up when we left the room."

"That's good to know," Martini interjected, "It had to be a big help for you when cutting the newspapers and magazines."

"Yes, Nick told me he gets tons of papers delivered every day in the ward. I asked him why he reads so much. He told me he does at least five different puzzles every day. The guy is so brilliant for sure. Doesn't belong in this hospital."

"Where is the pair of scissors your nephew gave you right now, Roberta?" Marie asked as she edged closer to the patient.

"Why, gosh darn, I'm not sure where they are now. Maybe Nick took them back to his room."

"Did you ever get mad and argue with Elsie?" Marie asked her.

The patient didn't respond right away, giving both of them a blank stare.

Boyd joined the questioning. "One more question, Roberta. Did you ever hit her or threaten her about anything?" *I gotta get this over with and move on.*

"Yes, Miss Martini and Nurse Bounder. That's what good friends do all the time, right? We could never agree on which dress or gown should be cut out and pasted in our scrapbook. I never hit her hard, though. You got to believe me even if some other patients up there ratted on me. My spirituality is embedded in love and not violence."

"Thank you for talking with us today, Roberta," Marie said. "Boyd, call the attendant and get her down here right away. Miss Peck has to get upstairs in time to begin her prayer meeting."

"A last question before you leave, Roberta." Marie was moving in for the kill with one last stab. "Do you kneel on a special prayer rug and face Mecca when you and your group are called to prayer?"

"Oh my God, nothing of the kind," Roberta gasped aloud and held her hands to her face.

Marie wondered if the charade was meant to fake her out—steer her away.

Roberta was on a roll. "I don't even know where this *Mica* person is located or what that's all about. We sit in comfortable chairs placed in a tight circle. We're close enough to hold hands with each other as we pray. Thank both of you for being so kind and considerate. I'll pray for your safety and well-being and implore my group to do the same."

Roberta left the room and met up with the attendant in the hallway. He escorted the patient back to her treatment area.

"Is this lady serious, or is she trying to throw us a curveball, Boyd? She claimed she didn't know what happened to the scissors. She admitted slapping Turk out of frustration. Maybe, just maybe in her paranoia, she decided to kill her. I'm starting to feel like a fruit cake myself after listening to these people."

"Marie," he said with a serious look on his face, "I think you need to be a little more objective in assessing the overall situation at Mission Oaks. These patients are in this hospital because they need our help. Roberta is a classic case of paranoia. She is harmless in our opinion, so are the others we've talked to. I don't know why you're having such a hard time getting that!"

"Bullshit, Boyd!" Marie pounded back at him. Somebody around here viciously killed Elsie Turk. That somebody will be held accountable by me if it's the last thing I do on this unforgiving earth!"

He opted for silence. *She didn't seem so lovey-dovey right now. I'd hate for her to have me centered in her pistol crosshairs ready to slam home a fatal round!*

CHAPTER 33

MARIE scooted to the back of her chair and gave Boyd a *let's get on with it* stare. He knew what was coming next.

"I want to talk to Nick Ryan and see how much he interfaced with Turk and Peck. Tell me why he's in this hospital undergoing treatment anyway."

"Nick Ryan was a twenty-year veteran on the MPD before getting ousted," Bounder said. "He had accumulated almost enough points to retire with a comfortable pension when adding his ten years of active duty in the Army Special Forces. The rough-neck was accused on several occasions of using excessive force while collaring suspected burglars. Tough guy indeed."

"What part of town did he work in?" she asked, knowing most area demographics from her brief stay in the city.

"His beat was for the most part on the east side of town which is inhabited by a large number of blacks. The locals there complained to Chief Astrade so many times he was forced to order an investigation."

"So why is he in here? From what I heard so far, he doesn't seem crazy to me like the rest of them. Ops, sorry, Boyd, I mean clinically unbalanced, or something close to that nomenclature."

"The psychologists who were part of the MPD investigative team determined Nick was suffering from a severe case of bipolar disorder. Many adults with this disorder have trouble coping with stress, experiencing mood swings, demonstrating a hot temper, and sporadic outbursts. He needs to get anger management under control."

Marie shook her head several times in agreement.

Boyd continued, "The MPD contract clinicians recommended a twenty-day stay in our hospital. They needed to determine if his mental disorders were pre-existing conditions before he entered the police force. They also wanted to establish baseline criteria triggering his frequent violent episodes."

"Okay, so far I get it. Please go on Mr. Boyd Bounder."

"I'll do that. Nick had to be restrained several times on the ward because of physical outbreaks against the staff. He tossed a chair through a partition on the second floor. He screamed he was being framed. The doctors have him sedated, and they are easing him back to some semblance of normality."

He reached for his phone and asked the ward attendant to bring Nick Ryan down to the conference room.

Nick refused to be interviewed. He sent word back to Bounder he wouldn't respond until a court order was obtained requiring him to report to the CIA dictator. He further stated he didn't know why they wanted to talk to him. He said he didn't know an Elsie Turk.

"Boy, the informal communication channels these patients have developed around here astounds me," she told Boyd. "It beats the hell out of any organization I've ever been associated with, even the CIA. Let's take a break and amble over to that cantina down the street. I need something to dull my senses, maybe a frozen margarita."

Boyd agreed a break was in order. He'd go to the restaurant. But, he wondered why Nick was putting up such a stink about the investigation. He figured he might be able to convince Nick to be interviewed and would make the attempt after they had some refreshments . . . and Marie composed herself.

Lucie Guerra stuck her head through the partially opened conference room door. "Excuse me you two. There's a long-distance call for Miss Martini from Chicago. An Irene Finerty needs to talk to her now. I sensed the call is important so I didn't hesitate to break in."

"I guess those margaritas will have to wait," she told Boyd as she got up and followed Lucie back into her office.

CHAPTER 34

"HEY, CIA superstar Marie Martini, this is the renowned Chicago sleuth," Irene Finerty chided. "Sorry I couldn't spend more time with you in person and not have to play telephone tag through the several airports. I want to update you on my findings, or I should say, non-findings."

"Don't disappoint me now. I made a big-time bet with Bounder here that you'd discover our murderer."

"Well, I–"

Marie stopped her cold. "Please don't tell me you hit a dead end with the meaning of those numbers fingered out in her blood, Finerty. I know about the reddish hair strands found under Turk's fingernails. I can't pin a murder rap on every redhead in San Antonio."

"The only thing that we've been able to ascertain for sure is that there were only nine numbers and not ten," Irene clarified. "I think that helps. Now we can rule out ten-digit telephone numbers."

"Yeah, right," Martini said with a groan. "All we have left to determine now is whose social security number can be traced back to the San Antonio area. Can you do that with some degree of certainty? Are we still going to be on the outside looking in?"

"Not sure yet where these uncertainties leave you." Finerty didn't like the CIA agent's harsh tone or gruff attitude.

"Well maybe your collection of nerdy geniuses up in the Windy City can find out what another entity in this world of ours is composed of nine numbers," Marie wouldn't let up. "Why don't you start with baseball? There are nine innings in a game. Maybe you can identify a baseball player down in Texas who loves to kill people with huge scissors."

Marie regretted being so facetious. *I need to dial down the stress factor. Finerty probably hates my guts.*

"For sure," Irene said, not offended by the push for facts. "The ball's still in our court on the number's piece of the mystery. One of our in-house gurus told us the numeral nine was considered a lucky number by the Chinese. Maybe this is a lead worth considering. Why don't you get off your duff and find the big bad Chinese redhead, and we can all go back to living the good life again?"

"Don't be a smarty pant, Finerty, we're doing the best we can under the circumstances. San Antonio is one of the few large cities that isn't blessed with a full-blown Chinatown. Perhaps we should frequent some Chinese restaurants and check out their fortune cookie inventory. Maybe one of the crumbly tasteless excuses for a cookie will identify the murderer for us."

"By the way, Finerty, have you ever interviewed a ward full of maniacs in your climb up that bureaucratic ladder? Give me a ring if you come up with anything I can put my arms around." She hung up with a slight thud of the phone and went back to the lobby area. Boyd was waiting for her.

"Good news I hope," Boyd said. He was anxious for some kind of closure on the case.

"Yes and no. They've ruled out the telephone number possibility and are wrestling with nine number scenarios. We have to solve this case here and eliminate the wishful thinking the Chicago group will find our killer."

She stared at Boyd's red hair again wondering how she could collect a few strands of it without his knowledge. Maybe she should come right out with it and inform Boyd he has become a definite person of interest, at least in her mind.

"Is something wrong, Marie? Why are you staring at me like that? Does my buzz cut get you aroused? We should forget about the margaritas and head out somewhere else other than the cantina–like hotel room perhaps?"

"Silly boy, wishful thinking. I lost my train of thought after talking to Finerty, and her flippant response that everybody was coming up empty."

Boyd dropped the hotel room idea–wasn't achievable.

"Let's get Nick Ryan down here by force if we have to," she said. "I'm getting impatient and want to move out on this with *mucho gusto!*" She even spoke some Spanish. Boyd wondered if she was tri-lingual, having been versed in Arabic.

"Alright, I'll run to the ward and talk with Ryan. I have an idea that might work to get him down here. You sit tight, okay?"

He left the conference room and took the elevator to the second floor. He found Ryan in the conference room finishing the Friday Wall Street Journal crossword puzzle. Ryan was deep in thought and didn't acknowledge Bounder's presence.

Meanwhile, Marie had a brainstorm. She remembered Boyd had an old beat-up cowboy hat in his office. Marie figured she could borrow it for a day and haul it over to the MPD crime lab. Unofficially, they could analyze the hair follicles or other remnants which could be compared to the DNA profile they already had on file for this case.

She'd check his schedule and see when he would be gone from the hospital, and then she would swipe the hat. If the samples turn up positive for a match, she could get a warrant for his hair sample and make the whole process official. They could move on to the next redhead in the queue if it turns out that there is no such match. Every redheaded person in the hospital or known visitors here the day or night of the murder would have to be tested. She hadn't ruled out a female and wondered if the DNA could determine if the red hair came from a male or female. She'd have to obtain that answer before taking more definitive action.

Boyd came in with Nick Ryan. She was impressed with his size and confident demeanor.

Nick was a tall, well-built specimen of a man, probably over six-six and packing no more than an evenly distributed two-hundred pounds over his body. The tall Irishman had light skin. The covering layer reported several purple liver spots fighting their way to the surface of the arms and to a lesser degree, his face. He appeared to be a heavy drinker at some point in his life.

Ryan was so fair-skinned that if left out in the blazing Texas sun for a long time, he'd hatch on the spot. He wore his long, dark red hair in twin braids extending downward from each side of his head. They were held together by flat rubber bands.

Marie was thrilled that Boyd somehow maneuvered him down to the conference room. She shot up to shake his hand and offer a friendly greeting. This gesture was a big-time mistake. He crushed her hand in a vice-like grip. She controlled the wince starting to mobilize in her face and jerked her hand away. Thank God she wasn't wearing that thick silver ring she got from the sheik, otherwise, it would've been flattened along with the finger joint.

"Pleased to meet you, Agent Martini," he said. "I hope I can be of some assistance here. Bounder said you were a special lady. I'd be a fool not to come down and sit face to face with a world-class beauty. He said you might arrange an early release for me from this rotten hell hole. Ain't that right, Boyd?"

"Hang on there a minute, Nick!" Boyd was quick to respond. "I told you she was the key person who could influence the powers-to-be to order your discharge from the hospital. Now it's up to you to do your part to make that happen."

"Yeah, right on," Ryan answered in anger. "Just like getting out of prison early for serving good time. Well, now that I'm here, let's talk. Who knows, something good might come out of this for yours truly after all. Things can't get much worse."

The fire in his eyes had disappeared. He smiled at Marie, and then scanned her entire body as he slumped back in his chair.

"Mr. Ryan," Marie asked, "How well did you know Elsie Turk?"

"She was a neat person. I'd see her with that black lady cutting out paper dolls, or something like that. Then they'd paste them into a book. Whatever kind of psychotherapy they employed on those two seemed to work. That Roberta somebody, I forget her last name, was as flaky as they come. I ignored her. She always pestered me to join a fucking prayer group with some other quacks she'd corralled."

Marie looked over at Boyd for a comment. There was none.

"Turk had a real hankering for me," Ryan went on. "The sweetheart would wrap those gangly arms around me and give me a peck on the cheek every time I brought them old papers. I think she wanted to screw me but was afraid the black saint would

146

damn her to hell for all eternity. She wasn't pretty as you, Miss CIA agent. She was way too old for this detective. I think the kitchen staff puts saltpeter in the men's food around here to keep it down. Know what I mean?"

Boyd had a difficult time not to laugh at the Irishman's dissertation. *This guy belongs in the Comedy Club!*

Ryan smiled again at Marie, almost reaching the proverbial leer stage as his eyes continued to scrutinize her body.

"Mr. Ryan, why are you in Mission Oaks Hospital?" Marie asked him with a penetrating stare he couldn't misinterpret. She was beginning to reach the boiling point with this cocky geezer.

"I've been a super good cop for many years, Martini, and I know how investigations work. You know goddamn well why I'm in this joint!"

Nick was starting to turn redder and began spewing saliva from the corners of his mouth. Bounder thought he might be witnessing the first signs of a stroke.

Ryan rose abruptly from his chair all of a sudden without any warning. The Irishman collided with Bounder as he stumbled toward the door exiting the conference room.

"I know my way back up there," he shouted back at them. "No need for either of you two prima donnas to escort me."

Bounder rushed to call the ward attendant and asked her to keep a sharp eye on Nick when he returned to the ward. He informed the attendant the patient might need a sedative to calm him down.

"Boyd, correct me if I'm wrong. I think he'd been drinking."

"I noticed the same thing. Do you think he and Munoz have a stash of booze hidden away up there?"

"Yes, perhaps they do. The entire area needs to undergo a thorough search. Dr. Pena reported Elsie Turk had excessive amounts of alcohol in her system when they performed the autopsy. I think we may have identified a primary suspect." She crossed her fingers and pointed to Boyd. "No wonder they kicked him off the police force."

"When does a person of interest become a legitimate suspect?" he asked.

"You just witnessed it here in front of us, my friend. I'd bet my next month's bonus on it."

Boyd smiled at her confidence.

"I need a break and one or two of those frozen margaritas," Marie sighed. "We'll see where this trail leads us to number one suspect–Nick Ryan."

She secured her documents in the briefcase and had Bounder lock them up in the file drawer. Marie would summarize her notes when they returned from the cantina, encouraged by the interview with the boisterous detective. Things were shaping up. She felt progress was being made but was hesitant to claim victory. She'd been burned before. *Maybe now Irene Finerty can surprise us with a report that clarifies the several issues we're still wrestling with.*

CHAPTER 35

IT was raining outside the crowded restaurant when they peered through from the inside the window. Huge puddles were forming in the street. Passing cars were splashing the wet residue on the sidewalks.

Larry Richards and Dr. Jim Smyth had decided to drive over to Peruzzi's Restorante in Leon Valley to have a late lunch. They brown bag at work, but Larry thought this would be a nice change of venue for them. In any event, they needed to disappear from the clinic. Each care provider had a tough morning.

"How'd you ever discover this place, Larry? It's far from where we work."

"I live nearby and often drive by it. Lots of cars parked outside. One night we decided to try it out. The food's outstanding."

"Thanks for coming, Jim. I thought your last patient would never leave your treatment room."

"Neither did I. The child's mother had a difficult time accepting the fact her little angel was a she-devil in disguise. Know what I mean?"

"I see the types often," Larry concurred. "Now, why did I choose this restaurant for a reason other than its proximity to my home? I had a sudden urge for some good Italian food and love how they prepare the veal cacciatore. My wife Pam thinks pizza was invented by Leonardo da Vinci, duly inspired after he completed his work on Michelangelo in the Sistine Chapel. That's about the only Italian food she'll eat anywhere or buy in the grocery store to fix at home."

"My wife loves Italian food any day of the week," Jim countered.

"Jim, it's a long haul from our clinic to drive here for lunch in the rain. You'll see from the quality of the food it was worth the added inconvenience."

Smyth looked again out the window and smiled. "We're in a terrible drought plaguing all of South Texas, and more so here in Bexar County. We should get down on our hands and knees and thank the Good Lord for all the wetness He can dump on us. Salado Creek near my house was bone dry. If this keeps up there'll be flooding to contend with. By the way, I thought your dad was going to join us here."

"He called and told me he'd be a few minutes late but to go ahead and order. Let's talk some business before we finalize our menu selections."

"Sure, what's on your mind?" Smyth looked concerned.

"I'd like you to join me in my clinic at Ft. Sam. I'm overwhelmed and need help. I underestimated the volume of patients referred to me for treatment. Either I'm doing a bang-up job, or there is an influx of sick kids within the military system."

Jim nodded. "Right on. I've witnessed you've cut down your hours over at South-Town Psychiatric Services. Phil Dean commented on that the other day. He said you were a great addition to the team. He hoped you'd never consider leaving us."

Larry said nothing.

"Let me sit on your proposal for a day or two, Larry. I'd like to help you out at the military base if I can swing it."

Rod walked in the front door of the restaurant and shook the water from his umbrella. He stashed it in the corner where several others were propped and headed over to the table where Larry and Jim were sitting.

"Damn rain," he said, "Reminds me of those monsoons over in 'Nam,' that seething hell hole. Hi guys, sorry I'm late."

"We both know how busy new hospital administrators are on any given day," Dr. Smyth said. "Congratulations on your appointment. Phil Dean is a tough cookie when it comes to supervising or mentoring other individuals. You passed his litmus test with high honors."

"No kidding, Jim, and thank you so much for your kind words. I thought he'd fire my butt after our clashing of heads on the hospital formulary issue."

Larry jumped in. "I heard through the proverbial grapevine you are doing an outstanding job over there, Mr. Richards."

"Thanks, Larry, but our hospital census is beginning to fall. I'm not sure how long they'll keep me around if it continues the downward spiral. Clemens, the old administrator at Mission Oaks got fired for less. We need to goose our occupancy rate somehow."

"Do you have a marketing representative with your staff?" Jim asked.

"No, not at present. I heard from my secretary Lucie that we had a marketing rep some time ago, but the hierarchy felt the position could be eliminated. She told me Harry Mooney went on record to say he brings in most of the referrals through his activities with the Alamo Heights Lions Club."

"That ego-maniac, numbers-cruncher thinks the whole world revolves around him," Jim said. "I suggest you re-visit the idea of hiring one, now. Two new mental health hospitals are scheduled to open here in the next six months."

"Shit, just what I don't need! I believe you've hit the nail on the head, Doctor Jim. I happen to know the right person for the job. I'm going to call her when I get back to the hospital, see if she's available."

Larry asked him if he was going to hire that Keena person away from the company where she is employed.

"Now why in God's creation would you ask me that question? How'd you learn about her?"

"Father Rod, you know we psychologists are blessed with physic minds. Just kidding. Pam told me about the tall, dark Indian beauty the other day. I finally got Pam to call and invite you over for dinner. It'd allow us to grill you further about this mysterious lady. Pam was able to pull out of that thick skull of yours some interesting things when she talked to you last week. You'd met an interesting woman at your condominium after you'd first arrived. You slipped up and shared more information with Pam than you thought. Care to fill in the blanks for us?"

"Go to hell, both of you!" Rod laughed back at them. "Let's order."

CHAPTER 36

ROD decided to take a different route back to the hospital. He never cared to go the same way twice. The rain had dissipated, and the sun began to peek out over the last black cloud in the sky. The traffic was heavy but moving at a good pace.

What in God's creation ever caused me to ramble on with Larry's wife about my experiences with Keena? I'm always close-mouthed about my so-called love life, even though I didn't have one. Did I spill my guts out about the drunken stupor I shared with Dalia Garza and her close friend months ago?

Rod swung east around Loop 410 and then headed south on Interstate 10. The city skyline was beautiful. A rainbow hung in shining delight above the downtown structures, almost reaching down and kissing the Tower of the Americas.

He was in a romantic mood. He wondered if he should call Dalia and see if she'd join him for dinner tonight. It was time he found out where he stood with her. They seem to be avoiding each other at the hospital. Probably good for both of them. He didn't want any solicitous rumors spreading around the hospital he and Dalia were an item.

"What's up Rod?" Lucie asked when he passed through her office and entered his own. She was sporting a sun-burned face from a weekend at South Padre Island. Rod remembered her athletic husband was a sport fisherman.

"Lucie, I got a great idea. I'm going to call an old friend from San Francisco and see if she'd consider becoming our new marketing director. You'd like her the moment you met her. She reminds me a lot of you."

Her sunburned cheeks took on a darker hue at his words. Lucie wondered what he meant by the comment but took it as a compliment. "I don't recall that you got that position authorized yet. Have you talked with Mooney about it? You know he thinks he calls all the personnel shots around here."

"No, not yet, I'll touch base with him at the appropriate time. All I want to determine now is whether or not the woman would be interested in relocating here. I can expedite the approval process if it's a positive response."

Lucie smiled in agreement.

"Harry is pretty happy with me now. I guess I can test the waters to see if he's willing to loosen the purse strings. We need to get a marketing expert in here. I'll hold off interviewing other candidates until I get a feeling from my friend about how she reacts to the call. Please grab the Rolodex and call Nancy O'Reilly at the Marine Memorial Club in San Francisco. Let me know when you reach her. Meanwhile, I'll be reviewing some pending contracts. Thanks, Lucie."

Rod pondered if this was a wise move. He had no idea about Nancy's track record at the Marine Memorial Club but was willing to take a chance. She was an ideal tenant of theirs at their old apartment in San Francisco. Everybody there spoke highly of her.

"Hello, Nancy, how the heck are you doing?" Rod said when Lucie signaled to him she had O'Reilly standing by. "I bet I'm the last person in the world you'd expect to get a call from, right?"

"Well, um, yes you are, Rod Richards," Nancy said in utter surprise. "How are you and Janice doing down there in Alamo country? I'd bet it's a different scene there than what you both experienced in San Francisco. Do you miss me and the apartment community as much as we miss you two?"

"I have to respond both yes and no, to be frank with you. Janice was alive and well when we managed the apartment complex. She died soon after our arrival in San Antonio. I don't want to go into the gory details. Suffice it to say we were all shocked. Nancy, we had great fun in the City by the Bay, even though we had to put up with that miserable Frenchman who owned the place."

"Oh my God, I'm so sorry for you, Rod. I didn't know. Are you doing okay?" She sounded so sincere Rod wasn't sure how to respond.

"I've adjusted, Nancy, but it's been difficult. Believe me!"

"Yes, I certainly understand."

"Now, what prompted my call? I'm looking for a super-good marketing person. I'm the administrator of a hospital in San Antonio and need someone who can bring in patients for us."

There was a hesitation on the other end of the line. He awaited her reply, then said, "That's about as simple as it gets, Nancy."

"Rod Richards, you couldn't have called me at a better time. The CEO running the Marine Memorial Club re-engineered me out of a job. They're putting the marketing position under customer relations . . . if you can believe that! I've been offered a generous severance package, though. My last day is at the end of the month. Tell me more about your hospital and what type of person you're looking for. All I've done in the past is retail and hospitality marketing."

"Marketing is marketing, Nancy. You convince the public that your product is superior to that being offered by your competitors. In our case, it should be easy to sell our hospital for a multitude of reasons. I'm done blabbering over the phone. Let me fly you out here this weekend or next. We can discuss the position face to face."

"Fine, Rod, I look forward to seeing you again. Maybe you can fill me in more about Janice after I get there. I thought she was a great person. I'm so sorry she's still not at your side. You guys made a great team."

Rod felt tears forming at each eye.

"Can't you overnight the airline ticket to me?" Nancy asked.

He was thrilled by her response. *She wants it!*

"Sure enough. I'll take care of the arrangements. Southwest Airlines is a Texas company, and we use them often. They don't serve meals. Their peanuts are great. Meet me at the baggage carousel when you arrive–say Friday. I'll make reservations at one of the fine hotels near our famous Riverwalk. See you then. Be sure to call me if any problem arises that would cancel or alter your flight for this weekend."

"Yes, Rod, I'm excited." She terminated the call.

Rod looked forward to being with Nancy again. She might be his solution to the hospital's shrinking patient census. They would teach her the *ins and outs* of the mental health business, at least from the economics point of view.

He told Lucie to make reservations for her at the Sheraton Gunter Hotel on Houston Street, not too far from his condominium.

Once again, he started to choke up at the thought of Janice. He knew O'Reilly was sincere when she sought more information about her untimely death.

Let it be. I'll move on, he whispered to Janice's photograph on *the small end table.*

CHAPTER 37

ANGEL Garza had journeyed a long distance from the dregs of Mexico, the environs of Michigan, and beyond to Afghanistan. His wandering mind kept reflecting on the onerous activities of the recent past, months after he'd abandoned his home country.

How things have changed for me. I'm far better off now than I ever thought I'd be after leaving home. I loved the history lessons they taught me here and the culture of this ancient and wonderful country. He remembered the story well, as though it were yesterday.

Afghanistan was considered the gateway to India in earlier centuries. The landmass of the country is almost the size of Texas. Islamic conquerors arrived in the seventh century. Al-Qaeda was formed by Osama bin Laden across the border in Peshawar, Pakistan. He was a Saudi by birth.

Bin Laden forged a close relationship with Mullah Omar in Afghanistan. He led the Taliban during their rise to power. It was not until the power surge of the Taliban that bin Laden had the al-Qaeda fully operational. Under his leadership and protection from the Taliban, he built up arms, gathered supplies, and organized camps to train recruits all over the world.

Al-Qaeda was composed of middle-aged men in the beginning. They'd fought in the Afghan war. Younger men were disenchanted with the spread of evil Western ideals and culture. They flocked to join them. Bin Laden had global aspirations, contrary to the mission of the Taliban. Their plan focused on regional control. He infused in the minds of his followers the certainty of a holy Jihad. The Western World must be brought to its knees!

Angel Garza again recalled those challenging days and long cold nights spent there. The training was unreal. He wondered if he'd survive the physical rigors. Angel questioned why'd he ever joined their crusade. Most of the time he was frozen half to death, lying in a curled-up fetal position trying to keep warm. It was an impossible task.

The mighty range of the high Hindu Kush Mountains of Afghanistan was brutal to any poor soul who had the misfortune to spend evenings in a pup tent. His sleeping bag, fortified with whatever warm clothing he could wrap around him was engaged in a battle against the elements.

"You must conquer both the fear of man and the uncertainty of nature and its harsh elements," the bearded al-Qaeda leader urged.

Most of the young men bought into this challenge. They were willing to suffer the consequences, regardless of the personal sacrifices that came with the idealism. They were on a glorious mission.

"Why couldn't they find a more desirable location to stage this important part of the training?" Angel questioned another recruit. The young man next to him shrugged his shoulders. He didn't know–didn't have the answer–didn't care why.

Afghanistan was a large country to offer a secluded, yet viable backdrop for the rigors of training. The rations included small pieces of cured mutton, stale bread, dried fish, and the terrible worm-infested rice proclaimed to be the best in the entire world.

In contrast, he remembered the warm evenings back home, the wonderful Mexican food, and the simple things he enjoyed there. He and his friend argued the only good thing they produced around these parts is opium. It was difficult to get his hands on the wonderful "cure-all."

"My friend Angel," his companion in arms said one day, "We will not only survive this rigorous training, but we will also exceed their lofty expectations. You got to hang with me, don't drop out."

Angel Garza's physical imperfections were discussed in detail by the al-Qaeda leaders before and even after he was recruited. They were concerned he couldn't accomplish the strenuous training requirements of their warrior initiation. He surprised everybody with his agility and perseverance.

"I know. . . I know how you feel about him," the camp leader said to several of his senior cadres. "I disagree with your conclusions. A crippled operative would be less likely to be profiled by law enforcement agencies as a dangerous terrorist. Yes, in contrast to our other frontline soldiers. He's a definite asset for us to use as we see fit."

The training cadre tried to make everything exciting for Angel and the other new members. They were true believers and vowed to die in the line of duty. That is if it was Allah's grand plan for them. He was more than ready, willing, and able to go to war. The hell with the twenty-seven virgins, he wanted to kill! He'd take less.

Al-Qaeda camp leader Mashudan was satisfied with the results of training achieved by the recruits. The newest members of the swelling al-Qaeda organization were ready to make a major impact on their worldwide movement. They had taught him to speak Arabic and how to overcome his physical limitations with a series of mental and physical gymnastics.

All trained recruits were loaded in a huge truck that traveled overland to Osama bin Laden's camp–an integral component of the out-processing procedures. Each person had a hood placed over the head when the caravan left their training camp. The hood was not removed until the convoy entered the outer defenses of bin Laden's highly secretive headquarters.

Sometimes the exalted leader himself would give the closing remarks if he were available. Otherwise, one of his prime deputies would render the highly energized closing declarations.

"Angel, come meet with me to get your new assignment," Mashudan ordered when they had returned to their encampment. They gathered together in his small tent. Angel was excited but concerned. He was sure they'd send him back to Michigan.

Over the years the radical Islamic organization developed a complex network to input demographic information on potential members. They knew his sister Dalia Garza was working and living in San Antonio, Texas, a southwestern province of the

United States. They also knew Juanita Comptos was a childhood friend of his sister's, and they were living together.

"We're sending you back to the United States to a location close to where you grew up," Mashudan said.

Angel was disappointed. He had hoped to be returned to the Midwest. He had many friends still living in the area. He was more than ready to take on the new assignment after six months of being re-born on an isolated mountaintop, halfway across the world.

"You'll have to be creative to gain back your sister's confidence and trust," Mashudan continued. "We've given you the skills to make this happen."

How in Allah's name they ever found out about my sexual abuse of Dalia is far beyond my imagination. These warrior leaders must be direct descendants of the great Mohammed.

"You will contact Juanita Comptos. She's your new handler in San Antonio, Texas. You'll contact her at the school where she's employed. Do not, I repeat, do not attempt to see your sister until Comptos authorizes it. Your sister is not one of us. Comptos will instruct you which approach to use to set up the meeting."

Angel stared at his leader.

"Do you understand me?" Mashudan said in a loud voice, picking up a negative vibe in the young recruit.

"Yes, I do," Angel replied with emphasis.

"I have one more important piece of information you need to know," the leader continued. "We also have an asset working at a local San Antonio hospital. Her name is Amfi bin Aziz. She's related to an important sheik operating in the Middle East. Listen up. He is one of us–be discreet!"

Angel committed all the instructions and vital information to memory. He wondered how his sister could not be involved in their glorious Jihad. In his mind, Juanita Comptos was a complete failure. She was unable to convert his sister to their cause. *Why did they select her to be my supervisor?*

He hated Dalia's childhood friend but would have to hold his emotions in check if he were going to be successful.

Your new name is now Hibat Allah," Mashudan said with pride. "It means *Gift of God* in our Muslim heritage. Now it is time to depart. Go proudly and strongly in the pursuit of your mission. *Allah Akbar!*"

CHAPTER 38

BOYD told Marie he had a meeting with the credentials committee after they returned to Mission Oaks from Cantina Classica. He'd return in two hours. She squeezed his hand as he left his office.

Marie figured this was the best window of opportunity to take Boyd's cowboy hat to the FBI. She had changed her mind about which agency should do the hair analysis. Marie ruled out the MPD–too many folks knew Bounder. She'd ask the FBI to coordinate with the medical examiner's office to run tests on any strands of red hair found stuck to the brim of the hat. Doctor Pena appeared to be neutral in terms of his loyalties. He shouldn't present a problem.

Marie also grabbed Boyd's coffee cup. She'd done this "trick" with other cases she investigated to help substantiate the DNA profiling.

"Got a search warrant allowing us to run the DNA tests?" Special Agent Vasquez questioned Marie after sitting down in his office.

"C'mon, Jorge, I don't want Lt. Hagen and his cronies over at the MPD to get involved with this matter. You can get it done for me. We'll see if the profiling matches the sample of hair which the medical examiner discovered under the deceased's nails. I'll hustle back and get a court order for the warrant if we get a bullseye here."

"Okay, Marie, you owe me, big time! We'll keep everything at the federal level for now. I understand your concern with our local cops. Whose cowboy hat is it, anyway?"

"It's confidential at this stage . . . CIA business," she said with a serious tone in her voice. "Record the name as Big Red One and leave it at that. One more thing. Don't forget to ask the medical examiner if he can verify if the red hair strand was male or female."

"Got it! By the way, are you doing anything tonight?" he asked her wearing a hound dog face begging for a milk bone.

"Get lost, agent, spend the night with that other female who wears the matching wedding ring on her left hand!"

Marie headed back to the hospital and found Bounder seated in his office scanning a patient's medical record. She hoped he wouldn't ask where she had been.

"What's going on, Boyd?"

"I'm reviewing the nursing notes from last evening. The charge nurse on the second floor wrote an incident report involving Nick Ryan and Eduardo Munoz. They had a heated argument. Ryan tossed Munoz off his motorized scooter. Nobody was hurt. Both had been drinking."

"What precipitated that?"

"I have no idea, but we're checking it out now. Their therapists will report back to me later. I'm more concerned about the booze aspect than the argument. I'm not satisfied with an earlier MPD report that dismissed the presence of alcohol in the patient areas. Earlier, Lt. Hagen took a different position and wanted to make a big deal out of it. He's backed off. I'm not sure why. I wonder who got to him, and why. I guess we'll never know."

"Interesting, to say the least," Marie said. "I'd probably flip that motorized moron out the second-floor window if I spent any time with him. How do you folks do it?"

Bounder looked shocked, then eased off.

"Nick Ryan will never get rid of that anger no matter what your mental health visionaries say about him," Marie said with conviction. "I'm going back to the hotel and do some paperwork. Will I see you tonight?"

"Does Santa Claus deliver toys on Christmas Eve?" He had visions of things other than sugar plums dancing in his head no less guiding a herd of over-eager reindeer through the cold night.

Rod came down the hallway and knocked on Bounder's door, just as Marie emerged from Boyd's office.

"Hello . . . goodbye," Marie said to Rod as she swung around him. "I gotta move out. The clock's running on this investigation. I can't let the battery die on me right now."

"What's that all about?" Boyd.

"You know her, Rod–busy, busy, busy."

"That's good. I stopped by to invite you to sit in on a meeting tomorrow. Chief Jesus Astrade from the MPD is coming over for lunch. He wants to talk to us."

"Is it about Turk's murder?"

"No, it has to do with the handling of mentally ill prisoners. He and the county sheriff think their jails are junior mental health facilities. He thinks we can help them."

"Does he want to put them in here for God's sake?" the concerned Chief Nurse asked with a look of disbelief.

"Who knows? Phil Dean will also be at the meeting."

"Do you want me to research anything before the get-together?" Boyd inquired.

"Nothing in particular. I think they want to use the vacated laundry building in the back for some type of function. Not sure you're aware I signed an agreement with several downtown hospitals to share a contracted laundry service. We're dumping all the equipment in the outbuilding. The outdated items have been a big headache for us and a noticeable drain of financial resources to keep it operating."

"Yes, Rod, I read the memo you circulated the other day. Let's convert the space to a topless bar and a dance hall, I love to line dance and shake these booties."

He lifted his feet and thrust his big cowboy boots on the desk. Rod noticed today he was wearing white boots adorned with the numerous horned-tailed ends of a rattlesnake. He killed the poisonous varmint last summer on the family ranch.

"I'd clunk my cowboy hat on my partner's head, flap my arms around her waist, and shout sweet things in her ears." Boyd continued his aspirations about a dance hall. He shot a glance at the hat rack in the corner and noticed the cowboy hat was missing. He wondered where he'd forget it this time. He'd left it at a dance hall three months ago in Bandera, Texas, and had to drive back the thirty miles to retrieve it.

"You're in a good mood, my man," Rod laughed.

"I happen to be feeling my oats." Boyd was thinking ahead to tonight with Marie. He'd surprise her with a dozen red roses.

CHAPTER 39

"WILL everyone in here please take a seat?" Phil Dean ordered with an authoritative voice.

"I'm sure you all know Chief Jesus Astrade, if not in person, then by the many news clippings he generates–somtimes good." He laughed as he glanced over at Jesus.

Rod Richards, Boyd Bounder, and Belle Chelby all nodded in unison.

Richards raised his hand to get Dean's attention. "I've not met this woman sitting next to the chief."

"Neither have I," Bounder chipped in.

"Sorry," Phil said, "I thought you all knew the charming psychologist. She's Astrade's right-handed man, er, ah, excuse me, Belle. I mean right-handed person over at the MPD."

Phil Dean was blushing, a phenomenon rarely experienced by the straightforward and confident physician. "She headed up the contractor group that performed the study we're going to discuss here. Jesus was impressed with the detailed findings and recommendations coming out of her final interview. He hired her as the full-time mental health consultant for his department."

Bounder had no interest in her, other than her professional qualifications. Rod took a few minutes to check her out. He guessed she was his age but didn't wear the visual bumps and bruises that befit their age group. *Of course, women tend to age in a different pattern than men, less noticeable, less quick. At least that's what he often told the fairer sex.*

She wore a long red dress flared at the knees. The sleeveless dress was cut short at the shoulders revealing strong arms. A gold chain link belt snuggled around her waistline. The long brunette hair was draped over her shoulders. There was an assortment of colorful rings occupying each finger, except the thumbs. A wedding band was not one of them. She wore little or no makeup.

She caught Rod's prolonged gawking in her direction.

"Do you have a question, Mr. Richards?" she curtly asked him.

"Oh no, I was trying to see if you were wearing a badge."

She picked up her purse and fingered a police badge pinned to the strap. She held it up for all to see. Rod couldn't read the lettering but presumed it to be legit.

"And I carry a pistol, too, Mr. Richards. I don't think you want me to pull it on you. Let's leave it at that for now."

Rod liked her quick wit and sweet southern accent. She'd be a challenge for any grown man wanting to play the romance game. *Hmm, might I?*

Belle Chelby was born in a small village in West Virginia across the river from the Ohio border. Her mother was Panamanian, and her father was the chief of police, well-respected by the townspeople. Belle wanted to be a cop as far back as she could remember. Her mother disapproved. The young girl walked to the police station after school and traded "shop talk" with the front desk sergeant. College changed her career goals. She still wanted law enforcement. Her school counselor channeled her focus from nabbing criminals to better understanding why they became criminals. Belle acquiesced.

"Where's Harry Mooney?" the chief asked, trying to change the direction of the conversation. He felt it was time to get this assembly moving. He'd noted Rod's fascination with his pretty psychologist.

"He's on one of those safaris he loves more than work," Phil Dean reported. "We all think he's hunting for one more horned animal head to grace his office wall. He'll be back in two weeks. Harry told me to arrange this meeting in his absence. I know he's already done legwork with Jesus on the subject."

Rod doubted it.

"Let's get down to business and address the reason we're all sitting around this conference table," Dean said as he surveyed each member in the room. He motioned for Chelby to begin.

"Your city commissioned a study to determine the best way to handle prisoners with mental health disorders. Crisis intervention teams know jails and other detention facilities across the nation have become pseudo-psychiatric treatment centers."

Rod nodded with interest. He knew where this was heading.

"Our team reviewed every record of incarceration MPD had on file. We went back ten years. We found fifteen percent of adult prisoners had some form of mental illness. The most alarming finding was that seventy-five percent of the detainees under twenty-one suffered fell in this category."

The room fell silent. Bounder became more interested. Chelby paused for effect and then continued her assessment.

"We have two options. Train every police officer to become a psychiatric assistant or construct a special facility to house them apart from the other prisoners."

The Chief of Police continued as an observer in the discussion.

"You folks are the experts in the treatment process and strive for positive outcomes," Chelby said as she glanced at Dean and Bounder. "We feel certain you can assist us."

"What do you have in mind?" Rod asked before the other two could frame a response. "We're a private, for-profit hospital funded from third- party insurance programs. We can't put dangerous people on our unsecured wards. The State Insurance Commissioner and the Joint Commission on Accreditation of Hospitals would disown us."

Belle Chelby observed him for a moment–liked his style.

"Harry Mooney felt we could convert the outbuilding that once housed our on-site laundry setup into inpatient detention beds," Dean offered. "Rod here had some fairly strong reservations. I have mixed feelings. Other clinicians on board think such a venue might work."

"Harry met with me several weeks ago," Astrade said, finally joining in. "He assured me it wouldn't be a problem. He hoped for a consensus in support of both Chelby and Dean."

Rod gave the chief a *what the hell do you mean* kind of stare. Chelby picked it up but didn't vocalize her thoughts.

"Mooney no doubt envisioned big fat dollar bills floating by his nose," Richards countered. "He has no idea of the complexities involved in such a proposal. The biggest thing he probably ever built in his lifetime was a model airplane!"

Blunt, way too blunt for a junior player in this league. I better tone it down a few notches.

Dean gave a half-hearted nod at Rod's comments. The others snickered, knowing Mooney, or at least his reputation.

"Jesus and I were in the Korean War. We knew of a hospital that had a prisoner of war wing separate from the mainstream hospital. Having two separate missions worked to everybody's satisfaction."

"Yeah, right," Rod said, "In Vietnam, our guys cut the ears off the wounded Cong they captured before they turned them over to the medics. This was a different kind of war. Let me remind everybody this is peacetime in the heavily regulated and litigious U.S. hospital industry."

"Then what do you intend to do with that empty building behind us?" Dean asked, putting Rod on the spot.

"I have something in mind," Rod lied. He planned to mothball the place for a while to save on utility, maintenance, and insurance costs. He had to study how best to use the space to generate more revenue for the hospital. He thought this proposal wouldn't generate money for the hospital.

"Dr. Dean said you were a rare find for the hospital and a man of many great ideas, Mr. Richards," Belle jumped in. "He said you were the most innovative person he's ever been associated with."

Rod smiled. *Boy, this lady can pile it high. I'll take it from her. Maybe it's a harbinger for something to happen down the road.*

All of a sudden the door to the conference room burst open. Howard I.M. Hill made his grand entrance.

Hill was undeniably a man's man, and nobody would argue to the contrary. He stood six-five with salt and pepper trimmed hair, not side-walled. A mean-looking scar ran from below his right eye to his lower right earlobe. Gold caps adorned most of his front teeth giving off an aura of invincibility when he smiled.

Although Howard didn't smile, he snarled. He was a few pounds overweight. His deep baritone voice filled the small room.

"Sorry I'm late people, but Highway 281 was fender to fender coming in from Loop 410. You'd think the city fathers and our esteemed police department could solve that simple problem." Howard turned to Astrade and rendered a sharp salute.

Astrade sat up straighter in his chair and then smiled as if to acknowledge Howard had a legitimate point. Arguing wasn't his style.

"I asked Howard to sit in on our little discussion," Dean said. "He has extensive experience with both prisoners and problem children. Isn't that right, Howard?"

Hill glanced over at Rod and winked his eyes. He loved the buildup. *They love me around here.*

"Give me and Mr. Richards the ball to run with," Howard asserted. "We'll have a solution for you that'll knock your socks off. At the same time, it will stand the test of time."

Rod wondered how Howard was already briefed on the subject. Then he remembered Hill and Dean were old buddies.

"I'd like to offer some additional input," Belle said. Everybody was anxious to hear what she had to say. Hill interrupted her.

"Miss Chelby," he boomed out as he looked over at Belle, "We'll bring you aboard at the appropriate time. I have a great idea percolating atop this old grey-haired head that will bring each of you good folks to your knees."

Same old Howard I.M. Hill, Rod thought. Was he grandstanding or did he have a workable idea? He loved to bring everyone to their knees, ankles, or even the damn floor when he was expounding on issues he felt strongly about.

"Let's adjourn," Dean said, "I know we all have busy schedules. We'll let these two geniuses mesh their ideas together and present a plan of action to our group. I trust that's fine with all of you."

Nobody objected.

Bounder thought the meeting was too short, nothing was accomplished. He did chuckle at Howard's verbosity and the inability of Dean and Astrade to cut him off.

"When can we expect to meet again?" Chelby asked. "The mayor and county commissioner are ready to discuss funding. When someone hands you a loaf of home-baked hot bread, you better snatch it, butter it up and eat it before it gets cold."

"You'll be the first to know," Howard assured her with a smile.

Both Belle and Rod thought Howard was pushing her too hard. Rod knew she had some firepower and didn't want it to explode in their faces. Phil Dean loved the drama and jousting of the main players.

They all got up and headed for the lobby.

Peppi, the cheery receptionist told the police chief to call his office. It was urgent.

Rod wondered where the coffee and donuts were that he'd ordered earlier. Did Peppi forget to tell the dining room again? She may be history.

Bounder thought this entire idea was a terrible, terrible mistake. Bringing in an academic to help wasn't the answer–too many real-life problems to resolve.

Chelby thought Richards might be an interesting pursuit.

Howard absconded with a bag of goodies for his troops back at the VA. They'd appreciate the donuts better than the super-clinical types.

CHAPTER 40

MARIE Martini was ordered to return to Langley again two weeks after her meeting with Vasquez. She was tasked to update one of the Counterterrorism Unit's sub-committees.

She received word from Agent Vasquez before leaving there wasn't a positive match of Big Red One's hair with the sample taken from Turk's fingernails. She was ecstatic! Boyd's cowboy hat got secreted back to his office by an FBI agent when Big Red was away from the hospital.

"What about the coffee cup, Jorge?"

"The cup broke into pieces when someone in the lab accidentally knocked it off the lab counter before they ran the test," Vasquez responded. "The clumsy technician swept up the pieces and tossed them in the trash."

She hoped Bounder wouldn't notice the missing coffee cup. Boyd had a habit of misplacing things. He'd think housekeeping returned it to the kitchen after cleaning his office. He hated to wash the coffee-stained cup for fear of losing a smidgen of distinct coffee flavor.

Boyd hopped a taxi to pick her up at her hotel. They headed to the airport. Traffic was light on Highway 281, a good sign. Marie was her usual slowpoke getting ready for the trip by not printing her ticket in advance. They proceeded to the airline counter upon arrival at the airport. She didn't want to go back to the East Coast. San Antonio was growing on her, including the big redhead.

He and Marie were in the process of saying goodbye at the security entry point, but she had one last mission. She was in a hurry to buy a latte at Starbuck's kiosk inside. Marie was hooked on the expensive concoction. He simply preferred the traditional brewed java—much cheaper, he'd argue. It was as good a fix for those in need of it.

"Greetings, guys, fancy meeting you two here," Rod said. He was picking up Nancy O'Reilly from San Francisco. "Where's Marie hustling off to now, Boyd?"

"Marie's heading back again to the D.C. puzzle palace. They have trouble chasing the bad guys without her help."

Rod wasn't aware Marie had to leave town again. He was anxious for the murder investigation to conclude. The patients and most of the hospital staff were still concerned that a vicious killer might still be in their midst—highly unlikely he thought. Perception becomes reality for a ton of people.

"What're you doing here, Rod?" Boyd asked.

"I'm picking up a candidate for our new marketing position. She's coming from the San Francisco Bay Area. I'm hoping she'll accept the position that was just approved. I've got to run. Have a good trip, Marie."

She didn't hear him. She was hassling one of the male screeners for delaying her. He wanted a full-body pat-down. She refused, slapping her credentials in his surprised face.

Rod headed over to the baggage pickup area searching for Nancy but didn't see her. He wondered if she'd missed her flight and failed to call him. Maybe he forgot what she looked like. It had been a while.

"Hi Rod," Nancy said cheerfully as she came up behind him and jabbed him in the ribs. "I had to stop at the ladies' room. You know the story about us Irish women—TB," she giggled.

"Huh? What do you mean by that comment?"

"Tiny bladder, but we learn to live with it, Mr. Richards."

They hugged each other, then walked over to the baggage carousel and pulled off her suitcases. The only dark green suitcases on the revolving conveyor belonged to Nancy. Oversized "N.O'R." initials were engraved in silver in the center of each piece of luggage.

"Thanks for coming, Nancy. I can't wait to show you around."

Nancy O'Reilly was a tall, slender woman with a mop of flaming red hair. A battalion of freckles adorned a smiley face void of makeup. She had lost weight since he last saw her in San

Francisco. Nancy wore a snappy brown tweed suit and low black heels. Rod thought she was dressed for colder weather but remembered San Francisco was cold this time of year.

"I'll bet you're hungry, Nancy. Salty peanuts are fine to munch on, but that's about all. Wanna stop for a bite to eat before I get you to your hotel?"

"No thanks, Rod, I'm not hungry. I always pack a sandwich when I travel by air. Sourdough bread laced with chunky peanut butter sticks to these little ribs of mine."

He conveyed a brief history lesson about Texas and more details of San Antonio and the Missions on the way to her downtown hotel.

Nancy O'Reilly was born and raised in Ireland. She'd arrived in the U.S. five years ago and never traveled outside the San Francisco area since she landed in California. They detoured to the Alamo and swung back to Houston Street. Nancy was surprised. She thought the Alamo was a huge fortress surrounded by a cobbled brick wall and guarded by a platoon of U.S. Marines.

Rod contemplated stopping at Teddy's Tavern but abandoned that idea. He checked her into the hotel and told her he'd pick her up at six for dinner.

He ran into Boyd conversing with Peppi in the front lobby upon arrival at Mission Oaks. It appeared Peppi was doing all the talking. She always found time to talk with folks after reading the daily paper and pecking away at a puzzle, regardless of the time of day. Peppi was a people person. It didn't matter who they were–staff, visitor, or one of the patients. She wouldn't hesitate to assist if they needed help. Most found a reason to speak with her.

"I wish Marie would stay in town until she completed the investigation," Rod said to Boyd. Peppi pulled away and tried to look busy.

"She's not dragging her feet, believe me," Boyd responded. "She obtained a court order to get a sample of Nick Ryan's hair for DNA testing before leaving town. He put up a big stink, accusing her of stonewalling him. We had to get a police escort, for God's sake."

Rod wasn't surprised. Ryan had stopped him one day and complained about being harassed by the staff.

"Dr. Dean decided to discharge him to their custody, pending the outcome of the medical examiner's DNA profiling," Bounder said. "I wasn't aware they could hold Ryan here without charging him. Astrade found a way to make it happen."

Peppi interrupted and told Rod a cute young lady was waiting for him in his office. Peppi was flipping a long pencil back and forth around her index finger. It never slipped and fell to the floor.

"Have fun with this one, Mr. Richards," she said to him as she tongued a piece of gum from one side of her mouth to the other. She replicated the same rhythmic tempo as the lead pencil scenario.

He wondered why his secretary Lucie hadn't informed him of the appointment. Then he remembered Lucie was on court duty today. *It's too bad for the local criminals undergoing trial in the county courthouse!* Lucie was known by her associates not to give leeway to suspected wrongdoers. She'd be dismissed by the defense attorneys before the proceedings began.

"Well, it's about time you got back here," Keena chided him. She rose from his desk chair and slapped a magazine she was reading to the floor. "I didn't know hospital administrators could wander around the city all day long. They should be looking after their precious building and the poor patients placed in their care. What's with you?"

"What a pleasant surprise!" Rod fibbed with a warm smile. "I didn't know you were planning to stop by today, Keena. You should've called me."

"Silly boy, I heard you're looking for a marketing director. I feared you'd forgotten about my many talents. I'm getting ready to resign from my position at work. They keep telling me I earned a big raise. They never came through. I've had it with them."

Rod was at a loss for words. He wasn't sure what to say. By all means, Keena had been cordial with him. He hadn't slept with her yet, though the opportunity had presented itself on more than one occasion. He was ready for some female intimacy. Something tugged him back.

She stood patiently waiting for a response.

"Okay, Keena, why don't you go down to our human resource office. You need to fill out an application form for the position and–"

"I can't believe you, Richards, after all we've done together!"

Her tan face turned a bright crimson. He could see the dark veins in her neck swelling. Rod thought she was going to drop a tomahawk chop on him.

Keena stormed out of his office without saying another word, slamming the door behind her with a loud thud.

"Keena, wait," he shouted after her. She was already in the lobby heading for the hospital front door. Peppi sat up and took note, a huge grin surfacing on her face.

Rod wondered if Keena had been smoking pot earlier today. He didn't smell alcohol on her breath. Something put a burr under her saddle. "Oh Lord," he mumbled out loud, "Women can be so darn unpredictable. No wonder men are driven to drink!"

He thought again about Janice. Then his mind drifted to Dalia Garza. He needed to get in touch with her. She might be the one person he knew around here that could make sense out of the gyrations in his bewildered mind.

"Who in the world was that?" Tom Lubay said as he stuck his head through Rod's office door. "A black-haired tornado almost knocked me to the floor!"

"You don't want to know, Tom. What's up?"

"The medical staff approved the revised drug formulary. Congratulations. It took some heavy-duty convincing. Phil Dean was at his best. He even threatened to take away the privileges of two female adjunct staff psychiatrists who started to rebel. How did you get Dean to go to bat for you?"

"It's because of my wonderful personality, Tom. Would you believe the disgruntled maintenance crew is starting to love me? I dared to terminate their after-hour laundry privileges. At the same time, I told them I was proud of the work they do to keep this place running."

Tom dropped off a copy of the formulary and left Rod's office. He didn't care to spend any more time than necessary with the new administrator. Tom sensed Richards was unhappy with him for some unknown reason. *Maybe he found out!*

Rod picked up the telephone to call Dalia in the ward. He dialed the number and then hung up. He remembered he had Nancy O'Reilly in tow waiting for him back at her hotel. *Time for a priority attitude adjustment. The job is more demanding than I'd expected.*

At least he planned to have a relaxing dinner and an evening with someone he knew well. It was important for him to sell her on the merits of coming aboard. He would quickly forget about Keena's little tirade and contact Dalia tomorrow.

CHAPTER 41

"**WHAT** a beautiful view of your fine city," Nancy O'Reilly exclaimed. Rod took her to the restaurant atop the Tower of The Americas in Hemisphere Park. He told Nancy the 750-foot tower was built as the theme structure for HemisFair 1968. It was the first officially designated World's Fair held in the Southwestern United States.

"You got that right," he replied. "Look down there at the huge Alamo- Dome. One of our former mayors was instrumental in getting the monster built. He planned on pulling in a National Football League team here. That hasn't materialized."

"Isn't that where my San Francisco Forty-Niners play when they come to Texas to play football?"

"No, they play up in Dallas. I guess you need a geography lesson to supplement my earlier history review about Texas. On second thought, I'll wait until you come to the Alamo City to live and work."

Rod had walked her through the facility and showed her where the marketing office would be located. He introduced her to the department heads and then set up the personnel interview. Bounder was extremely impressed with her. Rod had theorized redheads tend to stick together.

"I liked all the people I met at Mission Oaks. They seemed dedicated to the mission of helping poor souls suffering from mental disorders. Tell me again the name of that head nurse I met on the first floor."

"Her name is Dalia Garza. She's been with the hospital for about four years and does a good job. She's adored by all the patients. The woman's from Mexico but was educated here."

"I liked her, Rod. Is she married?"

"No, she's been divorced for some time."

He wondered why Nancy asked specifically about Dalia. He remembered from his days managing the apartment building in

San Francisco she preferred the company of other women. *I don't remember her spending any time with a man.*

"Thanks for showing me around the city, Rod. I love the diversity here and couldn't believe how it became so urbanized. Most of my close friends told me I'd see nothing but sprawling ranches and cowboys on horseback flipping long ropes over their heads chasing wild cows. The topography is so different in San Francisco. The city is surrounded by dark blue water and rolling hills."

Nancy checked her watch. She told Rod they'd better get back to her hotel. She hadn't packed yet for her early morning flight. It was getting late. Nancy had lost track of time. This was unusual for her.

Her interview had been a complete success. The department heads she talked with all felt Nancy would add a new and refreshing dimension to Mission Oaks Hospital.

Rod chided Nancy about the Irish whiskey she'd been sipping.

"You know what, Mister Rod? We'd darn sure be ruling the entire world if my Irish ancestors had never invented whiskey."

"Well, Misses O'Reilly," he countered, "Your ancestors still have some pull around here. They dye our San Antonio River a deep shamrock green once a year for the annual St. Patrick's Day celebrations. The Irish carry on about their heritage as well as any other ethnic group living in the city."

They both laughed and clinked their glasses together.

"Oh, Rod, before I forget it, I need to tell you about that new person Dupree hired to replace you guys as managers of our apartment. He fired her six months after he brought her aboard."

Rod stared at her in disbelief, then said, "I don't need to hear about the past. Let's think of how we're going to kick butts here and bring in a slew of new patients.".

She insisted on briefing him. "The reason he gave for canning her was beyond hilarious. Dupree claimed she wasn't doing enough for the residents. She charged a fine to anyone who forgot their keys if she had to come down and let them in the front door. She wanted to teach them to be more responsible whenever they left the building. She also refused to sign for parcel delivery packages."

He shrugged. "Guess you're right. I find it hard to believe the tight-wad would shed his thick skin and change face so soon after we'd left. Maybe he did appreciate us."

Rod's cell phone rang as they stood to leave the packed restaurant. He let it go to message.

"I thought you carried an old-timer pager," Nancy said. "I was wrong. Welcome to *new age* electronics."

"Thanks, I like it. Maybe the next generation of cellular phones will have music and even a mini-computer."

He dropped her off at the hotel and headed back to his condo. He decided to check his phone message in the parking garage before going upstairs. It was from Boyd Bounder. He wondered if he needed to get back to the hospital right away. He dialed Boyd's number.

"Boyd, it's Rod, what's going on?"

"Thanks for getting back to me. I received a call from Marie. She's coming back tomorrow. There's been a new twist in the murder case, and I thought you'd like to know about it right away."

"Don't tell me they pinned the crime on Nick Ryan," Rod said.

"That would be way too simple and much too convenient. Agent Vasquez called Marie and informed her about the results of the DNA test. I think I told you Marie got a warrant to test Ryan's DNA against the sample the medical examiner drew from Elsie Turk."

"Yes, go on, Boyd, I'm on pins and needles."

"Ryan wasn't matched. The red hair Elsie had under her fingernails belonged to another male. The police released Ryan from our control. He called that pesky reporter from the local newspaper that had been following the case. Nick told the guy he was going to sue the hospital, the CIA agent investigating the case, and the MPD for wrongful action. Thought you'd like to hear some hard facts before you came to work in the morning."

"Thanks for the heads up, Boyd. Lots to think about here." He hung up in deep thought.

This is beginning to get interesting. Now they got to run down every swinging redhead they can get their hands on, and do it quickly. I wonder if they tested old Boyd. He fell into the redhead category. This case is getting old, old, old! Marie Martini has to be frustrated at this time. I am!

Chapter 42

ROD climbed out of his car and took the elevator up to his condo unit. He saw Keena coming down the hallway struggling with a heavy basket of dirty clothes.

"Hi, Keena," he said cheerfully. "Why are you doing your laundry so late in the day?"

"Rod, I'm so happy to see you. I've worried every minute you would hate me after the episode at the hospital. Do you? I'm sorry for being a bitch. Can I make it up to you? I mean amends?"

He was leery about her intentions. She runs hot, then cold, only to reverse gears again. *How does a grown man deal with this? I've never met a woman like this one.* "Why don't you drop in after you dump those clothes in the washing machine? We'll have a glass of wine."

"You got it, Rod. I'll be right on down."

Rod pulled out a bottle of Hess Select cabernet and opened it. He grabbed two wine glasses from the cupboard. *Oh, hell, I'll go all out for it. You only live once!*

Keena came back in no time. They sat facing each other in the dining room, each wondering how to begin. Rod poured the wine and handed her a glass.

He thought she might take him to task about his drinking. Maybe she forgot he had been a tea sipper. Rod had begun drinking alcohol again but not to excess. It wasn't for his depression. "Social drinking," as he remembered an old friend label it. There were many "socials" back in St. Louis.

"To our health and your forgiveness," Keena said. She raised her glass to him. "You got any weed in here? I've been so busy of late–haven't fired up the bong in ages."

"Sorry, I don't go that route, Keena. We'll just have to drink. Let's start all over again.. I'll toss your hat in the ring. I'm sure you're still interested in the marketing opening we have at the hospital. I know in my heart you'd want to compete with the long list of candidates seeking the position."

She looked at him with a slight smirk on her face.

"Naw, I'm kidding," he exaggerated. "There are only five others who've applied for the position,"

"Nope, been there, done that marketing gig, Mr. Richards. I'm going back to school. I want to become a nurse. I'd like to specialize in psychiatric nursing. What do you think about that? Would I make a good one?"

"Umm, I'll have to think about that new venture, Keena. You took me by surprise."

They'd finished their wine. Keena excused herself. She told Rod she was expecting an important call and needed to get back to her unit. She also wanted to complete those tedious forms for admission to nursing school.

Yeah, righto. The bong had been in hiding and was about to come out of her dresser drawer. He laughed and poured himself another glass of cabernet.

CHAPTER 43

ROD grabbed the phone to contact Dalia. It was late. He was confident she wasn't in bed yet. He needed to determine one important fact. It couldn't wait. Was there gas left in their immoral tanks or just vapors from the past?

"May I please speak to Dalia?" Rod asked when the person on the other end picked up. He didn't recognize the responder's voice when she asked who was calling. The person seemed annoyed at his intrusion.

"She's not here. Whom should I tell her called?"

"Excuse me," Rod said. "Who am I speaking to?"

"This is Juanita Comptos. I told you she's not here right now."

"Would you please have her call Rod Richards when she returns if it's not too late?"

"Okay, will do," she said and hung up.

He waited until midnight. Dalia never returned his call. This is the second or third time he tried reaching her at home. He mulled over the idea maybe Comptos was throwing up a barrier to their relationship for some unknown reason.

Rod would try to catch her at work. He hated to mix business with pleasure. Not good. He didn't condone such interactions for his staff, but he felt he had no other recourse. He would find out tomorrow what's going on and where he stood with her.

Rod picked up Nancy O'Reilly at seven o'clock in the morning. They headed to the airport. Traffic was heavy coming into downtown, but they had no problem getting to the airport. There was a minor accident on the Basse Road exit. The boys in blue kept the traffic moving.

"What are your thoughts about joining us at Mission Oaks?" Rod was anxious to ask her. They" exited his car and were heading out of the parking garage to the airport entrance. She had been mum on the subject during the ride to the airport.

"Does that mean I got the job?" she smiled at him.

"It's yours . . . if you want it, Nancy. The staff at the hospital told me to find a way to get you on board. Why don't you go home and think it over for a few days and call me? Changing jobs and relocating to another city is a big challenge–believe me. Look at my track record!"

"I'll let you know by the end of next week."

Rod walked her to the security check lines which were starting to lengthen. He gave her a hug and a peck on the cheek, said goodbye, and then headed for the nearest exit. She waved at him and then disappeared through the screening gates. He got back to his car and wondered why Nancy never brought up the subject of Janice's death during her short stay.

Did she forget to ask or was she more interested in renewing a relationship with me? Maybe she had the hots for Nurse Dalia. What the hell, better get back to the hospital. Time will tell.

It was beginning to warm up early in the morning. Spring had waved goodbye and summer was in full swing. Air-conditioners across the city ratcheted up their defense against Mother Nature. Several red, yellow, and pink blooming plants near the hospital entrance were lapping up droplets of water released by the underground sprinkler system.

Rod was enjoying his second cup of coffee when he got the call from Agent Vasquez.

"I need to talk to you right away," Jorge said.

"I'm listening."

"No, not on the telephone, Rod. You don't have a secure line. Are you going to be there all morning?"

"I plan to be here most of it. C'mon over any time before eleven. This afternoon is out though."

"I'll be right over. Please have Boyd Bounder available when I get there. He needs to be read-in on our next move. Out here," he replied in military lingo and hung up.

Rod walked over to Boyd's office door. It was open. Boyd was knocking down a last slug of coffee and working a puzzle. He barely noticed Rod glancing over his shoulder.

"What kind of weird puzzle is that creature? There are no words, only numbers?" Rod didn't crosswords.

"I guess you've never seen this kind of puzzle before. They're called Sudokus. It's the newest rage in the world of our puzzlers. You need to grab a pencil and try one, Rod, it challenges your mind. We medical types maintain they might delay or even prevent dementia because of the mental whirling involved in solving them."

"What do you do with all of those numbers?" Rod seemed interested. *I could play his silly game.*

"There are nine large squares in each puzzle. Each square has nine cells in them. Some of the cells already have numbers pre-printed. You have to determine where numbers one through nine are placed in each vacant square. I'll show you later how to figure this bugger out."

"Ah, er, no thanks. It's all I can do to figure out how to run this place efficiently. Where'd you get that stupid-looking coffee cup you're sipping on? I've seen better-looking cups at our local thrift shops."

"Housekeeping corralled my last mug. I went to Wal-Mart and bought this one. It holds a full pint."

Rod informed him of the call he got from Vasquez.

"Yes sir, I'll still be here. Marie should be arriving at any minute. She told me she'd take a taxi from the airport rather than being picked up. I think we should wait until Marie arrives before we meet with the FBI rep."

Marie suddenly walked in on them as though responding to a pre-arranged signal. She gave Boyd a big Texas hug and winked at Rod.

She looked sharp as ever to Rod. As expected, Boyd was thrilled with her arrival.

"Jorge Vasquez is on his way over here," Marie informed them. "He called me when I deplaned and told me we need to sit down with Amfi bin Aziz for a long talk. He told me he also contacted you, Rod. Is Aziz working this morning, Boyd?"

"Yep, I made rounds with her earlier. The doctors are discharging Roberta Peck and Clark Hanson today. Cecilia Reyes and Norm Cook are scheduled to be released tomorrow. Amfi is finalizing the paperwork."

"How about that preposterous despot Munoz?" she inquired. "I think we should keep him under our thumbs for a while longer. I still think he's in cahoots with Ryan. Too bad that no-good gangster's long gone from our grasps."

"The VA extended Eduardo's stay here for another month," Rod chipped in. "That maniac is driving both our staff and the patients unhinged. Someone needs to steal those heavy-duty batteries from his cart and toss them in the dumpster outside. What's with Aziz, Marie? I thought the CIA had cleared her."

She cautioned them not to jump to any conclusions. Haste makes waste. They'd wait for Vasquez to bring them up to date. Rod agreed and returned to his office. Boyd told her to sit tight while he went to the toilet down the hall.

Marie was also curious about Amfi. The Saudi nurse's name never surfaced during her briefing at CIA headquarters. It was hammered into her head again the Kingdom of Saudi Arabia is the spawning ground of radical Islamic movements. Her leadership assured her they'd started to recognize the obvious. Marie had her doubts. *Whether they'll do anything about it is yet to be seen.*

She wondered if Amfi slipped through the cracks in the process of our government clearing her husband for training with the U.S. Air Force. She still felt Nick Ryan was the murderer, regardless of the DNA results. But what was his motive? He didn't fit the profile of a Muslim radical terrorist.

Marie was getting impatient about the sluggish progress being made by the investigation. They still had major work ahead of them. She'd been involved with other complicated murder cases in the past but this one had to be near or at the top of the pile. Hospitals of any type are not known to be hotbeds of murder cases.

CHAPTER 44

"DON'T you ever try to come over to this school again," an angry Juanita Comptos scolded Angel Garza. He'd been able to track her down in the school nurse's office.

"I can't afford to be seen with you anywhere around my school environment. You should've contacted me at my apartment. Let's get out of here and go somewhere where we can talk in complete privacy."

They left the school grounds and walked over to a nearby park. It was windy and humid outside as they meandered over to a wooden bench near a small fountain. Nobody else was in the area. It was still too early for mothers to be wheeling their little charges around in strollers through the park.

Angel learned an important piece of information from Mashudan. Juanita had been turned several years ago, underwent comprehensive leadership training, and was assigned to develop a new cell in San Antonio. She supervised the Saudi nurse at the mental hospital where his sister worked.

She was directed not to attempt turning Dalia Garza. The al-Qaeda leadership had their reasons for Comptos to live two separate lives. They did not trust Dalia Garza. They believed she was mentally unstable. Working in a psychiatric hospital only validated their apprehensions.

"I knew you and my sister were living together. I didn't want her to know I was in town yet," Angel began.

She said nothing.

"My leader told me you'd set up my initial contact with her. I know you're aware of our history. I'm told Dalia doesn't know of your involvement in the Jihad. In any event, I caution you . . . there is no way she'll be thrilled to see me."

"Your sister has changed a lot from when you knew her as a youngster in your hometown, Angel. She had undergone psychotherapy. Your sexual manhandling of her is a distant memory in her mind."

"What do you mean by that?"

"Listen to me, Angel. I encouraged her to forgive you. Yes, against my better judgment. I insisted she reflects on the many good memories enjoyed by your family and relatives. I know she loved your aunt and uncle. They were generous to take care of you two when your parents were away working in the fields."

Angel listened intently at each piece of information she discussed. He couldn't afford mistakes.

"There's one thing you should be aware of though," she said. "Your sister has no use for men, physically or emotionally. Don't pursue the issue of male relationships with her. It's irrelevant. Now tell me where you're living."

"I rented an apartment near Ft. Sam Houston. It's a great location for our purposes. Young military families are renting in the neighborhood. I believe I blend in there as well with the other young neighbors."

"Give me your cell phone number, and I'll call you in a few days when I want you to meet your sister. She's not a strong person. Your presence could harm her. She must be shielded from learning about your sacred mission. Understand!"

"Yes," Angel said with a dour tone. *Too bossy!*

"In the meantime, I want you to tour the Alamo and take mental notes of the structure and its surroundings. Don't be too obvious, Angel. Dress and act like a tourist. Go over there at different times during the next several days. I don't want any of their staff to get a mental picture of you. They mustn't recall any of your visits. Don't bring a camera. Do you have a car?"

"No, I stole a bicycle. I refrained from getting a driver's license because I have a fake passport –too risky."

"That's good thinking on your part. Should I call you Hibat Allah? On second thought, we shouldn't use our Muslim names until our mission kicks off. Then we'll be famous when the infidels hear about our exploits. I have a vehicle you can use when needed. You live close to downtown. Most of the places you'll need to check out on your surveillances are within reach of bicycle transportation."

Angel left her and decided to bicycle by Mission Oaks Mental Hospital on his way home. It was his primary mission after all. The Alamo piece of the plan can wait. He wanted to view the hospital building. The engineering diagrams he'd received during his out-processing were barely readable.

The parking lot was almost full. Nobody was visible in the area. Angel steered his bike into the second row of parked cars. He pulled into a vacant slot. The absence of activity allowed time to sketch parts of the building. He'd be familiar with the entire complex for future initiatives.

Angel was absorbed making notes in a small notebook when he heard the shrilling sound of a stressed motor amble up behind him.

"Howdy, mate, can I help you with something?" the voice asked.

Angel spun around to see this big guy wearing gigantic black goggles and a black leather helmet. He wore a "Hell's Angel" leather jacket hugging his large torso. The man was stuffed in a motorized scooter like the insides of a huge ring of pork sausage.

How the hell did he sneak up on me? I was super careful to ensure nobody was in the parking lot until this clown rode in.

"Oh, sir," Angel uttered in a surprised tone. "I'm an architecture student at Trinity University. We were assigned a project to sketch an unusual building in the downtown area. I selected this structure. It looks like a hotel to me. The sign outside says it's a hospital. What gives? Don't you think I should get an A on my report?"

Eduardo Munoz didn't respond to the question. He hated to be indoors every waking hour. He decided to get outside for fresh air. He'd been sucking on a Marlboro in the rear hospital parking lot when he spotted this guy. Something didn't seem right to him. *Why would a person bicycle into a parking lot and start making written notes?*

Munoz checked the guy over best he could. He began to fantasize. *Another frickin redhead, for Christ's sake! There are tons of them running around the hospital. He remembered reading something about the Nazis considering banning all redheads to wed for fear of degenerate offspring. Eduardo was convinced redheaded babies were the result of unclean sex.*

This person also appeared to have some deformities, but they were well masked in the way he carried himself. Munoz scooted closer to him, almost bumping the rear of the bicycle leaning on its kickstand.

"Sorry for the long delay in answering you about a grade for your report. Sometimes I lose my train of thought. My hearing is deplorable. I need a hearing device."

Angel stared at him, not knowing how to respond.

"By the way, I'm Major Price, U.S. Marine Corps, and I'm on a recruiting mission," Munoz said. "Don't let this outfit I'm wearing, and my motorized vehicle throw you off. We've been directed by higher headquarters to assimilate the appearance of the average American. The colonel feels we can be more effective in convincing you young troopers to join the Corps."

Angel was in complete awe. *Was this some kind of joke?*

"Have you served your country, young man? It appears to me you have some serious war wounds. You're too young for 'Nam.' Been deployed in Iraq or perhaps Afghanistan?"

Angel said nothing. *This guy is something else. He's got to be crazy. Must be one of the patients from across the street. I got to think up a good answer and right now.*

"Yep, Afghanistan—got hit by an improvised explosive device. The IED killed the driver. I got thrown out of the vehicle. I figured I'd use my GI bill when I left service to get educated. That's why I'm in this parking lot."

"Well, that's plausible. Thank you for serving our great nation, young man. I've got to run. They're about to begin Retreat. You remember how it was when you were in the service. They blow the bugle and lower the flag while everybody throws up a stiff salute. It's a call to march our bodies to the mess hall."

Angel watched the man ride out of the parking lot and head toward the hospital. The pea-brain in the chariot almost got t-boned by a black Mercedes.

He recalled those weeks of training in Afghanistan. Mashudan arranged for an American-born aide to spend numerous hours with him on those childish U.S. military customs and practices. That wise old man with the gray beard figured that a crippled recruit might someday pass for a disabled American veteran. He was right!

Eduardo headed up the hospital ramp–his vivid imagination was starting to run at a quick pace and then shifted into high gear.

That young carrot top is a fraud. Why the surveillance of the hospital? He was drawing some elaborate diagrams of the place. This stupid building is no different from any other one downtown. Architectural student my fat behind! This guy is up to no good. I should report it, but the colonel would ask me what evidence I had to make such an accusation.

CHAPTER 45

"GOOD morning Mr. Vasquez," Marie Martini said. The two federal investigators, Boyd Bounder, and Rod Richards had gathered in Rod's office.

"Everyone please take a seat," the FBI agent ordered. "I'll get right to the point. It can't wait. We've got some serious business to discuss this morning."

"What's up, Vasquez?" Marie asked. She was impressed with this agent but anxious to hear his report.

"We have reason to believe your nurse from Saudi Arabia may be linked to an al-Qaeda cell in the area. We've monitored several phone conversations she made last night while on duty upstairs. The first and most important call for our purposes was the one made to an unlisted number. Our technicians matched the number to other calls made to that same number. That action leads us to believe a terrorist plot might be in the formative stage."

"I didn't know you had listening devices set up here," Rod said. "When were they installed and did you clear it with anybody?"

"Hold on, please," Vasquez said. "Let me explain how we operate. We monitor all telephone calls from an off-site location. That's where we picked up Aziz. However, we wanted more sophisticated equipment placed here to pick up other voice traffic. Mooney gave us the okay before he went off on his safari. We worked with the MPD and got the warrant from the judge without any problem."

"Well, who was she calling and what did she have to say?" Bounder queried with some trepidation.

Marie hadn't said a word yet. She wondered why the FBI hadn't cleared the listening device with the CIA. Then again, it didn't have a thing to do with the murder of their sanctioned operative. At least it hadn't up to this point.

"The call was made to a Juanita Comptos," Vasquez said. "Nothing was discussed by either party that implied a threat. It was more of a social call. We found out Comptos has been employed as a school nurse for two years. We need to determine how Aziz knew this Comptos person. Why was she calling the woman? You folks at Mission Oaks might offer a clue."

"Beats me," Boyd said. "Rod, do you have any thoughts?"

"Not a one. I haven't been around here long enough to know Nurse Aziz. All I've been told is that her husband is in training over at Randolph AFB. I've never seen him at the hospital."

"Nor have I," Bounder said. "My guess he's under strict orders to stay close to the airbase."

"Let's not jump to conclusions here, Nurse Bounder," Jorge declared. "We'll determine what role, if any, the husband is playing. Will you arrange for me to have a private room. I need to interview Aziz right now?"

"Hold on a minute, Vasquez," Marie jumped in. "There are State Department ramifications here. Let's not rush into this without studying the various options available. There are other federal agencies including the Pentagon that might also come into play. I think we'd better run this up the flagpole and seek guidance from our superiors."

Vasquez let her take the lead. *Typical C.I.A. bullshit. Waste of time. Couldn't work there.*

"Boyd, see if you can run down Dr. Dean. He might have some ideas we hadn't thought of."

Rod supported Marie. "Great move. I know Dean's worked with Aziz on several mental cases. Let him do the interview. You and Jorge can coach him on how to conduct it without tipping her off. Maybe he can get to the bottom and find out why she got in touch with this Comptos lady. Dean has been here longer than all of us combined. I'm sure she will confide in him. Who's to guess, maybe he'll come up with a new wrinkle?"

"Wisely stated, Mr. Administrator," Marie Martini clapped her hands. "Jorge and I will give our bosses a head's up. We'll wait and see if the good doctor can shed any light on this mystery. Does that work for you, agent Vasquez?"

"That's affirmative. It looks as though we'll have to work together on this for a while longer." *Much to my chagrin.*

"Let me add another item of information that impacts our investigation," Marie said. "One of our research technicians uncovered an interesting piece of information on Elsie Turk when I was back at Langley. It hadn't surfaced before. She was an alcoholic. Elsie underwent treatment in a CIA-sponsored substance abuse program. We're not sure why this information was withheld from us. The research tech thought someone high up the bureaucratic ladder had it expunged from her records. Elsie was related to a former state senator from Virginia. Need I say more to you?"

Marie was stunned when she learned about Turk's drinking problem on her last visit to the CIA offices. Her mind wandered back to the time spent with Elsie on her assignment in the Middle East. Elsie was her handler back in Bahrain and never demonstrated a drinking problem. Marie never smelled alcohol on her breath during their few secretive meetings. What a shock!

"Whoa, hang on a sec," Vasquez said as he interrupted Marie's digressing thoughts. "The medical examiner reported she was drunk when murdered. We need to find an answer to the. . . w*ho done it and why* . . . questions."

They all agreed.

Marie turned to face Bounder. He was waiting for another order. She or Vasquez. Didn't matter. It was their folly.

"Boyd, do the best you can to make sure Miss Aziz continues her present work schedule. We don't want her to leave town, even for a weekend."

"I'll see to it from a scheduling standpoint. I can't tell her what she can or cannot do on her off-duty time."

"Maybe you should arrange for someone to shadow her, Marie," Vasquez suggested.

"No spooking. We'll just hope for the best at this stage of the game."

CHAPTER 46

AMFI bin Aziz entered the conference room and faced Doctor Phil Dean. She had an inkling why he wanted to talk to her.

He was happy she didn't wear the traditional Muslim burqa at work. It would only confuse the patients if they saw somebody walking around the wards in a headdress and mask. They didn't need another stimulus on top of their already fragile conditions.

"But I didn't call a person by the name of Juanita Comptos," Aziz said to Dean as she sat down across from him. "I was having a problem in the ward with one of our patients. I decided to call the head nurse at home for a policy clarification on the use of restraints. Some lady answered the phone and told me Dalia Garza wasn't at home and to call back later. She was rude to me, Dr. Dean."

The doctor had explained in general terms to Amfi why he was grilling her on the telephone call. He didn't mention it might relate to her personal life, the murder in the day room, or even a terrorist threat. He told her Dalia wrote her up about not following the proper treatment protocol on disruptive patients. Amfi ordered a male attendant to place a patient in restraints without sufficient justification.

"But I tried several times to contact Dalia. She never called me back. I was taught to take immediate action on possible dangerous situations if unable to get the concurrence of an attending physician or my nursing supervisor."

"Dalia told me earlier that day during ward rounds she was going to a symphony at the theater," Dean said. "She got home late from the performance. My guess is her roommate hadn't left a note that anybody called for her from the hospital."

"Well, at least I learned the proper protocol for use of the restraints. Dalia briefed me in detail on the procedures. We even practiced on one of the male ward attendants."

"Sorry for the confusion, Dr. Dean," she said and then got up and left the room.

Dean contacted Marie Martini and suggested the telephone call related to a specific hospital operating procedure. It had nothing to do with a terrorist situation. He told her Dalia lived with Comptos, and they were childhood friends.

Phil Dean suggested Marie pass this information on to whatever other authorities she was working with. Perhaps it would take some heat off the hospital.

"Did you know that Elsie Turk had a drinking problem and was drunk at the time of her death?" Marie questioned him before she hung up. "Weren't you assigned her primary physician?"

"I authorized her placement here, that's the only thing I ever did with Turk. One of the other therapists was aware of the situation and conducted rounds making bogus notes in her hospital records. We had to play the charade game every day she was here. It was difficult for the few of us who knew why she was at Mission Oaks. Our staff was beginning to question the validity of her admission about the time she was murdered."

"Doctor, did you know that she was a drunk?" Marie asked again. She felt he was trying to sidetrack her by not answering the question.

"Yes, I was aware of it."

"How did she get the booze on the ward, doctor?"

"What, am I on trial now?" Dean asserted with obvious anger.

"Sorry, Phil, we're all getting stressed out on the murder case. I have to ask these questions. Do you know how the alcohol got on the ward?"

"No, I don't have any idea."

When the perturbed Dean hung up he lurched back in his chair.

Did I make a dumb mistake by bending over backward for those God damn government spies? Life is complicated enough in our line of business. I don't need any more out-of-the ordinary challenges. I've enough stress to deal with around this place!

Amfi reflected on her visit with Dean on her return to the ward. She felt her responses to the doctor's questioning were effective. She was proud of herself. The damage control process was a constant challenge to her in this hostile environment. She needed to contact Comptos right away. She didn't want to use the telephone.

They were listening to all the calls! I wasn't thinking. I should've been more careful. Juanita will crucify me.

CHAPTER 47

THE al-Qaeda for United Liberty cell in San Antonio was operational. A demolition expert living in Houston rounded out their team.

Comptos decided to move all their activities to Angel's apartment near the military base. After her discussion with Amfi bin Aziz, she was frantic the enemy might be closing in on them. Amfi assured her no harm was done. They'd use pre-paid disposable phones from this point forward.

Angel bought a used motorbike from an Army medic. The soldier was on his way to the war in Afghanistan. The bike tires were a constant pain requiring additional air from a series of slow leaks. He got tired of having them fixed and opted for an upgrade in his transportation.

His thoughts again spun back to the hectic times he spent in that forlorn country. He hoped it would be months before he had to return. He learned through another holy warrior he trained with that Mashudan moved their base camp to a more remote location in Afghanistan. The Taliban warriors needed to reoccupy their old training site.

"I'm glad your relationship with your sister is starting to improve," Juanita said after he let her into his apartment. "The initial contact went smoother than I envisioned. I told you she is trying hard not to hold any grudges against you. She's found her niche working at the nut hospital and understands quirky human behavior far better than before."

"For untold years I've regretted that vicious attack on her when we were younger," Angel said with a solemn face. "I was out of my mind at the time. I never dreamed she'd find it in her heart to forgive me. Yes, I agree she's changed a lot. I can't believe how beautiful she is. You love her, don't you?"

"Yes, I sure do," Comptos answered without the slightest bit of hesitation. "She shared with you the details of our relationship, Angel. One day we might feel she's ready to join our crusade. I don't trust her enough to jeopardize our present objectives. She's well-respected at the hospital and confident in her treatment by that head doctor. I'm not sure what kind of garbage he's putting in her brain, but it's working."

He wondered if Dalia would ever become a Jihadist. Odds were against it. She hated violence.

"Your sister has overcome a lot of obstacles. I include the mistake she made one night with a first-class jerkoff she'd met at a local hotel bar., He's an administrator at Dalia's hospital . . . believe it or not. That's the first and last time she messed with any man."

They were interrupted when Amfi knocked on the front door. They let her in. Comptos peered back behind Amfi as though she was expecting more company.

"Did Muhammad bring the rest of the materials over from Houston yet?" Amfi asked. "All I saw the last time I checked the storage unit were some detonators, automatic weapons, tools, masks, and scaling ropes."

"Were you followed?" Juanita asked curtly.

"Of course not. I circled the block several times before I parked."

"I told Muhammad to wait on the C-4," Juanita said. "That's the last component we need. I'd rather it be stored somewhere in Houston until we're ready to begin assaulting our designated target."

They sat on the floor drinking the tea Angel had prepared. He laced it with a hallucinogenic compound that heightened their perception of the successes they'd achieved thus far.

Juanita decided they'd start using their real Muslim names when phase three of their campaign kicked off. It was only appropriate to wage the war against the infidels using the proud Islamic family names they were given after the completion of training.

The threesome was getting stoned.

Angel Garza kept pouring more tea into their cups. Oh, he wished he could've brought back only twenty ounces of the wonderful, home-grown opium sack he and a fellow trainee confiscated from an Afghanistan farmer. Thanks to Allah that they weren't caught by their supervisors.

"How did you ever get in the hospital to kill that CIA slut without being caught?" Amfi asked Angel with a slight giggle. She hated Elsie Turk.

"I'll tell you in a minute." He sat back and collected his thoughts. "It was a stroke of genius that Juanita figured out the Americans had suspected some movement locally about our glorious Jihad. Juanita's handler stationed in Mexico found out the Turk woman was a government spy. The person told Juanita that Elsie Turk had to be eliminated. We had no choice."

Amfi nodded in agreement.

"I'm glad Juanita arranged for you to be absent from the hospital the week of the murder," Angel said. "Helping her at high school was a great diversion for you. At the same time, the plan removed you as a possible accomplice. The hospital was part of the local community effort to make young kids more aware of mental health disorders."

"Angel," Amfi said, "I'm asking you again to tell us in great detail about the murder. "You did such a magnificent job. Everyone at the hospital is convinced she was killed by a patient or one of the other staff members."

"Of course, I'd be happy to. I'm getting there. Don't you remember I had your key to enter through the hospital back door, Amfi? It was dark. Nobody saw me until I arrived on the ward. I passed the arts and crafts room before I proceeded to the rear end of the wing. A gigantic pair of scissors was lying there next to some partially completed scrapbooks. A ward attendant got careless and forgot to secure the scissors under lock and key. I hustled in and grabbed the scissors. I figured I might need another weapon in case the fiber wire strangling attempt didn't work."

He'd learned that particular technique when he attended a required assassination course during training. He preferred this method over slitting throats. That was awful messy to him. He retched at the sight of human blood.

"Didn't you have that double-edged knife you were issued in training strapped to your ankle like most of our assassins?" Juanita asked. She wished Angel had slit the victim's throat and be done with it. She loved blood—somebody else's life supply.

"You guessed right!" Angel snapped. "I had it on me. I just told you I prefer other means but always carry it as a backup."

She shook her head and stared at the ceiling.

Angel Garza continued. "I'd been warned the federal agent was a black belt, martial arts expert. I had to be extra careful. Several of the patients were gathered in the rear of the day room drinking and dancing. I don't know where the staff attendants were at the time. They probably set up the party and took off. It had to be some kind of morale booster for the deranged lot of them. I heard some laughing and giggling in one of the patient rooms on my way to the day room. I figured two of the staff sex maniacs were going at it with each other."

"Wasn't anyone suspicious of you?" Amfi asked. "How did you identify the mark?"

"I repeat. Nobody saw me climbing the stairwell and walking down the hallway. Juanita had a photo of the government plant she showed me before our mission began. I committed it to memory."

"That was smart to do." Amfi liked her colleagues to think through every detail before executing a plan.

"The Turk lady was in a corner pawing at that big redhead," Angel laughed. "I heard her call him Ryan. They were both drunk. Another patient rode over to them in a motorized chair. This guy was nuts. He was dressed as a pumpkin and was drunker than the other two. More screwy patients became upset at the activities taking place in the day room. They stopped celebrating and left the area, closing the door behind them."

"What happened then?" Amfi asked. She was anxious. Loved the story.

Juanita butted in and took over the discussion. She knew Angel would start to ramble on proudly and aimlessly as though the whole Muslim world was in awe of his brave act.

"Angel saw the redhead pull out a syringe and grab the bitch's hand," Juanita said. "The big guy spread her fingers apart and shot up what appeared to be alcohol from the contents of the bottle he was drinking. Why he did that . . . we don't know. He wanted her good and drunk. I'm sure he planned to perform some outlandish sex act on her. He kept injecting her with that liquid until she waved him off. You need to know the agent was older than him but still attractive. Patients have sex with each other all the time in mental health hospitals. It's part of their therapy."

The laced tea they'd been drinking was playing uncontrollable games with their minds and bodies. It was unusual they all experienced the same sensations. First, they felt a heightened awareness of the colors in the room and of the clothing each wore. Every object shined with a chartreuse brightness. Two people in the framed picture on the wall appeared to be running at a fast clip. They would stop and then start again. The dog racing behind them to catch up was performing a series of front-end flips.

And at last, they became more rational as though some kind of a magic wand had passed over them. Their senses cleared. They'd drift off to sleep in due time.

CHAPTER 48

"**EXCELLENT** bottle of wine Marie," Boyd complimented her while flipping the steaks on the patio grill. She'd selected an expensive bottle of Carmenere, a Chilean wine vinted from the French Bordeaux grape. He wanted to take her to an expensive local restaurant for dinner. She insisted they stay home and relax.

Marie was staying with Boyd in his home located behind a high school football complex in an affluent neighborhood north of downtown.

His sprawling three-bedroom ranch-style house had been on the lot of an original *tear down*. Contractors were buying up older homes in this area. Most were in disrepair and were leveled. The property values of newer homes far exceeded their outdated counterpart structures. Hence, they follow by constructing expensive modern dwellings.

Boyd had asked Marie to stay with him rather than renting a hotel on the Riverwalk during her brief stays traveling between the Alamo City and Langley. She was comfortable with the arrangement.

She was falling in love with the big redheaded Texan. They were as different as light is to dark. She seemed to dial down her hyperactive nature whenever they were together. His *oh shucks* boyish attitude and casual lifestyle befitted her.

Boyd speared the T-bone steaks and brought them into the house. He placed them on the kitchen table next to the tossed salad. She liked the tenderloin portion. He preferred eating the meat off the bone.

He grabbed the newspaper and finished the Sudoku puzzle he'd started earlier that morning. The Word Jumble was the next victim.

Marie was talking on her cell phone in the living room—almost whispering. He couldn't make out the conversation with the other party. He drained his second glass of Carmenere, poured himself another one, and then topped off her glass.

"Thanks so much for passing that on," Marie said to Irene Finerty on her cellphone. "It gives us another avenue to explore. Maybe this will be the final link to our killer, and not too soon. The trail has cooled off."

Finerty told Marie one of her criminologists offered his opinion regarding the interpretation of the nine numbers associated with Elsie Turk's murder. He suggested the killer might be a Sudoku addict, like one who completes several puzzles a day. He was confident Elsie was attempting to identify her killer before she bled out on the cold game room floor.

"Who was that on the phone?" Boyd asked as she returned to the kitchen.

She froze in her tracks. The image of the puzzle with numbers he was working on jumped up and slapped her in the face. She paused to regain her composure.

"Do you remember that criminologist from Chicago? She gave me another potential lead to solving Elsie Turk's murder."

Boyd agreed.

Marie was careful how she phrased her next several questions. "What in God's creation are you doing with all those numbers–playing some kind of Keno game? I thought you could only play that stupid passive gambling game in Las Vegas."

Boyd laughed and showed her the puzzle. "I'm close to having this guy solved. It's an intriguing numbers puzzle. I'm not sure where it originated from, but it's challenging. I love it! Every day our local paper has one. It gets more difficult each succeeding day. This genius here can't solve the Saturday Sudoku puzzle.

"Let's eat," she said. "I'm starving. Boyd, that brunch we ate this morning is long gone from this body of mine. I wasn't hungry when we got up this morning. Should've eaten more I guess."

She then drained her glass of wine and asked for a refill.

Marie felt like getting drunk and passing out. A thousand thoughts were racing through her mind . . . like a speeding bullet train, hell-bent on destruction. Was her dear Boyd the murderer? The DNA study taken from hair samples in the rim of his cowboy hat cleared him of the red hair implication. Is he a suspect again because of a possible Sudoku connection?

She wasn't about to give in. There had to be another person involved, for which Elsie meant to implicate by the numbers. Maybe it had nothing to do with a Sudoku puzzle.

"Eat your meal, Marie, the steak's getting cold. I thought you were starving to death."

"Sorry, hun of mine, this old, cluttered mind is rambling on in overdrive mode. Out of curiosity, does anybody else over at the hospital do those stupid puzzles?"

"Marie, my God, they're the current rage. Everybody loves to solve them. I think Rod's addicted. Hey, wait a minute. Didn't Roberta Peck say Nick Ryan gave her newspapers after he did his puzzles? I remember Roberta telling us they needed tons of them for her and Elsie's scrapbooking activity."

"You're right Boyd. We need to find out if they were word crossword puzzles or Sudoku's—maybe both. Why would he have so many papers delivered? I never figured this guy was competent enough to solve a simple word puzzle even if given most of the clues."

"Let's go to the hospital right now," she said. "We'll get to the bottom of this once and for all."

"Hold on Marie, sit back down. It can wait until morning. I'm not going to waste any more time gabbing with you. I'm hungry."

He started to tackle the thick T-bone. Boyd forgot to cut off the tenderloin for her. It didn't matter, she nailed it with the carving knife, almost impaling his right hand.

They watched the evening news snuggled warmly in the overstuffed love seat and then went to bed. Boyd watched the sporting news every night but turned the television off after the weather report.

There would be no mad thrashing of bodies in the sack tonight. Neither could go to sleep. Boyd was worried she was becoming more and more frustrated. She hadn't solved the murder yet. Marie thought the killer had to be that deranged Nick Ryan. He had red hair but was exonerated by the DNA test.

Somehow, she had to dig deeper, much deeper into this complicated mystery. It couldn't be her big Texan lug. No way!

CHAPTER 49

ROD was in his office rewriting procedural guides when Boyd and Marie sauntered in. They plopped down in his hard-backed chairs and were whispering sweet things to each other. They were more relaxed this morning. Both were confident the arts and crafts room would reveal something to help solve the murder mystery. Rod heard the telephone ring. A few minutes later Lucie poked her head in and told him the call was for him.

"Who is it, Lucie?"

"Surprise, surprise," she laughed, knowing he would be excited.

The conversation was short. Rod started snickering out loud after he hung up. He had a wide grin on his face. His eyes were as big and round as a twenty-five-cent piece.

"Win the Texas lottery, Rod?" Bounder asked. "What finds you in such a good mood, my friend?"

"We now have a new marketing manager. Nancy O'Reilly called from San Francisco and accepted the position. She'll be here by the end of the month. Nancy asked me to find an apartment for her. Great, great news, don't you guys think?"

"Sounds good to me," Boyd responded. "I liked her. Did Harry Mooney approve the position?"

"To hell with him. That cigar-chomping owner is never in the hospital to know what's going on. I'm convinced he doesn't have a clue about the skill of marketing to medical professionals. Most people presume it's different than retail marketing, perhaps even contradictory."

Marie sat with arms crossed and could care less about the topic.

"Harry isn't running this hospital anymore, I am," Rod said with emphasis. "When he returned from his safari he was ecstatic about the hunt. He never inquired what was happening under this big roof. According to Mooney, he bagged the biggest, meanest lion ever killed in Africa by a foreigner. He told me he was retiring from the hospital business and I was now the main man here. That's hard to believe, right?"

Marie uncrossed her arms and asked him when Mooney planned to move out.

"I have no clue. He said something about converting his office into a wildlife museum. Who gives one heaping truckload of cow manure about Harry Mooney's hunting exploits? There is a *Hall of Horns* located in the city. People can go there if they want to gasp in awe over animal heads and gigantic horns."

"Been there, done that," Boyd laughed.

"By the way, what brings you guys here on this wonderful Texas morning?" Rod smiled. He was happy for Boyd that Marie came into the Texan's life.

"Sudoku puzzles," Marie said. "We're going up to the arts and crafts room to check out the scrapbooks on file up there. Roberta Peck told us Nick Ryan supplied the newspapers for their cutouts. I have a gut feeling we'll find completed Sudoku puzzles when we rip off the pasted papers in the books. Ryan may have been Elsie Turk's killer. We need more proof. There's a chance we can tie his puzzle fanaticism to the murder."

Rod was excited. "I'll go up there with you. I need to check out some patient complaints about not having access to the arts and crafts room."

"I hadn't heard anything about that," Boyd interjected.

"There are three or four patients who spend half a day trying to make pottery bowls, cups. and saucers," Rod said. "We're not equipped to handle pottery-making. There are no sinks or drains in the room. The patients are carting pitchers of water from their rooms and spilling some on the floors. That practice is another potential hazard we need to eliminate. No need for broken hips around here."

"On second thought," Boyd said, "I think I recall housekeeping had also complained about the mess they had to clean up after these ingenious sculptors did their thing."

Dalia Garza met them in the hallway when they arrived on the second floor. She was subbing for a sick colleague. She was escorting a patient back to his room. The patient was shadowboxing with a tall laundry cart parked in the hallway.

Bounder told Marie and Rod the patient had pugilistic dementia similar to former boxers Jerry Quarry and the great Ali–too many rounds in the square ring. They observed the laundry cart almost whipped him when a gallon bottle of laundry detergent slipped off the cart and landed on the poor patient's right foot.

"Hi guys, hi Rod," Dalia greeted with enthusiasm. "What can I do for you up here? Most of the patients are on the rooftop in the middle of a volleyball tournament. One of our gal patients is from California. She thinks she's God's gift to beach volleyball."

"I suppose she's long, tall, and bronzed to perfection," Marie quipped.

"To the contrary, she's short, fat, and aggressive. She watched the Olympics on TV–felt she was better than the ladies representing our country. Sure, we let her believe whatever she wants to when participating in her psychotherapy. Her doctor comments she's doing well . . . despite the fact she insists on being aggressive. She's married to a professional athlete. I guess this adds to her credence around here she's also a professional."

Boyd laughed. "Great bit of information. We want to check out the arts and crafts room, Dalia. We're trying to get to the bottom of Elsie's Turk murder. We think there may be a clue hiding in that room."

Dalia gave them a questioning stare. She recalled the terrible fatality. *Oh my God, this murder couldn't have happened the way they think it did. How could anyone be so violent to snuff out the life of another human being?*

"Ah, please, go right ahead," she said. "Rod, can I talk to you alone for a few minutes?"

Marie and Boyd proceeded to the arts and crafts room. Rod lagged. He and Dalia went to an open foyer and sat down on two chairs that lined the walls.

"Rod, I know you've been trying to contact me. Juanita is protective of me and–"

"Hold on there. Explain, please."

"She doesn't want me to have any contact with anyone who might cause a complication in my life. You may know we've been more than friends."

"No, I don't. Why should I be *persona non gratis,* for God's sake, Dalia? I thought there might be something between us worth developing. I can't recall how many times I've tried to contact you, only to be sidelined by your housemate. I think she's jealous of me and doesn't want you to talk to me or even see me again."

She hesitated, then opened up. "Rod, it's complicated. Juanita has been my bastion of strength over the years. I'm not sure how I could have survived without her."

"Can't you make your own decisions? Do you have any feelings for me, or am I just minced meat?"

"Oh, Rod, I hate to hear you say that so flippantly. You came to my rescue one night. I appreciated that, believe me. Juanita and I have become so involved with each other from a physical and emotional perspective. I can't think in terms of having a man complicating my life right now."

Rod stared at her. He had a difficult time digesting her excuses.

She became more relaxed. "I need Juanita more than anything else. My existence is worth continuing this relationship. Do you understand me, Rod?"

"Thanks for the clarification. I'll move on. You won't hear from me again, other than within the realm of our working relationships here at Mission Oaks. However, if you ever need me, I'm always ready to help you."

He left Dalia dabbing her eyes and went to join Marie and Boyd.

"Rod, come over here," Marie ordered as she stepped out of the arts and crafts room. "I want you to witness what we've found here."

"Sure. What's the deal?"

"We ripped open many of the pasted pictures in the scrapbooks accumulated by Roberta Peck and Elsie Turk. There must be at least twenty-five completed Sudoku puzzles on the back of everything pasted to the sheets in the book. It all points to Nick Ryan as the person Elsie Turk was fingering with her last ounce of blood."

"Yes, Marie, but did he kill her?" Boyd asked. "That's sure a huge assumption. How in the world could you even prove that in a court of law?"

"Wasn't he released by the MPD when they cleared him as the result of the DNA profiling?" Rod asked. "I heard his red hair was not the sample found under Turk's fingernails."

"True enough," Martini said. "However, I think we can find a correlation here with Ryan and the nine numbers etched in her blood trying to identify her killer. I'll consult with my superiors and their legal counsel. We have to determine if we have enough evidence before we go after Ryan, lest our case against him won't stick."

They headed back downstairs to Rod's office. Peppi intercepted them in the front hallway by the lobby. She must've had an entire package of Wrigley's finest chewing gum sloshing triumphantly in her mouth, dismissing any accepted rules of etiquette.

"Rod, a Miss Simpkins is sitting in your office. She says she needs to talk with you. I think I've seen her in the hospital before. Lucie told me to get her out of the hallway and put her in your office. She was causing a ruckus and is agitated. I tried to calm her down, but she told me where to go to and it wasn't heaven!"

Rod mouthed to himself—the last time I saw her she was calm, cool, and collected. She wanted to become a mental health nurse. What in God's name sidetracked her this time? If there ever was a poster child for adult attention deficit disorders, it had to be Keena.

"It's about time you got here," Keena blasted as Rod opened his office door. She was sitting at his desk writing notes on a large yellow notepad. Her hair was dyed a bright red. She wore a tight red sweater, black flared pants, and tattered red tennis shoes.

He hadn't seen her lately . . . thought she was busy, out of town, or just avoiding him.

"Keena, what can I do for you today?"

"I know you're going to hire that lady from San Francisco for the marketing position. You should've known better! All those people from that far out city are either gay, transvestite, cross-dressers, pot smokers, or arm shooters, for Christ's sake!"

"Well, Keena, I didn't think you cared. Correct me if I'm wrong. Didn't you tell me you were no longer interested in the job? By the way, what's with the new doo?"

"I'm shocked you've noticed, Richards, for all the attention you've given me of late. Do you like it?"

He decided not to answer that question. She looked like a street trollop. "Keena, it's been hectic around here. I'm up to my armpits in management challenges. The unfortunate murder hasn't been solved yet. We're trying to get ready for re-certification by a national accrediting body. The local press hasn't been kind to us, implying we're trying to sweep the whole murder episode under the rug. And no, I don't like the new hairdo. I'm hoping it's a cheap wig."

Keena ignored the implication. She bolted from his desk chair and walked to the window, staring outside for several minutes.

Rod was waiting for the next volley to begin. He expected a heavier barrage. He wasn't safe in a bunker. He wasn't wearing a flak jacket or a steel pot on his head.

"Rod, will you come over tonight for dinner? I bought the best steak the grocery store had behind the meat counter. I'll broil it and fix mushrooms sautéed in garlic. I got a bottle of Bombay Sapphire gin we can sip on and bring each other up to date. Maybe you'll get the opportunity to see and understand the real me. What do you think?"

"All right, I'd be glad to but under one condition." *Deep down I have mixed feelings about getting too involved with her.*

"What might that be?"

"That we play it cool and relax a bit."

"Got it, see you around sevenish," she said with a sweet smile permeating her entire face.

Rod stared at that sleek proportioned body as she left his office. An extra ounce of human flesh could not have been poured into those tight pants. *Why was she so insecure? She could captivate the universe if she knew how to control her emotions and apply herself accordingly.*

Lucie stuck her head in Rod's office breaking his chain of devious thoughts. He never heard the telephone ring.

"There's a Belle Chelby from the MPD investigator's office on the line for you. Do you want to take her call?"

"Did she say what she wants, Lucie, I'm kinda busy right now?"

"She didn't tell me, but she did say the chief of police told her to contact you."

"Right, tell her I'll be with her in a few seconds."

He heard some loud voices in the proximity of the reception area but was afraid to stick his head out the door. Perhaps Peppi and Keena were a little obnoxious wishing each other a pleasant goodbye.

CHAPTER 50

An hour had passed when the loud slam of a car door jerked Angel, Juanita, and Amfi back to reality. They leaped up to check the source of the noise and were relieved to see the taillights of a car parked across the street. They sat down again and resumed their discussion of the murder.

"What were you doing at the time all this craziness was happening in the hospital day room, Angel?" Amfi asked.

Juanita had deferred to Angel allowing him to tell the rest of the story. After all, he'd earned the right to brag about his big accomplishment. She had already forgotten some of the more intricate details Angel shared with her about the kill. Didn't matter–it got done?

"I planned to sneak into the hospital room you advised me she occupied and kill her there in bed. She wasn't in the room when I had peeked in. I headed further down the hallway. I heard loud music in the dayroom and saw people aimlessly frolicking around–almost like drunken seamen. I decided to go in and see how they'd react."

"Sounds exciting to me," Amfi muttered. Juanita said nothing.

Angel paused, his speech began to slur. Excitement overwhelmed him. Then he continued. "This pumpkin man rode over to me in a motorized cart and said in a garbled speech that he'd met me somewhere before. I remembered seeing him in the parking lot after I got in town to begin my study of the hospital. He then asked me if I was looking for anyone in particular in the hospital. I told him I came here to visit my sick mother. He asked me if her name was Roberta Peck. I said it was–didn't know her–took a chance. He hesitated, then looked at me with a blank stare through that eye slit in the pumpkin head. It must've been related to the comment about Peck."

"Pumpkin man?" Amfi laughed. "Was it a Halloween party?"

"I don't know anything about American parties. The idiot told me the white robe I was wearing fit in well with this Halloween motif." Angel was on a roll. "It wasn't a robe but a large white bath towel. I'd grabbed it from the room where I thought the target was located. I forgot to wear a long-sleeved shirt that morning. Needed to hide my bad arm. I didn't want to be identified as a cripple if anyone saw me dressed in normal clothes."

Americans celebrate Halloween in October," Comptos told him.

Angel shifted into overdrive. "By now, the redhead and the agent were rolling on the floor grabbing each other's private parts." He was shaking, almost breathless. "All she had left on was her pajama tops. The man had taken his shirt off and shoved his underwear and trousers down to his ankles. He couldn't get them over the black combat boots he was wearing."

"Wow, way to go!" Amfi mouthed as she started to enjoy the play-by-play description of the murder.

"The pumpkin man got so annoyed at both gropers he shot out of the room like a cannon. It's a good thing the room had two swinging doors. He would've taken a normal door off its hinges."

"What happened next?" an impatient Amfi asked, showing more animation as the *happy powder* diluted in the tea invaded her entire body. "Were they screwing each other?"

"No, no way. It gets better. The two drunks on the floor rolled under the opened ping pong table that had been shoved in a corner. All of a sudden they started arguing and shouting at each other. Then the redhead stumbled to his feet, pulling up his underwear, and pants. He shouted at her, using words I didn't understand. She ignored him, turning her head to the side like she was pouting. He left the room pointing his finger at her several times, though she didn't see him leave."

Angel was out of breath–had to pause for a few minutes.

"I'm shocked the staff nurse, or any orderlies didn't walk in on them," Amfi said, now with a serious look on her face.

"Me too," Juanita agreed, "But Angel was lucky."

"Believe me, I was aware of that. I had to move faster. The bitch sat up and was groping around trying to find her pajama bottoms. Her back was facing me. She had no idea I was in the room. I then raced over and grabbed her around the neck, flipping the wire over her head. She kicked it outta my hands without looking up at me. It all happened in a millisecond."

"How was she able to do that while being in an alcoholic stupor?" a confused Amfi asked him.

He side-stepped her question and then continued. "I reached into my pocket and pulled the scissors out. I figured it'd be a better murder weapon than using my little knife for the assault. She began to cry, begging me to leave her alone and to get out of the room. The whore reached up and pulled my hair all of a sudden without any warning. The jerk was so hard I thought my scalp was being ripped off my head."

"I bet that hurt!" Juanita stammered. "Ouch . . . ouch." She'd been enjoying the narrative account.

"For some unknown reason, she never turned around to see who was trying to kill her," Angel went on. "She reacted like a caged animal with great instinct. She clawed at my eyes with her other hand. They're still sore. Then I plunged the scissors as hard as I could into her chest, got to my feet, and raced out of the room."

"Didn't anybody hear you?" Amfi reasoned. "Surely the ward attendants had to be on their way back to supervise their charges?"

"I thought you'd never ask, my dear friend. They still weren't in sight. I couldn't believe my luck."

"Yes, the great Mohammed was present in a spiritual being," Amfi smiled.

"I got up and headed for the fire alarm after I killed the bitch. It was located on the wall near the ping pong table. I planned to set it off but then feared everybody in the hospital would flood the hallways and detect me. I took my hand off of the fire alarm and sneaked back down the hallway."

"Maybe that was a mistake not creating a diversion," Amfi said.

"Hey, I'm here . . . okay? Two attendants were arguing with each other as they walked outta a patient's room. I think the male orderly tried to rape the other one. They didn't see me. I ducked into a utility closet. After they were far past my location, I headed down the end of the hallway. The last act saw me racing down the stairwell and leaving the hospital. I'm done."

"Fantastic," Amfi yelled out.

"Oh, by the way," Angel said before the other two could react. "I wore gloves during the entire time I was in the hospital. Just in case you were wondering but didn't ask. Fingerprints are easy to lift. They can come back to haunt you. End of story."

What Angel didn't realize at the time of the Elsie Turk murder, Eduardo Munoz circled back and returned to the day room entrance. He held the door ajar with the front tire of his cart. He jerked back in horror when he saw the scissors impaled into the woman's upper body, put his cart in reverse, and sped back to his room.

The two ladies were now in a state of deep meditation. Angel wondered if they even heard the rest of his triumphant story. The wonderful soothing effects of the warm tea made the women at ease, numb, or no longer interested.

He looked in disgust at them. They looked like little Buda statues, their legs crossed, and hands folded in front of them waiting to pray.

Angel was waiting for some type of eruption from them. The mood swings from the "dirty" tea have unpredictable sequences. *Maybe I overdosed them. Stupid me!*

He decided to close his eyes after some hesitation and joined them. Soon he envisioned himself standing before the great Allah waiting for his eternal reward. There were virgins anywhere. They'd come soon enough.

All of a sudden a warm hand clamped down on his shoulder. It startled him. He looked up. It was Amfi.

"I think I should get going soon. My husband will wonder where I'm at. He knows I get home late sometimes. The poor

Yousef hasn't the faintest idea what I'm doing. All he ever wants to do is fly, fly, and fly. Yousef is striving to be the best navigator in the world. He loves the bravado of American pilots and their dedication to service."

He stared deeply into her face. He wondered if she was happy with her husband. She came from royalty, he didn't–being a simple Bedouin. The marriage had to be arranged by some highly influential Arab chieftains. The reasons weren't known. There had to be motives.

Angel was getting horny. He hadn't lain with a woman since that whore in Detroit stole his wallet and took off when he was asleep. Amfi was by no means a beauty, but she would do for now.

He didn't care much for Saudi women. Most of the females were as big as, or even bigger than their husbands. No wonder the Saudi men went out of the country so often. More gratifying sex, although at a steep price was available in England. It was one of their favorite getaways. Plenty of booze was at hand to whet their appetites wherever they went.

"Why can't you stay a little longer?" he begged Amfi. "We can discuss our next move."

She stared at him. The fog had lifted.

He then got up and put his good arm around her. She flinched.

"I'll fix dinner and then you can go home to him." Angel was aroused. He thought she was attractive in a Western sort of way. Big black eyes, long arms, soft skin, and average breasts.

"Angel," Juanita said in a loud voice. She'd heard him smooth-talking Amfi. She noticed his awakened manhood in the despicable tight trousers he loved to wear.

He bolted back from his erogenous thoughts.

"Let her go home to her husband, you damn fool! We've got serious business to attend to. The sooner we get started on our final plan, the better for all of us. Good night."

She hustled out the front door with Amfi on her arm. Her car was hemmed in by two other cars. She couldn't leave the curbside to exit. Two soldiers leaped out of the front vehicle and confronted Juanita. They'd been waiting outside with patience for several hours.

"Sweetheart, what's your hurry?" the taller man of the two said. "I and my pal here are looking for a little company. How 'bout lending us your cute little companion for the evening? You can run on and clean another house in the neighborhood. We'll take good care of her for you."

Juanita reached into her purse and pulled out a Smith and Wesson, Model 20, .44 Magnum. She pointed it at the smaller man's head. Her two-handed grip on the weapon was steady.

"Holy shit, lady, put that thing back in your purse before it goes off!" the taller soldier pleaded. "We're out here just looking for some fun. Don't mean any harm."

She swung the pistol and leveled it toward his crotch. "I'm going to count to five. If you morons aren't out of my sight by then, I'm going to put a hole in both of you big enough to drive a truck through. Got it?"

The soldiers raced to their car and sped off.

Angel went to bed on his woven mat, alone, tired, and frustrated. He wanted a woman so bad it ached. He rationalized it'd have to wait for a more opportune time. He's a hero now.

He reflected back to the goofball in the motorized scooter at the hospital. All of a sudden he jumped up off the hard floor. The murderer remembered the pumpkin man was parked ahead of him when he sped out of the dayroom.

Did he double back and witness the murder? If so, this guy might cause a problem. He can identify me being up there at the time of her death. I need to go back to the hospital and kill him, otherwise, our holy Jihad plan could be jeopardized. Maybe even be aborted.

CHAPTER 51

ROD was perplexed as he headed back to his condo. He almost clipped a guy riding a motorbike as it raced into the hospital parking lot. He'd swerved around him to enter the busy street. His mind was running rampant with various unrelated questions.

Why does Belle want to meet with Howard Hill and me next week? Did it have anything to do with her recent study? What does Keena want with me? I can never figure that woman out! I guess I'll find out tonight.

The telephone rang when he walked into his condo unit. It was his son on the line.

"What's up, Larry?" Rod asked him. "I'm sorry I haven't talked with you lately. Things have been way out of control at the hospital."

"Dad, that's what I'm calling about. How well do you know a police psychologist by the name of Belle Chelby?"

"I met her once, Larry. Why . . . what's up?"

Rod figured he knew why Larry was calling but didn't want to pre-empt his son's story. Maybe he could fill in some of the blanks that hadn't been addressed earlier.

"Belle called me earlier today and asked if I would meet with her at your hospital next week. She told me you'd also be at the meeting with Dr. Jim Smyth and Howard Hill. Jesus Astrade at MPD told her they're ready to move on to a new project which involves Mission Oaks. He's her boss. She wants me and Smyth in attendance to provide some technical guidance on the treatment of mentally disturbed adolescents in a restricted setting."

"Why does she want Howard to sit in?"

"She didn't come right out and say it. She alluded Astrade felt Howard would be an ideal candidate to run the new program. She told me Dr. Dean threw Hill's name into the mix. I guess they know each other from days past."

Rod slumped down on his couch. He almost dropped the phone when Larry mentioned Howard's name. Belle never told him anything about that possible plan. She never mentioned Hill's name during their earlier telephone discussion.

"Larry, needless to say . . . it should be an interesting meeting. I know Hill well but can't picture him dealing with a bunch of pimply-faced teenagers. I guess we'll have to wait until next week and see what's coming down. How are Pam and the kids these days?"

"They're all doing well, Dad. Pam asked me to invite you to lunch Sunday. John might be coming in from Green Bay this weekend. Are you available?"

"I'll be there, thanks much. I haven't seen you guys for a while. Anxious to hear how things are going at Ft. Sam with your government contract. I'll bring a couple of bottles of wine and some beer with me."

There was a long pause on his end of the line. Rod waited in silence before Larry wished him well and hung up.

Rod shaved and showered. He dressed in a blue guayabera shirt with gray trousers and wore black tasseled loafers without socks.

He picked up a copy of the Sports Illustrated swimsuit edition and paged through it, killing time until he went over to Keena's. He didn't have the faintest idea how this evening would turn out but hoped for the best. One never knew with Keena!

It was seven-fifteen. Rod grabbed two bottles of a Napa Valley merlot, locked his door, and headed down the long hallway to Keena's place. There was a helicopter whirling downward to the brightly lit rooftop helipad of the nearby All Saints Medical Center.

The hum, hum, hum of the motor, and the swish–swish–swish of the blades reminded him of 'Nam once again. The Army medical air ambulances and their heroic pilots saved the lives of thousands of battered American bodies. The swooping *birds* were affectionately known as "Dust Off" helicopters by the wounded warriors.

Wouldn't that be something if his old Army buddy, Tim Jackson was sitting in the cockpit of that chopper!

The hallways in his building are different. They're open to the outside and exposed to both the elements and the hustle and bustle of a busy downtown city. Flower boxes are positioned atop three-foot-tall outer walls. Some contained plants, others had colorful flowers. A person didn't have the typical closed-in feeling of hallways found in most residential buildings. He wondered if Keena had tried growing her weed here. Thought it'd be an ideal location.

Rod knocked three times on her door. There was no answer. He knocked three times again, this time much louder. He knew the doorbell was not functioning from the last time he visited her. The door swung open as he was prepared to rap a third series of "I'm out here waiting."

"Hello, Rod, please come in. Sorry for the delay. I had my head in the oven and didn't hear you at the door. I damn near singed off this beautiful red bird's nest."

"Well, I ah–"

She greeted him with a warm hug and a fierce kiss on his lips. The black and red clothing attire was gone. In their stead were a loose-fitting purple blouse and white pants. She was barefoot with black painted toenails. Keena had skipped the aromatic candles and soft lights this time. Mood music was playing from a nearby Bose Wave music system.

"I'm glad you came, Rod. I feared you'd cancel at the last minute. I don't know why for sure. I had this weird feeling that you were seeing somebody else and didn't have time for me. You are way too handsome to be ignored by the fairer sex!"

He let out a brief sigh and then laughed out loud. "To the contrary, Keena, I'm glad you invited me over. I haven't had a home-cooked meal in ages. My culinary skills need a serious makeover. It smells great in here."

Rod set the bottles of wine on the kitchen counter, strolled over to the living room window, and peered outside. "You have a better view of the Riverwalk than I have from my unit. The trees outside my rear balcony need a serious haircut. They block most of my view. I get the biggest kick out of the tourists staring in disbelief at these gigantic trees. I guess they're telling each other Texas was supposed to be rangeland."

"What'll it be Rod? I have some martinis chilling in the fridge, or we can open a bottle of wine you brought over. Me, I'm in a gin mood tonight. I love the taste of those juniper berries."

"Keena, I'll join you. Pour me one. The wine can wait. I haven't had a good martini in ages. Do you have any large stuffed green olives?" *Rod assured himself once again that he wasn't a recovering alcoholic but a recovered and severely depressed half-maniac.*

"I do, although I prefer a twist of lemon in mine. The citrus wakes up the taste buds before the alcohol assault, Rod. I'll get them from the refrigerator right away. She winked her eyes at him and disappeared into the kitchen. Do you like my music? I purchased the CD just for you."

Tony Bennett was announcing to the entire world how he left his dear heart in San Francisco. Keena wondered if he'd ever found it again.

They sat out on the back balcony sipping their drinks. She opened a bag of pretzels, poured them into a wooden bowl, and set the bowl down on the little stand between their lounge chairs. The sun was starting its descent from the tall building to its right. A slight breeze was lazily pursuing the twisting river below them.

She took a big hit of her drink, turned, and then looked Rod straight in the eyes. "I suppose you think I'm a flaky Jane, right?"

"What makes you think that? You do surprise me at times, Keena, but I'm getting used to it. There's never a dull minute when you're around." *He tried to anticipate what was coming next from that pretty mouth of hers. He gave up. No track record to alert him.*

"I'm jealous that you're bringing in that lady from San Francisco to be your new marketing director. Somehow I envisioned I'd be the person sitting in that chair next to you every day at the hospital."

"But you said—"

"Yes, yes," Keena stopped him. "I know what I told you about going to nursing school and becoming a mental health nurse. That was back then, but now I've changed my mind. I enrolled in a new cosmetology school downtown. I went there to have my hair done the other day. They were professional—schooled me on their trade."

"Wow! I had my hair cut there once. Hey, I'm thankful the buzzed crop dared to grow back."

"The girl who fixed my hair had been a surgical nurse at Rhodes Hospital. She got tired of caring for sick patients every day and taking orders from those overpaid physicians. The gal decided to give it up. Now, she makes elated whenever someone walks through the door. She's only a student. Hard to believe. Don't you think she did a wonderful job on my hair?"

"Um, of course, I do, Keena. You look great!"

He wasn't kidding. She looked fantastic. The top button of the purple blouse was not fastened. Rod observed Keena wasn't wearing anything underneath the sheer blouse. *This lady doesn't have to run around wearing one of those dinky little camouflaged push-up bras.* He was hoping they'd end up between the bedsheets tonight.

Rod was on his second martini and felt great. She wasn't "coming on" to him. Maybe he liked that. He preferred to be the aggressor when it came to sex. Keena's newfound vocation excited her. It gave her a certain radiance he found heartfelt and soothing.

"Let's eat, Rod. The meal is ready now. The timer just went off. Didn't you hear it?"

He snapped out of his brief mental lapse and helped her set the table. She brought a bottle of merlot from the kitchen. He opened it, pouring them a glass, and set the bottle down next to the water pitcher.

While balancing the filled wine glasses in one hand, they clicked their glasses together with the other hand and then finished off the martinis. The couple sat down next to each other and ate.

"Excellent meal, Keena, you are a number one cook. Where'd you learn to cook like this?"

"Thanks, Rod, glad you're enjoying it. My mother made me take those boring home economic classes in high school. It was a knockdown-drag-out fight. Pop wanted his girl to take auto mechanic courses. He argued every female in his family should know how to rotate and change flat tires. He insisted they also need to learn when and how to change the engine oil. Mom won out. I'm done talking. Pass me the bread."

They finished their plates and brought the dirty dishes into the kitchen. Rod suggested they convene to the couch. They had drained one bottle of merlot during the dinner and were working on the second. She snuggled up next to him.

"By the way, Keena, how did you know I hired Nancy O'Reilly for the marketing position?"

"I thought you'd never ask me," She giggled like a teenager. "I know everything about you and what goes on in your little fiefdom over there at Mission Oaks."

"Well, who the hell–"

"Shh." She took his hand in hers. "I ran into my cousin at the grocery store the other day when shopping for dinner items tonight. He told me how happy and excited you were when O'Reilly informed you she was coming to San Antonio to work."

"Okay, refresh my memory again. Who's your cousin?"

"I thought you remembered. Boyd Bounder. Isn't he a great guy? He lives close to the grocery store. Cousin was trying to find a certain wine his newfound love preferred. Marie Martini is a neat gal. I hope they get married."

It was getting late. Keena brought out an opened bottle of cognac with two snifters.

He'd had his fling with cognac one time. He was serving in the army and stationed in France. He forgot how the French liqueur could play tag with one's mind. He had downed a half bottle of cognac one night on his first weekend pass off base. The military police had to escort him from a French pokey.

"Rod, I've gotta show you the new paneling I had installed in my bedroom. It took the workers three days to finish the job. I love it." She grabbed his hand and led him to her bedroom.

"Very nice, Keena, I love the design. It could be several shades lighter. Don't you think? The hand-painted paneling depicted three Indians galloping after a scattering herd of wild buffalos. It looked beyond realistic.

"Are the Indians from your grandmother's tribe?"

"Why'd you ask that?"

"I could tell by the colored headbands they're wearing and the length of the wooden spears being thrown at the animals." He enjoyed the art of exaggeration.

"Gosh, you're so smart, Mister Richards! I find it exhilarating you took the time to research my family tree."

He nodded his head in agreement and gave her a quick wink.

"You know what, Rod, I think the paneling fits in well with my bedroom furniture. The tracked lighting installed along the ceiling border accentuates the scene. Wouldn't you agree with me?"

"Shouldn't I, Keena?" he laughed. *Rod could care less about the ridiculous paneling. On top of that he'd donate every piece of furniture in the bedroom to the local Salvation Army.* The room reminded him of Grandma Richards' smoke-filled quilting room, less the Indians in pursuit of their hoofed prey.

Keena had only one thing in mind for tonight. The energy she derived from the bedroom scene excited her. She began to perspire, then placed her long arms around his neck. She slowly unbuttoned the guayabera, flipping it on a nearby chair.

Rod reciprocated by slipping her blouse over the dyed redhead and dropped it on the floor next to the chair. He had no second thoughts, none. The many libations he had consumed melted any stored-up inhibitions. The act of any self-imposed piety resembled a misplaced iceberg disappearing in the middle of the Sahara Desert!

When it was finally over, the two exhausted and intertwined spent bodies fell asleep in each other's arms.

Rod woke up in the middle of the night and surveyed the damage. A faint light was peeking through the louvered windows. She was sprawled out sideways on the bed, snoring like a lumberjack. A smug smile was imprinted on that lovely face.

When and where the Indians learned the *Kiowa Klutch* position will probably never be known or reported. It was the most sensual and exciting love-making technique he'd ever hope to experience. Neither of them would be able to stand up straight for a week, let alone walk in a straight line!

Rod barely made it out of bed to dress and go home. He had no idea where his clothes and shoes were located. He didn't want to turn on any lights for fear of waking her up. He got down on his hands and knees crawling around on the floor trying to find his clothes.

Several of the items were found on the other side of the room, thrown under the bed. One shoe was found in the closet dirty clothes hamper. He couldn't locate the other one. He didn't care–it'd turn up.

Rod tip-toed into the living room and found the second shoe near the bedroom doorway. He got dressed. His head was throbbing. The rest of his body was numb . . . love numb.

He opened the unlocked front door and walked barefoot back to his unit. Streaks of light were beginning to overcome the darkness of night. To his surprise, another medical helicopter was taking off from the rooftop of the nearby medical center. He didn't care anymore about the Vietnam occurrences of the brave Dustoff crewmembers. Their heroics under intense fire were well-documented. History will repeat itself in time. The Baltics? The Middle East? War never ceases to plague generation after generation.

A ground ambulance was racing down Navarro Street, followed closely by a screaming police car. The few passenger cars on the road raced for cover. Excitement reigned all over the place. *Some poor sick old soul died tonight. So be it. Keena breathed a fresh new life into this beat-up dead body of mine!*

CHAPTER 52

ROD was perched at his desk pouring over notes for the upcoming hospital board meeting. He was upbeat about last night's session with Keena. He was reliving the scenes in her bedroom when he was jolted by a loud rapping on his office door.

"Come in please," he responded to the knocker, quickly abandoning his lewd recollections of the previous evening.

"Morning, boss," a beaming Mario Caseres said. "One of my loyal night housekeepers cornered me yesterday and shocked the living daylights out of me. She dropped two empty 750 ml. bottles of Bushmills Irish Whiskey on my desk. My employee wanted to bring to my astute attention . . . booze was coming into the hospital on a regular schedule. She knew it was against our policy. The dear woman hesitated to tell me about this earlier. She feared I'd accuse some of the housekeeping staff of drinking on duty."

"Where did she find the bottles?"

"They kept appearing in the trash can in the second-floor dayroom. The bottles were wrapped in hospital toweling. They wouldn't be conspicuous to anybody nosing around. The fools were thinking we wouldn't notice the towels being tossed away. They had to be too stupid or too drunk to think we wouldn't catch it."

"Thanks for bringing this to my attention, Mario. I have a good idea who the culprits might be."

"That's not all, Rod."

"Huh?" *What the hell next?*

"She told me she witnessed Tom Lubay showing up on the ward talking to that big redheaded patient we had up there. She thinks Lubay might have been the idiot bringing in the booze. He always had a package under his arms when he showed up. This activity was happening at night. It made her wonder why the staff pharmacist was meeting with a patient after normal working hours. Be aware she doesn't want to get into any trouble for reporting these incidents."

"What's her history, Mario? Do you think she's reliable? Maybe she has some kind of vengeance grudge against Lubay—an ax to grind or something just as ridiculous."

"This lady has been with me for over two years. She's by far my best worker. I trust her judgment and would back her up completely."

"Thanks, Mario. Please thank her for reporting this to us. Tell her there will be no repercussions. We need to protect the integrity of our workers and the health of those patients placed in our trust."

"I'm with you, boss. Though I think you need to keep a closer eye on that pharmacist. He might be peddling drugs for all we know."

Caseres left Rod's office whistling a merry tune he'd heard before but couldn't place. Mario thought he was in for a big raise. Whistleblower?

Rod sat back in his chair wrestling with the options confronting him on the alleged problem with Lubay. He couldn't accuse him of feeding booze to the patients without substantial evidence. He decided the best course of action would be briefing Marie Martini. She could run with the information from the investigation point of view. He'd have to deal with Lubay in his way.

His telephone rang and kept ringing.

Why didn't Lucie answer the damn thing?

He picked it up. It was Phil Dean.

"Howard Hill and I are going out tonight to take in a San Antonio Mission baseball game. Care to come along?"

"I didn't think Howard liked baseball."

"Yeah, he doesn't give two hoots for the game. I told him both Chief Astrade and Belle Chelby were guests of honor by the club ownership. Need I say more?"

"Count me in, good doctor. I'd also like to get to know her a little better."

CHAPTER 53

"THAT fucking tourist bus damn near ran me down!" Angel Garza cursed as he swung into the hospital parking lot. He found a slot in the rear to park his motorbike. This was the night he decided to kill that space cadet who drove the motorized cart.

It was still light outside, but the sun was beginning to bid adios to the long day. He opted to take a walk, wait for the sun to set before he snuck into the hospital. Angel passed the Cantina Classica and decided to go in and get a warm cup of tea. *These Texacans are complete idiots. They always order their beloved iced tea with tons of sweetener. Stupid infidels, ugh!*

At dusk, he headed to the back entrance of the hospital. He unlocked the door using the key Amfi had given him and entered. Angel tried to recall which room was warehousing the idiot with the big, motorized vehicle.

Yes. Warehousing is the correct word in this case! Only a living, sane human should have a clean hospital bed. Not this moron.

A silenced .38 caliber, snub-nosed police special was tucked in the back of his belt. He wore a long-zippered jacket to hide the weapon. Angel felt a bullet hole in the middle of the forehead would be quicker and more efficient than using the wire, even his sheathed knife. The target was beefy, could put up a fight. It was cool enough. Anyone wearing a light jacket shouldn't become suspicious.

"Can I help you young man?" a middle-aged female orderly in a green scrub suit asked Angel.

What's with the scrub suit? Are they cutting open the fruit cakes' heads to check their brains for parasites?

"Oh, no thank you. I was on my way to my mother's room."

"Well, you'd better sign in. We don't want just anybody coming in off the streets to see our patients. Their security is of utmost importance to us. There's a clipboard at the end of the hall."

"Thanks, I'll go down there and register." He laughed to himself. *Idiots!*

Juanita wanted a hit team to accompany him to the hospital. He talked her out of it. Angel assured her the fewer people involved, the better. These fraudulent people-healers didn't have the slightest idea of total warfare. It wouldn't present any opposition to a trained assassin. She relented, allowing him to proceed alone on his secret killing mission.

Angel saw the motorized unit as he headed down the first-floor hallway. It was parked next to a hospital bed in a room further down the ward. *Aha, in luck.*

He looked up and down the corridor to see if anyone was around. It was empty. He slid around the corner of the opened door and saw a huge clump of manhood underneath the covers. The big head was turned away, facing the outside wall. Angel heard heavy breathing emanating from the bed.

The assassin tip-toed in, reached around behind his back, and withdrew his pistol. He smiled nearing the bed. *The fat slob is going straight to hell! This is going to be way too easy for me.*

Angel took several soft steps and reached the bedside. He pulled the pistol out. The pistol hammer was already back in the ready position. A hollow-point round was about to slam into that swollen head.

All of a sudden as quick as a lightning rod, Munoz spun around and zapped the unsuspecting Angel with a Taser. ZZZZT! Thousands of electrical volts played havoc with his body. The would-be assassin slumped to the floor.

Eduardo vaulted out of bed like a gifted athlete. He grabbed a roll of elastic bandage sitting on the bedside table and tied Angel's arms and legs. Then he secured a half-filled steel bedpan from the bottom of the bed near his feet. Eduardo slammed it down on Angel's head, straight and hard. An untrained enemy soldier went down.

Urine shot from the bedpan and spewed everywhere.

The fit of spastic seizure subsided in the attacker. The victim went limp. Eduardo thought for sure he killed him.

Munoz mounted his steel horse and sped down the corridor to get help. The female ward attendant was entering the corridor with a hot cup of coffee in one hand. A piece of pizza was flopping in the other. Eduardo told her that he captured one of the Israeli Mossad undercover agents dispatched on a secret mission here to assassinate him.

"Call the Military Police right away and let the colonel know," Munoz ordered the shocked female.

"Eduardo, quiet down. Go back to your room right away. Stop playing military games."

He spun around her, barely hitting her right knee, and sped for the front lobby. The poor lady dropped the pizza slice on the floor. He was going to mount the troops himself, screw everybody. *Why the hell did they ever allow women to join a man's army? No help here.*

All of a sudden Doctor Dean came through the front door of the hospital. He was on his way to make evening rounds. Eduardo corralled him. "Follow me, Colonel, I captured one."

Dean ran after Munoz, not having the faintest idea what the excited patient said, or what was going down. He skidded on the pizza slice lying on the floor, posing as an enemy booby-trap. He swore aloud and picked himself up off the floor.

When they reached Eduardo's room, Dean saw the body sprawled on the floor and the weapon lying next to it. He made a quick assessment, kneeling while placing two fingers on the man's carotid artery. There was a faint sign of life.

The noxious smell of urine was strong. He started to retch. The female attendant peeked in and screamed as loud as she could. The verbal blast scared the living hell out of Munoz and the doctor.

Eduardo picked up the pistol and carefully released the cocked hammer. He shoved it in his pajama bottoms.

"Call MPD," Dean directed the ward attendant who was still stunned. He then slipped his cell phone from a shirt pocket and punched in Jesus Astrade's number to tell him what had happened in the ward.

The chief told Dean he'd send Lt. Hagen over right away. Hagen was at the station working overtime. Astrade was at a fundraiser with his wife. He'd come over to the hospital later.

Detective Hagen and a young female associate showed up ten minutes after the call. The victim was now sitting up on the floor, sipping a glass of water Dean had given him.

"I'm getting fed up running over to this spooky place every other week," the Lieutenant declared. Hagen slapped a pair of handcuffs on Angel after hearing a brief description of the events. He hauled him to his feet by his withered arm, then roughly shoved him down on a chair next to the bed. There was a smattering of fresh blood oozing from Angel's red hair. Doctor Dean poured antiseptic on it and applied pressure until it subsided.

Hagen looked at Munoz with a quizzical stare. He wondered if this guy was an innocent bystander or involved in the incident. "You got a legal permit to carry that Taser?" he asked a proud Munoz.

Munoz responded, "The colonel issued it to me last week. He received an intelligence report to expect an armed aggressor to storm our walls. The plan was to take out our communications shack during the darkened evening."

"What a load of bullshit, you fool," Hagen said. "Would someone please tell me why the intruder was trying to murder this patient?"

His associate whipped out a yellow notepad and started to jot down notes. Angel began to regain his senses and composure. Munoz crawled back in his bed, rolled over on his side as if he were trying to go to sleep. He lay silent for several minutes.

Suddenly, Eduardo shot up and began screaming as loud as his vocal cords would allow him. HAYAHH! He jumped back in his cart, nearly knocking the young female detective to the floor in the process.

"That no-good, half-man enemy soldier slumped in that chair over there tried to kill me. He also murdered that poor Elsa Turk lady up in the second-floor dayroom. I saw him stab her with a big pair of scissors. Put him in the stinking brig! Bread, and water only. He's not to have visitors. Construct the hanging platform."

"I demand a lawyer right now," Angel spit out. "I'm not saying anything to anyone till I get legal advice."

The female cop read him his rights.

Hagen told Dean he'd call the chief of police before he did anything further with the suspect. When he ended his cell phone call, he contacted the FBI office asking for Special Agent Jorge Vasquez.

The agent on call said he'd notify Vasquez post haste. Then Hagen dialed Marie Martini's cell phone. She didn't answer. He left her a message to contact the FBI as soon as possible.

Hagen wanted to wash his hands of this entire case as soon as possible. It was getting complicated. He didn't need these kinds of challenges. *Just give me a simple homicide where the killer is one of those homeless simpletons living under the fucking freeway.*

Dean called back the chief of police. He told him there was no need for him to come to the hospital. Relax for the rest of the evening. The doctor reported everything appeared to be under control.

Astrade concurred but couldn't relax. He told Dean he'd head to the police station when the prisoner arrived. He hoped nobody called the local news station.

The doctor didn't want snoopy reporters following Hagen to the hospital to scoop out a story. Those newshounds would find out soon enough. They always do.

The police detectives took Angel to the police station after searching his body. They threw him into a holding cell upon arrival at the station. Hagen ordered the desk sergeant to accomplish the booking procedures. The detectives headed back to their office relieved of another stressful situation.

"That deformed killer will get his pro bono lawyer when I'm good and ready to make it happen," Hagen declared to his young associate. "Git off my back."

She started to object. Hagen cut her off.

"Would you rustle us some hot coffee? I have a package of Oreo cookies in my drawer. I'll get 'em for us. It's going to be a long night for both of us."

Eduardo Munoz was sitting on his bed after everyone left. The hospital area became quiet again. He returned to some semblance of normality. A gigantic smile was spread almost from ear to ear.

I did it. I finally did it. I'm now armed with a weapon of mass destruction. They'll surely send reinforcements. He slid Angel Garza's snub-nosed pistol under his pillow.

CHAPTER 54

THE following day Marie Martini and Jorge Vasquez met in Rod's office. They were ecstatic about the capture of a suspected terrorist at Mission Oaks Mental Health hospital last night.

Rod was away from the hospital attending a meeting downtown with a group of other hospital administrators. Bounder was making ward rounds on the wards.

Both the CIA operative and the FBI special agent felt the upper echelon ruled wisely in agreeing to a joint investigation. The heads of each government institution put aside the usual animosity of competing against each other. Domestic terrorism is a larger issue than a single murder of a federal undercover agent. However, there were too many unknowns at this point in the investigation for each party to go their separate ways.

"Let's bury our personal feelings towards each other, Marie, and get this case closed," Vasquez said. "I'm willing to let you take the lead. Your friend and esteemed co-worker Elsie Turk was taken out viciously. You've kept your emotions in check, although you've shared with me that the lady wasn't a close friend."

"Agreed, are you ready to jump in on the red hair issue?"

"What are you talking about, Marie?"

"For the life of me, Vasquez, do I have to teach you Criminology 101 all over again? You should've immediately recalled one obvious fact about the medical examiner. The doctor has in his possession a DNA sample of the red hair Turk snatched from the killer's head!"

"Um . . . yes, I do. I vaguely recall that situation. Oh yeah, they tested your man Bounder to see if he was the murderer. Good fortune for you. He got a free pass on that one."

"What in the world do you mean by the inference, 'he got a free pass,' you bastard?" Marie snapped back at him.

"Sorry, it slipped out of my mouth before I could stop it from running off."

"Good morning folks," Boyd Bounder greeted them. "I was passing by Rod's office on the way back from the upstairs wards and heard my name called."

Neither of them had mentioned Boyd's name. He probably heard the word "bastard" coming from inside the room and interpreted it as "Bounder."

"If you fine investigators need me for anything, I'd be glad to help? I'm thrilled we got that killer behind bars. Eduardo Munoz should get a medal for his courageous actions last night. The proud guy was riding up and down the corridors blowing a bugle. A male orderly yanked it out of his hands, then thanked him for the heroic achievement."

"Thanks, Boyd," Marie said. "We're fine. You got the big job right now, settling down the patients. You told me they reminded you of a cattle herd ready to stampede at the sight of a raging mountain lion. My FBI cohort and I will get this done, won't we Jorge?" Marie was still hot under the collar.

"See you for lunch, Marie," Boyd said. "Feel free to join us, Mr. Vasquez, I'm buying today."

Bounder bid farewell and continued down the hallway whistling a soft tune he'd heard on a radio program driving to work yesterday.

Maria was prepared. "Here's the game plan, Jorge. You get the necessary warrants to have Doctor Juan Pena match hair samples from the killer. Arrange for a team to search the perp's apartment. Oh, excuse me, I meant to say, alleged killer. Have some heavy hitters plunk him in a cold room and interrogate him. Waterboard him if you have to. You better get some answers."

Vasquez was jotting down her instructions on a small notepad. "Maybe we don't need to get a warrant from the judge to test his DNA. I'll get it clarified. Everything we do has to be legitimate–above board. We can't afford any slip-ups."

"Sure, and by the way, Jorge, seeing we don't know his name yet, let's call him 'Crip' for the sake of discussion. I'll contact

Irene Finerty in Chicago and bring her up to date on the latest developments. Maybe she can plug some formulas into her magic computer and spit out a solution."

"What formulas are you talking about?"

"I'll sketch it out for you, wonder boy." She got up and went over to a portable chalkboard in the corner of Rod's office and grabbed some chalk.

She then scribbled on the chalkboard the formula—*nine numbers + red hair genes + Sudoku − Bounder − Ryan / by the social security numbers of Bounder + Ryan + Munoz = killer.*

"Oh, I see clearly," he fibbed. "What a great idea, Marie. I wish I'd thought of that. You CIA folks think outside the proverbial square box, don't you?" he laughed.

I have absolutely no stupid clue what in God's name this little darling is thinking of, but if it works, who gives a shit. Maybe I'll get some of the credit!

CHAPTER 55

"AMFI, we need to get you out of town right away," Juanita Comptos said. They were in Juanita's apartment rehashing the terrible chain of events that would change their lives. "Thanks be to Allah! Someone at the hospital called you last night and alerted you about Angel's capture and arrest. I don't know how they knew he was a friend of yours. Maybe it was a coincidence."

Amfi looked confused, said nothing.

"Dalia hasn't called me yet," Juanita said. "I'm sure when they find out Angel is her brother, she'll be taken into custody. We have to act fast. Use your disposable cell right now and start calling whomever you have to. You need to return to Saudi Arabia right away. We can't afford to compromise our mission—they may break stupid Angel. He's not a hardened radical yet. The infidels secretly torture our soldiers to extract important information from them about our network and future planning scenarios."

"But, what are we going to do about my husband, Juanita? Yousef's not finished with his training. He loves it here, and his instructors rave about how quickly he's absorbing the many intricacies of aerial navigation. He won't leave until he completes his training. He's a difficult one."

Juanita got up and strolled to the window.

"You don't have the slightest clue about the Bedouin mind," Amfi continued. "They're stubborn to the core. They will sacrifice their lives for their friends and what they believe in."

"Hush up, Amfi, this is a much bigger predicament that faces you and your beloved Lieutenant. We are in a holy war! Nothing, I repeat, nothing will interfere with our assigned mission. Get on the phone. Dalia will be coming home from work in three hours. She can't see you here with me. The poor dear is having a relapse. Angel's presence in San Antonio was a positive thing for her. Yet, she's starting to recall the vicious act he perpetrated on her innocent body. I need to get over to his apartment right away and sanitize it."

"What should I tell Dr. Dean and the rest of the staff the reasons for my leaving?" Amfi asked her. "I'm sure they'll want an explanation. They're short of nursing personnel right now."

"Refrain from explaining to anyone. If pressured, tell them you were notified your mother had a massive stroke. She needs you there right away, right? Don't hang around. Get the hell out of here! This shouldn't be a problem. You have royal connections."

"You're right, Juanita, I'll make it happen. But, I'm not going home tonight. Yousef will detect something is amiss. He knows me too well. Can I stay here with you?"

"You absolutely cannot! Get a motel room. Let me know where you're staying. We both have things to accomplish. Let Yousef worry about you for once in his stupid lifetime."

"What about you, Juanita? What are you going to do to avoid being captured if Angel is broken?"

"It's summer. School is out. I'm off until late August. I plan to go back to Mexico for a while until things cool off. I'll notify Muhammad in Houston. We'll shut down until further notice."

"Don't forget about the items we've accumulated in the storage shed. They're all important to us."

Juanita laughed. "Good thinking, my friend. I'll get the key when I go over to Angel's apartment. He has it hanging to a key hook on the rear of the front closet door. As far as I'm concerned, we'll leave the stowed gear in the storage shed. It should be safe there. We will, I repeat, we will succeed on our holy mission. Nothing will stop us, even with Angel taken out of the picture."

They hugged each other and Amfi left. Juanita jumped in her car and headed over to Angel's apartment. She hoped she wasn't too late.

She arrived in Angel's neighborhood and circled the block three times. It was a mandated practice to rule out any suspicious activity. Juanita then parked a block away. She entered his apartment and checked for the key. It was missing. *He better have it on his person!* She knew Angel had a long slit hidden in his belt. He kept up to three keys and a one-hundred-dollar bill.

His apartment was almost bare of furniture. He slept on his prayer rug on the corner floor of the bedroom. A beat-up bathroom cabinet was sitting under a partially-opened window.

Juanita opened every closet door in the small apartment and then searched through the cabinet drawers. She only found the Quran and two dispatches from Mashudan. She scanned them rapidly. *Nothing new here.* She shoved them in her purse.

The notes from Mashudan to Angel surfaced some memories of her recent past. She remembered each challenge in her rigorous training in Afghanistan. A pledge had been made. She swore she'd never again undergo such a humiliating experience. Her male cadre pushed her without mercy because she was a Mexican, and a woman.

Juanita stowed the Quran and the prayer rug in the trunk of her car and sped off. She saw two MPD cruisers pass her while she turned the corner and pull up in front of Angel's apartment.

"Praise be to Allah," she screamed out loud. It was time to get out of there.

CHAPTER 56

ROD'S meeting with the other hospital administrators ended on good terms. Everyone was excited that a suspect in the murder of the CIA agent was now in custody. The local newspaper carried extensive stories about the arrest of the terrorist.

The administrators formalized their central purchasing agreement. The All Saints Medical Center was tasked as the lead agent. All agreed they had the best track record on buying needed services for their facility.

The group also reviewed the central laundry expenses. The system was saving them at least twenty percent on their laundry costs. Quite noticeable to the group was the reduction of stolen sheets and towels from each facility. One negative, however, was the drawdown of employees from established staffing quotas. The departure of proven talent created morale problems.

"So, you finally got your degree, huh Richards? What did Doctor Dean do, slip the Provost at the university a folded grand under the table?"

The administrator from the Rhodes Hospital was a former infantryman in Southeast Asia and fought in the Mekong Delta. He wore two purple hearts and walked with a noticeable limp. The GI Bill also served him well. They had much in common.

"Go to . . . you know where, Dutchman, I paid my dues long ago," Rod pointed at the big blond still wearing an outdated flattop on his wrinkled head.

"Oh, how cold," Dutchman cried. "I'm told by a reliable source you showed up at the University of Michigan wearing a dented steel pot and dragging muddy combat boots on their polished floors. It's no wonder they tripped over each other rushing to your side before graduation. Those professors couldn't wait to hand you the master's degree on a silver platter."

The group bantered back and forth for several minutes and then adjourned.

Rod headed back to the hospital. He wondered how the criminal investigation was going. Thank God he wasn't involved in that mess. He had enough issues on his plate to worry about. Harry Mooney finally agreed to sell his shares of the corporation to doctors Dean and Smyth.

Mooney wanted that stupid zoo he called an office, to be converted to a large museum. *It's not going to happen. I'm planning to use the space for a multi-media room for staff conferences and employee training.*

He urged Dean to appoint two non-medical community leaders to the board of directors. He felt there was too much "medicalese" on the current board. Medical professionals seem to have tunnel vision on too many administrative initiatives. Community leaders would lend much credibility to the hospital and enhance its image in the community. They become un-salaried, part-time marketers for the hospital.

"Howdy, Rod," Boyd said as he stuck his head in the doorway. "Have you heard the latest news about the investigation?"

"Sure haven't. How 'bout bringing me up to date."

"Marie called from the police department. It seems the murderer is one of those radical Islamic terrorists. The interrogating detectives played tag-team around the clock and wore the perp out. He spilled his guts. You wouldn't believe the amount of information they pulled from him. I was shocked."

"Now, that's what I call making some major headway, Boyd. Did they waterboard him?"

"Nobody knows or is willing to tell how they extracted the information from him. The key here is they have something tangible to work with. It could save historical properties and human life."

"This is getting interesting. What else did she tell you?" Rod relished the information—at last, great news for the hospital.

"They found one of those storage stall keys hidden inside his belt and some money. The young fool never scratched off the number of the unit. Somehow or other, they were able to match that key number to a specific rental business near where he lived.

"What did that lead to?"

"The team raced over and woke up the manager. He couldn't find the extra key on file and broke into the shed. The officials found detailed architectural plans of the Alamo, the Tower of the Americas, and the terminals at the San Antonio International Airport. They had gained enough evidence to conclude a devastating terrorist act was being planned."

"Good gracious." Rod was stunned.

"You won't believe this," Boyd continued, "But one of the boxes stacked in the far corner of the storage shed still had a shipping ticket taped to the back of the box. It was shipped from an address in a Houston suburb. The FBI office in Houston was notified. They traced it to another terrorist who served as the explosive expert. They have high hopes the last team member in the cell was discovered. He's behind bars as we speak."

"Did they pry loose any more useful information?" He knew Bounder had been briefed by Marie but wasn't sure how much detail she passed on to him.

"They ain't getting more information from the guy. He's dead!"

"What do you mean dead, Boyd? Did the waterboarding scheme kill him?"

"No. The guy hung himself in his cell. The detectives were using another room to question him. The regular interrogation room was being painted and temporarily out of service. Team members brought in one of those portable floor lamps because the substitute room had inadequate lighting. They needed a long extension cord to reach the only electrical outlet in the place. It had been used as a large storage room and had no windows."

"Okay, so what happened?" Rod pushed him to go on further.

"All but one officer left the room after the team finished their barrage of questioning. They had told the remaining policeman to escort the handcuffed perp back to his cell. The perp and the uniform headed for the opened door as the uniform got a call on his cell phone. It's alleged he turned his back on the prisoner for only a brief second. The floor lamp had been turned off. There was adequate light coming in from the hallway."

"For Pete's sake, Mr. Head Nurse, are you writing a book on the entire killing drama? Please get on with it! I've plenty of work yet to hammer out today. How the hell did the terrorist die?"

Boyd let out a big sigh. "There's still some conjecture in the report Marie read about the exact sequence of events. Authorities maintain the bad guy quietly and with speed jerked the electric extension cord from the wall electrical socket and shoved it into his jail pants' waistline. The officer clicked off the cell phone, turned around, and led the perp back to his cell. He took the cuffs off the prisoner and shoved him into his cell."

"Whoa," Rod shouted. "I think I know what's coming down the verbal pike. It ain't going to be good."

Boyd ignored the comment and continued. "It was during evening rounds of the jail when the officials found the terrorist dangling from an exposed ceiling water pipe. The extension cord was secured around his broken neck. We concluded he used the toilet top to climb up and secure the cord to the pipe. It provided him the necessary platform for his death leap."

"Why did the interrogation team leave the prisoner alone with an inexperienced cop?"

"That's currently under investigation," Boyd stated as he concluded his lengthy report.

"Wonderful, that's some story," Rod whistled. "Have they found any accomplices? Have they determined if the terrorist cell is operating in San Antonio or somewhere else in Bexar County? These radicals often find an isolated farm or dilapidated home far from an urban area to use as their headquarters. Security and secrecy are mandated for such campaigns."

"Hold on, my man, I can't answer all those questions. But I learned more details about the plot."

"Please go on. Don't leave me hanging in mid-air!"

"Sure enough. Marie told me they think one of our nurses might be involved. Nurse Amfi bin Aziz didn't show up for work yesterday or today. Naturally, I was concerned. I had to juggle our staff to ensure that we had adequate nursing coverage. Her husband told us she hasn't been home for several days. Either Marie or that FBI agent whose name I can't remember got a head's up about Aziz."

"Did Dalia show up for work?" Rod asked. "I'm very concerned about her."

"That's the strange part. She didn't show up either. Will you check on her for me?" Maybe Marie has the answer, but she's been busy today."

"Why not? I'll do that. Are the cops after Aziz?"

"Yes indeed. The MPD is putting out an APB on her as we speak. They're checking every means of public transportation that leads into and out of the city. They'll get a location on her pretty soon. Marie is convinced of it."

"What's her next step?"

"She and Jorge Vasquez are trying to develop the exact sequence of events that happened the night of the murder. They're pretty adept at this sort of thing. The government sleuths won't neglect even the slightest unanswered question."

"Yeah, I don't doubt that."

Bounder continued. "I learned there are four major issues that continue to bother them. How valid is Eduardo Munoz's testimony regarding the night of the murder? Was Nick Ryan involved in the actual murder? Is he an active member of the radical cell that's operating in our city? And the final issue is directed at the Chicago criminologist. Is she willing to admit now that more detailed facts have surfaced in the investigation to draw a conclusion?"

"I can't think of any more pieces needing to surface," Rod laughed. "I'm a simple man for all seasons!"

"I've got to run," Bounder said. "Munoz is being examined by a forensic psychiatrist from Dallas at the request of Dr. Dean. He wants me to sit in on the session. I guess he wants me to give Eduardo some moral support."

"That's a great idea."

"Dean is concerned Munoz might be riding one of his many fantasizing trips again," Boyd said. "They intend to bring in

MURDER IN A SAN ANTONIO PSYCH HOSPITAL

another psychiatrist who teaches at the UT Health Science Center Medical School. The local professional has worked with Chief Astrade in the past. That collection of esteemed brains should be able to validate Munoz's story—or possibly generate a new one."

Boyd left, anxious for the Munoz interview.

Rod sat back in his chair. He raised his feet and plunked them on a wastebasket. He wondered why he ever got involved with this odd collection of human beings, all working under one roof. Destiny? Maybe a new and rewarding calling.

He thought again about his night with Keena. She keeps surfacing in and out of his busy mind, somehow weaving through the myriad of nerve cells clogging his brain.

I wonder what drove her to become a hairdresser. I fail to understand what makes that goofy lady tick. I'm too deep into her now to write it off as one big carnal achievement. What would a sane man think? But then again—!

CHAPTER 57

WITH all the excitement and turmoil going on at the hospital, Rod worried about Dalia, and why she hadn't shown up for work. He picked up the phone and dialed her home number. Surprisingly, she answered immediately, instead of that mean-spirited lady who covered for her all the time.

"Hello, Dalia, this is Rod Richards. How are you doing? I haven't seen you around the hospital today. You haven't been at work, and Boyd asked me to find you. We need to know if everything's alright?"

"Oh, Rod, is this you in person?" Dalia Garza was weeping into the telephone. She was upset and welcomed his call.

"Yes, it's me. What's wrong with you Dalia?"

"Juanita took off. She left me a note, said she had to go to Canada right away. It seems her mother was on a cruise to Alaska and had a massive heart attack. They took her off the ship in Vancouver. Her father is incapacitated, and there aren't any relatives available to help her. She loved her mother deeply."

Dalia began to cry harder. He had no clue about Juanita's family background or current status, nor did he care.

"Do you want me to stop by your place?" Rod asked her. "I'm finishing up here at the hospital."

"Yes, please come right away. I don't know what to do, Rod. I'm so confused right now. I haven't seen my brother for several days. Where is he off to now? I wonder if he was in an accident. He drives that motorbike around like he's in some kind of fatalistic road rally. He doesn't even wear a helmet."

Dalia was hysterical by this time.

Rod was concerned. "I'll be over as soon as possible. You need to sit down for a while and take several deep breaths. Put the teapot on the stove. We'll sip some hot tea and figure things out, okay?" *I didn't know she had a brother.*

There were two MPD cars parked out front when he pulled up to her home. One officer forgot to turn off his blaring siren.

The other car had both rear doors swung wide open. It appeared to him they sped over here, converged on the house, and kicked in her front door.

Neighbors were pouring out of their homes like worker ants exiting their disturbed mound. They scurried to see what was going on in this normally quiet corner of the neighborhood.

His first impulse was to run up to her wide-opened front door and ring the doorbell. Maybe somebody tried to murder her, or hopefully, something less drastic happened–like a simple break-in. He pulled the car into her empty driveway after mind-wrestling with a course of action. He forgot to carry his cell phone in his hasty departure to get there. He probably would've called her from the car.

He questioned whether he should distance himself from the neighborhood. Things didn't look right to him. He decided to rush into her house and find out what was going on. She obviously needed him. He wouldn't disappoint her now.

Rod jumped from the car and raced to the opened door.

The last thing he remembered before he hit the floor in a sea of whirling bright lights charging through his stunned brain, was that somebody, maybe a midget, was gaping at him in sheer delight.

CHAPTER 58

DOCTOR Juan Pena was briefing the County Sheriff on his take regarding the status of the terrorist murder investigation. The sheriff had no actual role or jurisdiction in the case. Pena felt for political reasons the sheriff should be read in on the facts and circumstances. Pena received a call from Marie Martini while they were knocking down a pitcher of margaritas at the Cantina Classica.

"Good afternoon, doctor, this is Marie from the CIA. Your secretary told me you were at an important staff meeting. She gave me your cell number anyway. I haven't heard from you of late and need to follow up on several issues. Can you spare a minute?"

"Of course, young lady, shoot. By the way, how's your part of the investigation going? We've completed the autopsy on that young man who'd hung himself in the jail. What a way to go, huh?"

"Yes and no," Marie countered. "The good news is that another terrorist has been taken out and a major catastrophe averted, at least for the time being. We have some interesting information he 'offered' just before he hung himself."

"That happens once in a while, ah, in our line of creepy business," he laughed.

Marie ignored the sarcasm and continued. "The bad news is we weren't able to learn much about his organization, nor any future plans to cripple America. He was a low-level operative. The perp had limited knowledge of the big picture."

"By the way, what's the deceased's full name and address?" Pena asked. "We'll need this information before we can close the autopsy case files on him."

"We've obtained demographic information on him with the help of the FBI and other federal agencies. His official name is Angel Garza, born in Matamoros, Mexico. Angel is the older brother of Nurse Dalia Garza. She works at Mission Oaks Mental

Health Hospital. His parents were migrant farm workers. We don't have a legitimate age for him. Official records and related documentation had been purged from his records at the municipal courthouse in Matamoros. We have an idea why, and by whom."

"I heard the Alamo was targeted for destruction," Pena said.

"Yes, that's what we got this far in our probe. We don't know if there are more religious zealots still operating in our city. Our folks are tracing additional leads as we speak. Did you find out anything of value for us during the autopsy?"

"Not a thing, Marie. We're still waiting for the toxicology screens to come back. The young man had an athletic body. He appeared to have overcome his handicapping condition. The wrist on the hand of his shriveled arm was broken. All we can piece together from the information the MPD provided us is the injury that happened in the hospital room. No need to put a cast on it now."

"I'm concerned about fingerprints and hair follicles, my good doctor. Did the investigators find any prints on the scissors? How about prints anywhere else in the hospital dayroom?"

"Not his, Marie. He must've been gloved."

"How about the hair follicles? Did the DNA screen show anything? This is crucial information for us."

"Yes, my dear. The red strands of hair poor Elsie Turk snatched from Angel Garza's head were a perfect match. They belonged to him. She damn near yanked his scalp off, at least judging from the placement of the loose vertebra supporting his neck. The condition is recent, best we can tell. My testimony will stand up in court. It'll support the fact he killed her."

Marie relaxed. "Well, this guy believed he'd be enjoying the company of sweet young virgins. The murderer won't be sitting before an overzealous jury deciding his guilt or innocence. Think of the time, energy, and expense we've saved by his own hand."

"Call me if you need anything further, Miss Martini. I'll let you know if I find anything of worth after I receive that toxicology report. I'm not sure what good it'll do at this stage of the game. The guy's dead. What more do you want?"

"There are always more facts hanging around in murder cases. Good investigators don't always put the cases to sleep just because the main suspect is put in jail."

"Oh, I forgot one more thing that may or may not be of significance to you."

Marie perked up.

"The position of the scissors buried in the front of her torso led us to believe the killer snuck up from behind her. He would've swung the weapon over her head and into the chest."

"Really?"

"Yes indeed. Also, we concluded he was right-handed because of the angle it entered her body. We're sure it wasn't a frontal assault. She couldn't see it coming until the last moment. We're sure she didn't recognize the person who killed her. If it came from the front, Turk would've grabbed the scissors and lacerated her fingers. Maybe her whole hand. There was no evidence of that. The pooled blood came from her chest."

"Thank you, doctor. That added fact will be helpful when we put together the sequence of events that happened the night of the murder."

Marie called Vasquez later that day. "We need to get our heads together and share the information we've gained thus far. I now have several important questions answered. How're you doing on your end?"

"Fine, Marie. Are you interested in catching some pea soup over at Schermer's? I'm beyond starving and need a break. How about meeting me there in twenty minutes? I'm sure you've been to Schermer's before. I'd bet money Mr. Bounder introduced you to one of our more popular downtown deli's."

"Um, I don't remember that he did. Anyway, that sounds good to me. Where's Schermer's?"

CHAPTER 59

ROD Richards recovered from the uninvited head conk and gazed up in shock at the officer holding the big black nightstick. The short male policeman was smiling at his newest conquest scrambling to stand up. The uniform had been hiding behind the front door guarding the entryway when Rod raced into Dalia's house. His scrambled brain ordered both eyes to return to focus. He wondered how long he was knocked out.

"Shake it up, buddy, and give me your wrists right now," the male officer ordered.

Shorty slapped a pair of cuffs on Rod and escorted him to the couch. He ordered him to sit down. Rod didn't see Dalia anywhere after a brief scan of the house. *Where'd they take her?*

He couldn't hear anything either. Maybe the huge swelling goose egg above his right ear was the cause of the hearing loss. He stood up and grabbed the back of a chair to steady himself.

Rod stared in anger at the little guy who must've had a height exemption to enter the police academy. The uniform had a head the size of a watermelon. His service hat was propped on top of his head like a golf ball sitting on a tee. It was obvious he enjoyed being in total control of someone.

"Whatta ya staring at, mister?" the cop asked.

Rod didn't respond. He was still trying to clear his mind and regain full hearing. He'd been cold-cocked in the past. The sequence for semi-conscious to realty had a definite code of behavior.

There was a loud commotion coming from the direction of the backyard. All of a sudden, a hysterical Dalia appeared in the kitchen. A tall black female officer was standing next to her. A ruddy-faced detective staggered in behind them. Rod assumed he was a detective. The man wasn't wearing a uniform. To his misfortune, it wasn't Lt. Hagen. He'd never seen this officer before.

The female officer was intimidating giving all the commands. This woman could have been wearing another uniform–that of a Dallas Cowboy football player–probably a defensive tackle!

"Sit down on the couch," she ordered Dalia. "Trying to run away from us wasn't the smartest thing to do under your set of circumstances, young lady."

"It looks as though we've hit the jackpot here, Officer Randolph," she said in a triumphant tone looking down at the shorter policeman. "I'll call the station and alert them we have two terrorist suspects on the way over for booking."

"Hold on one damn minute, officers!" Rod shouted to the law enforcement team now surrounding him. "We're not terrorists by any stretch of your collective imaginations. I haven't the slightest idea where you got your information. We're both U.S. citizens and work at Mission Oaks Mental Health Hospital. Call your chief of police, right now! He knows both of us. We're not leaving this house until you speak to him!"

"Keep quiet, mister, or else!" the male officer threatened.

Rod kept assuring them they weren't the bad guys.

Officer Randolph tapped Rod on the other side of his sore head with the big stick. "Look here, mister, he said again with more emphasis, who the fuck do you think you're talking to? It's about time you showed us some respect."

"My name is Rod Richards," he shot back at Randolph. "I told you before, we're not who you think we are . . . for God's sake."

He'd had all he could take from these authority figures dressed in blue. He was boiling hot and had a difficult time holding his tongue. Dalia was in a daze, crying, and mumbling incoherent phrases.

The black female officer placed both hands on her gigantic hips and shot a vicious stare at Rod. It would've dropped a mule. She drew her service revolver and shook it at him. One huge mitt was enough to envelop the weapon. It looked like a kid's squirt gun hiding in the back of her hand.

"Mr. Richards, your ass belongs to me now. I could holster this gun and squeeze that chicken neck of yours so hard your head would pop off like a festered pimple. Or, you can just seal that motor mouth of yours and listen to me once and for all. Do you understand me?"

Rod elected not to respond to her. He'd get shot down before he uttered ten words.

Dalia remained silent throughout the bantering back and forth. She appreciated his being here and defending her from these ridiculous cops. Juanita wasn't here to help her. She felt close to him. He was her only friend now. She'd been trying to reach out to him for friendship and support, as she cooled her relationship with Juanita.

The other accompanying male law enforcement officer with a ruddy face finally spoke up. Rod was impressed. At least this man seemed to know what was going on here. He stepped in front of the female officer and turned to Officer Randolph. "Read them their rights."

Shorty stumbled halfway through the Miranda verbiage. He gazed back and forth at Rod, then Dalia. He wondered if they were listening to him.

The phone clipped to the female officer's service belt suddenly began to ring. She crammed her pistol back in its holster and spoke to the caller for several long minutes, uttering, yes sir–no sir, four times.

"What's up?" Shorty asked her.

"The boss said to uncuff them and bring 'em back to the station right away. He didn't think they were terrorists based on some quick calls he made. Let's get going."

Several reporters and television crew members greeted them with a string of questions as they stepped outside. Shorty kept pushing Dalia from behind. The black police officer was prodding Rod to hurry up and climb in the back seat of the squad car. The detective followed. A smile emerged from his opened mouth.

A large crowd had gathered around the TV trucks parked behind Rod's car in the driveway. The detective put his hand over the microphone jammed in his face by a cute, but aggressive reporter from one of the local stations.

"Please, everyone, go home!" the detective urged them. "I can only tell you this. We've had an anonymous caller report a domestic disturbance at this address. My team defused it. We're taking the couple in for further questioning. They told us about drug dealers soliciting in your neighborhood. I've nothing more to report to you at this time. Thank you and please make way for us."

Chief Jesus Astrade was waiting for them in the main hallway when they arrived at the police station. "I'm so sorry, Rod, please forgive us. We acted on a call from the FBI to send a unit to Dalia's house. They uncovered evidence that a radical Islamic group was using the location for one of their operational bases in the city. We had no clue what to expect."

"Oh my God," Dalia shouted. "What are you talking about? My close childhood friend Juanita Comptos and I live there alone. There aren't terrorists living with us. I can't believe this! Juanita is a school nurse. You know where I work, Chief Astrade. How in the world could anyone believe we're those kinds of bad people?"

"Come over here and sit down for a few minutes," the chief urged Rod and Dalia. "Officer Randolph, please round up several bottles of water for our guests."

The detective and the female officer excused themselves. They'd been compliant. Both left the room without glancing back at Astrade.

"Dalia, where is Juanita right now?" the chief asked. "We need to talk to her—the sooner the better." He was trying to assist CIA Agent Martini in hunting down the other suspects in the terrorist plot. Dalia remained the last bastion of hope in locating Juanita.

Rod answered for Dalia. "Juanita had an emergency call from Canada that her mom had suffered a heart attack while on a cruise to Alaska. She flew up there a few days ago to be with her. At least that's what she'd told Dalia."

"I know this will come as a complete shock to you, Dalia," the chief said in a soft voice. "We suspect she might be tied in with a local radical Islamic group planning a major attack in the Alamo City."

Dalia Garza was stunned at the chief's accusations.

This is so overwhelming. I never suspected anything. Had Juanita changed when Angel came to town? Was my brother also involved in this terrible plot?

"Rod, please take me home now," she pleaded with him in a shaky voice. "I'm not in the proper right frame of mind to be grilled by the police."

Recognizing her instability and emotions, the chief ordered a cruiser to bring both of them back to Dalia's home. He told Dalia not to leave the city. They'd planned to talk to her again.

"Get those two officers and the detective back here," Astrade directed the desk sergeant stationed near the front entrance. "I want them standing tall in front of me this very minute!"

The chief was highly disappointed with the actions of some of his uniformed personnel during the lengthy murder investigation. There had been some initial confusion in determining how his department would interface with the two federal agencies. He ran a well-respected police force. The MPD was recently recognized by the Federal Bureau of Investigation as one of the most effective law enforcement agencies in the country.

Astrade had received feelers f1rom officials in both Chicago and Philadelphia regarding his availability and desire to head up their respective police departments. The hard-working lawman preferred to serve his hometown residents. After serious consideration, he politely passed on the generous opportunities presented to him.

Dalia asked Rod to spend the night with her after the police car dropped them off at her home.

CHAPTER 60

INTERSTATE 35 from San Antonio to Austin was one hell of a big mess. An eighteen-wheeler hauling a load of Rhode Island Reds was lying on its side next to a huge culvert. The cab had disengaged from the unit and hung gingerly from a bridge railing.

Several dozen chickens were picking their way out of the ditch they were thrown into. Emergency flares were spaced strategically along the north highway lanes. Passenger vehicles and other motorized units could continue north at a slower pace. At least traffic was moving.

Marie Martini couldn't believe the large number of heavy transport vehicles that rolled down each side of the freeway, so far south in the United States. Most Californians had no idea of the extensive commerce that took place in Texas, especially in South Texas.

It was early morning dark outside. Marie was en route to Waco, Texas, for an important rendezvous. She'd went into great detail discussing everything with Boyd the previous evening. He needed to know all the facts.

"Honey, I've been summoned to Waco to meet a group of fellow CIA operatives for a planning session. The subject involved possible radical terrorist threats in the entire Southwest."

"Do I need to be worried?"

"Boyd Bounder, you have no need to fret. This is routine work in my line of business."

Marie had been summoned to a meeting with three special agents from the Dallas field office. Langley's assets intercepted four highly classified communications emanating from the Saudi Arabia embassy in Washington. An embassy courier jet was directed to pick up a "special package" at a little-used commercial airstrip east of Waco. CIA analysts determined that information based on other scattered intelligence bits. The package in question might be the Saudi nurse who worked at a mental hospital in San Antonio.

Earlier, Langley had contacted Marie to locate the nurse. Amfi was not at Mission Oaks Hospital or in the city. Marie had advised her supe-

riors the Saudi nurse might be on the run. Thus, the trip to Waco was organized. Now Boyd had the big picture.

Dawn broke through dark clouds as she passed Temple, Texas. Traffic was light, but a group of happy motorcyclists buzzed by her in a big hurry. None of them were wearing helmets.

She stopped at a Starbucks to slug down a double-tall latte, a strong coffee concoction with steamed milk to maintain her stepped-up adrenalin flow. Her Sig Sauer 9mm pistol was strapped to the hidden waist holster. Boyd had acquiesced and gave it back to her when Richards had become the administrator. She was overdue for some meaningful action and couldn't wait for all hell to break loose. This is what she was trained for!

Two teams of three special agents were tasked with this important mission. **Team Alpha** met Marie at a highway rest area south of Waco. The black Suburban with government license plates, driven by the Dallas-based team, was parked at the far end of the rest stop.

She pulled in next to their big vehicle, got out, and climbed into the back seat. "Hi, I'm Special Agent Marie Martini from San Antonio. I'm glad to finally meet up with you gentlemen. We've had numerous phone conversations to put this together."

The three men introduced themselves to Marie. She remembered working a case with one agent a few years before she shipped off to Bahrain. They had teamed up to take out a known Libyan exterminator in Washington, D.C. Marie told the agent-in-charge she was ready for some big-time dogfights. He looked at the other agent who had worked with her in the past and gave him a—*this lady is for real* body language gesture.

They'd mapped out their strategy over secured phone lines. After leaving the rest area, **Team Alpha** would proceed to a huge unoccupied maintenance building south of the main runway. It was located five hundred yards from a small passenger terminal.

Team Bravo of the CIA task force had been sent several hours earlier to reconnoiter the entire airfield. Their mission was to decide which maintenance building would serve as the primary site for both teams to begin operations.

From intelligence info passed on from Langley, the "special package" was to be delivered to the airfield passenger station at dusk on their arrival day. The agent's downtime would give them a period to relax and rehearse their plan.

Team Alpha leader opened the discussion. "Our team will initiate the snatch as fast as Marie is able to make a positive identification of Aziz. We'll kill the Muslim bodyguards and abduct her after they arrive inside the terminal. All conditions must be perfect. I was given specific instructions from Langley to take her alive at all costs."

"What do we do after we collect her?" Marie asked. She had forgotten that part of the plan in her excitement to return to action.

"We'll all return to the rest area where we first met. Your mission is completed at that point. You'll be free to return to San Antonio. We'll take the captured Amfi bin Aziz back to Dallas for further interrogation and processing."

Team Bravo relocated to a large tool shed left of the passenger terminal several hours before dusk. They were assigned the mission of capturing the vehicle that transported Amfi to the passenger terminal.

They had discussed several contingencies. If the delivering vehicle raced out of the immediate area upon hearing gunshots, the team would allow the driver to proceed about one mile. They'd pursue the terrorists at that point. The team would "pinch" the fleeing vehicle between them, and a roadblock set up by the local sheriff. Back-up would be provided by a squad of Texas Rangers.

They'd take them down immediately if the vehicle remained behind to collect the other terrorists after delivering Aziz to the plane–no questions asked–no Miranda options given.

A white van approached the passenger terminal shortly before dark. The van parked in front of the facility. Amfi and two tall, bearded men emptied out of the rear of the van. They entered the empty and dimly lit passenger terminal. Marie used her night scope to ID Aziz walking between her bodyguards. The team members breathed a sigh of relief.

The two CIA teams were in constant communication with each other. **Team Bravo** had visual contact with the passenger terminal.

"Hold tight on your position," **Team Bravo** leader ordered the other team, "We don't like the setup for a takedown inside the terminal. Wait until the terrorist group heads for the runway before you confront them. No use alerting them till we can get 'em all."

"Roger that," **Team Alpha** leader responded, "Better to take them in the open, provided we have enough background light to see them. I'm confident the weather gods are on our side."

A small jet aircraft began its final approach fifteen minutes after the terrorist group entered the terminal. The runway lights had been switched on minutes before the aircraft arrived. The entire area was illuminated. The terrorists spilled out of the terminal and headed to the nearest runway to await the descending plane.

"It's time to go," **Team Alpha** leader ordered as they saw Amfi with her two accomplices run into the open. Earlier, they had repositioned themselves away from the maintenance building to a secluded vantage point next to the runway fence line. The team raced after them and began to close the distance to the terrorists.

"Halt or we'll shoot," the team leader shouted at the scurrying radicals. "We've got you surrounded," he lied, hoping they'd stop in their tracks.

The terrorists ignored the order and kept running. Amfi was lagging behind. She was unable to maintain the speed of the faster men.

Marie was in the lead, sprinting ahead toward Amfi when **Team Alpha** began firing at the enemy. ZAP, ZAP, ZAP! Amfi pulled away from her bodyguards in a state of confusion. She sped back toward the terminal building. The poor woman was caught in a cross-fire between the accompanying bodyguards and the CIA pursuit team.

Martini caught up with the Saudi nurse and ankle-tackled her to the ground. She hardly felt the incoming round strike her in the upper leg when they both hit the tarmac. At the same time, Amfi was gagging and bleeding profusely from a wound in her chest area.

"Amfi, Amfi," Marie shouted. "I'm going to help you. First, tell me who sent you here for the flight. Give me the name of your point of contact back in San Antonio."

"I . . . ah . . . am hurting so bad," Amfi cried as she clutched her chest with both hands. She screamed when she withdrew her hands and saw the hot stickiness covering them. Blood was everywhere. Marie compressed both fists into Amfi's chest trying to halt the flow.

"Kill me. Please kill me right now," she pleaded faintly as she looked up at Marie.

"Hold on, Amfi, please hold on. Help is coming. One of our team members is a doctor."

The surprised terrorist group only possessed handguns. They were rapidly felled by the heavy automatic weapons carried by the special agents. BAM, BAM, BAM!

The approaching jet had been maneuvering to touch down on the runway when the pilot witnessed the intense battle taking place below. He aborted the landing. The small plane shot skyward, soon out of sight.

The white van driver who'd delivered the terrorist group to the terminal heard automatic weapon fire from the direction of the airstrip. He sped away in a frenzy.

They were caught in **Team Bravo's** trap within minutes after the van's departure. Local law enforcement agencies assisted in the mission. The terrorists in the van decided to make a stand. They were outgunned and outnumbered. The extremists were shot numerous times with high-powered rifles and lay strewn on the bloody pavement.

Back at the runway, one of **Team Alpha** agents who served as the team medic knelt next to the wounded nurse. He was quick to assess the situation, glancing first at Marie, and then at Amfi.

"Is she going to make it?" Marie asked.

"I sure as hell hope so." He then turned his attention back to the bleeding Saudi nurse. "We were ordered to take her alive."

The medic ripped Amfi's blouse open and applied a wadded gauze with heavy pressure to the bullet wounds in an attempt to stop the bleeding. Three gaping holes in the chest were oozing blood faster than the medic could arrest the bleeding. Amfi teetered back and forth between alertness and unconsciousness. She died grasping his blood-spattered arm.

"Here, let me take a look at you, Agent Martini," he said after he disengaged from the dead Amfi. "Looks like you stopped one of their bullets. They were flying around non-stop. "

"I'm fine . . . compared to her. I'll live to fight another day."

The round that kissed her leg resulted in a minor flesh wound, missing her femoral bone and artery by a wide margin. The medic cut an opening in her slacks, dabbed in some disinfectant, and slapped a bandage on her leg.

"That'll hold you till you get back home," he assured her. "It could've been much worse than a small wound. The good Lord was with you on this one, Marie."

Team Alpha bypassed the other team and took a different route back to the rest area where Marie's car was parked. The decision was made to take Amfi's remains back to Dallas. The CIA Field office was better equipped to handle the fallout that would occur.

Team Bravo was tasked with hauling the bodies of the other dead terrorists back to Dallas. The corpses were loaded in the rear of the large CIA panel truck. It motored out of the area.

The local law enforcement officers stayed behind to clean up the bloody mess and collect the shell casings.

Marie checked her wounded leg before she headed back to San Antonio. There was no evidence of further oozing. She felt relieved in the absence of any major pain coming from the minor wound. Her left elbow bothered her more than the gunshot wound. She'd jammed it when hitting the hard runway surface with Amfi.

Marie pulled out her Sig Sauer and inspected it as she was heading south back down Interstate 35. She sniffed the open end of the barrel. Not a single powerful round had been fired from the weapon.

Oh, damn it, damn it! Caught in the middle of a raging gun battle but shut out again. I might as well turn in my weapon and petition to become a glorified desk jockey.

CHAPTER 61

"HOW does your thick pea soup taste, Marie?" Jorge Vasquez asked. *Just being nice to her. I don't give two hoots about the stupid soup. Not spicy enough. She's a beltway bandit, Not prone to visit old eating places.*

They were sitting at a table near the front door of Schermer's on Market Street. Marie was still thinking about the Torch of Friendship monument she passed on the way to Schermer's. Both thought it was an unusual gift from the Mexican government to commemorate their relationship with the United States.

"Oh, it tastes okay, I guess." She hated both bean and pea soup They made her gassy. She forgot to shove some Beano pills in her purse before she'd left. Marie figured she'd eat it anyway. She knew it was a healthy choice.

The thick soup was a house special. All the locals rave about it. The Reuben sandwich was "out of this world." However, the sauerkraut in the sandwich which was allied with the pea soup might make everyone around her unhappy later today.

Vasquez took the time to congratulate her on the Waco mission. "I heard you got shot."

"Just a nick in the thigh. I went to one of those 'Doc in the Boxes' and flashed my credentials. I told them not to notify the MPD. They sewed a few stitches in my leg and gave me a tetanus shot. I was sent home with some extra-strength Tylenol. Boyd went ballistic. He insisted I resign from the CIA. You'd think I lost the damn leg."

"You're a tough woman, Marie. I'm glad it worked out."

Marie took out a bulky manila folder from her briefcase when they finished eating. She paged through numerous files and pulled out a brief labeled *For Your Eyes Only.* Meanwhile, Jorge hightailed over to view the attractive dessert offerings. He came back empty-handed.

"Let's talk business," she said.

"Got it," he replied and flipped open a notebook. He fingered through a dozen pages until he found what he wanted. Marie sneaked a peek at the tablet. She wondered how he could ever interpret the hieroglyphics scribbled on each page. His handwriting was worse than any physician progress notes jotted in her medical records. She referred to them many times.

"Yesterday morning I spoke with our esteemed Chicago associate Irene Finerty," Marie began. "She reviewed in great detail everything we passed on to her. It didn't take long for her to decide Elsie Turk was murdered by the Jihadist who hung himself in jail."

Jorge finished his soup and let her continue the summary.

"The terrorist stabbed Elsie from behind with his right hand. His left arm was deformed if you recall. The angle of the impaled weapon came in from behind Elsie and from the right. He was a redhead. The medical examiner matched his hair sample with that cluster found underneath Elsie's fingernails."

"What about Nick Ryan," Jorge asked? "Wasn't the patient your number one suspect?"

She took a minute to reflect on the case. "Finerty concluded the nine numbers etched in her blood identified someone she'd been in contact with being a Sudoku fanatic–perhaps the killer. You know what I'm referring to, don't you? It's that ludicrous numbers puzzle that nobody can put down until they solve it. We got confirmation from the hospital staff that Ryan was addicted to Sudoku's."

"So, what about Ryan?"

"Roberta Peck told us Ryan provided her and Turk numerous newspapers to cut out designs for their scrapbooking. We went to the arts and crafts room and tore apart those scrapbooks. There were many completed Sudokus on the pasted side of the pages."

"Okay, so how does that clear Ryan?" Jorge asked with a quizzical look on his face. "I presume this is where you had mixed feelings."

She didn't respond to his question. He was getting impatient.

266

"I'll get to that. We grilled Eduardo Munoz numerous times about what he saw in the day room the night of the murder. We came at him from several different directions. Every response he gave us was consistent with the previous ones we'd interrogated him on."

"That gross freak of nature!" Vasquez remarked. "I wouldn't trust one thing that crackpot reported to me. I learned he develops and plays out 'cops and robbers' scenarios. A crippled-up murderer would make a great play."

"Hold on there, Mr. FBI man. Munoz has been evaluated by Dr. Phil Dean, his attending physician. He's been analyzed by both an outside forensic psychiatrist and a psychiatrist from the local medical school. All three concluded Munoz's story should be considered valid. Remember, he reported Ryan had left the day room in a fit of anger. We guess Turk refused to have sex on the floor with the big redhead. Getting her good and drunk didn't help his cause."

"So, why rule him out?"

"Elsie Turk did her best to identify who she thought was her killer in her fleeting last few minutes of life. For some reason, Turk didn't notice Ryan leave the day room after their argument. We think she was in such an alcoholic stupor she failed to hear the killer sneak up from behind her and plunge the scissors through her sternum. She, excuse my pun, 'fingered' Ryan as the killer! Elsie knew Ryan was a puzzle addict and tried to warn the police it was he who stabbed her to death."

"I'd feel more comfortable if we get both Ryan and Munoz to undergo an extensive lie detector battery to fully clear them," Vasquez suggested. "The FBI specializes in this technique. They have the resources and proven expertise to electronically pull the truth out of those lowlifes being questioned."

She said nothing.

"You know what, Marie?" he continued, "I've never trusted doctors, especially psychiatrists. They always support their patients, right or wrong."

"Look, Jorge, the shrinks are legally liable for their actions. They wouldn't dare cross the line in matters that would perjure themselves. Let's be content with what they've reported."

"Well my CIA co-worker, why in the hell do the shrinks carry such exorbitant liability insurance?"

"Get over it, Vasquez. You talk like a complete idiot at times. We need to finally close the investigation. I'm sure both of our agency chiefs would agree to that course of action."

"I hear Munoz is being given the *Outstanding Citizens' Award* from the mayor for his heroic role in this escapade, ignoring Marie's tongue lashing. "Perhaps the Lone Ranger is sane after all."

Marie nodded her head as though to agree. She still had her reservations about Munoz's mental shortcomings. "I think you're aware he gave them a hard time when they tried to get him to surrender Angel's pistol. Munoz denied having it at all. He claimed one of his Army Rangers "beat" him out of it while playing craps. Both the Ranger and the dice had to be loaded." She laughed at her insinuation.

"Sounds plausible," Jorge commented.

"I've learned one rule long ago working with criminals. You can't rule out anything, no matter what. Boyd and I have talked about this many times. You're dealing with a warped mind when you interact with killers of all makes and models. He maintains all murderers are mentally unsound. I tend to believe him—that is, to a certain degree. There are exceptions. Our glorious court system has proven that."

Jorge gave her a "thumbs up" as though he bought her entire spiel. *FBI work is a hell of a lot more complicated than what the C.I.A. spooks do running all over the world trying to catch stupid spies.*

"Are you doing anything tonight, Marie?"

"Get the fuck lost!"

CHAPTER 62

"LARRY RICHARDS, did you take the turkey out of the oven yet, sweetie?" Pam asked as she yelled down from upstairs. "We don't want to eat a burned bird, honey if you get my drift."

Larry had written orders to set the table, not to babysit the turkey. That was his designated job. She worked hard enough in the kitchen.

Rod and John were sitting on the couch laughing and drinking a glass of wine. John was a devout beer drinker in the past. He finally turned the corner and imbibed on a glass of good red. John was in town over the weekend to visit a college friend who coached football at one of the local San Antonio high schools.

"Don't you dare forget the knives and spoons, dearest," John mocked his younger brother? "Make sure you wash your hands before touching the silverware, love!"

"Go to hell, big cheesehead. Better shut up your big yap if you want to eat. Dad, cuff him behind the ears for me, will ya? The big dude thinks he's still with the oversized goons in the smelly locker room with stinky jock straps hanging from the rafters."

Rod remembered Larry hated the violence of football. He'd been a decent college basketball player.

Larry, John, and Rod retired to the back patio after the big meal. Pam was playing the good wife role. She agreed to clean the table and wash the dishes. She regretted letting the kids get away from the house before doing their chores. The woman didn't want to be around Rod. He was drinking again. The feeling was mutual. Rod didn't care for her one iota. He missed Larry's first wife. She never wore the pants.

"Tell me, Larry, what's the latest between you, Howard Hill, and that female police psychologist?" Rod asked him.

Larry was sweeping off the patio rug. John was opening another bottle of merlot and smoking a big stogie.

"I heard you guys have had several meetings about using our hospital for that new venture," Rod continued. "Don't you think it's about time you brought in the hospital administrator for his detailed input before this notion gets any further down the road?"

Larry finished and sat down on a lawn chair. He grabbed a glass of wine John had poured for him and took a big hit. He preferred wine to that sweetened iced tea Pam loves to drink.

"That's one of the reasons why I wanted you to come over this weekend, Dad. I figured we could cover some things in a more relaxed environment. I'm not in front of a troubled kid in the clinic or on the phone talking to a concerned parent. Dr. Smyth has been a godsend helping me out over at Ft. Sam Houston."

"What's her name again, Larry, that police psychologist?" Rod asked. "Aren't she and Howard an item? That smoothie Hill could talk a deaf man out of his blasted hearing aid."

"Oh, wait a minute, Belle Chelby–that's her name," Rod answered his question before Larry had a chance to respond. *He wondered how in the hell such a remarkable beauty could sash-shay before his love-starved eyes and not remember her full moniker.*

"Not as far as I know but stranger things have happened in our business. Phil Dean asked Howard if he'd be interested in coming to Mission Oaks to head up a new program. You remember the earlier discussions about forming a partnership with MPD. It concerns hospitalizing juveniles instead of keeping them behind bars at the jail."

"Sorry, I forgot about that–been knee-deep in other important things." He didn't forget but wanted to pull out more specifics from his son. *I don't feel comfortable about this arrangement.*

"Yes, I know you're a busy man," Larry agreed.

"The events involving the terrorist activity at the hospital disrupted everybody's routine," Rod said. "I still have a hard time visualizing radical Muslims embedded with us. Only time will tell what kind of impact this mess will have on our hospital."

John finally wiggled into the conservation. "For crying out loud, even our newsy local paper in Packerland has been having fun with your unfortunate situation. One day the storyline read . . . *Terrorists Operating Out of Mental Asylum to Blow Up Sacred Texas Alamo.* That's why I called you the other night, Dad. I knew you were in the hospital business and worried you might be involved in some way."

"I think we should wait until our visit by the JCAH is completed before we take on another initiative," Rod said. "First things first. We'll all be looking for new jobs if we blow the survey. I hope Howard hasn't submitted his resignation from the VA yet, too premature. We'll go ahead and meet soon and hammer this thing out."

John was getting bored. They weren't talking about sports.

"Belle Chelby seemed anxious to get this project off the ground," Rod continued, "But we can cool her skids. Has anyone thought of a feasibility study? The MPD paid good money for an outside consultant to report that something could, and should be done about adolescent incarceration in jails. We should do the same thing about dumping them in a hospital. Our monies are pretty tight right now, though."

"Perhaps you brainy therapists can get a grant through one of your national associations," John opened up. "Everybody knows there's a lot of dough out there for do-gooders like you two creatures. Anything works that improve the lives of us poor souls suffering the indignities of our fellow men."

"Good points you two brains have surfaced," Larry responded. "Let's wait and see what happens next."

Pam came out to the patio and eagle-eyed the empty wine bottles strewn on the carpet next to Larry. She hesitated, took a deep breath, and started back to open the sliding glass door leading into the kitchen.

"Like father, like son," she uttered loud enough for the three to hear. The large door almost shattered when she slammed it shut behind her. They looked at each other and said nothing.

"Well, I heard my wake-up call, sons of mine. Love you both tons. I'm outta here."

Rod skirted around the patio to the backyard fence gate, opened it, and then jogged to his parked car in the driveway. His mind wandered off again as he headed back downtown.

What a first-class challenge Larry has to put up with every day of his complicated life. And son John, why doesn't he ever bring his wife down to San Antonio on any of his visits? Maybe she hates the thought of having to spend time with me. He wondered if Keena was home tonight. He'd call her.

CHAPTER 63

JUANITA Comptos hid in the rear bed of a filled grain truck. It was waved through the border checkpoint by U.S. officials and crossed the Rio Grande. She fled San Antonio after Angel Garza was captured and subsequently took his own life in prison.

She expected trouble re-entering Mexico. She still had a reliable contact on temporary duty recruiting for the Jihadists in the Brownsville, Texas, area. Her contact was a sleeper agent. He infiltrated a group of local hoodlums known as MS-13. The goal was to help Al-Qaeda shuffle their operatives back and forth across the U.S.-Mexico border.

To hide in Matamoros was out of the question, even though it was her hometown long ago. She couldn't trust anyone there because of her father's criminal background. It would be better for her to head deeper in-country and find a safe-haven. Juanita wouldn't be noticed there.

"Where can I catch a bus to Mexico City?" Juanita asked an old lady hauling a bundle of dirty clothes on her shoulders.

"*Aqui, aqui,*" the woman said pointing to the opposite street corner. There were no visible signs.

Juanita recalled the tragedies of the past few days while she rode in an old, dilapidated bus traversing south on bumpy roads. She had a hard time keeping her eyes open. Fatigue was setting in. Yet, she still remembered in detail the unfortunate events that took place back in San Antonio. She started to recall the dire circumstances.

The fool Angel raced back against my advice to kill a suspected witness. His youthful exuberance and impatience precluded him from developing an effective plan to assassinate the patient. How will Dalia react when she learns of his death? She was starting to come apart long before the final stages of the mission kicked off. Dalia no

273

longer had any feelings for me and lost all interest in sex. She claimed her work overwhelmed her. The weak bitch will have to suffer on her own from now on. Good riddance!

She started to nod off again and entered a deeper, pseudo-unconscious state. The mental confusion was caused by the effects of the illegal drug she'd been feeding herself since she'd left San Antonio. Juanita bolted to attention when the bus slammed into a big pothole in the road.

The bus traveled through a small village. It stopped to take on more passengers after more uncomfortable hours. Small kids and stinky animals crammed the lorry. She thought for sure she'd get sick from the foul-smelling insides of the moving vehicle.

"Hang on to the rack above your head," an old man sitting behind her shouted. "It's going to be a rough ride for the next few hours."

She reflected with great admiration of Amfi's performance in their dangerous undertaking. A smile formed on her face. She thought back to their last days together in San Antonio.

I had her arrange a courier flight with diplomatic immunity to pick her up at an isolated airfield in northern Texas. It was accomplished through her royal family connections. I knew through my contacts the flight was sanctioned by one of her dearest uncles in the Saudi embassy. I'm comforted in knowing she's safely back home now among her dear people.

Juanita was in a deep state of rationalization as she continued her semi-hypnotic séance.

Amfi is so much better off without that no-good military husband of hers. I hope he goes down in flames learning how to navigate one of the infidels' planes! He should've been sent to South Florida to our special pilot training school. He shouldn't have allowed his superiors to convince him he'd be effective to the organization by learning how the U.S. military operates.

The passenger sitting directly across from Juanita was cradling a small baby goat on her lap. She gently nudged the animal in the ribs with a walking stick. The scraggly-looking lady started to mumble a few words. Juanita was struggling to hear the soft words.

"Lady, lady, wake up now," she stammered to Juanita. "We're at the end of the line. The bus reached the old terminal here in Veracruz. It ain't going any further. Everybody's got to get off."

It'd been a long journey. She couldn't go any further anyway, happy the trip was over. Both her body and mind were exhausted from the stress of the past week. Mexico City wasn't too far away. She hated it there. The cool breezes coming in from the Gulf of Mexico were in contrast to the humid weather in South Texas. The allure of a coastal city convinced her to find temporary quarters.

She decided to settle down for a few days. Contacting her handler for further orders could wait. In true Mexican fashion, a bottle of good tequila would help soothe her frayed nerves.

All hopes of success were certainly not lost—just a temporary setback. She would come back stronger and with a greater sense of urgency. The holy war must be won by all means available!

CHAPTER 64

WHEN Rod returned to his condo, he yanked off the envelope that was scotch-taped to his front door. He ripped it open and read the note.

Rodney, my love, I had to leave town in a rush. You will find the key to my condo unit under the big orange flower pot next to my umbrella stand. Please feed my tropical fish every other day. There's a bottle of good gin on the kitchen cabinet. It's your favorite one, so help yourself. Oh, I forgot to stop the paper. Would you gather them up and also pick up my mail. The mailbox key is next to the gin bottle. Thanks, darling. It's xxxxxxxx for you when I get back!

Rod was mad. He went ballistic when someone called him by his full first name. He wadded up the note and tossed it down to Navarro Street. A city bus was slowing for the signal light and crushed the balled-up note into the pavement.

He did have a life of his own. It wasn't dedicated to feeding her squiggling underwater creatures. He didn't even remember the aquarium in her living room the last time he was there. All he remembered was the wonderful time they had together in her bedroom. Again, he had mixed feelings about their relationship.

Rod wandered down the hallway to her unit, found the key, and let himself in. The fish food was where she said it would be. He dumped a handful of the package into the small aquarium and checked to see if the bottle of gin sat where she said it'd be located. It was there. He opened her freezer door and filled a glass full of ice cubes, poured some gin in the glass, and sat down on the couch.

He was in awe at the ferocity of the little piranhas when he glanced over at the aquarium. They attacked the food pieces he'd tossed to them with great intensity. *Thank the good Lord I was smart enough not to put my hand in the water to dump in the fish food.*

The sun was setting comfortably over the trees on the Riverwalk. Birds could be heard serenading each other. Two squirrels were playing tag on the stubby tree limb near her rear balcony.

Rod locked up her condo and headed back to his unit. The street below was quiet. He glanced over through the window of the TV station across the street as he went down the outside hallway. Two news people were scurrying around the office on the second floor. *What great news items were they going to report to the world tonight?*

Rod saw the message light blinking on his answering machine when he got back to his condo. He switched it on, surprised at the caller's voice. He couldn't believe the pronouncement.

"Hi there, Rod, this is Dalia. I'm over at Teddy's Tavern. Come join me if you can. I'm all alone. I'll be here for at least an hour before going to the mall for some light shopping."

He turned off the answering machine and sat down on the couch and deliberated. *I had supported Dalia through the trauma of Elsie Turk's murder. Juanita abandoned her. She's since learned her brother was an al-Qaeda operative. Should I go over there? What the hell!*

He locked the door and decided to walk the several blocks over to the tavern. It was pleasant enough outside. All he had to do was avoid those damnable crackles. The blackbirds can drop a load on you before you know what's coming.

The activity in Travis Park turned him off. The homeless were having some kind of field day–loud music and louder speeches. Something about the right of free speech was all he could hear working its way out of the megaphone.

Rod crossed the busy Alamo Square proceeding to Teddy's Tavern. He expected to see her at the bar.

There she was, draped on the same barstool where he'd first met her. She was not alone in the tavern. Two other people were at the bar, probably tourists or conference attendees. They love the place even though the cost of drinks was pretty steep. *What the hell. They're enjoying the special ambiance of the tavern.*

"Rod, I'm so glad you came. I've been sitting here drinking a margarita and remembering how we first met. It seems like so long ago. We never got to know each other that night."

"I remember it well now, Dalia, although I didn't remember too much back then."

He told the same black beautiful barmaid to pour Dalia another margarita and mix him a dry martini. The lady remembered being told about the incident at the bar some time ago. It must have been one gigantic scene!

Rod didn't care for margaritas. She enjoyed them. Maybe he should try one last time. Everyone around these parts drank them.

"Have you heard anything more about your brother, Dalia?" He hoped he wasn't stomping on a hurtful woman.

"No, nothing new," she said without emotion. "I was asked by the MPD to identify his remains. I'd written him off until he showed up one day in San Antonio. I suspected something was grossly wrong about the relationship Angel had with Juanita. Sure enough, both were up to no good. Shoulda known."

"Have you heard from Juanita?" Rod continued the questioning, hoping it wouldn't disturb her. He felt he might be pushing her too far but wanted to find out how grounded this beautiful lady was now. Some major trauma happened in her life.

"Nope, and I don't care anymore. She abandoned me, big time. I'm ready to move on. Please, Rod, can we go back to your apartment? I've had my fill of this place."

He was stunned by her question. He couldn't believe the words he had just heard. *What was on her mind?*

"Hmm, yes, of course. Are you sure you want to come home with me?"

"Yes, Rod, if you don't mind. I don't like to sit in these bars for long periods. It's difficult to have a serious conversation with the background noise. I wish they didn't allow smoking in here. Let's go, okay?"

CHAPTER 65

ROD paid the bar bill. They ventured outside, hand in hand. There wasn't any wind blowing. It was still humid. The sidewalks weren't crowded. He found this weather picture unusual for this time of year. Weather change is inevitable, especially in Texas.

"Did you drive over here, Dalia?"

"No, I grabbed a cab. My car is in the garage for repairs. It was side-swiped the other day. I think it was dinged by one of those obnoxious news people. Maybe it was one of my neighbors. I don't know. Nor do I care–just get it fixed. Are we walking?"

"Sure. My condo is only a few blocks from here. Is that alright if we walk? I could hail a cab for us."

"No, walking would be fine. I love to stroll by the Alamo, especially when it's lit up at night. It gives me a real sense of purpose, Rod." She took a firmer grip on his hand as they began to walk.

He had no idea what she was referring to about *sense of purpose*. Was it the gallantry of the undermanned Alamo defenders? Perhaps she gained a new lease on life. Whatever it is with her, she seemed stronger, more self-confident to him.

Rod gave her a quick tour around the place when they returned to his condo. They went out on his balcony and sat down. It was a beautiful evening. A cool breeze was more evident now, fighting its way through the stubborn humidity.

Several tourists were enjoying the Riverwalk down below. One couple must've gotten engaged or married. You could hear the newlyweds bantering back and forth. They were loud. Could be their first big argument.

Dalia spent a part of the evening talking about herself. He was all ears. He didn't know about her background. It was all interesting. *I guess she's doing well, considering all the horrible things she's had to experience in the short period of her life.*

They finished a bottle of wine and were feeling mellow. She placed his hand in hers and looked him straight in the eyes. "Rod, will you take me to bed?"

He was shocked, taken off guard. He never envisioned or even planned to romance her this night. Knowing her a little better would've been helpful.

"Ah, are you sure you're ready for this?"

"Yes, Rod, I am," she said softly. "Is there a problem? Are you seeing someone else? I'd hate to interfere with any relationships you might be involved with."

He didn't answer her questions. He got up after a few silent moments and led her to the bedroom.

The male ego in him wasn't used to having a beautiful woman act the aggressor role when it came to sex. He always did a good job in that department.

Rod drove her home early the following morning. She exited his car without saying a word. She opened her repaired front porch door to her house, turned around, then gave him a "V" for victory sign.

Traffic was light. His head was heavy. All he could think about was that vicious-looking rattlesnake tattooed to her belly. It struck out at him time after time during the long night. It never did bite him though.

On the drive over to her home before dropping her off, Dalia had offered to fix him *huevas rancheros*. He needed something much stronger to silence his thumping head. A syrupy breakfast at the nearby IHOP wouldn't resolve the issue this time.

Rod swung his car over to Interstate 37, exiting at Loop 410. He began to wonder as he was driving. *Should I be developing this relationship with a key staff member at the hospital I manage? I remembered a close, successful friend who was axed by his company for doing the same thing. Perhaps I should cool it!*

He was on his way to Tio's Mexican Restaurant on Bandera Road. Rod remembered Larry telling him about the great recuperative effects of *Menudo*. He swung into Tio's parking lot and left his car between two red pickup trucks, each with hunting rifles racked inside on the rear window. The trucks were the size of a Greyhound bus.

The owner greeted him at the door and led him to a booth. Estela gave him a menu. Rod told her it was unnecessary. He was going to try some *Menudo,* knowing those medicinal qualities kick in faster than a cat chasing a mouse to a hole in the wall. The pounding in his head had gotten worse on the trip to the restaurant.

"Well, what do you think about our specialty?" Estela asked him.

"Not too bad. I sure hope it works its magic pretty soon."

"I guess you had a pretty rough night."

"Yes and no. I'll never be able to figure out women, especially the younger ones. They do a one-eighty-degree turn on you just when you think you know them."

"Allow me to throw out a few words of wisdom that might put your mind at ease, young man." She slid into the booth next to him. The restaurant was busy. Her long-time help appeared to have everything under control.

Estela began her friendly sermon to a set of anxious ears. "Women don't like to feel you have them figured out. They think once this happens, the mystery embedded in the relationship disappears. Routine sets in. The only exception to this premise is . . . if she falls in love with you. She becomes vulnerable at that stage of your relationship."

"Hmm, I've never looked at it that way. Thanks for the interesting analysis, Estela."

Rod left the restaurant shaking his head back and forth. He was beginning to feel better. He thought he'd get sick when she told him they use honeycomb tripe, the tenderest cut of the cow's stomach to make the *Menudo.* However, the story she told him about women made sense to him. It could have been muddied by her description of the food items.

Maybe they should hire Estela at Larry's mental health clinic. She'd be an immediate hit and successful to boot!

He headed back to his condo to change clothes. He had to return to the hospital and prepare for the big meeting with Hill, Chelby, Smyth, and his son.

Traffic had picked up, but he was calm, cool, and grounded. He needed to put some kind of "governor" on the committee's engine to slow down the expansion idea.

His priority was to get through the upcoming JCAH visit. He was prepared to argue and cajole with the committee. The revenue stream would dry up that without a positive outcome from the JCAH site visit. Insurance companies and other third-party payers mandate their enrollees receive care from accredited facilities. There were few exceptions.

CHAPTER 66

BOYD Bounder was busy scanning nursing notes on one of the problem patients upstairs when Rod came waltzing by. He looked up and saw Rod. "Did you have a nice weekend, partner?"

"Yes, and an interesting one for sure, my man. I'll fill you in some day over a cool one down at Cantina Classica. How was your weekend with Marie?"

"Absolutely great. Why do you inquire?"

"Aha. Want to define 'great' with a close friend?"

Bounder paused, reflecting back to last evening. Their love-making was both passionate and gentle. Their entwined bodies moved together like synchronized swimmers gliding through heavy waters in a choreographed swim meet. They were exhausted after the event. It didn't matter if the sex act was planned in advance or spontaneous–on the kitchen table, in the living room on the couch, or in the bedroom.

"Well, are you going to–"

"Oh, uh, sorry about getting sidetracked, Rod. Almost dozed off."

"You're excused," Rod said, not able to pick up any body language. *Musta been one big hootenanny!*

"Marie got word her request for transfer was approved. She's being reassigned to a local CIA field office. I can't tell you where it's located because I don't know the specifics. It's close enough for her to commute from our home though."

"That's wonderful, Boyd."

"Sure is. The higher-ups were pleased with her role in squelching the radical terrorist's plot. She received a special commendation detailing her heroic actions for preventing Amfi bin Aziz from escaping the country. The President signed it personally."

"Great, great news. Good for her, and I should also add . . . good for you. On another matter, I read with interest in the newspaper both Eduardo Munoz and Nick Ryan passed their lie detector tests. They were cleared of any wrongdoing in Turk's murder. I was happy Munoz finished his stay with us without being arrested, indicted, or anything so dramatic. I know you're happy he was sent back to the VA facility."

The big Texan commented Marie was happy both characters were out of her hair. *Talk about some far-out personalities. I can finally relax also!*

Rod smiled back at him and told him he needed to write a book about what strange and exciting things happen every day at Mission Oaks. Nobody would believe it.

"By the way, Boyd, getting back to your much earlier comment–what do you mean by the words, *our home,* Mister Head Nurse? Did you coerce Marie to add her signature next to yours on the mortgage note?"

"Oh, shut up your mouth, Rod Richards. Let's move on. Phil Dean asked me to sit in on your big meeting this morning. Do you have any problem with that?"

"Sure don't. I always welcome your input zeroing in on matters involving clinical issues. I'll see you later today."

Rod decided to check up on a maintenance problem one of the ward attendants called in and left on his recorder. He saw Dalia on his way through the ward. She was in a deep conversation with one of the patients trying to get undressed in the hallway.

The grey-haired skeleton of a woman couldn't get the yellow pajama tops over her thick head of hair. Some of the large buttons on the front got tangled up with at least ten gigantic hair rollers. All were strategically located in one mass on the right side of her head.

Rod stepped into an empty patient room and keeled over laughing at the hilarious scene. He was about to bust his gut. Thank goodness neither the patient nor Dalia saw him.

He vacated the room and caught up with Dalia when the activity and voices quieted down in the hallway. She was by herself at the nurse's station making notes in the patient's record.

"Good morning, Dalia," he said cheerfully. "You look refreshed this fine day. I trust you're feeling as good as I am. You won't believe this, but I had a dream last night that we—"

"Oh, Rod, I also had a wonderful time last night. You gave me a gigantic reason to start enjoying life again. I hope you don't regret anything that happened."

"No way. Everything was beautiful, Dalia. I hope we can see each other again, and soon. We need to keep things under wraps here, though. You know how crazy gossip zips around these hallowed halls."

She nodded with a smile. "Yep, even our patients have a way of picking things up which are none of their business. Let's keep our relationship at arm's length at the hospital. We'll see how things progress on our off-duty time."

Dalia grabbed his hand and gave it an affectionate squeeze before returning to record notes in the patient's medical record.

He forgot why he was in the ward and hustled back to his office to prepare for the meeting. Love, or maybe infatuation in his case can cause bouts of forgetfulness. It wasn't a senior moment. That's for old folks.

It was now late afternoon. Rod finished wrapping up some last-minute duties for the long day. He reflected on the discussions that took place during the earlier meeting.

Of major interest was how best to utilize the vacant outbuilding. He felt overall the assembly went well. Belle Chelby was the hit, playing out her role in a professional manner. She up-staged Howard Hill, a difficult feat for any human being.

Larry and Dr. Smyth offered meaningful input during the meeting, as did Boyd Bounder. Rod grudgingly agreed to hire an architect to begin developing the conversion of the outbuilding to a twenty-bed ward. He would drag his feet as long as he could get away with the delay. Belle reported the city and county would fund seventy-five-percent of the construction costs and fifty-percent of the operating costs after the adolescent unit opened. The hospital would retain all the revenue garnered from Medicaid and any other third-party payer.

It was getting dark outside when the flamboyant, former majority owner of the hospital Harry Mooney barged into Rod's office. He plunked down in a chair across from Rod's desk. Harry was dressed in the attire of a weathered ranch hand on his way to repair barbed wire fencing in the back forty. He was sucking on an unlit stogie like a newborn piglet draining the last ounce of milk from a sow's teat.

Rod was engaged in a deep discussion on the telephone.

"How'd the big powwow go, boss?" Harry asked, oblivious to the fact Rod was engaged with the telephone conversation and ignoring his divine presence.

In due course, Rod flipped a "V" sign to Mooney and continued talking on the phone. He was discussing potential dates with a representative from the JCAH firming up the schedule for their visit to Mission Oaks.

"I'm moving out tomorrow," Harry said to him, despite being ignored. "You can begin the conversion of my office to an animal kingdom concept right away. Here are the detailed drawings of how I want the place to look when the work is completed. It'll be the highlight of every tourist fortunate enough to find their way to our hospital and visit the display."

Rod continued to talk on the phone, half taking in Mooney's dissertation. Harry was annoyed and started to stare him down.

The former owner rolled up the sketches and tossed them on Rod's desk. He tried to light his cigar. It wouldn't fire up. The accumulated slobber softened the end to the degree it was starting to unravel. Mooney tossed the cigar in the wastepaper basket in disgust. He pulled a replacement out of his bib pocket.

Rod finished his telephone conversation. He picked up the rolled papers Mooney had tossed on his desk. Rod scanned the documents with disgust. *This egomaniac belongs in one of our beds upstairs.*

Rod had plans for the location. It wasn't going to be a memorial for Harry Mooney's hunting conquests.

"Thanks, Harry, I'll hang on to these drawings. How are things going now that you're in semi-retirement? I haven't seen you around the hospital in ages."

"The best thing I've done recently is getting rid of my share of ownership in Mission Oaks. I know for certain everyone here will miss my leadership. Great things accomplished here in my time. The show must go on . . . as they say in the theater business."

"You've got that right, Harry," he said half-heartedly.

Glancing at his watch, Rod said, "I'm already late for an important meeting. Thanks so much for stopping by."

He casually flipped Mooney's prized drawings on the floor near the entrance to his private bathroom. Harry gave him a stunned look. Rod got up from his desk, shook the accountant's big paw, then left the building. He almost ran the entire distance to his car in the parking lot. He couldn't get away from Mooney fast enough.

Rod had a dinner date with Howard Hill at the Stables Restaurant. He wanted to hammer out some issues on the proposed juvenile unit for Mission Oaks. There were too many unknowns at this time. He was uncomfortable and non-compromising.

CHAPTER 67

"HELLO, Dipstick," a booming voice resounded from the corner bench of the restaurant waiting area. It startled everybody in the big room. There were several men in business attire seated in the lobby waiting to be called to their table.

Two older, grey-haired prissy women wearing Fiesta-colored pillbox hats came out of the lady's restroom and stopped short in absolute horror. The stare they gave Howard Hill would've stunned an Angus bull. The seated men laughed loud and long causing the head waiter to appear from the other room and check on the disturbances.

"Howard, you've got to control yourself in public," Rod bantered. "Do your therapists on the psych ward at the VA facility know you've left the building? They said you were too doped up with morphine to talk on the phone when I called earlier to speak to you."

Rod turned to the stunned oldsters.

Howard said nothing.

"Sorry if he upset you, ladies," Rod said politely. "I'll get him back to the hospital as soon as possible. He's harmless."

The two old ladies clutched arm to arm, left the eating establishment in a snit. Rod hoped nobody from the hospital was dining there today. All he needed was for staff to witness Howard carrying on like some ridiculous vaudeville act.

The head waiter came over and joined Howard. He whispered something in his ear and then walked back near the reception counter.

"What do you mean the old coots are high society types?" Hill shouted so loud for half the restaurant occupants to hear.

"Quiet down, Howard, I'll explain later."

He had no plan to brief Howard on eclectic professionals residing in an overpriced neighborhood thinking they represented the upper crust of San Antonio society.

"March over here this minute, soldier, or I'll call an ambulance to haul your ugly ass back to your facility," Rod ordered with authority. "And they'll put you back in those uncomfortable leather restraints for being AWOL."

Hill lurched from the bench and marched stiff-legged over to him and gave him a big salute. The businessmen were expecting a confrontation. They quickly retired into the interior of the restaurant looking for the number of their table which had been called out.

Howard was one of the few persons in the world who could create gigantic waves when there was no wind around to cause them.

"Glad you could make it over here on such short notice, Howard. I need to run several things by that warped old mind of yours–things that bothered me in the past few weeks."

"I heard you were on the sauce again, Rod. Your son confided in me several days ago before our big meeting at your hospital. You can't get a clear view of the world looking through the bottom of a shot glass, my friend. Care to talk about it?"

"Ah . . . well . . . um, only a few glasses of wine now and then. That's not why I wanted to break bread with you. I'm concerned about our new joint venture with the city."

"Are you upset that I'm going to be the clinical director, rather than Larry?" Howard asked with a stern look on his face. There had been a heated discussion at the initial planning meeting about who would head up the new unit. There wasn't a consensus on the leadership issue as far as Rod knew.

"No, I'm not upset, nothing of the sort. My son is busy at Ft. Sam, even with Jim Smyth helping him. He told me you were the perfect choice to run the program because of your relationship with both Phil Dean and Jesus Astrade. They always listen to you when seeking input on controversial matters affecting their work."

Howard smiled and then nodded in agreement. He loved to hear compliments thrown in his direction. Not criticism by goofballs blowing hot steam at him.

"If anyone can balance those two different personalities, it's you, Mr. Hill. Besides, we all know you're adept at dealing with all kinds of troubled kids, big or small. Larry and Smyth plan a minor role in the operation."

They were called to their table by a concerned head waiter, not knowing what to expect from the two when they were seated in the crowded dining area.

The businessmen who witnessed the scene in the lobby were seated at the next table. They fell silent when Howard and Rod slid their chairs under the checkered tablecloth.

"I'll be back to take your order in a few minutes," the waiter said as he glanced over to the next table. He wanted to ascertain if there was a negative reaction from the businessmen. There was none.

The service was slower than Rod remembered from past visits. The wait was worth it. The food was as good as ever.

They finished their meal in relative silence. Howard tackled his well-done New York strip like a blitzing linebacker devouring an opposing quarterback. Rod finished a T-bone steak that passed a maximum of five swipes over the heated charcoaled grill.

"What do you want to talk about, Rod?" Howard asked as he wiped a smear of steak juice from the corner of his mouth. He then burped out real loud and grabbed his throat. The action startled everyone seated near them. Two men at the next table stopped eating and jumped to their feet to look at him.

"Whoops, sorry about that folks . . . thought I might need one of you to administer the good ole Heimlich on this poor old man. I'm fine now, all systems are back to normal."

"Howard, get serious for once, okay? You're flaking out half the people in this fine-eating establishment. I wouldn't doubt management is on the phone to the MPD as we speak."

"Rodney, in our line of business, a little Tomfoolery goes a long way to maintain our sanity."

Rod recalled Howard I.M. Hill never forgot his official first name. Damn U.S. Army records!

Their waiter cleared off the table after they'd finished. The restaurant was emptying. Coffee conveniently arrived without being ordered. Instead, Howard asked the waiter for a pot of hot tea for them. He also asked for some hot biscuits with a side of blueberry jelly.

"You got the floor, soldier, shoot," Hill declared.

Rod began. "I ran several financial scenarios through a special software program after our big meeting with the MPD folks. I'd purchased the computer package for my courses over at Trinity. My CPU massaged a ton of dollar figures, timeframes, number of patients, and the average length of patient stays. It burped out other supporting data I didn't need at the time. I wanted to calculate our return on equity and even stage several break-even points."

"Well, what's the bottom line, Professor Einstein?"

"We can't do it, Howard. No way!"

"I'm sure you have a reason for that spiel of negativity."

"Yes, I do. The juvenile unit would be operating at a loss. That is unless the city and the county underwrote the entire cost, plus throwing in some profit for us. We're a private hospital and have to generate our sources of revenue. I didn't factor in the legal ramifications–like maximizing our liability insurance and staffing an in-house legal capability. I could mention a few more off the top of my head."

"Are you finished?" a restless Howard Hill asked.

"Almost done. We'd be better off if the unit were built by the MPD on their property and then staffed by our personnel. I don't think we need to get into the business of incarcerating criminal adolescents."

"You'd better go back to the drawing board, Rodney, my good friend, and close associate. Make this whole venture happen. Do it soon! Belle Chelby has sold everyone from the mayor on down to the lowest ranking blue uniform her plan would evolve into a nation-wide phenomenon. It would put the MPD on the map. Didn't you read the study Belle did for the chief of police?"

"No, not yet. I asked Bounder to review it and highlight the major provisions for me. It's as thick as the holy bible, Howard."

Hill shot back. "Well, I couldn't have done a more thorough job of writing it myself."

"Right you might be, but you seem to have forgotten the infamous words of the Army manpower survey team when they came in to evaluate your staffing levels. I'll never forget their opening remarks . . . 'gentlemen, we're here to help you.' Then you wonder how far you have to bend over before they stick it to you."

Howard Hill gave him a gracious smile and then sat back in his chair with both arms firmly entrenched on the table. Several minutes passed as he reflected on the good old days.

He did a brain dump many years ago of the military traditions he learned the hard way and all the ridiculous rules and regulations he disagreed with. He got the job done his way! It may not have been completed by published procedural guides and sanctioned lesson plans, but they worked. He felt managers are measured by the outcomes they produce. Not by the processes that are used to achieve the desired results. If anyone can skirt long-time ingrained step-by-step functions, it's Howard I.M. Hill.

"Are you shacking up with her, Howard?" Rod asked, breaking the long minutes of silence.

Hill was shocked at the insinuation. It came at him like a bolt of lightning from the sky. Nothing could've hit him harder in the face.

"Screw you, Richards! I would've sent you an official fucking engraved announcement if I wanted you to know about the intimacies of our relationship."

He then got up and bolted out of the restaurant in a bigger snit than the two dignified old ladies displayed earlier vacating the place.

Rod knew it was not wise to delve into Howard's personal life. He thought they were good enough colleagues to discuss their successes and personal issues. He was wrong. Hill wasn't about to flaunt his good fortunes. Belle found the long-lost key to open the steel framework to Howard's miserable soul.

CHAPTER 68

ROD picked up Nancy O'Reilly at the airport and headed straight to Dalia Garza's house. Traffic was light on the freeways. He heard on the radio earlier a cement truck veered off the road near Loop 410 and Harry Wurzbach Road. The truck spilled its gooey contents on the access road.

He was elated she'd agreed to the marketing position. He knew she would have misgivings about leaving San Francisco. That would disappear over time once she got rolling. Nancy would fall in love with the friendly Texans and of course, the Alamo City.

Dalia was gracious and thoughtful to offer her house as a temporary place for Nancy to stay until she found an apartment of her own. Dalia had the extra bedroom since that monster childhood friend disappeared for good.

"We're almost there," he said as they turned on to Durango and headed for her neighborhood. "You met Dalia Garza on your earlier visit several months ago to check us out."

"Sure did, Rod, I liked her. I called and talked to her several times after I returned to San Francisco to clarify some ah . . . female issues before I made my decision. She was helpful. We should get along well. Dalia seems to be my type, don't you think?"

"Yes, I do, Nancy, you two seemed to hit it off better than I'd expected."

Dalia was home when they arrived and escorted Nancy into the house, as though they were long-lost, cousins. Rod lugged her heavy luggage in and set the pieces down in the living room. He had to make another run to the car to get the carry-ons. Dalia had him carry the suitcases into the master bedroom.

"I'll leave you two gals be for now. I've got to get back to the hospital. The JCAH team is scheduled to arrive tomorrow. There will be a ton of last-minute things to go over. See you ladies, soon. Plan to have dinner at Los Lobos on Blanco. Nancy will love the neighborhood atmosphere there. The delicious Tex-Mex food will grab her attention."

He pulled into the hospital parking lot, turned off the ignition, then sat in his car for several minutes. Two kids were skateboarding in the rear of the lot. They had hauled in a portable homemade launching platform. He had to review the liability coverage on the parking lot. At least they were loose and having fun. *Don't see many youngsters playing outside anymore—damnable electronic games on their cellphones!*

Rod wondered if it was a good idea to have Nancy stay with Dalia. He was becoming more attracted to Dalia despite mixed feelings. She was a sweet, forgiving, and kind person. Also a wonderful lover. He couldn't determine which qualities he needed most in his life.

Peppi greeted him at the front porch doorway of the hospital. She was coming outside for a smoke. *She loves those stinky little cigarillos. She and that slippery Harry Mooney share something in common.*

"Hello there, Mr. Richards, what's happening? You ready for the big inspection tomorrow?"

"I am, Peppi."

"I remember the last time they were here," she said. "Harry and that egotistical administrator were running around like dried-out corn cobs were stuck up their . . . you know whats."

"We're as ready for them as we'll ever be, Peppi. That's why we formed those planning committees and had meetings around the clock. Bounder suggested we arrange for a mock JCAII inspection by a team of our peers from the other downtown hospitals. They found discrepancies. We had no idea they existed and got them corrected."

"Thanks to Boyd, we're well prepared now, huh chief?"

Peppi was trying to figure out if she liked Rod Richards better than Boyd Bounder. They're both hunks. Give me either one!

Rod closed his office door when he got into the hospital. He needed time for himself without interruption. He wondered if he did the right thing on the proposed juvenile detention beds for Mission Oaks. He met with the board last week and told them he was against the initiative. He detailed his rationale. Several members agreed with him, but Dean and Smyth were upset. They felt it could and should be done. He was able to gather the necessary votes to table further action on the proposal for another six months.

Belle Chelby called him the night after the board meeting and chastised him for not supporting her.

"I've been given the reins to run this hospital like any other commercial business, Belle. I have to balance revenues and expenditures, making sure we have a healthy bottom line. Don't take it so personally. It's a great idea. You researched it as thoroughly as one would expect. Mission Oaks shouldn't be the site for this innovative venture."

He hadn't heard from Howard yet. Maybe he never would. It didn't matter.

Why don't the clinical types understand the dollars and cents it takes to keep this place afloat? Some days I would love to switch places with them and see how many fractured lives could be made good again. Then I wouldn't have to worry about the cost element.

CHAPTER 69

TODAY was D-Day for Rod and Mission Oaks Mental Health Hospital. The JCAH team had arrived. This was the first time he was comfortable with an important inspection. He felt the entire staff had prepared above and beyond the call of duty for the visit by the JCAH team. There were few complains about overtime requirements.

He learned the inspection criteria were less stringent than if they were a medical-surgical hospital. Hospital-based infections create multiple problems. They rarely existed in mental health hospitals. Other types of infections such as food poisoning and contagious microbes were always lurking around, waiting to raise their ugly heads.

The physical security of the patients was a big issue for mental health hospitals. After all, this was not a prison, and patients had many rights. Few exercised them. The others were passive and allowed the staff to function as they felt necessary.

"We're pleased with the wide range of privileges offered the patients here," the inspection team leader said after the first day.

"Thanks for the kind comment," Rod replied. "Supervision is a key requirement here. Mission Oaks has competent staff. It takes a special type of human being to work with the frailties of the lesser endowed. Our staff knows the importance of dignity."

"We've noted that and are highlighting it in our report," the team leader responded.

The JCAH survey team granted Mission Oaks its continued accreditation status at the end of the tedious five-day review. The hospital board of directors was delighted. It was the first time the hospital received full six-year accreditation. The more experienced former administrator wasn't able to achieve this level of success.

Rod met with key staff members after the survey team left Mission Oaks. Pharmacist Tom Lubay was not invited.

"There were several findings by the review team, most were minor deficiencies," Rod told the assembled group. "They can be addressed and corrected without much effort. All but three issues were resolved before the inspection team submitted their final written report."

"What finding was the most significant?" Bounder asked.

"The pharmacy operation took the biggest hit. The inspection team was not happy with the way the staff handled controlled drugs."

He had placed Tom Lubay in charge of the entire controlled drug process from the pharmacy to the ward and from the ward nurse to the patient. The written chain of control was incomplete in several cases involving the Vicodin drug.

He was glad a third party "nailed" the creep. Rod long suspected Tom Lubay had been skimming off some of the narcotics and selling them on the black market. He also suspected Tom was involved in an illicit arrangement with two pharmacy company representatives.

Rod had given Tom Lubay an ultimatum. Resign or face the outcome of an internal inquiry and subsequent investigation by the feds. Lubay opted to resign and take his chances elsewhere.

Dalia Garza weighed in, couldn't hold back any longer. "What were some of the other issues, Rod?"

"They pinpointed the male bathroom off the dayroom on the second floor. The team wrote up a finding that the physical layout violated the Americans with Disability Act (ADA). The doorway into the toilet stall was too narrow to accommodate a wheelchair."

"How do you intend to resolve that?" Phil Dean queried.

"I'll have our maintenance supervisor Mario remedy this situation by extending the partition out another two feet. He'll install a larger entry door into the stall. The same modification will be done in the female restroom."

"No problem, boss," Mario Caseres smiled from the back of the room. "I got it covered."

He had invited the receptionist Peppi to sit in on the meeting. *After all, she was one of the original human building blocks of the hospital. I like to give her extra visibility from the staff.*

She's not one to turn the other cheek when accolades were on the horizon.

Peppi loved the attention. Her warm and fuzzy feeling for Rod had jumped ahead another noticeable notch above that of Boyd Bounder.

"They did have a female representative who used the facility," Peppi reminded everyone. "But the pretty little thing spent most of her time propped before the mirror, checking, and reapplying that God-awful makeup she wore."

Everyone in the room howled at the overpaid hallway monitor, though they loved her antics.

Rod laughed about the toilet issues. He had chided one of the shorter male inspectors he wasn't going to lower the urinal to accommodate a midget, regardless of what the ADA might dictate! He also wondered if Eduardo Munoz had a problem wheeling into any of the restrooms.

CHAPTER 70

NANCY O'Reilly was an immediate hit. The staff at Mission Oaks loved her. The patients weren't sure what she was bringing to the banquet. She was quick to understand the intricacies of a trim mental health organization.

It didn't hurt that she came from a dysfunctional family environment in Ireland and yet survived the challenges at a young age. Her nasty father abused the younger brother but left her alone.

Nancy worked closely with Larry Richards at Ft. Sam Houston. Through their efforts, the unit referred more youngsters to Mission Oaks. Larry treated children and adolescents, though he found the need for parents to receive supportive therapy.

O'Reilly organized and expanded the outpatient component at the hospital. The unit supported evening and weekend sessions for working mothers and fathers. The dayrooms were multi-purpose rooms and large enough for large group sessions.

"Nice job on re-arranging the day room upstairs, Nancy," one of the senior nursing supervisors said. "The patients love it."

She authored many changes not listed in the typical marketing job description. Most were boring, repetitive.

One of her former acquaintances from San Francisco landed at a new hospital in a suburb north of downtown. The social worker friend was responsible for discharge planning. Soon, patient referrals were coming to Mission Oaks from her friend.

Nancy decided to stay longer with Dalia. The redhead loved the neighborhood where they were living. Some of the restaurants reminded her of San Francisco. The informality of outdoor seating and an extensive wine list were head-to-head. She encouraged Dalia to remodel her home to make it more livable for them. They enjoyed each other's company even though they had diverse ethnic backgrounds.

Though Dalia was dating Rod, she missed the soft, sensitive intimacies she'd shared with Juanita. She thought for sure she'd never find the intensity of female compatibility again. At the same time, Nancy missed her female companion at her old apartment but decided it was time to move on. The dear lady friend in San Francisco was becoming too possessive and jealous of her.

Dalia and Rod were having dinner one night at Mabela's Restaurant. Rod loved their homemade pies. He always took home one of the fruit selections after eating dinner. He'd bring Keena a big slice if she were back at her condo. She had a gigantic, sweet tooth.

"Rod, I'm not sure how to say this to you," Dalia said hesitating too long.

"What in the world are you trying to tell me? Just say what you have to say and be done with it."

There were several more minutes of silence. She squirmed and fidgeted. "I think we need to slow down our relationship. You're starting to get too serious, Rod. I'm not yet ready for that level of commitment." She was explicit. He knew it.

She was becoming more and more enamored with Nancy O'Reilly. He didn't see it coming. There were the obvious signs to others around him. Rod reacted as though he was blind-sided by an out-of-control, eighteen-wheeler.

"See you later, girl," he retorted too loudly. He stormed out of the restaurant leaving her stewing in the corner booth.

Dalia sat there in disbelief after he left and stared at one of the cluttered walls adorned with murals. Her mood shifted from being confidently serious to a state of unbridled depression.

To make matters worse, yesterday she'd heard from her old aunt in Matamoros—the one who'd never contacted her in the past. Juanita Comptos had been murdered in Mexico City.

The national press headlined the story for several days. Juanita had been soliciting for banned drugs and got caught up with members of a vicious Mexican Mafia splinter group. They'd suspicioned Juanita was fronting their territory. She'd become a hard-core drug addict. To make matters worse, she couldn't fork over enough pesos to buy the needed fix. Her entire support system had vanished into thin air. Juanita couldn't grasp reality. She was a "goner."

CHAPTER 71

"HELLO, Rod. this is Belle Chelby calling. How've you been doing of late, my friend? I haven't heard from you, ah, in ages. Do you have a minute to spare?"

He was finishing hospital employee evaluation reports at his condo and welcomed the interruption. He wondered why she called. "Yes, I do, Belle. Where are you?"

"I'm here across the street at the TV station. I finished an interview about our proposed juvenile unit at Mission Oaks. Everyone is so excited about the plan. It will be broadcast on TV tomorrow night. Can I come over? I need to talk to you."

Rod told her how to get into his building and the condo number he resided in. He thought it was peculiar that Belle would call him at the last minute and invite herself to his home. Rod speculated there was a problem regarding her relationship with Howard Hill. He'd find out soon enough. He was relieved he'd sent Howard a sincere letter of apology about his inferences to sleeping with Belle. He wasn't aware Howard forgave him.

"Please, come in, Belle. Make yourself at home. Can I pour you a glass of wine? I have some of California's finest. I even have a select Carmenere from Chile. Most of the locals haven't the slightest idea such a fine wine even exists. Perhaps you'd prefer something stronger?"

"Pour me a shot of Wild Turkey. No ice and fill it to the brim." Then Belle slumped on the sofa and kicked off her high heels. She looked worn and exhausted.

He observed with interest she was dressed in a scarlet red dress with an expensive gold chain link belt tugged around her narrow waist. She was clothed to kill, knowing anyone standing in front of a television camera would want to look their absolute best. She didn't wear makeup and still looked beautiful. Belle had the air and demeanor of a much younger woman.

"The drinks are on their way, Belle. I'm glad you're making yourself at home."

He hadn't had a drink in several weeks but found an opened bottle of Bombay Sapphire in the cabinet. He poured a few jiggers over ice and threw in a lemon wedge for good luck. He pulled down the bottle of Wild Turkey and fixed her drink.

Rod turned off the television set and planted himself in a chair opposite her. The sporting news was coming up. He could watch that later in bed. He routinely taped all the newscasts and two favorite programs for later viewing. It allowed him to skip the hated commercials.

"What's on your mind, Belle? You look distressed. Is it about your job or our mutual good friend, Howard? I know you two are pretty close. Or, should I say . . . were?"

She looked away from him.

He didn't dare bring up the devastating conversation he'd had with Howard at the steak restaurant. She no doubt knew about it. Anyway, it was history.

Belle swung back at him. "I hesitate to say this to you Rod, but I'm not going to beat around the bush. I know you think the world of Howard. You'd donate your right kidney to him if he needed it. You would give him more than any other ordinary citizen would, Rod. Yes, even his family members."

"He is family to me, Belle! What in he hell is going on?"

"Howard asked me to marry him. I have feelings for him, but I don't love him. I don't know how to tell the man. He's so strong and positive and sure of himself. Howard's accomplished so many positive things in his life. I respect that. Yes, we're good friends, even intimate. I need something more than Howard can give me."

"Like . . . what exactly do you need, Belle?" *Rod wondered if he was about to step on an enemy land mine this time. He'd avoided them in 'Nam.*

"I don't know for sure, Rod, I just don't know."

"I'm confused, Belle. What exactly would you like me to do? You best sort things out in the meantime. Howard is not predictable putting his arms around female emotions."

All of a sudden there was a loud pounding on his condo front door. A key could be heard being inserted into the lock. The door flung wide open.

"Rod, I'm home." It was Keena. She stood in the doorway with open arms. "Come here, you brute. Give me a gigantic hug and a big wet kiss. She slammed the front door shut behind her. "God, I missed you so much!"

There wasn't a sound in the condo. "All quiet on the Western front."

She rounded the corner and looked in shock at Belle sprawled out in total comfort on the couch. Rod was in a chair next to her.

"Who's this lady in red?" Keena asked with a sharp tongue. "I happen to go out of town, and you decide to hunker down with another woman. Who in the hell do you think you are, Richards?"

Rod jumped up and started to explain the situation to her. Keena spun around and raced out the front door. It almost came off its hinges.

He sheepishly strolled over to Belle, now sitting up in awe. *What in the world was coming down? I can't win for losing!*

"Keena is, or I should say . . . was a good lady friend of mine," Rod said with a sly grin. "She also has a unit in this building. We've dated several times. She is spunky and fun to be with but can go off like a volcanic eruption at times."

"Rod, I'm so sorry," Belle said. "I shouldn't have come over to cry on your shoulders. It's my problem. I should be able to find a solution on my own accord. Why am I getting you involved?"

"Have you talked with Howard about your feelings? He needs to hear it straight from your mouth."

"Yes, I started to go into detail the last time we were together. He became upset. I thought he was going to hit me. He doesn't understand somebody would have the nerve to utter no to Howard I.M. Hill!"

Rod agreed in silence.

"He's a fine man," she continued, "But I don't envision our relationship to be permanent. I've treated people like Howard my entire professional life. Too many warning signs are starting to appear. Can you help me out here?"

"No, Belle, I can't. You have to deal with Howard the best way you can work it out. Don't let your emotions take precedence here. Why can't you act as though he is one of your most challenging patients? Guide him through this emotional highway to a conclusion that will satisfy you both."

"Rod Richards, that's good advice. I'll keep trying to figure out a way to resolve it. Howard is a good man. We both know that!"

Belle got off the couch feeling much better about her situation with Howard. She felt the discussion with Rod helped her out more than he'd agree.

Rod slumped back into his lounge chair, took several long breaths, and lowered his eyelids.

What am I doing wrong? Why am I always the whipping boy in these complicated love entanglements? Maybe I should become a total recluse like the infamous Howard Hughes, or a cloistered monk sequestered on a high and secluded mountaintop somewhere in India!

It is what it is. Dalia's history. Keena's too much for a man like me to handle. Howard has Belle locked up. I guess I'm simply the odd man out.

EPILOGUE

THE calendar on Rod Richards' desk read March 15, 2007. The new juvenile unit was in operation at Mission Oaks Mental Health Hospital. Rod had re-evaluated his earlier negative position on opening such a unit. He moved aggressively ahead with the plan. He'd won some battles but lost the war.

The Mayor of San Antonio and the Chief of Police Jesus Astrade cut the ribbon to open the remodeled building. They were ecstatic ushering in the new program.

Doctor Phil Dean and Rod Richards were secondary bystanders, anxiously giving way to the other dignitaries in attendance. Every local politician claimed part ownership in the new venture. Several asked for a section of the ceremonial ribbon.

Belle was there with Howard Hill. Larry Richards and Doctor Smyth were also in attendance.

Rod figured it'd take at least three years to recoup their investment in the project. Construction modifications were always estimated too low. He budgeted a ten-percent inflation factor increase. It proved realistic.

Belle and her group felt Mission Oaks would be in the black financially at the end of the first year of operation. Rod was convinced Belle and her other psychotherapist brethren had no idea how to amortize expenses relating to operating income.

The local press was positive in all their written reviews regarding the establishment of a new and innovative concept for the care and treatment of law-breaking adolescents. The murder of the CIA agent was stagnant information not fit for new ink. Placing young adults in caring hands was more newsworthy.

The San Antonio paper would later earn special recognition by the Associated Press on their coverage of this new and exciting accomplishment for the City of San Antonio.

Mission Oaks became widely known as a positive medical asset within the community. Nancy O'Reilly was given more ammunition to run aggressively with her marketing thrusts. The daily average patient census rose to all-time highs. The smattering of red ink soon disappeared from the accountant's ledgers.

Howard Hill turned down the directorship of the new unit at Mission Oaks at the last minute. His acquaintances were at a loss for words. The old soldier decided to remain at the VA facility. Their addiction unit was being merged with a new holistic element. Howard was given a promotion to oversee the combined entity. Belle resigned from the MPD and joined Howard as co-director of his new organization at the VA.

Larry Richards was appointed director of the Juvenile Unit. Doctor Jim Smyth took over the Ft. Sam Houston clinic. He was also appointed medical director of the Juvenile Unit at Mission Oaks. He'd later relinquish the directorship to preclude accusations of "conflict of interest."

Elsie Turk's CIA replacement in Bahrain was successful in linking Sheik Salamah to an extensive and intricate money-laundering sting. The arrangement involved three separate international banks. One bank was located in the United States.

The sheik's illegal arms shipments were halted. The chemical laboratories that manufactured his lethal bacteria agents were raided. Important secret material was collected. The facilities were razed to the ground. Salamah had his legal team file a wrongful death suit against the United States government for slaying his only daughter, Amfi bin Aziz. All this occurred while he was under investigation before an international court of law.

Amfi's husband's navigation training at Randolph AFB in San Antonio was abruptly halted. U.S. authorities hesitated but then agreed to the extradition process. They returned him to Saudi Arabia. The establishment was unable to determine whether or not he had an active role in the terrorist's planned attack.

Rod was nearing the end of his third year in San Antonio. He felt an unbelievable pride in his accomplishments. Poor Janice had passed on and had left him in a world of hurt. He climbed out of the quicksand and made something of himself.

He loved all of the challenges that came his way. He was known throughout the medical community as an accomplished administrator. The downtown All Saints Medical Center offered him a position as the assistant administrator. The City Hospital wanted Rod to head up its outpatient clinic activity.

Keena had forgiven him one more time. He was never out of line with her. Of course, that conclusion was his opinion. Rod ended the relationship with her in a cordial approach to a complex dilemma. His, not hers.

Dalia and Nancy became lovers. Rod was weaned from the woman with whom he was falling in love. He'd never understand the caring and yet fragile Dalia. She was one of the most passionate lovers he ever took to bed. She gave him her entire body, heart, and soul, all with no questions asked. She demanded nothing in return. Yet, in the final analysis, Dalia would find more lasting security in the arms of another woman.

Belle had reconciled her major differences with Howard Hill. They moved in together. The old warrior was ready for the largest challenge of his manhood–marriage.

Marie Martini and Boyd Bounder were getting betrothed.

It was time for Rod Richards to move on. Nobody wanted him anymore. Nobody cared for him. Nobody needed him. He lapsed into a deep sense of remorse. He could only think of his true-life partner.

Oh Janice, my dear Janice, my loving wife. I miss you so much. Why did you leave me at the time of my greatest need? You've always been there at my side helping me achieve success. Tell me what I should do. Tell me what you want me to do!

He had to get out of Dodge, and right away, lest the demons try to overtake him. He was grappling with his subconsciousness. *Where should I go? What should I do? Somebody, anybody, throw me a lifeline!*